Wallace Family Affairs

Affairs

Volume VI

First You Laugh, Then You Cry

Carey Anderson

DEDICATION

This story is dedicated to Nookies, Velvet, Thade, and a few of my maternal family members. Between all of you Darryl's voice lives on, and brings much laughter to my life even when things aren't funny.

Join me on Facebook –
www.facebook.com/careythewriteranderson

Twitter - @CareyTheWriter

Blog - http://careyanderson.blogspot.com

Website – http://www.careythewriteranderson.com

Author Central (Amazon) -
http://www.amazon.com/author/careyanderson

Editorial – Treasures of Joy Editorial

Cover Design by Cover Couture
(www.bookcovercouture.com)

Photo Copyright: S.Borisov / Shutterstock

Photo Copyright: Olesya Kuznetsova / Shutterstock

Photo Copyright: Natykach Nataliia / Shutterstock

Photo Copyright: severija / Shutterstock

ACKNOWLEDGMENTS

I would like to thank my baby-girl who is my life's ultimate expression of a dream realized. Thank you for sacrificing mommy time so that I could have the time to work some things out on paper.

I would like to thank my Soul Sistah #1 who has been my captivated audience since middle school. Without your love, support, encouragement, and FIRE I never would've completed Volume I or II, etc. Thank you for bringing me laughter when I couldn't get outside of my head.

I would like to thank my Sister-In-Law for taking time out of your busy family life to humor me with a read through of my latest thoughts and expressions. (SS1 & SIL THANK YOU for the trip to St. Helena where we spent the day lost in my imagination. I will never forget it, and it was exactly what I needed. THANK YOU!)

I would like to thank my dear cousin for reassuring me that my little hobby was relatable and entertaining. You are definitely a speed-reader, thank you for taking time out of your busy life to be entertained by my imagination.

I would like to thank last but not least Mrs. Laverne Dyes! Mrs. Dyes the day that you read my short story to my class changed my life. Thank you for giving me a positive outlet for all the angst going on in my life. You have forever changed my life, I am so thankful to have ever known you.

Chapter 1

Nellie

I was the apple of my daddy's eye no doubt about that. Whenever he saw me he brought me something really nice and expensive. But why wouldn't he? At the time I had two older brothers, but he says they're knuckleheads. I was his little princess. My mother stood over to the side visibly inspecting his gift. He knew if it wasn't top notch she would call him on it. Since my daddy is married to my big brother's mother I didn't get to see him all that much. At that time, she didn't know I existed. My brothers knew, but his wife didn't.

When my grandmother was on her deathbed she asked my daddy to bring me to the hospital to see her one last time. My daddy didn't want to deny his mother her dying request, and there was no way to bring me there without his wife knowing about it. My momma did my hair real pretty and long. She put on my cutest pink outfit and then I watched her put on her makeup. When she was dressed I told her she looked really pretty, she smiled and thanked me. Then we went to the hospital to see my grandmother. The guard at the guard station said there was a bunch of people in the waiting room and there were only three people allowed in the room at one time. My momma took a deep breath, held my hand, and then we walked into the waiting room. Everyone looked at us for a minute without saying a word at first. Then my Auntie Natalya came over and gave us a hug. My biggest brother Junior came over and picked me up. He gave me a hug and kiss. He told me I looked really pretty. Everyone came over and said hello to my momma and me, but my brother Nathan stayed by his momma who had no clue who we were. My Auntie went to tell my daddy that we were here. When my daddy came to the waiting room he thanked my momma for coming and then he took me from my brother. My daddy looked sad when he looked at his wife, who looked surprised. Then he carried me down the hallway to his mother's room. He told me that my grandmother was sick and she was about to go to sleep. But she wanted to say goodnight one more time to her little princess. My grandmother smiled when she saw me, but she looked really sick. She told me she loved me and she was going to miss me. My daddy's wife came in the room, she asked my father who was I. He told her that I was his daughter and

that my name was Nealesha but everybody called me Nellie or
Princess. His wife looked at me like she wanted to hit me. She got
so mad she stormed out of the room. My daddy hurried out of the
room with me in his arms behind her. She went back to the waiting
room and got in my momma's face. She was cursing and
screaming at my momma. My momma didn't say anything; she
stood there grinning at my daddy's wife. No one said anything to
stop her from talking to my momma that way, not even my daddy.
Then she yelled at everybody in the room cause they all knew and
no one said anything. No one even warned her. When she started
crying my daddy put me down and asked her if she was done. Then
he told her to get over it cause it was done, and now the secret was
out. Nathan comforted his momma while everyone else stayed
away. My momma went with my daddy to say goodbye to my
grandmother. Junior held me while his momma stared at me like I
was a bug to be squashed.

After that I started going over my daddy's house every other
weekend. His wife was always mean to me, but my daddy tried to
keep us apart as much as possible. My daddy still came and spent
the night at our house sometimes, and he still brought my momma
gifts and nice things. One day my daddy took me to the park. He
told me that his wife was having a baby and that I should be
excited to be a big sister. I did not like the idea at all. I was the
baby, and I was the Princess.

I hadn't seen my daddy in a long time and when he finally came to
get me he told me his wife had a girl and that they name her
Nassya. I was not happy, not one bit. I was the Princess, and the
only little sister. Now this baby was here and my daddy's wife was
happy. She would say, your daughter this and your daughter that in
reference to me. But then she would say our daughter this and our
daughter that in reference to Nassya. My visits over my daddy's
house started to become less and less. I would cry and ask my
momma where my daddy was. Then she would call my daddy's
house and most times she argued with my daddy's wife. She was
mad that my momma called their house.

Before I was born my momma worked for my daddy in his office,
but when she got pregnant with me she no longer needed to work.
My momma said my daddy paid for our apartment and her car.
One day while I was watching cartoons my momma picked up the
phone to make a call and she started hitting the button over and

over again. She threw the phone in the kitchen and she ran in her bedroom trying the phone in there. My momma knocked on our neighbor's door and asked them if their phone was working and when they said yes, she came back inside. She knew there had to be a mix up at the phone company cause my daddy always paid all the bills on time. The next day when I came home from school there was no electricity. And there was a note on the door stating that our rent hadn't been paid. We drove to my daddy's office. I didn't go in the office with my parents but you could hear them arguing all the way out to the lobby where I was sitting. The people in the office were all trying to listen without looking like they were listening. My daddy told my momma that he and his wife were really trying to make things work. And unfortunately, that meant that he could not support my momma anymore. He said he would pay child support but he would not cover all of momma's bills. My momma screamed at him and asked him how he could break up with her without even discussing it with her. My daddy shrugged but he didn't answer her. She asked him when he was going to come get me, and he said he would call her. She asked him how is that possible when we didn't have a phone anymore. He shrugged, and then he shut the door to his office.

My momma cried and we went to my grandmother's house. My momma begged my grandmother to let us stay with her for a while. Although she wasn't crazy about the idea, she didn't like the idea of me being homeless. We packed up our beautiful apartment and moved from Albany to Richmond. Suddenly and almost instantly my life completely changed. I was at a new school and I knew no one. All the girls gave me evil looks, except for one girl. During recess I was going to go hang on the monkey bars by myself but the girl asked me if I wanted to play jump rope with her and some other girls. The rest of the girls looked at me, but she was the only one to talk to me. When we lined up for lunch she told me to come stand by her. She introduced herself as Kendra. In the cafeteria she asked me where I was from. Kendra was browner than me, shorter than me, and never as cute as me. But she was nice. My hair was long and thick, and hers was short and fried. All my clothes were new and name brand, hers were fine but no labels. The only thing we had in common were our grades. She was on the honor roll and so was I. If she got a 92 on her test, I had to have a 93 or better. Kendra would always say it was not a competition. But there was no way she was ever going to think she was better than me. When I brought home my good grades my momma would tell me how proud she was of me. She would tell me to get good grades, get a good job, make sure the man I married had money, but I also had to be smarter than her and make sure that I made his money work for me. And the only way to know how to do that properly was to get my education.

Kendra lived a few houses over from me, so on Saturdays I would come to her house or she would come to mine. We would play outside as long as we could; all day if our parents didn't have anywhere to go. I know her family liked me better than her, cause they were always so nice to me and paid me a lot of attention whenever I came around. All the boys at school wanted to be my boyfriend, but I would only agree to be the girlfriend of the boys who could afford to buy me candy from Shacks, the corner liquor store by our school. My momma said the little boys at King school were practice guys cause none of them even really dressed right to be taken seriously. She told me to study long and to study hard cause I needed to be able to catch a bigger fish when I was put in a bigger tank in college.

"How much money did your parents give you for clothes?" I asked

"Clothes? They gave me money for the bus, and something to eat." Kendra said.

"I thought we were going to take pictures?"

"Yes, but not today. I don't get my allowance until next week."

"Are you going to at least get your hair done? You can't be looking all homely in my pictures."

"I'm going to do my own hair and I will be just fine."

"Whatever, you can look homemade if you want to. I'm going to look extremely crisp and fresh and you can try to keep up as usual." I said looking out the window.

"You waste money on ridiculous stuff. I don't care what you think."

When we got to the mall, I drug Kendra from store to store as I looked for shirts that would make us look amazing. I was getting frustrated at the selections in the stores. Kendra always went to the clearance racks while I searched the rest of the store. Kendra held up lavender shirts that were surprisingly cute. Since they were reduced in price, and they didn't have pink, I bought both of our shirts and accessories. I wanted to check out the shoe store to get an idea for shoes in case I felt we needed them as well. Then I heard my name but I kept walking. Kendra said a guy was calling me. "Nealesha?"

I turned around to see my big brother Junior looking completely stunned to see me. "Junior?"

He rushed me and picked me up. "Where have you been? You disappeared!"

Seeing him made my heart burn and immediately I felt sad. "Your daddy kicked us to the curb when your momma had your sister."

"Our sister and I'm sorry he did that. I've been trying to find you."

Hearing that he was looking for me made me smile. "You have?"

"Of course! I miss my little Princess." Then he looked at Kendra, "who's this?"

"Oh this is my friend Kendra, Kendra this is my big brother Junior."

"Nice to meet you pretty little lady." He smiled.

I sucked my teeth; "she ain't prettier than me so I don't know why you even went there."

Junior got a stuck in headlights look on his face. "Princess that was rude!"

"She's always rude!" Kendra said walking in the store.

"You can't treat people like that." Junior said to me.

Then Nathan and Nassya walked out of the fragrance store. My blood boiled when I looked at her, not only did she not know who I was. Her shoes were newer and nicer than mine. I wanted to kick her over the railing. "Princess?" Nathan said coming to give me a hug.

I hugged him, "hello." I kept my eyes on Nassya.

"Nassya, this is your big sister Nealesha." Nathan said

Nassya faked the happiest face ever. She hurried to me to hug me. I didn't want to hug her, but both of my brothers were looking like they expected it. Nassya kept looking at me with stars in her eyes, but I wasn't buying the act. When Kendra came out of the store Junior introduced her to Nathan and Nassya. When Kendra and Nassya seemed to hit it off I felt completely annoyed. I asked them why they were at the Richmond Mall and they said they were looking for gifts for their parents for their anniversary. Again I felt like the outsider to their family circle. As if he read my mind, Junior offered to take us to get something to eat with them. I declined but Junior wouldn't leave us alone until I agreed. Nathan made me write my phone number and address down on a napkin so they could find me again. I didn't want to discuss my business in front of Kendra or with their little sister sitting right there, so I kept changing the subject. Any topic that highlighted how wonderful and fabulous I was, was preferred. After a while Nathan stopped talking to me, as if he thought I was ridiculous. But Junior and Nassya kept talking and looking at me with love in their eyes. Nathan was having a side conversation with Kendra and I didn't like it. He was asking her about her grades and school, but I still didn't like it. After a while I realized that little Nassya was looking up to me as a big sister. I liked the idea of that so I warmed up to her a little bit. We walked around with them as they each picked out gifts for their parents. Junior said this was his senior year in high school and he wanted me to come to his graduation. Nathan told him he should check with their parents before he said something like that. But Junior told him to shut up and it was his day and he could have whomever he wanted there. He said he would call with more details later. They gave us a ride home and Nassya gave me the biggest hug right before I got out of the car. Kendra looked like she had so many questions, but I told her I had to go talk to my momma which I did. I told my momma everything that happened.

Kendra

My parents were high school sweethearts; my momma said she loved my daddy from the first time she laid eyes on him. My daddy said time stopped the first time he saw my momma. They fell in love in school and married right after they graduated. They waited a while before they had me, but my momma said my daddy was so excited when she told him she was pregnant. When I was only a little over a year old my mother was pregnant again with my sister Kaleah, and two years later my sister Kalani. People referred to us as the stair steps, but my parents couldn't be prouder of the three of us. Both of my parents work so we all had to do our part. My dad left early in the morning so my momma would see us off to school. And then my dad would come home not too long after we got home from school. We did our homework first and then our chores. The three of us worked together to make sure that when our very tired parents came home that everything was taken care of. My family wasn't the poorest family but we definitely weren't rich. I learned that money comes and goes, so not to base too much of my happiness on it. While most of the kids at my school were overly concerned about the labels on their backs and feet, I was looking after my sisters. I didn't worry about being the biggest and the best, I just wanted to be good. Now my friend Nellie on the other hand, she always feels like she has to be the best at everything. Everything is a competition for her; if I think a boy is cute she has to know that he likes her. Her momma doesn't care if Nellie has boyfriends; my parents said I couldn't have one. Every time she notices something with me she has to have bigger and better. My momma says not to pay that type of behavior no mind. She said girls like Nellie end up used and alone when they get older. She told me to continue to be nice to her in hopes that she will see one day that there is another way to be.

I try, but sometimes I get tired of letting her shine when I know if I let go a little my light would out shine hers. My momma says to just hold on and watch. She tells me to look at the family examples of various Aunties, and cousins. All of the ones she points out are single sometimes with kids and fractions of what they used to look like. Kaleah acts like she doesn't hear momma though. She thinks Nellie is wonderful, and she just about sits at her feet taking all of her non-sense in. When I see Kaleah imitating Nellie in her clothes or especially her hair I run interference. I'll mess up her hair or accidentally spill something on her clothes where she has to change. Kaleah thinks I'm jealous of her, but that isn't the case. Even though out of the three of us, Kaleah is the lighter skinned, then Kalani, and I'm the darkest. I happen to love my brown skin and I wear it with pride. Kalani is always the peacekeeper and she tells both of us that we are both beautiful in our own ways.

****

The sun has gone down and again my momma has beaten my daddy home. Lately when he comes home he's in a bad mood and he acts like he can't be bothered. On the weekends he gets up, works on the yard, and then he picks a fight with momma so he can storm away. I don't know what's going on, momma packs us up and we go over Aunt Quilla's house. A few times we've spent the night.

My Aunt Quilla is my daddy's little sister. She and my momma are so close you would think she was my momma's sister. My Aunt Quilla lives on the other side of our long street. It's a distance to walk so we normally drive. We play out back with Aunt Quilla's kids Ahjanae, Audra, Ahjani, and Aunrey. Ahjanae and I were the oldest so we were always in charge. I liked being at my aunt's house, but the tension between my parents makes me worry. Ahjani watches my face, and he then comes up with the best games for us to play. His games always require tons of imagination. I normally forget how sad I feel until I see my momma's red eyes. Audra always finds a way to work singing into the mix. She has a beautiful voice and she knows it. Through her influence Kaleah practices and practices. Kaleah is developing a pretty good voice as well. Another thing to add to her arsenal.

Aunrey is just mean and a grump. He never wants to play with us and he's mad all the time. The only time he's nice and happy is when Aunt Quilla tells him his father is coming. We all lay low if his father didn't come for whatever reason. Then he's really angry or ornery. Ahjanae says he acts just like his daddy. She said whenever his daddy feels like he wants to get back with their momma and she tells him no, then he acts ugly. She said she called the police one-time cause he was choking their momma cause she told him she would never get back together with him. Ahjani pulled a knife on him, Audra had an iron skillet. Aunrey was the only one still on his father's side even though he saw what he was doing to their momma. Ahjanae told her daddy about the incident and he threatened to take her and Ahjani away if it happened again. Of course that made Audra sad cause her dad is dead, there was no one to save her. Thankfully Aunrey's father got locked up after that so they didn't have to be separated. On the flip side that means Aunrey has been a terror. And that little sucker is strong! Thankfully he's my cousin so even though he's mean to me he will not allow anyone to do the same. We don't go to the same school, but the people at my school leave us alone because of him. Aunrey is friends with the Baker family. The Baker family is this huge family that have real blood related cousins all over Richmond. Everybody knows who they are and they can be just as mean as Aunrey. His dad used to take him over the Momma Baker's house all the time since he was a baby. The only family as big as theirs is the Mason family. The Baker's and the Mason's are good friends, and one of the Aunties lives a couple of houses over from Aunt Quilla. My Aunt said that since Ms. Lorraine found religion her house has calmed down a lot. I wonder what that means cause from where I sit there's always people at her house, coming and going. Sometimes there's arguments and fights outside her house. But Ms. Lorraine don't play. Male or female she's had to get with some of the more ignorant ones to remind them why they needed to respect her house. She's always nice though and she always waves to us when she sees us outside playing.

"Aquilla, Ahjanae is getting so tall." My momma said

My aunt smiled, "thanks. She's gonna be tall like her daddy." Then she looked at me. "You remind me of our momma's sister. If I believed in reincarnation you'd be my living proof." Aunt Quilla always says that, I just smile cause what else am I supposed to say. I continued to help Ahjanae clean the greens while they sat at the table and loudly whispered. We didn't let on that we could hear because we were nosey. "I'm sorry Kharee. I don't know what my brother is thinking. You've always been good to him. I don't know why he's doing this. So what if you're all he knows, he should be proud that he could say he's disease free! What are you going to do?"

"As soon as I have proof he's out!" She said weakly.

"Why do you say it like that?"

"Aquilla, I have three girls. What am I supposed to do? Date other men and risk bringing a pervert around my girls? I would never forgive myself if something happened to them."

"You don't bring everyone you date around your girls, only the one you think is special meets them."

"Aquilla, I don't like talking like this. I hope we're just going through a rough patch. I hope Jerry isn't compromising our marriage."

Aunt Quilla rubbed my momma's hand, "I know sweetheart me too."

****

"Do you have these shoes in a size 8?" My momma asked the sales guy.

"I'll go check," he told her. Then he disappeared to the back.

"Go see if you can find any sneakers you like." My momma told me as she continued walking around looking at the shoes on the shelves.

Kalani needed new sneakers more than I did so I was looking for a pair that I thought she would like. "Kendra right?" I heard a male voice say.

I turned around and it was one of Nellie's brothers. "Yes, and you're? I'm sorry I forgot your name."

"Nathan, are you here with Nellie?" He said looking around.

"No, I'm here with my momma."

He exhaled, "good! I need to ask you a very important question." He looked me in my eyes. "Why are you friends with her?"

His question surprised me. "I don't know. She was the new kid and I felt sorry for her, so I was nice to her and it went from there. You don't like your own sister?"

"Not really, and it's not because she has a different mother. It's her constant need to be the center of attention that I don't like. When we saw you guys in the mall it had been years since we had seen her. I had forgotten that she's always been that way. I love her, but I don't like that. So again I ask you why are you friends with her? You're nothing like her."

"How do you know what I'm like?"

He smiled at me, "I can tell."

"She can be really sweet sometimes. So I excuse her rudeness most times."

His eyes went all over me, which surprised me. Nathan had to be in high school, why was he looking at me like that? Next year I would be in middle school, shouldn't I look like a little girl to him?

"Figures, you'd have to be kind hearted to be friends with her." He looked around the store, that's your mom?" He gestured with his head.

My momma was looking completely stunned at us. "Yes, please come meet her."

He smiled, "alright."

"You work here?" I asked as we made our way over.

"Yep, every weekend. You gonna come visit me?"

I was surprised, "you want me to come visit you? Why?"

He smiled at me, "what's your last name?"

"Hutchins," I said as we approached my momma.

"Hello Mrs. Hutchins, I'm Nealesha's big brother Nathan." He said smiling at her.

My momma looked relieved. "Oh! Ok! Nice to meet you. I was wondering why my daughter was talking to a high school looking boy. What grade are you in?"

"I'm a sophomore at Albany High."

"Oh that's nice." My momma said still showing how relieved she was.

"You have a very patient daughter, hopefully some of what she's got will rub off on my sister."

My momma smiled, "Nellie just needs to see that there's another way to be. She's fine; between the two of you I think she'll get it. It was nice meeting you Nathan." My momma said as the sales guy came out with a shoebox.

Nathan told the guy he'd wait on us. The guy said ok and went to help another customer. Nathan chatted with my momma and me the rest of the time we were there. He even gave us his employee discount on the shoes I picked out for Kalani and the ones my momma got for herself. Nathan smiled at me real big when my momma was surprised that I picked out shoes for my little sister instead of picking out a pair for myself. When my momma went to the bathroom, Nathan told me I had to come back to see him. I told him I'd bring his sister, and he kind of frowned. He said if that was the only way I could make it, then he guessed it was ok. But he'd rather I didn't bring her. I was confused but I agreed anyways.

Chapter 2

Nellie

My momma sent me to the shop to get my hair done up right. She made sure my clothes were new and crisp. She even had to chip in her lunch money for the next couple of weeks to make sure my outfit was on point for Junior's graduation. I was going to be stunning, no doubt about it. I got a little irritated when Junior told me to bring Kendra. First of all, I didn't want her in my family business like that, and I didn't understand why he even devoted her name to memory. Her outfit was fine, but not as cute as mine. I know why I was nervous but I had no idea why she was so nerved up. My momma was coaching me in the bathroom about how to be when I saw my daddy for the first time in years. My grandmother knocked on the door and said my brother was at the door, and then she looked at my momma like she was waiting for an explanation. I kissed my momma and I told her I'd be back after dinner. When I walked into the living room, immediately I was irritated with the way Nathan was talking to Kendra. He was smiling at her and paying HER attention. UM HELLO! He was here for me; she's the afterthought. I stepped in front of Kendra and I told Nathan I was ready. He frowned and then he told us to come on. Kendra got in the back as she should've and Nathan looked like that bothered him. I asked him how come Junior didn't come to get me, and he said Junior had to be at the school too early. When we pulled up to the school I touched the card in my purse that I picked out especially for Junior. I hoped he liked my card; it was all I could afford after I spent everything I had to look this fabulous for his graduation. Nathan kept smiling at Kendra and trying to talk to her too much for my liking. So I kept interrupting and answering his questions as if he asked me and not her. Nathan looked at Kendra completely irritated and he asked her why she was friends with me. I told him she needed someone to look up to. Kendra sucked her teeth, and then she told Nathan on days like this she wonders the same thing. I turned around and looked at her in disbelief. How dare she say something like that to my brother? She wiggled her neck at me and I wiggled my neck back at her. Then I asked Nathan why it mattered to him. He said I was being very rude to Kendra. "WHY DOES IT MATTER TO YOU WHAT I AM LIKE

WITH MY FRIENDS? YOU ARE MY BROTHER AND YOU'RE SUPPOSED TO HAVE MY BACK!"

"Wrong is wrong! And you are so self-centered I doubt you even get it. You should never treat anyone the way you treat Kendra. But I'm sure this lesson like every other one will go over your head. You let your mother brain wash you into thinking this is how you're supposed to treat people and you're too dumb to look at her life and see that she is the LAST person you should be taking advice from."

Fire turned in my stomach! "DON'T YOU EVER TALK ABOUT MY MOMMA! SHE'S THE ONLY PERSON TO BE THERE FOR ME WHEN YOUR FATHER DUMPED US BECAUSE YOUR MOMMA COULDN'T LEAVE WELL ENOUGH ALONE!"

"You've got it so twisted! You can't even see that you should be mad at your father not my mother! He had and still has choices, but all you look at is the competition. Stop taking your frustrations out on Kendra, she had nothing to do with this."

"Stop defending Kendra! I am your sister! You're loyalty is supposed to be to me!"

"I will not defend you when you're wrong, and you are wrong!" He growled at me.

"Take me home!" I demanded, "I did not come with you so that you could make me feel like I'm less than a person just because your father chose your momma over mine."

"No, Junior asked me to bring you so I'm bringing you. If you want to walk to the Bart station in those new shoes that I'm sure you didn't break in, then be my guest." He said parking his car.

"Fine!" I said getting out of the car and preparing myself to walk. When Kendra started to follow me, Nathan grabbed her arm and told her not to. That made me madder, "you're supposed to be my friend! If I want to leave why would you stay just because he told you to? I hope you don't think he likes you! He is my father's son. They use you and then they toss you to the side like yesterday's news. You're a little sixth grader, what could a high school boy want with you anyways?" Kendra exhaled and then she started walking with me.

"Fine! I'll just tell Junior that you were too scared to come support him on his special day. I'm sure he'll understand." He said locking his car doors like he didn't care.

I stopped walking, "I'm not scared of your parents!" I yelled. "Then prove it!" He said looking both ways to cross the street to go to his school.

I exhaled and then I turned to follow him across the street. Kendra didn't say anything she walked with me in silence. People had balloons and stuffed animals for their graduates. I wished I had money for a balloon at least but I sucked it up. Nathan sat us in the lower section of the bleachers in the gym and then he said he would be right back. As soon as he was gone I started drilling Kendra about him. She said I was making a bigger deal out of everything than I needed to. She said she and her momma went by his job and she's seen him around a few times after that when she went back to the store. After a while I noticed Nathan escorting his parents and sister to a higher section on the opposite side of the bleachers and then he sat with them. I pointed them out to Kendra, and I told her I was the wicked stepchild. I tried to act like my feelings weren't hurt, but they were. I wanted to cry, but I wasn't going to give them the satisfaction of one solitary tear. When they called Neallan Langston Parker Jr, Kendra and I stood up and cheered loudly. A lot of other people cheered for him as well, so we didn't stand out. When the ceremony was over I grabbed Kendra's hand and we rushed to Junior. He picked me up and kissed my forehead. He said I looked very pretty and he was so thankful that Kendra and I came. I didn't like that he included Kendra in my moment with him. But I decided to let it go. The look on his mother's face was priceless when she realized it was me with Junior. I know my daddy was surprised to see me as well, but he seemed like he stood there holding his breath for a minute. Nassya ran up to me and gave me a big hug. She told me she's missed me; I wanted to be mean to her. But she put those big brown eyes on me that said she meant it. My daddy didn't say anything to me, but he extended his hand to Kendra and introduced himself, then his wife did the same. When they asked me how I got there and I told them Nathan picked me up, they stared at him like he was a traitor. Then Junior explained he made him do it. I guess Nathan really doesn't like me, if Junior had to "make him" do it. Junior said he was riding with us to the restaurant, and his parents looked shocked that he wanted to include us in his celebration dinner. Nassya begged her parents to let her ride with us. They were suckers for her brown eyes as well, they agreed. Junior told me to let Kendra ride in the front with Nathan so that we could sit in the back like the celebrities we were as they chauffeured us around. Nassya told me she really liked my hair, and then she complimented everything I had on like she was making a mental note. It was too hard to ear hustle on Kendra and Nathan and talk to Junior and the little brat. So I talked to Junior, I got excited when we pulled up to Murphy Carlos. My daddy used to bring us here all the time, but it all seemed so long ago. Kendra hesitated and I heard her tell Nathan that she didn't bring enough money for a place this nice. He told her that his parents were footing the bill, but she didn't ever have to worry about money when she was with him. I interrupted them and told them she was with me and she would never be with him. Nathan looked at Junior, and Junior came over as the peacemaker as usual. My daddy told the host to add two more people to his reservation. When we sat at the table Kendra thanked Junior's parents for allowing her to come, and the first smile I've ever seen on his mother's face was big and wide. That made me angry! When they came to take our drink order, I ordered a strawberry daiquiri while everyone ordered sodas and Kendra said she only wanted water until Junior's mom convinced her to get a soda as well. I couldn't believe how nice she was being to Kendra!

"So where do you live now?" My daddy asked me.

"Richmond," I said feeling upset.

My daddy didn't really care; he was just making small talk. "That's good."

"Do you live in Richmond too?" Nathan's mom asked Kendra.

"Yes, she lives down the street from me." I answered for her.

Nathan's mother gave me an irritated look. "Are you an only child?" She asked Kendra.

I cut Kendra off and I answered for her again. Nathan's mother snapped at me and told me she wasn't talking to me. I told her that Kendra was irrelevant, and she should be trying to get to know me. After all she was my stepmother. Then my father leaned in, "you wonder why you haven't seen me? This is exactly why! You act too much like your doggone mother! Let me have to talk to you again and I'll treat you like the stranger you're making yourself become. My wife is trying to make the best out of you being here, but we will not allow you to treat people like this in our presence, as if we condone anyone acting like this! This is a lovely young lady. Let them have their conversation or you can leave now! Either way I don't want to hear another peep from you!" Everybody was looking to see how I reacted. My face was stinging I was so angry. I kicked my shoes off under the table. I reached and picked them up. I stood up so Kendra did too. In the loudest voice I could muster I cursed my father as hard as I could. I called him every name I could think of. And when I couldn't think of anything else to say I said, "PEEP! PEEP! PEEP!" And when he sat there looking unaffected by my words, I picked up my glass of ice water and I threw the water in his face. Everyone in the restaurant gasped. When he moved to stand up I ran. I ran out of the restaurant barefoot and out into the parking lot. Kendra was right behind me. When I stopped running she ran up to me and put her arms around me. I didn't want her to see me cry, but I couldn't help it. He's my father; he's supposed to care what happens to me. The only ones who cared were Junior and that little brat. But neither one of them came after me. The only person acting like they cared was Kendra. I was walking and crying on her shoulder. She said we could call her mom from the hotel next door. As we were walking I stepped on glass. My foot started bleeding. GREAT! Could this get any worse? Kendra put me on her back and she gave me a piggyback ride in her nice shoes and clothes to the hotel. The girl behind the counter let Kendra use the phone to call home. Then she got the first aid kit. She put on gloves then she got the glass out of my foot. She put alcohol on the cut then she blew air as I screamed about the burn. Then she put gauzes and a bandage on my foot.

When Kendra's mother came she asked me if I was ok which made me cry more. Kendra's mother was not related to me and she cared more than my family did. When they dropped me off at my grandmother's house, my momma was gone and my grandmother was on her way out. She asked me what happened to my foot, when I told her she told me not to walk around outside without my shoes on then she left. Neither one of them came home that night. Eventually I cried myself to sleep.

****

"This is my daughter Nealesha." My momma said with pride. My momma's new boyfriend smiled at me. "She looks just like you."

My momma smiled, "that's what makes her gorgeous, no thanks to her father. She'll be in the seventh grade in the fall. Yadda, yadda, yadda! Anyways!" My momma said steering the conversation away from me. I sat there quietly cause they weren't talking to me. Mister too cool was foaming at the mouth looking at my momma and she was eating it up. When she had to use the bathroom she told me to come with her. But Bobby told me to stay and pick out a dessert. My momma eyed me like I might say the wrong thing and ruin this for us, and then she walked away.
"Yo momma is FINE Mmmmhhh!" He said watching her walk. Then he looked at me. "You're not far behind her. So tell me," he sat back in his seat. "What do you like?"
"Everything!"
He smiled, "you're a little diva like your momma I see." I smiled back, "well you know in this world you don't get something for nothing. If I get you what you like, are you going to do what I like?"
I felt like my skin was crawling. "What do you like?"
He sat back, "we can talk about that later. Just be a good girl and keep this between me and you." Then he put a hundred dollar bill in my hand. "Put that away for a rainy day. There's plenty more of that if you can keep secrets."
All I could think about was all the clothes and shoes I was about to get.

Kendra
As I walked down Aunt Quilla's street I saw boys playing football in the middle of the street. Some of them were shirtless and the others had shirts on. I heard Aunrey yell "LOOK OUT!" as the ball came hurling at me. I moved in time for the ball to hit my shoulder so hard it spun me around and knocked me on the grass. I heard footsteps as everyone ran over to me to see if I was ok. Aunrey helped me up as my shoulder was KILLING me! All the guys asked me if I was ok. I sucked it up out of embarrassment and lied and said I was ok. When I made my way inside, I heard them erupt into laughter. Which only hurt my feelings more. Ahjanae asked me what was wrong, and she tried not to laugh as I told her the story. But she said the way I described it made it sound hilarious. I sat at her table embarrassed to get going, but I sucked it up. Ahjanae asked me where my stuck up friend was, and I told her

that she was with her momma. Ahjanae said she didn't know why I was friends with her. I nodded my head in agreement, but I didn't say anything. She looked at my face and asked me what was wrong. I told her my daddy didn't come last night. Normally he comes home irritated or late, but last night was the first time he didn't come home. I told her my momma's too depressed to even get out of the bed this morning. I felt horrible, I asked Ahjanae if she thought my parents were really going to get divorced? She said she didn't know but she hugged me and told me that anything that happened at this point was for the best. I wanted to cry but no tears would come out. I took a deep breath and then I asked her if she was ready. As we walked out of the door the guys were saying, "alright D!" To one of the guys, but I didn't look to see which one. I was hoping that they didn't look at me and start laughing again. Ahjanae and I walked ahead to make our way to the Bart station. "Where you two going?" The voice said from behind us.

We looked back and Ahjanae stopped walking to respond. "The Bart station, you?"

"The Bart station, I'm about to go home. Who's your friend?"

"This is our cousin Kendra, Kendra this is Darryl."

"Girl, the way you spun around I thought you were part Tasmanian devil." Then he chuckled, I gave a courtesy smile and then I turned to start walking again. "Dang! Did I hit you in the arm or the butt? Jen she got a BIG OLE BOOTAY!" I gasped; I couldn't believe he was serious. My reaction made both of them laugh. "How could you not know how blessed you are?" He said with a smile.

I shot Ahjanae a look cause I couldn't believe she was laughing with him. "Darryl leave her alone, she gets enough slack at home because of it."

"You don't get the world handed to you with a body like that? Everyone should just bow down to you when you walk past them." Then he got on the ground like he was worshipping me. "Kenny B! Kenny B!"

"Kenny B?" Ahjanae asked, "I'm afraid to ask."

"Kendra's Booty!"

Ahjanae cracked up laughing again, "You are so stupid!"

"Shut up!" I said irritated.

"Aw Kenny B, don't be like that." He said putting his arm around my neck. "Listen, I'm sorry for hitting you with the ball like that. I thought my cousin was gonna catch it, but he was such a punk talking about I was throwing too hard. But I'm glad I hit you, that booty has made my day." He smiled

"Where are your brother's?" Ahjanae asked him.

He kept his arm around my neck, "Drew's probably still out celebrating his graduation which is why I'm on five point toes instead of rolling with him. D-Rick is going to catch up to me at the Bart." Then he looked down at me, "you know my brothers?"

"She don't know none of ya'll."

"What you mean? Who doesn't know us?"

"She doesn't. Kendra's a good girl." She said like I wasn't there. He looked back at my butt. "We'll see how long that last."

I took his arm from around my neck. "You are so rude! You don't even know me, and I don't appreciate your comments."

Darryl grinned at me. "You're right, she don't know us." He took a deep breath. "I apologize KB for objectifying you." He tried to make his face sincere. Right as I was going to accept his apology, he smiled. "It's just that it's very rare to find such beauty in a booty like that. Did your momma spank you just so it would sit up just like that?" He clapped his hands, "well done momma! Well done!"

I growled at him and stormed off. Ahjanae told him to be nice to me as he cracked up laughing. They ran to catch up with me. He told Ahjanae that he couldn't apologize for admiring my assets it wasn't right. I rolled my eyes at him, he's heck of childish. When we got to the Bart station his brother was there buying his ticket. Darryl said he was buying our tickets since he had the pleasure of seeing me run. Ahjanae told me to let him pay for us as she told him we were going to El Cerrito Plaza shopping center. His brother was the complete opposite of him. I wondered how they even got along. His face was very serious and he didn't do any unnecessary talking. Darryl introduced me to his brother D-Rick. He nodded at me and said hello. Then he looked at Darryl with a so-what expression. Darryl asked what we were doing in El Cerrito. Ahjanae said we were going to see my friend. Darryl looked at me and asked me if it was my boyfriend. I wiggled my neck and told him it was none of his business. That made his brother laugh for five seconds, then he went back to his unamused expression. Darryl told Ahjanae that he liked me, he said I had spunk. When Ahjanae and I got up to get off the train, Darryl kept bumping his brother to look at us. D-Rick shook his head and said I was a little girl.

As we walked from the Bart station to the shopping center Ahjanae told me everything she could think of about them. She said they were Ms. Lorraine's nephews and nobody smart messed with them. She said even Aunrey knew better than to mess with them and outside of them he backed down to no one.

Nathan smiled when we walked into the store. Ahjanae said he was so cute. Nathan asked his friend to show Ahjanae around the store while he led me by the hand to the back to a corner behind the bookshelves. He set me on the table, put his hands on my butt, and then he kissed me. I was in shock; I've never kissed a boy. Then he forced my mouth open with his tongue and he kissed me some more. This was all new. I felt so stupid cause I didn't know what to do. He smiled at me then he told me to massage his tongue with my tongue and to follow his lead. Then he said I was doing it right, his hands were all over me. I had never been felt up before. When he put his hands under my shirt I jumped. He started laughing. Then he said he got off work in a few minutes and then he'd take us around. I said ok, and then he smacked my butt when I walked in front of him. I got a sinking feeling as I heard that stupid boy's voice talking about my butt in my head, but I liked the attention this high school boy was paying me. Ahjanae and I walked around the shopping center while she told me more about the Masons. She said she was scared for me when I was throwing attitude at Darryl. She said he's crazy, she said he must've felt bad for hitting me with the ball. I told her that ball hit me hard and I'm sure my shoulder is bruised. Nathan found us after a while and he asked us what we wanted to do? We shrugged and then I told him we had to be home in a little bit. He sucked his teeth. We decided to go to the park. We had a bunch of fun running around and being silly. As Nathan drove us to Ahjanae's house she leaned forward. "Are you Kendra's boyfriend?"

I gasped, but I wanted to hear his answer. He laughed and looked at me. "Yea sure, why not?" When he pulled over around the corner from Ahjanae's house he leaned over and kissed me. Ahjanae got out of the car and waited. His hands were all over me again. I liked the attention but I didn't like his hands being all over me. But this is my boyfriend, isn't this supposed to happen?

****

"I hardly ever see you anymore. Why are you at your aunt's house so much these days?" Nellie asked.

"My momma goes over to talk to my aunt. Then Ahjanae and I do stuff together."
"What kind of stuff?"
"We hangout, stuff like that." I didn't want to mention her brother.
"Why don't you bring me around your family? You afraid I'll out shine you there too?"
I cut my eyes at her. If she even knew half the things her brother has said about her she would shut up! "Why would you say something like that?"
"I'm just playing." She smiled, but I knew she wasn't. "Can I come with you? I'm so bored over here with my grandmother all day."
"My cousins don't play, I don't think they want to put up with your shenanigans."
She put her hand up, "I'll be good! I promise!"
"I have to ask my Aunt." I called Aunt Quilla and she said it was fine as long as Nellie behaved herself. I told Nellie to be at my house in the morning. That night I called Nathan after my momma went to bed like I normally do. I told him I couldn't come see him tomorrow cause his sister was coming with me over my cousin's house. Nathan was mad and he told me to ditch her. I told him I wouldn't do that cause I was the only friend she had. He said she was a selfish spoiled brat and she wasn't my friend. "Nathan she's your sister! Don't treat her like that."
"Half's don't count!"
I gasped, "That is so mean! It's not like only half her blood is linked to you. That is your sister bonded by blood. Did you ever think she might act like that because you treat her like this?"
"She's always been like that. She acts like her mother. That's why my dad dumped her." He spit.
I felt bad for Nellie, "but that doesn't excuse him dumping his daughter as well. That was heartless."
"What would you know about my father? You're just a stupid kid! You need to shut up and only talk about the stuff you know!" Then he exhaled, "I don't have time for this have fun with your friend. I'm breaking up with you!"
"Why? Because I was stating facts?" Tears started welling up in my eyes.
"Because you're a little kid. I'm a man and I need more out of a relationship than you're ready to deal with!"
"Like what?"

"Sex! You get too nervous about me touching you. When are you going to let me in?"

I felt like he punched me. "I, I, I..."

"I, I," he said mocking me. "Have a good life, call me when you're ready!" Then he hung up in my face.

I went back to my bed and cried myself to sleep. In the morning, I was dragging I couldn't understand why he broke up with me over something so stupid. When Nellie came she was so busy being a diva she didn't notice my defeated demeanor. My momma dropped us off at Aunt Quilla's. Kaleah and Audra entertained Nellie while I cried on Ahjanae's shoulder. She said Nathan is a jerk and he didn't deserve someone like me, or my virginity. She said it should be with someone you love like her and Jabbar. I looked at her in disbelief, she smiled an embarrassed smile. I sat up, I wanted details. Then Aunt Quilla told us to walk around the corner to the corner store to get some tissue paper and bologna for lunch. We snuck out the door fast so that Nellie wouldn't see us. All those boys were outside again. We barely hit the sidewalk when I told her to share. Ahjanae smiled real big and then she described the whole scene so I could feel like I was there. She told her momma she was with me, and she went over his house. She said they were on the couch watching TV with his little sister. Her little friend came over and they went out back. Jabbar locked the door and they started making out on the couch. She said he had her bra up and pants unbuttoned then he asked her if she loved him and she said yes of course. She said he told her, he loved her too. Then he pulled her pants and panties down. She said when he touched her down there he said she was ready. She said she wasn't sure if that's what he meant until he started sticking it in. I asked her if it hurt, and she said it did a little bit, but not like our momma's try to make it seem. I asked her if he used anything, and her face dropped. She said she didn't think of that. Her eyes were wide as she swallowed. I asked her if she was scared and she shook her head yes. She even broke out in a little sweat. I rubbed her back and told her it was gonna be ok. I asked her if it at least felt good? She said it was ok, but she loved how sprung he was acting when they were done. He made everybody homemade hamburgers and French-fries. He told his little sister that he and Ahjanae were married. She said she loved the sound of it.

Then I heard, "KB! Where you been girl?" He said staring at my butt. I rolled my eyes at him, "Aw KB! Don't be like that! I've missed your assets!"

I sucked my teeth and looked at Ahjanae, "can we leave?"

"DON'T LEAVE ME GIRL! NO! DON'T DO IT! At least let a brotha watch you walk away!" Then he laughed.

"Darryl you like my cousin or something? I've never seen you pay so much attention to any girl."

Darryl's face got serious, "I don't know do I?" He put his finger up to his chin like he was thinking. "How does one act when they like someone?" He asked Ahjanae

She laughed, "Like you're acting right now."

He looked at me, "I guess if I liked you it wouldn't be ok to get on your nerves?" I shook my head no. Then he smiled and I knew it was a wrap. "But I like getting on your nerves, then watching that big ole booty bounce away. Can we have it both ways?" I crossed my arms and shook my head no. "Aw! KB! Don't be like that!" When I stormed away to the counter he said, "and there she goes! Mmmhh! Your cousin is BLESSED!" I was waiting for Ahjanae and they were talking. Instead of bologna like her mother told her to get she got ham. She got cheddar cheese, sourdough bread, and three different kinds of chips. She got two bottles of soda, and a bunch of candy. I didn't know what was going on. We didn't have the money to pay for all of this, and if he tries to hold up the store I'm running and I'm telling my Aunt I had nothing to do with it. He put gum and mints on the counter as well. Then he paid for everything. Ahjanae said we were going to eat good thanks to my booty. I rolled my eyes again. "Do that again!" Darryl said smiling real big. So I rolled my eyes again. "You do that just like my momma! That's it! I think I'm in love!" He smiled; I rolled my eyes and reached for a bag. "I know I'm in love!" He said smiling at my butt. "You break up with your boyfriend yet?" I said no and Ahjanae said yes. I cut my eyes at her. "Well which one is it?" He said taking all the bags even the one in my hands.

"Technically we broke up last night. But that was only temporary. We're getting back together as soon as he calms down."

"Why would he break up with you? It's because you told him about us isn't it?"

I looked away, and we continued walking. Then I heard somebody say "look out". I turned just in time to see a pit bull charging at us.

Ahjanae and I screamed and jumped on top of the nearest car. Darryl stood still hands full of groceries and he stared at the dog. The dog stopped right in front of him wagging its tail. He told the dog to sit, and it did as it was told. He told the dog it was a good dog as the owner came running up out of breath. "Thank you," the girl said trying to catch her breath.

"This your dog?" Darryl said looking her over.

"Yeah, she got out the fence and took off. I didn't think I'd catch up to her." She said putting her leash on the dog who didn't take her eyes off of Darryl. "How did you get her to sit?"

"I told her to." Then he looked at us. "You guys better get down before the owner of that car sees you." Then he returned his attention back to the girl, "You don't know how to control your dog?"

"She's my brother's dog. I was just feeding her for him." Then she smiled at Darryl.

Darryl looked at me, "you see this? This is how you're supposed to act." Then he smiled at me. "What's your name?"

The girl looked at us as we got off the car, "Orkisha." She said We introduced ourselves then she lingered while looking at Darryl. He smiled at me again. "What you got going on today? You wanna come hang out with my friends and me? We're about to eat lunch."

"Can I bring the dog?"

I wanted him to look at me so I could tell him no, but he said yes. Darryl asked her how old she was and she said fifteen, he smiled at me again. Ahjanae looked at me and smiled too, then she bumped me and told me to smile. I was irritated cause she got this big ole dog walking with us. And Ahjanae's momma told us to get bologna for lunch and she didn't do it. I thought the groceries were for us but if he's inviting random females he must be taking her back to his aunt's house, so we didn't get what we were told to get. He walked us to Ahjanae's house then he told us he was going to tie the dog up and he'd be right back. GREAT! Now we have to entertain this girl. Ahjanae invited her in, she looked around. Kaleah, Audra, Kalani, and Nellie came inside. "Who's this?" Audra asked.

She stuck her hand out, "Orkisha."

"Audra, and these are my cousins Kaleah and Kalani, and our friend Nellie."

"Nice to meet you."

31

Aunt Quilla heard the introduction and came out of her room. She eyed Orkisha and asked her where she lived. When she explained Aunt Quilla said she was kin to Juju, she smiled and said he was her big brother. I know she wanted to know how we knew her. Nellie made herself comfortable next to Orkisha on the couch. She was blatantly sizing her up. Darryl knocked on the door and Ahjanae let him in. She was about to introduce him to her momma, but Aunt Quilla said she knew who he was already. "You're Ms. Lorraine's nephew aren't you?"

"Yes ma'am! I am the favorite!" He smiled.

"Weren't you hanging upside down from that tree that use to be in her yard? Screaming something crazy?"

His smile got bigger, "yep that was an ordinary Wednesday. But that was a long time ago. Now I hang from buildings, houses, and bridges. You know ordinary stuff."

Aunt Quilla started laughing, "You are crazy you know that. You here for Ahjani? He's in his room."

"Actually I was hanging out with the girls." He raised his eye brows at her.

"Oh! That's why this child is here. I was wondering."

"Momma, Darryl bought everything at the store." Ahjanae said giving her mother back her money.

Aunt Quilla looked shocked, "thank you baby." Then she gave Darryl a hug.

"Mmmmhhhh! Ms. Quilla you smell good! I tell you if I was six years older."

She laughed, "six years?"

"Yeah eighteen. Old enough to be legal, and young enough for you to show off."

Aunt Quilla belly laughed, she rubbed his head, and then she went back in her room.

Darryl scanned the room, "you're Ahjanae's sister I can tell. You two can only be related to KB." I frowned at him, "I mean." He laughed, "Kendra. And you are?" He said pointing to Nellie. "Nellie," then she smiled.

Ahjanae asked me to help her make the grilled ham and cheese sandwiches. Everyone except Nellie and Orkisha followed us into the kitchen. We were whispering about Darryl and Orkisha. Nellie kept trying to keep Darryl's attention by talking to him and Orkisha was sitting there looking annoyed. We were putting the perfectly prepared sandwiches on a plate in the middle of the table. And putting enough out, when Darryl directed his attention to Orkisha. "So, how's your summer treating you?" He asked her.

"Good," she said. Darryl hopped out his seat like it was on fire. He quickly moved to the other side of the room. "What's wrong?" She asked.

"Your breath! Did something die in you?" Orkisha looked embarrassed. "You shouldn't go around assaulting people like that!" He said still holding his nose like it was about to fall off if he let it go.

Nellie started laughing, the rest of us looked on in horror. "I'm gonna go!" Orkisha said running for the door.

Darryl held on to his nose as he shook his head, "go brush your teeth."

Nellie was completely amused by the scene, but I was annoyed. He didn't have to be that mean to her. I bet she cried all the way home.

I was waiting for Darryl to sit so I didn't have to sit next to him. But of course the last two seats were next to each other. Darryl rubbed my chair and told me he wished he was the chair for the next however long. I held my breath and sat down. Ahjani turned on videos to watch while we ate. When a Torrie Rowe video came on we all got up and started dancing. "We know the dance to this song by heart." Kalani said going into the living room.

Darryl smiled, "you guys like Torrie?"

"Her music's alright, but her videos make them sick! I'm excited whenever she has a new project cause that means we're going to learn some new moves." Audra said dancing her way into the living room.

"So you're saying you like the choreography more than you like the songs?" He asked everyone.

"Yep! It's sick!" Kaleah said doing the routine.

Nellie and I didn't leave the table. "You guys don't dance?"

"I'm eating," I said not wanting him watching me while I danced.

"I'm not much of a dancer." Nellie said because she had no rhythm. "I dance like a white girl."

Darryl frowned, "what does that mean?"

"I don't really have rhythm." She said matter of factly.

"You're ignorant! That's a dumb stereotype!" His eyes glazed over, "you look at people and see color don't you?"

"Chill out! I was trying to poke fun at myself I didn't mean to offend you." Nellie said in her first apology in my presence ever! Darryl sat there glaring at her, and it was unlike anything I've seen before. His demeanor became cold and stiff. "Hey Darryl, can you dance?" I asked hoping to bring him around.

"I dance like a white boy," he said cutting his eyes at Nellie.

"Well let's see what that looks like." I said taking his hand.

When I stood up he smiled at me, "you gonna back that thing up on me?"

I frowned, "no!"

"Oh come on KB!" He pleaded.

Nellie sat at the table watching us dance. Immediately we stopped dancing and we all stood there frozen watching him glide around the living room. Not only could he dance, he was really good! "I thought you said you dance like a white boy?" Kalani asked

He shot Nellie an evil look, "I do!" Then he looked at Kalani, "don't let ignorant people shape your perception of a person based on the color of their skin. You'll get a lot further in life without stereotypes."

"Perception? Ok," Kalani smiled and went back to dancing.

I didn't understand why Nellie's comment offended him so much. But you could tell he put her on his yuck list. Eventually we laid out on the floor randomly and we were coloring in Audra's coloring books. Audra asked Darryl why he wasn't coloring and he said he couldn't stop staring at it. When she asked him what, I looked at him and he was licking his lips acting like he wanted to take a bite out of my butt. Audra told him he was nasty, and he agreed with her. I didn't feel so annoyed about his comments especially once he showed no interest in Nellie. The only guy to do that before was her brother, and of course he wasn't gonna be interested.

Someone pounded on the door, we jumped and Darryl stood up. Ahjanae opened the door. "Is that fool still here?" Someone yelled from the door.

Aunt Quilla heard the noise and came out, "what fool?"

"The punk who yelled at my sister and took my dog!" The guy said looking really big and mean.

"Juju we don't want no problems." Aunt Quilla said trying to protect Darryl who was putting on his shoes.

Darryl walked to the door, "I don't know about no punks, but I'll get your dog for you." Darryl said dryly.

"This him?" Juju asked his sister who was standing on the sidewalk with two other guys. Orkisha shook her head yes. "I need to see you outside!"

"Juju no! I'm sorry! I don't know what's going on, but we can settle this..."

"Ain't nobody talking to you Aquilla! I suggest you stay out of this or else I'll come back for you!"

Aunt Quilla grabbed Darryl who was fearlessly walking out the door. "No! I'm calling the police!"

"Ms. Quilla it's ok. I'm gonna lay him out for disrespecting your house, then we can finish coloring." He said calmly, as he removed her grip on his shirt.

Juju smiled real big as he backed up. "You can't be from around here, everybody else knows better. I normally don't beat little kids but I'll make an exception for you!" He said dancing around the grass.

Aunt Quilla told Ahjanae to bring her the phone. As soon as Darryl's feet hit the grass he didn't seem shorter than Juju anymore. When he hit Juju you heard it, and the surprise that flashed across his face was priceless. His sister and friends were speechless. The smiles that were on their faces a few minutes prior were gone. Now Orkisha was pleading with him to stop beating on her brother. Darryl was fast, strong, and mean! Grown Juju didn't stand a chance. Then Darryl's brother and two other guys casually walked across the street. You heard Juju's arm break, I thought I was going to be sick. Darryl was going for the other arm right as Juju's friends got the courage to try to help him not seeing his brother and other two guys behind them. "Whoa D! What's going on?" His brother D-Rick asked calmly as his serious eyes scanned the scene with approval.

"Please make him stop!" Orkisha screamed in horror.

Darryl laid both of the guys out, and then he stormed towards Orkisha. "WHAT YOU BRING THEM HERE FOR?"

D-Rick put his arm out to catch his brother before he reached her. "That's a stupid female calm down." He said calmly.

"I'm calm!" Darryl said staring at Orkisha.

D-Rick looked at him, he smiled. "If you're happy and you know it clap your hands."

Both of them started cracking up laughing. Even the fools on the ground looked at them like, "WHAT?"

Darryl wasn't angry anymore. "Oh let me go get his dog. That's what he came for anyways. I'll be right back." He ran across the street.

"Who are you?" Aunt Quilla asked.

"I'm D's brother, these are our cousins."

Darryl came back with the dog. He handed the leash to Orkisha. He looked at Aunt Quilla, "can we finish coloring?"

Aunt Quilla blinked at Darryl. "Are you ok child?"

"Yep!" He kissed her cheek, "I'm ok. But I won't be fine until they leave!" He barked at the guys who were helping their friend up.

"If it's ok with you, we'll make sure they leave. And you guys can go back inside to whatever you were doing." D-Rick said to Aunt Quilla.

Aunt Quilla looked lost for a minute then she said ok. Darryl grabbed Kalani's hand and told her to come on. When we went back inside I stared at Darryl like he was a stranger. "Don't look at me like that KB." He said looking at his picture. "You gonna be scared of me now?" He sounded like the thought of it made him sad.

"Should I be?"

"No, I like that you're not scared of me."

"Ok," I said going back to my picture.

When Aunrey came home from wherever he was, he was happy to see Darryl. Then everyone told him about the fight, for the lack of a better word. Aunrey asked Darryl what would happen if Juju and 'em come back? Darryl said his brother was handling that and we'd be fine. Darryl smiled when he saw me listening. He patted the floor next to him for me to come closer. I told him if he mentioned one thing about my booty I was leaving. He told me he made no promises, but he would try to control his lust. The expression on his face was different; even though he was smiling he wasn't being overly silly. He asked me a lot of questions about myself, and I liked him like this. And I guess apparently I'm pretty funny cause he kept laughing at the things I said. Nellie sat over to the side watching us like a hawk. It was nice talking to Darryl, and getting to know the other side of him. But I couldn't help but think of Nathan the moment Darryl left. I told myself I wasn't gonna call him; he'd have to figure out how to get in contact with me if he wanted me back.

Chapter 3

Nellie

What universe is this? A guy likes Kendra and acts like I'm not me? No! No! No! This will not work, this cannot happen. Whenever "D" comes over his Aunties house he goes over to Audra's looking for Kendra. I've seen him checking me out, but he acts uninterested. I wonder if his first love was white or something. I don't understand why my comment offended him so much. Or why he likes Kendra when she doesn't act all that interested in him. She's stupid, he's got money cause he's always buying something for the house whenever he comes over whether it's pizza, going to the store to get stuff to cook or whatever. He dresses neatly, but when he's my man, I'll make sure he put some labels on. He's cute when he's serious, but when he's my man he will be more serious. But honestly if his brother D-Rick would look my way! OH! OH! I like the strong silent type. When I say hi to him he says hi but then, his eyes burn a hole in you. I don't know what's wrong with the men in this family that they don't appreciate pretty when it's staring them in the face. D-Rick is about to be in high school, so I think I'll stay in my lane with D.

"What do you want me to bring you back?" D asked Kendra.

"Nothing," she said trying to play hard to get.

She needs to quit playing because if he asks me I will ask for something. "Where are you going?" I asked

"Hawaii," he said still waiting for a better answer from Kendra.

I bumped her, "let him bring you a necklace or something." Kendra shook her head no. "Don't pay her no never mind. Bring her some earrings or something."

He looked at me for a minute like he was irritated. "Was I talking to you?"

Ugh! Why does he always respond to me like that? "No, but I was only trying to help." I sunk in my seat.

"Kendra you don't have to be so standoffish though." Ahjani said eating a bowl of cereal. "You keep acting uninterested and my man's gonna really think you don't like him. When we all know you do."

"HOLD ON! KB be talking about me?" Darryl smiled

Kendra looked horrified, "No! No I don't! Shut up Ahjani!"

"She like you D! I heard them talking." Ahjani said with a smile.
D spun around, "FANTASTIC!" He shook Ahjani's hand. "You
are alright with me Adobo!"
Everyone started laughing. "Man, when you gonna get my name
right? It's Ahjani, ah-jah-nee, Ahjani." He said laughing.
"My bad!" D laughed, "Put some music on, I wanna dance with
KB. It's time for you to work it. I'm gonna be leaving soon to get
ready for my trip. This will be our last dance until I can get out
here again."
Kendra was still embarrassed. "I don't feel like dancing." She said
in protest.
D looked at me, "here's your first dance lesson." He pulled me up.
"Maestro! Music please!"
Ahjani put music on and even though I was embarrassed I'd do
anything to have his attention. I couldn't do the fancy footwork or
anything, but I caught the rhythm with my hips. Especially when
he showed me how the first time. I wonder if this is what sex is
like moving to someone else's rhythm. D smiled at me when I got
the hip movement, he told me I was ready for something. I was
ready for whatever he wanted as long as he kept his hands on my
body. When the next song came on Kendra popped off the couch
and she went to the other side of the room dancing with Ahjanae
and their sisters. D left me to go dance with them. I tried not to
show my irritation. I had to dance with Ahjani to play it off.
Kendra's auntie wasn't home so our little dance party quickly
turned into a Freak Fest. I had to pretend I was ok with Ahjani
freaking on me. But I couldn't believe Kendra. D was smacking her
butt and she didn't get mad. When she turned her back to him, D
screamed out that he was in love! He kept narrating their dance and
explaining how happy he was. Kendra fell on the ground laughing
at him. When he helped her up he kissed her. I felt like I was going
to be sick. Everybody was stuck not knowing how to respond.
They were kissing for a long time. This couldn't have been the first
time they've done this. My first kiss was clumsy. Kendra pulled
away looking at everybody looking completely embarrassed.
While D stood there smiling at her really big. Everybody started
laughing. Kendra grabbed Ahjanae's hand and stormed out of the
living room. I followed them to Ahjanae's room. Kendra screamed
into Ahjanae's pillow kicking and screaming. Ahjanae laughed at
her and told her she's in trouble now. Forever the good girl, Kendra

said she didn't mean for that to happen. I asked them what the big deal was and Kendra just stared at the floor. "I don't understand what the problem is. He's fine! Got money! And he likes you! What's the problem?"

"He lives in Oakland, it could never work. Once school starts I'll need to focus anyways." She exhaled, "a summer fling!"

When we went back in the living room D was dancing with Kalani and playing big brother. Then his brother knocked on the door. He told D it was time to go. I wasn't ready for him to go yet. He said he'd be gone for a while. He went around the room hugging everyone goodbye acting like he was crying. When he hugged me I pressed my body in on his real close, and I quickly kissed his neck. D jumped but he didn't reject me. That's when I knew he would be mine.

Kendra

He couldn't even look at me. "I don't want you guys thinking that this is about you. I'm going through something right now, and it's best if I stay away for a while." My father said

"Why daddy? Why? Nobody could love you more than we do! I won't ask for any more clothes or anything. Please stay!" Kaleah pleaded.

Tears filled his eyes as he picked her up. "I'm coming back, I promise!"

"Don't tell them that!" I spit at him. "Don't insult our intelligence just so you won't feel bad about what you're doing to our family!" I snatched my sister out of his arms. "You're leaving us, and you're not coming back. Spare us the pain of wondering when you're coming back! You've been gone this whole time without a word. And you expect us to believe that now that you're taking your things you're coming back! Stop lying!"

"I am still your father!"

"No you're not! I can't wait for my momma to divorce you and marry a real man! So we can have a real father! Did you ever stop to think, what kind of woman takes a man from his wife and three kids? She's gonna get you! Break your heart! Just like you did to ours! And you deserve it all!" All I saw was light. It was like sound stopped existing. My face was on fire and I was looking up from the ground.

"You will not disrespect me I am still your father!"

My father has never hit me before. And the fact that he chose now to do it surprisingly made me furious! Even I thought I would be scared. "You are a coward! Thank you for confirming why I should hate you! You can't stand the truth so much that you'd hit me for speaking it! I will never forgive you for hitting me! I grabbed my sister's hands to walk away. Kaleah snatch her hand away and ran back to her father. Kalani looked confused. I picked her up like she was a baby and I carried her towards the ramp to walk home. Kalani cried her eyes out as she clung to my neck. When we got home my momma asked me what was wrong. Kalani screamed that her daddy slapped me. Our momma's eyes turned black. She asked where Kaleah was, and Kalani said she was with her daddy. Momma told us to stay in the house. She went outside and stood on the sidewalk waiting. When he pulled up she told Kaleah to go in the house. He didn't even get a chance to get out the door. She started hitting him, kicking and screaming! All the neighbors came outside. He kept telling her to stop, but she told him to never touch her children again! Kaleah was screaming asking her to stop. Every time my momma smacked him upside the head my tears felt cleaner and cleaner. My momma had my back! I loved her so much. Finally he put his car in gear and drove off with his door open. Then my momma screamed at Kaleah telling her she told her to go inside. Everybody was looking at my momma then our neighbor Ms. McCall started clapping for my momma. Momma ignored her and came inside with us. We sat on the living room floor crying together.

****

Momma sat at the table with the bills and a calculator. She kept taking deep breaths as she tried not to cry about our finances. When I asked her what was wrong, she took a deep breath and said nothing. She told me to go play. I went in my room and I got my bank. I sat it on the table. I told my momma to use it. There were no more deep breaths to take she started crying. I told her we're a team and I would figure out a way to help out around the house. My momma cried and cried, I told her it would be ok cause we were a team.

The next morning, I went in the garage, I took out the lawn mower; our lawn hadn't been mowed since my father did it. It took a minute but I got the hang of it. Kalani got the tool that lined the edge of the grass and she did her best to get that going for me.

When I finished mowing I took over for Kalani and she gathered all the cut grass and put it in the trash. When we were done Kalani and I celebrated our victory. Ms. McCall was sitting on her porch watching us. Then she called out to us to come over to her yard. We walked around the fence. The weeds were as high as the fence, and her yard was a mess. She asked how much we would charge her to do her yard. I shrugged cause I didn't have a price in mind. She said if Kalani and I would clean up her front and backyard she'd take us school shopping. She told us to call our momma and ask her if it was ok. Kalani and I ran to the house and I called my momma at work. She started crying and she said it was ok. She asked about Kaleah, I told her Kaleah said her daddy was going to take her shopping.

Kalani and I went through her front yard like a tornado! I used all the tools their father left in the garage. I learned the hard way to watch out for rocks while using the weed whacker. I whacked, Kalani cleaned up. When our momma came home Ms. McCall was still sitting on the porch watching us like she had been all day. She told our momma she should be so proud cause she had hard working daughters. She said she's asked all the knuckle head boys to help her and none of them were interested. She said she's needed a new fence but she was embarrassed about her yard so she left this ugly too high fence. Ms. McCall invited us over for dinner as an additional thank you, and when momma tried to decline she wouldn't hear of it. We didn't really have anything to eat so momma gave in and accepted her invitation. Momma went and got Queen Kaleah who was reading books all day and then came back. Ms. McCall's house smelled like an old lady. She had newspapers and magazines everywhere. Her house wasn't dirty, but she had too much stuff crammed everywhere. Her dinner smelled delicious though. She had pulled pork in the crockpot. Ms. McCall said she used to have friends over all the time before Mr. McCall died. Then she said she got depressed, and then she was too embarrassed to have anyone over. Momma said she understood. She said if it wasn't for her girls her house would be a complete mess right now. She said she didn't have the energy to deal with anything at home. "Kharee is he coming back?" She asked

Momma hesitated when she looked at us. "He says he's going to, but I don't know."

Ms. McCall frowned, "what a man says and what he does sometimes is two different things." She exhaled, and then she looked at us. "What kind of a man turns his back on such beautiful little girls?" She shook her head. Then she looked at me, "so little momma I smell ambition all over you. Do you have a plan?"

"I was gonna knock on your door and ask you if you needed any yard work done around here, but you beat me to the punch. I was thinking we'd clean yards to earn some money for the house."

"What about when the winter comes and yards aren't kept up like the other seasons?"

"I haven't thought it all the way through." I admitted.

"I have an idea. I have friends who need all kinds of odd jobs done around their homes. When you finish my yards, help me get my house in order. I'll invite my friends over and you're guaranteed to get more business. How does that sound?"

I looked at my momma and she smiled through tears to say it was ok. I asked Kaleah and Kalani if they would help me. Kaleah sucked her teeth. She said her daddy was going to send money for her and she didn't need to work. Kalani happily said she would be my assistant.

The next day we finished the front yard. And then it took us three whole days to clear the jungle that was her backyard. As promised Ms. McCall took us shopping. Kalani and I only got the basic things we needed. Socks, one pair of shoes each, a few pairs of jeans and tops, backpacks, binders, paper, pencils, and pens. When Ms. McCall couldn't convince us to go crazy she handed us each a hundred and fifty dollars. She said we did way more work than fifty dollars each in clothes. She said next week we'd need the whole week for her house. When we got home I told Kalani to put forty dollars in her bank for emergencies and then I told her we should give the rest to momma for the house. I told her about momma crying about the bills. Kalani couldn't give me the money fast enough. When momma came home she was sad like she has been. Kalani and I went in her room while Kaleah entertained her imaginary audience in their room while she sang and jumped around. We gave momma the money and she cried as she hugged us. I told her to take forty to get Kaleah something's for school and let her think her daddy sent money for her.

She wasn't kidding we needed a whole week to clean out everything. When we finished Mrs. McCall's house everything sparkled in there and since she loved the smell of lemon everything she bought to clean with had that smell. I bought lemon scented plug-ins and placed them around the house. We brought momma and Mrs. McCall inside and they both cried. Mrs. McCall paid us five hundred dollars. I've never seen so much money in my life. She said she would pay us sixty dollars a week to come over and maintain her house.

The next day Mrs. McCall had her friends over for lunch. I guess they saw her house before because they were amazed at the transformation. She told her friends she could finally get her white picket fence she's always wanted. Like she said her friends were lining up for our services. It felt great.

Nellie

"Wake up!" My momma said shaking me awake. "Bobby wants you to come shopping with us. But I'm telling you right now, I don't want tantrums, no smart mouth comments, and no bad attitude or else you're getting nothing. Understood?"

I shook my head yes and then I hurried to the shower. I called Kendra and I told her I was going with my momma today. Everybody had already gone school shopping except me. For a minute it looked like my momma didn't care, as she would run through the house in all the new clothes Bobby had bought her. I got dressed and I quietly waited on the couch. When Bobby honked his horn my momma told me to come on. I quietly sat in the back as I watched my momma slobber all over this man. I would've said something but school clothes were on the line. Bobby asked my momma where she wanted to go shopping and she said in the city. I got excited because we hadn't shopped in the city since I was little and my daddy was footing the bill. Bobby looked back and asked if I was shopping in the city too. She exhaled and told him to take us to the Hilltop mall, which was Richmond's mall. I tried not to show disappointment on my face, because in the end I needed whatever he was willing to buy me. I asked him what was my limit and he said the sky. When my momma started to protest he told her my shopping wouldn't affect hers. My mouth started watering as I looked around the store. I picked up six different kinds of jeans. I tried them on and loved each pair so I went and got every color in every style. I got tons of shirts to mix everything up. I got every pair of shoe that called my name. I got four different jackets and two coats. I couldn't stop smiling as we walked to Bobby's car each of us with bags and bags of clothes all for me. We dropped my bags at the house and then we went to the city. Everything looked better than I remembered; I followed them around as my momma floated from rack to rack picking out everything her heart desired. When she finally went in the dressing room Bobby pulled me into his lap. He asked me if I loved all the stuff he got me. And I said yes, he asked me if I was going to show him how much I liked everything. I asked him how I would do that. He said tonight after my momma went to sleep he'd come see me. I immediately felt scared; he kissed my cheek and told me we'd go slow. Then he pointed at a dress I was looking at earlier and he asked me if I wanted it. I looked at the dress and I thought about how good it would look on me. It was my favorite color PINK! He said I could have the dress "if". I didn't want to think about what "if" meant, but I agreed because I really wanted that dress. Bobby paid for my stuff before my momma came out of the dressing room. He held my bags a long with the bags he carried for my momma. We had dinner in the city, and then we had to swing by his friend's house to make a pickup. He put the small black bag on the floor in front of my momma's seat and told her not to touch it. I wanted to know what was in the bag but since my momma didn't question it, I left it alone. When we went by our house to drop off my momma's bags and get nightclothes Bobby came inside with us. My momma introduced Bobby to my grandmother. "Mary where are you going?" She asked my momma not taking her eyes off of Bobby.

"We're going to spend the night at Bobby's." My momma said nonchalantly.

"We're? You're not taking my baby over this thug's house!" My grandmother said.

My momma sucked her teeth, "Momma! It's fine he's got a three bedroom. Nellie will sleep in her own room."

"And get shot up in her own room! You wanna be stupid and risk your life with him you go ahead, but my grand baby stays home!" Bobby didn't say anything; he stood there watching my momma and grandmother argue over me. He looked at me once briefly but he mostly kept his eyes on my momma. My grandmother saved me that night.

Kendra

Kalani and I took the last week of summer off to hang out with our cousins. Ahjanae said she and Jabbar do it whenever they can. She said it was so much fun. Immediately I thought of Nathan, I wondered if he thought about me at all. Ahjanae said that Darryl came by a few times looking for me. I told her I wished it was Nathan. She said I was crazy, she thinks D actually likes me. She said Nathan is taking advantage of a little girl. I didn't like that she was calling me a little girl, but hey! He's going to be a junior next week and I was going to the seventh grade. Ahjanae told me junior high would be a piece of cake for me. She was going to be a sophmore at Kennedy High school, and Ahjani was going to be a freshman. Ahjanae asked why Nellie didn't come over with us. I told her that I talked to Nellie briefly over the phone and she said she's been with her momma and her momma's new boyfriend. Ahjani knocked on the door like only he knocks. Ahjanae and I were laying on the floor listening to the radio facing the window. "Come in!" Ahjanae said

"KB! Oh my goodness KB! Don't move I wanna remember you just like this! Mountains of booty!"

"Stop it!" I laughed as I sat up.

He exhaled like he was sad as he sat next to me on the floor. "You guys start school next week don't you?"

"Yep, when do you guys start?"

"The week after." He shook his head, "what am I supposed to do without my booty view?"

Ahjani fell on the floor laughing, "you are so stupid!"

"You're laughing and I'm in pain! Move in with me KB! Bring that booty to Oakland where it belongs."

"I'm sure your momma would like that." I said

"Ok, come stay on the days she's out of town. I can convince my granddad and dad that you're cool. Once they see that booty they will understand! Whew!" Then he said he'd be right back. He came back with a small gift bag. His smile was real goofy like he was embarrassed. "I brought you something."

No one has ever given me anything I got butterflies in my stomach. "Thank you Darryl, but you didn't have to bring me anything."

"I know but it didn't cost me anything, I thought you would like it." He said bashfully.

I smiled and I took the tissue paper out of the bag while Ahjanae and Ahjani looked on. It was a beautiful seashell like I've seen on TV. I put it up to my ear and I really could hear the ocean. "It works!" I said in surprise.

"It's a conch shell. I found it on the beach when I was with my little sisters." He blushed.

"I didn't know you have sisters?"

He exhaled, "my momma's boyfriend has two girls. We're a family. Do you like it?"

"I love it!" I gave him a kiss on the cheek.

He blushed, "what was that?"

"Uh? A thank you kiss."

"You know what I want, turn the radio up!" He said grabbing my hand. I let him grab my booty one time and he said he was never gonna wash his hands again.

That night I listened to my shell until I started dozing off then I put it on my nightstand next to my bed. Darryl was sweet, but I missed Nathan.

Chapter 4

Nellie

He rubbed his hand over his face. "Why won't she move in?" Bobby asked about to blow a gasket. I shrugged looking down at my French fries. "I mean do you even like your grandmother? Say the word right now and I'll have a bullet put in her head!"

My heart started pounding because I didn't doubt that he would do it. "Of course I love my grandmother, she's the only one I got." I said softly.

He stared at me, "well she needs to mind her own business. Things could be so much easier if you guys just moved in."

"My grandmother says my momma can go if she wants to, but I can't come."

"And I don't want her there if you're not coming as well. You need to beg her to move in. Your grandmother is not your parent. How she gonna run this?"

I shrugged again; my grandmother has told my momma that I can't go stay with her and Bobby when my momma moves out. I don't think my momma even wants me to come with her. She looks at us funny all the time. Then she gets mad at me, and all of a sudden I'm not the little girl she's always loved. Now I'm fast and I do too much. I don't say too much since Bobby started picking me up from school and sometimes during school. I don't want my momma to be mad at me, but he told me if I didn't do it he'd break up with my momma and she's been so happy since he's been around. He always makes sure I have money and anything I want, but it's always "if" I do what he likes. I try not to think about it, I try to think about something else. It doesn't even hurt all that much anymore. If I relax and let it happen then I'm not as sore afterwards. But when I get all nerved up about it and try to feel some way about it, it hurts so badly. If he's in a bad mood he can be rough too. I keep my face even cause if I show that he's hurt me he gets mad. Sometimes I fake being sick so I don't have to go to school, I never know when he's gonna pop up. Just when I think I have his pattern down he pops up out of nowhere. He asks me all of the time if I have a boyfriend and I know I better say no. He gets mad if he even thinks I was looking at a boy. He tells my momma it's because I'm like a daughter to him. I wish she would just know and take me away from here. But she's so busy going on shopping sprees and spending his money. I don't think she's even noticed except for every once in a while she'll ask me what's wrong. I just say nothing because Bobby said he'd kill my momma if she ever took me away from him. He's killed other people before so he said killing my momma would be like 1, 2, 3.

When Kendra saw my report card, she looked at me and asked what was wrong. I shrugged at her cause I don't know what else to say. My momma yells at me and puts me on punishment, but Bobby tells her to leave me alone. Kendra keeps asking what's wrong and watching me. I wish my own momma would pay that much attention cause then maybe she'd figure it out.

I sat there moving my French fries around waiting for Bobby to say something else. "Who's this?" He asked about to go off.

"Princess?" I heard my brother's voice.

I looked up so happy to see him. I started to get up and Bobby glared at me. "It's my brother." I said softly as I sat back down.

"What are you doing here? Why aren't you at school?" Junior asked me looking real serious.

"It was teacher's work day or something. I'm here with my momma's boyfriend Bobby." I said, "This is my brother Junior."

"What's up?" Bobby said looking him up and down like a jealous boyfriend.

"Where's your mother?" He asked not taking his eyes off of Bobby.

""Probably at the shop getting her hair done."

"Why haven't you called me?"

"Phones work two ways, you could call me too. I figured you guys didn't want me around after what happened."

"What happened?" Bobby asked.

Junior looked at him and then continued to talk to me. "We need to talk about that night. Things got out of control. I should've said something."

"I don't know who you think you are! But you don't ever disrespect me! When I ask you a question, you answer me!" Bobby said getting in my brother's face.

I started crying, "Bobby please don't hurt my brother!"

"Hurt me? Who are you?" Junior said not backing down.

Bobby was all in his face, "I'm your worst nightmare! You got to go through me to talk to her!"

"You're her mother's boyfriend?" Junior said sarcastically.

"Don't worry about who I am! All you need to know is, I ain't the one to be messed with!"

Junior grabbed my arm real tight, "you ain't going nowhere with this fool! I don't like him!"

Bobby's eyes got big, "apparently you don't know who I am. I'm not one to be tested. I will lay you out!" He said as he pulled me towards him.

"Please Bobby! Don't hurt my brother!" I cried.

"He's not gonna do nothing! SECURITY! THIS MAN HAS KIDNAPPED MY SISTER!" Junior yelled at the two police officers patrolling the Oakland mall.

"You're dead!" Bobby said as he walked away before the police officers came over.

"Bobby please!" I cried after him.

"What's the problem here?" One officer said.

"Why aren't you in school?" The other asked.

"I wasn't feeling well so I left early." I said.

"I thought you said teacher's workday?" Junior asked.

"It is, I'm confused!" My head started swirling around.

"Who was that man?"

"My mother's boyfriend."

"Why were you here with your mother's boyfriend?" I held on to Junior and I cried. All the tears I always hold back came bursting out.

"Cause," I said crying my eyes out.

"Cause? Did he hurt you?" The officer asked me. I couldn't even lie anymore, I shook my head yes. "How did he hurt you?" I couldn't say it, I cried and cried my eyes out.

The police called my momma down to the station and then they told her. I could hear her screaming all the way down the hall. Junior stayed with me. When he told me he called his father I didn't think he would care or even come. I was so surprised when he walked in the door with tears pouring down his face. He picked me up and squeezed me so tight I couldn't breathe. He kept saying, "I'm sorry Princess! I'm sorry!" My momma came in the room while he was holding me and went off. She started screaming and hitting my father. She told him he didn't care about whether I ate or lived before, how dare he come around now. He completely ignored my momma and focused on me. He told me he wanted me

50

to come live with him. I asked him what about his wife; he said she wanted me to come too. My momma said that he couldn't take me. The female officer told my father as long as he was my father he didn't need her permission to take me. Junior led me out of the station by the hand and my father blocked my momma who was going off as we drove away.

****

"Do I look like you Princess?" Nassya said twirling in the middle of the room.

"No!" Then I smiled. Things have been interesting to say the least. When my momma didn't have me anymore my grandmother kicked her out. Bobby dumped her and he's running from the police. My daddy got the judge to say my momma was unfit and that she couldn't see me until Bobby was in jail. I miss my momma, the old momma before Bobby. She was the only one to understand how jealous people are of us.

My daddy held me in his arms and cried his eyes out when we got home that night. His wife even cried for me which still surprises me. I thought she hated me. My daddy said everything was such a mess, but he was going to fix it now. He isn't always the nicest, but at least I know he loves me. I thought he hated me. Sometimes I get sad cause I don't understand how I feel, it's not like I liked Bobby or what he did to me, but sometimes my body craves a man. Daddy told me to stay away from boys and to get my grades back on track. But sometimes I need somebody. I don't have to even like him all that much; I just need the cravings to go away. I buy my own condoms cause my daddy would die if I got pregnant. Most of the girls don't like me, and I find myself missing Kendra. She was my only real friend, ever. She didn't care that she could never be as pretty as me, we were still friends. I've had more fights over girls being jealous that their boyfriend likes me or wants me than I ever have. My daddy's wife looks at me with tears in her eyes all the time now. Sometimes she hugs me and tells me that I gotta let the pain go then I'll get better. I don't even know what she's talking about. My daddy doesn't ask me anything about Bobby; he acts like he didn't happen. Junior normally goes with me whenever I go anywhere. Nathan still acts like he's tolerating me. But even he is nicer to me. Nassya, this little girl is too much! She worships the ground I walk on. I love it! I can't be mean to her, I've tried. But she's so cute. She's only half as cute as me, but hey it's not her fault.

"What about this?" Then she jumped in the air.

"No, I wish I could dance like that. I have two left feet."

Nassya giggled, "What does that mean?"

"That I can't dance." I admitted.

"Why can't you dance?"

"Just because I'm black doesn't mean I automatically can."

Junior knocked on the door. He asked if we wanted to go with him to Oakland. We excitedly put on our shoes. Junior didn't show favoritism. He showed Nassya just as much love as he showed me. Junior picked up his check and then we went to Durant Square, when I saw him walk past me. I tried to hold back my excitement. I told Junior that Nassya and I were going to the bathroom. He nodded as he haggled over the price of a chain with a vendor. I grabbed her hand then I rounded the corner. I didn't know which way he went. So I started to guess. "Why are you following me?"

"Hey D! I didn't know you saw me." I smiled real big. He's gotten taller.

"Of course I saw you. And who is this?" He said bending down.

"Nassya," she said.

"Say that again?" He looked confused.

"Nass-cee-ah, Nassya," she said like she always does when people ask her to repeat her name.

"This is my little sister."

"Aren't you a pretty little thing." He said gently flicking her chin.

"Yep she looks just like me."

"You haven't changed, is KB here?"

"No, I haven't talked to her in a long time."

"She moved away?"

"No, I did." I said.

"Oh," he said looking like he was about to leave.

"Can I talk to you for a sec?" I asked.

"Isn't that what you're doing right now?"

"Stay right here." I said to Nassya.

Then I walked up to him and kissed his neck. "What are you doing?" I put a condom in his hand. Then I bit his neck. "Your sister."

"Go with Junior, I'll be right back." I watched her walk in the store up to Junior.

Then I kissed D again. "What's your name again?"
I smiled, "Nellie!"
"Why?"
"Cause you're sexy!"
"I like Kendra."
I tried to kiss him again, "it's just sex! I won't tell if you won't."
"I should've known. My momma made breakfast this morning.
Now a little afternoon delight." He laughed, "If you tell it'll suck to
be you!"
"You don't have to threaten me. I know how to keep secrets."
He looked around then he took me through a door that said "Staff
Only". He took my condom and inspected the wrapping. He
handed it back to me and pulled out his own. I was so happy I wore
a skirt today; I put my underwear in my pocket. I kissed his neck
while he put the condom on. He was so strong he picked me up
and had me straddle him. My craving subsided as soon as I felt
him, he felt like a man. This feeling was new; everything felt good
from beginning to end. I kept saying, "Oh D! Oh D!"
Then he said "Oh me! Oh me!" I guess making fun of me. Then he
put me down and bent me over; he said something about catnip and
making me purr. I thought he was going to burst through my
throat, but I loved every moment of it. Time seemed to fly while
we were being naughty in this hallway where anyone could
discover us. He took off his condom, asked me if I wanted more. I
very eagerly said yes, he smiled and said I was still purring. We
went at it again! We went at it two more times, and I knew my
brother had to be looking for me. When we were done, I stood
there expecting him to say how good it was to him or something.
He pulled up his pants, wiped his forehead and walked away. Then
he put up two fingers, "alright then Noel, it was good seeing you."

Kendra

Kalani and I were getting ready to leave. We had to go over Mrs.
Sutherland's house to clean her house and her car. Queen Kaleah
could never be bothered with demeaning work as she called it. She
said her father sent money for her so that she didn't have to work.
Kalani told her he doesn't send money for anybody and she needed
to get a grip. Kaleah refused to believe us, she'd wait at home
every Saturday thinking today was the day he would come home.
Kalani would get sad and say she missed him as well. I'd hug her

and tell her it was going to be ok, cause he was a loser for leaving us with nothing. Aunt Quilla would feel so badly for us. She said their father wasn't raised like that and she didn't understand how he could do this when he sees what she goes through raising kids all by herself.

I was getting my cleaning gloves when there was a knock on the door. Kaleah screamed with excitement, I thought it was her father so I pulled out a knife. A bit dramatic I know, but I had choice words for him and he wasn't going to hit me again without feeling the pain. I looked into the living room to see Nathan standing there looking every bit as good as he did the last time I saw him. My heart sank; I was in my cleaning clothes with a scarf on my head. Nathan smiled at me like nothing bad ever happened between us. Nellie came up to me and gave me a big hug. "Were you on your way out?"

"Yes, I still have my service for the elderly. Where have you been? Where did you go?" I asked.

"I moved to Albany with my father." She said with a smile.

"You left without saying bye. Your grandmother up and moved seemed like in the middle of the night. We never saw a moving truck, one day there was a for rent sign in the yard."

"Yea there was some trouble with my momma's boyfriend, but that's water under the bridge."

"I've missed you so much!" Kaleah said hugging Nellie

I rolled my eyes, "I'm sorry I can't hang out. I have to go to work." I said trying my best to ignore Nathan who was watching me.

"MOMMA!" Kaleah yelled towards the back of the house. "CAN I GO WITH NELLIE?"

Momma had finally come to terms with the fact that her husband wasn't coming back. Aunt Quilla convinced her to go out with her a few times. Hook, line, and sinker, she met someone. I say someone cause we haven't met him yet. She said only the special ones get to meet us. They go out from time to time, but she always comes home early and she's always smiling. It's nice to see her happy again. Momma came in the front and she gave Nellie a hug. She asked her why she disappeared on us, and she said there was a lot going on. Momma asked Nellie where they were going. I didn't like the idea of Kaleah going with Nellie, but she had already been brain washed so what difference did it make? Kaleah was too

juiced to be going with Nellie. "Maybe we can all go eat when
you're finished working?" Nellie asked
Nathan stood there staring at me waiting for my answer. "No, I'll
be tired and needing to relax."
Kaleah excitedly left with Nellie. My momma asked why Nathan
kept looking at me. I told her I used to like him, but he told me I
was a little kid. She said he was too old for me and most likely in
to things that were more advanced than she wanted for me. She
said she got a bad vibe from him. She doesn't even know him how
could she say that? Momma talked with Mrs. Sutherland while
Kalani and I cleaned her house and car. Mrs. Sutherland was in a
wheelchair so she appreciated each visit. When we finished, Mrs.
Sutherland said that my momma had lovely girls and she should be
so proud of her little go-getters. My momma was proud she stood
there with her head held high. Since we were starving and I was in
no hurry to get home, I asked momma to take us to the Palace
Golden for a late lunch and early dinner. Momma told us about her
friend, she said if things keep going like they're going she'd let him
meet us soon. Kalani asked her why we had to meet him at all.
Momma explained that we were the most important people in her
life. She really liked her friend which is making him more
important to her as well. She couldn't keep important people
separate. Kalani said she didn't want a new dad. My momma told
her we have a father, and he was a friend. Although she hoped we
liked him. If we didn't like him that was ok too. Then she sighed,
she said she already knew Kaleah wasn't gonna like him. I told her
that Kaleah lives in a world of denial, and she couldn't worry
about her.
I asked momma to drop us at Aunt Quilla's, I didn't want to be
there when Nathan came back. It had been too long and nothing
from him. He couldn't think he could just pop up and I'd be happy
to see him. My momma agreed, and she dropped us off. She said
she'd bring Kaleah before her date. Jabbar was over with his little
sister. They were all in the backyard hanging out. Ahjanae asked
me why I was in my work clothes. I told her I was avoiding my
house cause Nathan was bringing Kaleah home after her day with
Nellie.
Ahjanae was showing us some stupid dance when Nellie, Kaleah,
and Nathan walked out in the backyard. When I asked why
momma didn't bring her she said she was running late. Nathan shot

Jabbar evil eyes because we were sitting next to each other. Ahjanae saw it too, but she didn't say anything. Nellie got comfortable asking who I was sitting next to. I introduced her to Jabbar; Nellie was too excited for me when she said he was cute, and that she was happy for me. Jabbar and I looked at her like she was crazy. Ahjanae and Ahjani started laughing saying we did make a cute couple. I couldn't believe Ahjanae, and then she winked at us. Jabbar was uncomfortable and I couldn't blame him. He got his sister and then they walked home. When Ahjanae walked them to the corner Nellie bumped me saying I was wrong for letting her believe he was my man. I told her I didn't say he was anything. She jumped to conclusions. Nellie was drilling me asking me question after question. When I asked her why she was asking so many questions she said she hadn't seen me in a long time and she missed me.

Once the street lights came on we had to play freeze tag. I mean it was only right, right? We played out front in the street and all over the neighbor's yards. Aunt Quilla's broken down car was base Nellie was it, cause she was the easiest target, she didn't run that fast. I was sitting on the car when Nathan came and sat next to me. "How you been?"

"Ok for a little girl I guess!" I snapped at him.

He frowned, "did I say that or something?"

"You know you called me a little girl don't try to play innocent now."

"Look Kendra I didn't know why you stopped calling me. But if I said something that offended you I apologize."

"IF?" I exhaled, "you know good and well you broke up with me and you called me a little girl. You broke my heart for no reason. That's when I realized I'm too good for you. Just because you're older than me does not make you better than me, or my superior. If and when I decide to have sex, it will be because I want to. Not because some insecure high school kid thought I would be easy prey because I was young and inexperienced…"

He cut me off, "whoa! Kendra's found her voice, ok. Ok! I was wrong. Can I apologize now?" I looked at him like he was stupid. "I apologize for hurting you. I…."

A car pulled up on us real slow, "KB? Girl!" Darryl got out of the car so fast. He came to me and picked me up off the car. He has gotten taller. He doesn't look like a seventh grader for sure. "I haven't seen you in forever! Where have you been?" Darryl said smiling at me.

"At home, there's been a lot going on. Are you going to your Auntie's house?"

"Who are you?" Darryl asked Nathan.

"I was about to ask you the same thing." Nathan said with attitude, I remembered Darryl beating down… whatever happened to Juju? I haven't seen him since and his sister doesn't speak, she keeps it moving. Anyways I didn't want a repeat.

"Darryl this is Nellie's big brother Nathan."

"Who?" Darryl asked.

"You don't remember me?" Nellie said with attitude.

Darryl looked at her, "oh right. What's your name again? Noel? And this is your brother Nat?"

"Nathan," he corrected him.

"Right what I said Nat, but nobody cares so whatever!" He said returning his attention to me. "How's school? You ready for the summer?"

"School's good, I can't complain. I'll probably be working hard this summer, but I'm looking forward to it." I said, Nellie had the most hurt look on her face when Darryl didn't care about who she was. "D-Rick, give me a pen and paper." He said walking to the car. He walked back to me writing down his number, "What's your number?"

"Who says I want you on my phone?" I said playfully.

"I know you want me! What's your number?" He smiled at me. I gave him my number. He gave me his and he put mine in his pocket. He hugged me and then he said he had to go. "Later Nat and Noel!" Then he walked across the street to his Aunt's house.

"Your momma lets you have calls from boys now?" Nellie asked me.

"No, but I guess I gotta talk to her before he calls." I smiled. "I'm it!" I called out as I ran after my sisters and cousins.

Chapter 5

Nellie

"Princess, we always send Nassya away to camp for part of the summer. Would you like to go? You could probably be a camp counselor." My daddy asked me

I frowned, "a summer with a bunch of kids? I don't know daddy."

"It will look good on your transcripts and it will give you something to do away from here. I think time away will do you some good."

"Are you trying to get rid of me?"

"No, there's more to life then the Bay Area. I want you to get out and meet new people. You'll soon learn that there's more than one way to be." It still felt like he was trying to get rid of me. "Please Princess, do it for me. Nassya will finally get to show off the sister she's been bragging about her whole life. And you will get to meet new people."

I told him I'd think about it. But I didn't want to go. I was trying to figure out how I was going to get to Kendra or her cousin's house in hopes of getting next to D again. He was so strong and powerful; no one has even come close to him. At night I think about him until I fall asleep, just so I can dream about him. In my dreams, he doesn't even know who Kendra is. Everybody is so jealous of us. Cause he's so FINE, got money, and power. While his girl, that's me, is drop dead gorgeous. I don't know why he likes Kendra so much. He makes such a big deal over her butt. Ok so it is big, but I got a nice booty too. My clothes are always name brand and tight. Kendra does her own hair, no labels, and even though she's a little pretty who would know it. She sits in the background so much, it's a wonder he even noticed her. I get my hair done all the time, when I walk in the room people notice. He's a fool for liking her over me. I bet it's because she can dance and I can't. That doesn't make me any less black because she can and I can't. What did she do? Dance her way into his heart. Thinking about it was irritating me. D should be with me, it's a waste of time for him to look at her.

Nassya's mother knocked on the door. I told her to come in; she came in and sat on the bed next to me. She gently grabbed my hand and started rubbing it. This is still a weird place for both of us. Seeing her be so nice to me always makes me feel bad. I remember when she started being nice to me, and why, and then I'm sad. Then I start missing my momma who seems to have disappeared off the face of this earth. But I like her being this way to me, I just hate that it makes me so sad when she does it. She asked me to come hang out with her today. I said with Nassya of course. And she looked me in my eyes and said no, just me and her. I like alone time with anyone I get time with, anyone except Nathan. All he does is find a way to work Kendra into the conversation to ask me fifty million questions about her. I don't know why he does that, but I stop talking when he goes there. I am his sister; he should want to get to know me. Kendra could never be a better little sister cause I know he couldn't possibly like her. I told my stepmother I would go. She smiled really big like she wasn't sure if I'd want to go with her or not. We immediately got in her car and left. We had breakfast at the restaurant in Berkeley off of Shattuck across the street from the Bart Station and the bank. I always forget the name of the restaurant, but we come here all the time. Our waiter was so cute, and he kept looking like my glance in his direction made him blush it was cute. "Somebody's got an admirer." My stepmother said smiling. I smiled and didn't say anything, cause if she wasn't here I'd probably take him out back and do him. But I was being cool today. She asked me what I thought; I shrugged and told her he was cute. I didn't know what she was getting at. Then she made her voice real soft. She asked me what did I do when I thought a boy was cute? I told her I didn't do anything. She said her childhood was pretty rough, and a lot of bad things happened to her. She said she was lost for a long time, she didn't understand herself or how to be. She said she used to get in fights with girls all the time because of boys. I looked at her cause she didn't look like the type. My stepmother wasn't ugly but she wasn't on me or my momma's level of gorgeous so I guess I just dismissed her pretty altogether. She said it's hard when you feel like no one understands you huh. And I nodded, cause I know no one at home understood me. She said she had low self-esteem when she was younger and it wasn't until she learned to love herself that things in her life got better for her. Like meeting my father and falling in love. Getting married and having a family. I felt bad for her, cause I know I have high self-esteem, there's no one better than me. Whenever men look at me they're instantly turned on. That would never happen if I had low self-esteem. I listened as she went on and on about things from her life. I understood some of it, but not all. It was like she was trying to tell me something, but I couldn't grab the message. I let her go on and on cause I was enjoying my time with her. Then she asked me if she needed to get birth control pills for me. I didn't say anything at first because I wondered if she was trying to trick me into admitting something. She smiled tenderly and touched my hand again. "I'm trying to tell you that I've been in your shoes. You have a long bumpy road ahead of you. The last thing you need is to try to understand yourself with a baby on your hip." I looked away, "I'm not telling you to go out there and have sex. But it's unrealistic to think that at this age you'll understand what that monster did to you. I know you're going to act out if you haven't started already. But you have to protect yourself." Then she exhaled, "plus you dropped a condom out of your pocket the other day. I convinced your father that it was Nathan's. Condoms are a good way to protect yourself, but two methods are better than one. Continue to use them to protect yourself from diseases, but you also need another barrier as well. Do you want me to make the appointment?"

"My daddy will be mad." I said quietly.

"He doesn't have to know baby. I won't tell him if you won't, he would never understand this." She said gently.

"Will you do this for Nassya?"

"Once I know she's sexually active yes. I don't want her to become a parent until she's ready to be one."

"Please don't tell my daddy and make him mad at me. He just started loving me again."

"Honey, he never stopped loving you. He's always loved you, things got too crazy. I didn't help things either. I was so hurt about everything; I wasn't looking at the big picture. You are here and you didn't ask to be, I'm praying it's not too late for you. We need to get your grades back on track. You can still have a victory over all of this. That monster doesn't determine the rest of your life!"

After breakfast we went to the city and did a little "retail therapy" as she called it. We bought a few things, but she kept drilling into me to keep myself clean, no matter what to always use condoms, and to take my pill every day.

****

Nassya was so excited when daddy told her I was going to camp with her. She said this was going to be the best summer of her life. I have to admit that her excitement to have me at her camp with her was heartwarming. But what sold me on the idea of going is when she showed me the picture of her friends from last year. The guys my age were mostly cute, and I thought about all the adventurous sex I would have. I was hoping during my six weeks away that I would find someone better than D.

The camp sent a T-shirt for each of us, and the note said that extra shirts would be provided at the camp. I packed all the things I would need in the suitcase set my daddy let me pick out once I agreed to go. It was designer and I felt like a million bucks putting my things in it. I packed my perfume and feminine products that my stepmother bought me. Nassya in a very animated fashion told me some of the stories about this camp. Her little stories were cute and the way she told them did grab your attention.

When we pulled up to the camp Nassya got excited as she pointed people out. Some of these kids were from different states all over the country.

All I know is it took us a long time to get here, and then when we got out of the car it was ridiculously hot. The girl at the registration desk acted like she drank a bunch of sugary Kool-aide before she sat down. She was extremely excited and cheering about almost everything she said. I was assigned to be the junior counselor of Nassya's cabin. Nassya was so excited she did a happy dance. There were four other little girls assigned to our cabin. Our parents kissed us goodbye and they left us, they said they would be back in six weeks. Six weeks sounded like a long time, especially when I didn't see not one cute boy yet. Nassya showed me around the camp, and she showed me the most important room, the snack room. She said the freezer was full of all the popsicles and ice cream we could eat and we were welcome to get as much as we needed since it was so hot. They had the cheap popsicles, but then they also had the good stuff that had whole pieces of fruit in it. I got a pineapple popsicle and I was in love. I braided both of our hairs into one long braid it was too hot to deal with hair on our necks. As Nassya's little friends arrived they all came in the room one by one exclaiming how excited they were, and how happy they were that I was the junior counselor assigned to their cabin. At dinnertime, we were sitting at our table and then he walked in. He was the junior counselor for one of the boy cabins. He wasn't all that tall but he was cute. I wanted him the moment I laid eyes on him. Unfortunately all the other girls seemed to share the same feelings. Fortunately more and more cute boys started arriving, but I had my heart set on the first guy. I watched him all night and when he saw me he smiled. That did it; I wanted to do him tonight. But this lady said the staff needed to meet with all the junior counselors to go over information for the next six weeks. First they had everyone say hi to me and welcome me since I was the new counselor. I decided that everyone at this camp should call me Leasha, for whatever reason I didn't want to think about home. Then everyone introduced their selves to me. My summer man's name was Aldo (what kind of name was that?). I kept shooting him looks and he kept smiling. I was very disappointed when I went to bed that night with unsatisfied cravings, but I knew tomorrow would be different. I made sure I paid attention to which cabin was Aldo's. All day I kept smiling at Aldo and shooting him looks. That night I waited until everyone was knocked out in my cabin then I snuck into Aldo's cabin, I woke him up and then I told him to follow me. We went behind the snack room and I dropped his shorts. He looked surprised and unprepared for what I was about to do to him. I put the condom on him and then I straddled him. His eyes rolled back in his head as he slid down to the floor. His eyes were big like he didn't know what to do. I asked him if he was a virgin and he said an embarrassed yes. I told him to lay back and I worked him over. I had to cover his mouth because he didn't know how to be quiet. Fortunately, even though he blew right away the first time he was ready to go again right away. I liked showing him what to do and how to do it. By the end of our six weeks he was like a pro. We did it every night. Even when I was on my period, thanks to the pill it was barely there anyways. Aldo kept telling me he loved me and he promised to keep in touch after camp. I didn't care if he did or he didn't. I was just happy to have someone to screw while I was out there.

Kendra

I don't know how, but I talked my momma into agreeing to allow Darryl to call me. It made me more surprised than I thought. Then I waited for him to call me. When he finally called me, "of course you waited for me to call you first!" He said teasing me.

"Of course! I'm a lady you call me first!" I said
"Yes you are.... until... I PUT THE MUSIC ON! And then you back that THANGGGGGG up!" He said cracking himself up.
"Look Darryl, if the only reason you wanted my number was to talk about my butt I can find better things to do with my time. Cause I thought I begged my momma for permission for a gentleman to call me not a pervert!"
"Begged your momma?"
"You are my first male caller." I said proudly.
"Well dang! Should I sip on tea and eat crumpets when I call you at high noon?"
"Whatever makes you feel like a gentleman."
He cleared his throat and then he made his voice real deep.
"HELLO KENDRA! THIS IS DARRYL! MAY I PLEASE SPEAK WITH KENNY'S BOOTY!"
We laughed and I proceeded to spend the next two hours laughing with him. My momma heard me laughing and she sat in the living room to listen in on my conversation. At first she tried to act like she wasn't listening. Eventually she was laughing as well. Darryl asked who was laughing in the background. I told him it was my momma. He asked to speak to her. I told him he better not say anything crazy. He said scout's honor, I asked him if he was ever a scout and he said no. We laughed again. I gave my momma the phone and first she smiled, then she chuckled, then she was laughing so hard that tears came out of her eyes. After he and I got off the phone my momma was still laughing. She asked me if he was always like that and I told her pretty much.

****

"Where's Nellie?" Ahjani asked.
"I don't know, but I haven't called her."
"Who is that?" Darryl asked.
"You remember, her friend who can't dance." Ahjani said.
"Oh," guilt flashed across his face. "She looks like a bird!"
"WHAT?" Ahjanae said holding her stomach laughing.
"A pretty bird though." Ahjani said.
"If you say so." Darryl said.
"I didn't know you liked Nellie?" Ahjanae said.
"You never asked, I got friends just like Aunrey. Why you think I be here?" Ahjani said.
"I never thought about it."

Darryl frowned in disgust. "You mean like you wanna be her boyfriend and bring her flowers?"

"Yeah," he said

Darryl shook his head, "that is a troubled bird. I wouldn't invest any emotions in that kind of feathered friend. But there's someone for everyone. You got a backup for today?"

Ahjani looked at Kalani, "you'll be my ride buddy right?"

"I guess that leaves us." Audra told Kaleah.

We were going to the Great America amusement park in Santa Clara. Darryl told us to get permission to go and he'd take care of the rest. We were on Bart on the Fremont line, making our way out there. At the Fruitvale station, a big group of kids got on the train. They were loud and having fun. Then they sat around us. They kept saying hey to Darryl. One girl walked up to him while staring at us. "Who we got here?" She said looking at us.

"This is KB's family, and her cousin's boyfriend." He said nonchalantly.

"Which one is KB?" She asked

"Kendra, this is my cousin Lanie." He said pointing at me.

She looked at me then she looked me up and down. "Hey," then she watched me.

"Hey," I said.

"Not one label." She said like that was a strike against me

"They're a waste of money." I said watching her.

"I guess." Then she looked at everybody. "Interesting family, ya'll from Richmond? You know Oakland and Richmond be funking."

"I wasn't aware of that, but that's not my life anyways." I said

"Hhhhmmmm, you run with anybody from North Richmond?" She asked.

"No I live on the South side of Richmond."

She looked at Darryl, "she's alright." Then she looked at me, "for now!"

"Oh joy! KB passed the first crazy test! Let's dance!" He and Lanie grabbed hands and started dancing in the aisle. Then the rest of the people with her started clapping their hands. "Hey! Hey! Hey!"

When we got off the train our group was huge. When we got to the park, Darryl went to the guest services window. One person came out and gave each person a wristband. Darryl told each person not to take their band off; it was good for admission and food.

Everyone got excited when they saw the merry-go-round. We

posed for our group picture then we ran to the carousel. Something as simple as the merry-go-round was complete and total fun with them. Whenever we were having fun though I kept catching Liz, Lanie, and or Pearla watching me. So I engaged each of them in a conversation one on one. Half way through our day we were cracking jokes and acting like friends from long ago. Lanie said something to Darryl and he blushed when he looked at me. Then he walked over to me and put his arm around my neck and kissed my cheek. "KB you make me want to bite you!" His cousins started laughing. "Jabbar feel me on this. Does Ahjanae make you want to bite her?"

Jabbar smiled, "I bite my baby all the time! Lick the heck out of her too!"

"Oh yea? What she taste like?"

Jabbar looked at Ahjanae, "caliente cinnamon chocolate!"

Everybody erupted into laughter.

"What does Kendra taste like?" Pearla asked

Darryl smiled at me, "I haven't tasted her yet."

"WHAT? How long have you been together?" Liz asked

"We're not together." I said

"WHAT?????" Everyone said in unison.

"Since when you do stuff like this?" Lanie said talking at the top of her voice.

"I don't! But now that you put me on blast I can't act like this means nothing. Thanks everyone!" Darryl teased

We finished eating and then we decided to beat the heat on the water log ride. Darryl could not wait for me to sit in his lap. As soon as I sat down he put me in a bear hug and started kissing my neck. His touch felt good, I forgot we were on a ride. "Kendra!" He said in my ear, "you taste like chocolate passion fruit!" When our log reached the docking station. Darryl handed the kid money to let us go again. Then he kept kissing my neck and biting on it. I loved the feeling.

Audra and Kaleah decided to sing for us on the mini stage. A few girls walked up and they started talking mess about them. Ahjanae and I got in two of the girl's faces. There were six of them and they were all big and mean looking. We told them to leave our sisters alone. Darryl and Jabbar came back with our lemonades. Darryl smiled at me while I was standing in front of this big ole girl. When the girl pushed me, I pushed her back. Then security came and broke everything up. The girls continued to talk mess while security made them backup, and I guess they decided to go to the bathroom. Darryl told us it was time to go make a video. As we walked towards the video station a lot of Darryl's cousins went towards the bathroom. We made a video; Audra and Kaleah were singing some serious love ballad slow song, while we danced full speed to a fast song playing in our head. Darryl was twirling Kalani around and dancing fast. Jabbar and Ahjani were standing posted with arms folded. And Ahjanae and I skipped around being completely silly. Audra and Kaleah had no idea that all of this was going on as they belted their hearts out. When we came out of the room there was a crowd of people outside watching our video and cracking up during the play back. Audra laughed when she saw it, but Kaleah didn't think it was funny. She was mad that people were laughing. Darryl told her to lighten up. Kaleah sulked for the rest of the day. At the end of the night, Darryl and I shared a funnel cake, and I thanked him for getting us into the park and everything. He said we were welcome.

****

Thursdays have become my favorite day of the summer. Kalani and I keep our schedule clear on Thursdays and then we go over Aunt Quilla's. Most Thursdays Darryl goes over his Aunt's house as well. Sometimes he can't come because he has to go with his momma to work or he had to do things with his dad. But he comes when he can. When he's away with his momma I don't get to talk to him all that much.

I love how he pays Nellie no attention. The mere mention of her name once he remembers who she is seems to disgust him. He says she's not my friend, but he doesn't know that she can be nice sometimes. He doesn't have anything to back up his claim so I let him say it but I move on.

"Hello?"

"Hello, this is Kendra may I please speak with Nellie?"

"It's about time you called." Nathan said with a smile in his voice.

"Is Nellie home?" I said rolling my eyes.

"She's away at camp. How have you been?"

"I'm fine, when will she be back? I'll call then."

"Kendra, I'm sorry for hurting your feelings. I wanted to come to you and apologize, but I was scared."

"Scared of what?"

66

"Scared that you would act exactly how you are right now. I miss you, I want to be your boyfriend again."

"Why?"

"Because I like you."

"You like me so much that you broke up with me over something petty. Then you didn't even try to make it right. I gotta go!"

"You're gonna hurt me like this? I'm putting my heart on the line and you don't even care. Kendra please don't hurt me like this." His voice cracked as he pleaded.

"What about how you hurt me?"

"I am so sorry!"

"You only care cause you know somebody else wants me." I said

"Who? That goofy little punk? I'm not worried about what a little boy wants. I am a man! I am laying my heart on the line like a man too. Can I come pick you up?"

"No!" I said even though I wanted to see him.

He sensed my hesitation. "How about I come and take you to lunch tomorrow? We can clear the air and get back together."

"I can't go to lunch with you. My momma's not going to let me go anywhere with you."

"Can't you tell her you have a job?"

"Kalani and I work together."

"You can bring her."

"Ok," I heard myself say.

Kalani agreed to go with me as support, and Nathan picked us up around the corner from our house. He took us to a burger place in Albany. Then he proceeded to beg me to get back with him. He even got on the ground on his knees begging me. I did miss him and I thought about him all the time. After lots and lots of begging, I heard myself give in and say yes. Kalani looked at me in complete shock. I'm sure she thought about Darryl just like I did in that moment.

****

Nellie's stepmother pulled up to Aunt Quilla's house. I went outside to say hi to her. She smiled real big when she saw me. Nellie got out of the car looking all around the neighborhood. Then she smiled at me and hugged me. Her stepmother told her to call when she was ready to come home. Nellie told us all about the camp she was a junior counselor at and all the fun she had. Ahjani was trying to be cool but I guess he decided that at some point

today he was going to make his big move. We told her about our
day at the park with Darryl and some of his family. We even
showed her our goofy video. She said we had to do it again now
that she was back, but I told her I hadn't talked to Darryl cause I
hadn't. He was constantly on the go with his parents or his
grandfather. Nellie told me to tell her when cause it sounded like
we had a lot of fun.

Aunt Quilla left to go grocery shopping, she took my sisters and
Audra with her. Jabbar came over and we sat outside in the
backyard. Ahjani nonchalantly put his arm around Nellie's neck.
She smiled at him and kept talking. Ahjani's face completely lit up.
Ahjanae asked him to get cards so we could play a game. He told
us he'd be right back. Nellie watched him walk in the house then
she asked me what was up with him. I told her that he liked her,
and she looked surprised like she never considered that he would
like her. She started shaking her leg and then she said she'd be
right back. After a little bit, Ahjanae said she'd be back, she came
to the door and asked me to come. As soon as I stepped through
the door the sound of the bed rocking was undeniable. I bucked my
eyes at her, Ahjanae put her finger up. We crept by the door and
Nellie was on top of Ahjani working the day lights out of him. My
mouth fell open; I didn't know she wasn't a virgin anymore. I asked
Ahjanae what we should do. She told me to let Ahjani finish. She
was irritated and tapping her foot. Ahjani called out, but then they
kept going. I asked Ahjanae how long does it take. She looked
irritated when she said Jabbar never last that long. Finally they
were still for thirty seconds. Ahjanae opened the door, "what do
you think you're doing?"

Nellie threw the covers over them as they both laughed. "Ahjanae,
can you give us a minute?"

"No! What if momma would've come home while you guys were
at it! She won't let Jabbar come over any more if she catches wind
of stuff like this! You can't disrespect our house!"

"I'm sorry," Nellie said. She looked really sad and like she was
going to cry.

"Get dressed and come back outside!" Ahjanae demanded.

When we walked out the room I asked her if we could trust them to
come right out. She frowned and then we stood by the door. Nellie
started crying then Ahjani asked her if he was that bad? They
giggled a little then he asked her what was wrong. She told him all

she ever does is get people in trouble. He told her that he wasn't in trouble. She said Ahjanae was mad like she was going to tell. He asked her if she was his girlfriend, and she hesitated. I had to hold Ahjanae back cause she didn't appreciate the hesitation. Then Nellie said she didn't want to hurt Ahjani, he's always been nice to her so she wanted to do something nice for him. He told her she would hurt him by saying no. They were quiet for a minute then she said she was his girlfriend. When they finally opened the door we were standing there still waiting. Nellie looked embarrassed, she told me not to look at her like that. I took her hand and we went in the bathroom. "Was that your first time?" I asked, she looked at the floor and shook her head no. "When?"
Her eyes filled with tears, "I don't wanna talk about it." She said lowly.
"You're being awfully nice this visit, are you ok?" I asked.
She shrugged, "I've missed you."
I felt her forehead like I was looking for a fever. "You have to be sick." I smiled, "I missed you too. So...." I smiled bigger, "you and my cousin huh? You better not break his heart."
"How can I protect his heart if mine is already broken?" She said taking a deep breath.
"Who broke your heart? Talk to me."
"I don't know where my momma is. Or my grandmother for that matter. I live with my dad, which is fine. At least he loves me again, and my stepmom and I are fine. But where's my momma? She's mad at me! So mad she doesn't want anything else to do with me! My dad's gonna end up hating me again, and then I'll have nobody!" She cried.
"Not true! We're friends almost like sisters. You wouldn't hurt me, nor I you." I said wondering if liking her brother counted.
"That's what you say now, but watch!"

Chapter 6

Nellie

It's like I can see myself doing stuff, but I don't know how to tell myself to stop. I try to be with Ahjani as much as I can. At least if I'm with him and we do it, I'm doing it with my boyfriend. And sex with him is never quick. I'm always tired when we finish. He's learned to tune into how I purr. I've taught him about catnip, and everything that I loved about Darryl's euphemisms for sex. He tells me he loves me all the time, and I say it back. But I feel so numb, I don't know if I mean it. "Why do you love me?" He keeps saying it and I've already had sex with him it can't be to get me to do it.

"You're smart, funny, a brat, and because you love me."

"You forgot the most important reason." I said

"I did?"

"I'm pretty!"

"That helps, but that's not why. You've always been pretty, but I didn't like you until you started being nice when you thought no one was paying attention. Why do you love me?"

"Because you tell me you love me even when you're not trying to have sex." I exhaled. Talking like this is exhausting. "What do you want to be when you grow up?"

"Either a dentist or play in the NBA."

"Are you any good?"

"I'm the best! I'm going to play at Kennedy next year, you're coming to my games right?"

"Just tell me when. So if you don't make it to the NBA then you want to be a dentist. Why?"

He laughed, "cause dentists make bank! And there aren't too many black dentists in Richmond."

"I don't know what I want to do yet. Would you be mad if I didn't know what I wanted to do when I graduate?"

"I don't know about mad, but I hope we'd have a plan by then."

"We?"

"I'm going to be away at school. You may not get into the same school as me. I may bounce around schools for a minute. We'll need a plan, but we can think about that closer to my senior year."

"Do you really think we'll be together that long?" I asked.

"Why do you act like it's so hard to believe that someone could love you as much as I do?"

"Because the people who are supposed to love me no matter what pick and choose when they wanna love me, if they ever loved me at all."

"We can't choose our parents. My father likes to deal with us on his time. When my momma was pregnant with me the responsibility became too much for him. Who dumps a pregnant woman? He sends child support so he doesn't look like the jerk that he is. I see him maybe twice a year. The only real father I've known was Audra's dad. He always treated me like I was his own. He was killed over some bull! The Bakers handled that one, still didn't bring him back." He exhaled, "but that's how she met Aunrey's dad. My momma was so hurt behind losing Audra's dad, by the time she realized what was happening she was already pregnant."

I put my head on his chest, "but you still had your momma. My momma told me to be one way. Everybody else acts like that's the wrong way to be. I don't know how to be." I cried.

"This you is fine."

"Ahjani I can't be like this in front of other people. They'll try to hurt me and try to get over. You can't tell people about the stuff we talk about either!"

"Ok," he said rubbing my back.

"Why does it make me mad at you when you're like this with me. I feel like I want to punch your face in right now!" I said speaking the truth.

"Because you're open right now. It makes you scared, I know because I feel the same way. I see your head turning when guys come around. Every time I want to grab a fist full of your hair. But just so we're clear. I'm not cheating on you, if you cheat on me.... It sucks to be you!"

****

I let his question float on the air, if looks could kill he'd be dead twice over. "Hello? Hello? Anybody home in there? Lights on but nobody's home?" Nathan said sarcastically

I spoke through clinched lips. "I am your sister, and the only time you talk or anything with me is when it serves you! Don't ask me about any of my friends, none of them would be dumb enough to fall for you!"

"You're crazy all those little girls want me. Does she have a boyfriend or not. It's a simple question."

"Bonnie has better things to do with her life than worry about a loser in high school who's too weak to prey on the girls at his own school cause they all see right through you!"

Nathan backhanded me and sound disappeared for a minute. "You are beneath me! I don't know why I waste my time trying to talk to you. You are a worthless hooker just like your mother! This is why nobody likes you! You run your mouth too much!"

"And you're pathetic! You have no game that's why you prey on little girls cause you're afraid girls your own age will know the difference!"

Nathan lunged on me and started choking me. I scratched his face and his arms, anything I could reach. Junior ran in the room while Nassya screamed from the doorway of our bedroom. Junior beat Nathan up and he didn't know why he was fighting him. My stepmom made him stop, and then our father asked what was going on as he surveyed the scene and he picked up Nassya who was crying so hard she was shaking. Nathan yelled at everybody that he hated me and he didn't understand why I had to be there. Junior hit him again! Daddy gave Nassya to her mother then he pulled Junior off of Nathan. He asked Nathan what was wrong with him, and that I was his sister and I had every right to be there as much as he did. Nathan screamed that this was his house and he wanted me gone. My daddy told him that this was his house and he wanted all of his children. "Her mother was some hooker you forgot to strap up with! Why do we have to deal with her just because you messed up?" Nathan barked

"Son you've got this whole thing twisted up in your mind! Her mother was not a hooker, and she's here on purpose. You were the mistake! And I continue to pay the price because of you!"

Nathan looked like our father shot him. "You have the same mother!"

"WHAT???" Nathan and I said in unison.

"I'm sorry Princess! I know this only makes matters worse for you." My daddy said.

I looked at Junior and sure enough he looked like his mother, Nathan looked more like me than Nassya and Junior. My head swished! "I don't understand!" I said

"Mom?" Nathan said with tears running down his busted face.

"I'm sorry baby. But you've been my son since the moment he brought you home."

"So wait a minute! He's my mother's son? He's lived with you all his life! You broke up with my mother and left me out there like an outsider while he's here not knowing who his mother is?"

"Nathan was an accident. Your mother wasn't ready to be a mother when he was born. So I took him. Your mother never bonded with him and she wanted a child of her own. So even though my wife thought my relationship with your mother ended when I brought Nathan home seeing you confirmed that nothing changed."

My heart burned, "what else can you people possibly do to me!" I screamed. "Is Mary my real mother? Are you my real father? What's my real name?"

"NO! That hooker is not my mother! NO! I've always hated her!" Nathan screamed.

"And now you know why!" My daddy replied.

"NO! NO! NO!" Nathan stormed out of the room. Everybody went after him.

I grabbed my purse and then I snuck out the back door. I climbed the fence and ran down the Bart Trail to the Bart station. I called Ahjani and I begged him to catch Bart and meet me in downtown Berkeley. I waited for him on the platform while I cried my eyes out. When he got off the train I jumped on him like a big baby and I cried on his shoulder. He stood there holding me and rubbing my back. Eventually I got down and we walked the streets of Berkeley until I found a cheap motel that would give a room to me even though I was a minor. I sat on the bed telling Ahjani everything that happened. He said that would explain why my brothers were around my mother. He said normally fathers don't bring their children around their mistresses on purpose. I had sex with Ahjani until he couldn't anymore, even though I was sore beyond belief it didn't matter. Nothing was fixing the pain I felt. I needed to confirm this story with my momma but I didn't know where she was. Maybe that's how she could not even fight to see me anymore she has babies and then she gives them away. Ahjani called home at eight o'clock and his momma went off. She told him to come home immediately. I begged Ahjani to stay with me and not to leave me. He asked me to come with him. I told him his momma would only make me call my parents. He pleaded with me, and then he put his foot down as he grabbed my purse. "I can't leave

you in this sleazy motel! Get up or I'm calling your parents
myself!"
I tried to get my purse from him but he wasn't having it. He paid
for my room and then he walked to the Bart station all the while I
was all over him trying to get my purse. When we got to his house
his momma met us at the door cursing both of us. The only time
she stopped was when she asked for my parent's number. I
hesitated and then Ahjani gave her the number. I looked at him like
the traitor he was. He told me there would be no way to recover if
we didn't tell her. Her tone completely changed when she hung up.
She told Ahjani to leave us. She told me to sit on the couch. As
Ahjani started to walk away with my purse she told him to give me
my purse back. He told her that he didn't want to give it to me
because I would try and run away. She looked me in my eyes and
told me I wasn't going anywhere, and then she told him to give me
my purse back. He handed me my purse then he shot his momma
pleading eyes. Ms. Quilla sat on the couch next to me. She said my
parents were very apologetic and thankful that she called them.
She said it sounded like things were pretty bad at home. I slouched,
were they going to put everybody in our business? Ms. Quilla
apologized for not allowing me to explain when we came in the
door. She said my parents sounded relieved to know that someone
had me. My father walked in the door with a serious face and my
stepmom was covered in worry. Both of them rushed me and
hugged me. I guess they both love me after all.

Kendra

"Kendra, it's Nathan." Kaleah said putting the phone down.
"Please tell him I'm sleep or something." I didn't fee like talking
to him. Lately all he wants to talk about is when we finally do it.
And I'm not in no hurry, seems like everybody is doing it, and I
don't see anybody's life improving because of it. I don't want to
worry about getting pregnant. I don't need that stress right now.
Plus nothing with Nathan makes me feel like I'm missing out on
something better. If anything I liked talking to Darryl more, when
he used to call me. He'd say things about my body but we'd talk
about other stuff. And he was so goofy. Half the time it wasn't
what he said but it was the way he says things that makes you fall
on the ground cracking up. I miss that stinking knucklehead, but
the distance stops us from ever having anything real. I hear from

him every so often, but not enough to say we have anything. Nathan on the other hand, I mean I like him and I like when we talk about other stuff other than sex. But it seems like he calls me when it's on his mind and then I do my best to refocus his thoughts to anything but that. Sometimes I give up and say my momma needs to use the phone or something. Even though she's out a lot with her boyfriend.

"She told me to tell you that she's sleep!" Kaleah said then she hung up the phone like she couldn't be bothered.

My mouth fell open; she's so rude sometimes. Kalani cracked up laughing. Nathan called right back and I felt obligated to answer the phone. "Hello"

"I need to see you!" He sound upset.

"I can't leave." I said alarmed by the sound of his voice.

"Can you come outside? I just need to see you." Then I heard him sniffle.

"Ok, but you can't stay long. My momma will be home in about an hour."

"Ok, I'm at a pay phone around the corner." Then he hung up.

When I walked up to his car, the streetlight shined on his face as he got out. His face was swollen and knotted up. "What happened to your face?"

"Junior!"

"Why were you fighting?"

"Nealesha and I were arguing and he got mad, cause I wasn't holding back with her. He caught me off guard and beat me up."

"Why were you arguing?"

"You know how she is, how can you not argue with her? Tell me something, do you think Nellie and I look alike?"

"Well not right now, your head is all lumpy." He cut his eyes at me, Darryl would've laughed. I exhaled, "out of all of your siblings you and Nellie favor the most. But all of you look like your father." He put his head down as he exhaled. "What difference does looking alike make? My sisters and I have the same father and mother and we all have our own looks. We favor but you gotta look hard to see it."

"What about me and Junior?"

"Yes, I just said you all look alike. Why does it matter?"

He growled, "I can't go to school out here! I need to get away from here!"

"Why what's wrong?"

"Nellie is taking over everything! She's turning my parents on me! I HATE her so much!"

"Nathan, don't talk about your sister like that. She's worried about her mother…."

"FORGET HER AND HER RAGGEDY MOTHER! I HATE THEM! ALL THEY DO IS CAUSE PROBLEMS EVERYWHERE THEY GO! Her mother better hope I never see her again!"

"Why would you hurt her mother?"

"Because of all the pain she's caused my household and me!"

"Have you been drinking?"

He looked at me with fire in his eyes. "I don't know why I even came here. Again! You keep disappointing me. One minute I think you're mature and have a good head on your shoulders. And then other times you say stupid stuff like that! I'm done! Look me up when you completely grow up!" He said getting into his car.

"AGAIN!" I couldn't believe I let him do this to me again.

****

"Are you sure?" I asked her. Ahjanae cried on my shoulder as she shook her head yes. "What are you going to do?"

"My momma is gonna be so mad at me!" She cried

"Yes, but she'll get over it. I keep panicking thinking she knows already. But my life is about to be over! She's going to kill me!"

"What does Jabbar say?"

"That we should tell our mothers together. But I think they'll take turns beating on us."

"At least he didn't run away from you and leave you hanging."

"Yea I guess. I'm scared!"

I hugged her and told her it was going to be ok. Even though I didn't know for sure that it was going to be. I stayed with Ahjanae as long as I could then I went home. Tonight my momma was bringing her man over for dinner. She had stretched things out as long as she could. It was now time for him to meet us. She was so nervous about us meeting him that she took the day off from work; She did all the housework in preparation for tonight. Kalani and I were curious to know who this man was, Kaleah was falling apart. Even still, after all this time she believed her father was coming back. She said he promised and she believed him. I honestly wondered if he would as well. But when their divorce became final and there was no word from him one way or another it didn't take a genius to figure it out. Dinner was in the oven and the house looked and smelled fabulous. Kalani and I were watching TV in the living room when we heard the knock at the door. I ran to the room and asked Kaleah if her stomach was feeling any better cause he was here. Kaleah put her pillow over her head and cried some more. I shut her door to give her some privacy. I turned around to see flowers come in the door and then him. He was a little shorter than my momma, so he wasn't tall. But he was very nicely put together, and his hair cut was fresh like he just got it done. His face looked very serious even though he was smiling. He was peanut butter complexion, and his outfit was coordinated very nicely. He gave my momma a kiss on her cheek and then he looked at Kalani and I. Momma excitedly introduced us. "This is Jason, and Jason these are my girls."

"It looks like you're missing one?"

"Kaleah is having a hard time dealing with all of this. So she's laying down."

"I'm sorry to hear that, it's nice to meet you two. I'm glad you feel up to meeting me. You're mother has told me so much about you two. You're the two that help out around the house, and help your mother manage the home right?" Kalani and I nodded yes. "When your mother told me that, I knew she had very special ladies in her life."

Kalani and I smiled and thanked him for the compliment. We sat down for dinner and he did a good job of engaging us in conversation. When he went to the bathroom our mother told us to honestly tell her what we thought. Kalani said he was nice and I nodded in agreement. Momma smiled real big like she was so excited to hear it. When he came back Kalani asked him what he did for a living. He said he managed a barbershop in Oakland mainly, but he was head of a few of the other locations as well. He said there was one right here in Richmond. He asked us if we had heard of Drew's barbershop. I told him all the guys either went to Drew's or Mark's mainly out here. He asked what cleaning services we offered. Kalani explained that we did it all, from yard work to car detailing. All he needed to do was state what he needed and we could handle the rest. I loved hearing her pitch our services. He asked if we could fit his car in on Saturday. Unfortunately we couldn't, during school; Saturday was one of our busiest days. So Kalani fit him in on Sunday, he said he was very impressed with our set up. He said we hadn't even gone to college yet and we were very organized. We had a nice dinner and for dessert we had fruit salad. Jason hung out with us for a while and then he left. When momma walked him out Kalani and I asked each other what we thought. He seemed nice enough. Kaleah came out and warmed up the plate momma left for her. She looked horrible, she had been crying her eyes out and she didn't look like she intended to stop. She called us traitors, and she said she could tell he was evil by the sound of his voice.

When momma came back inside she was smiling from ear to ear. But then Kaleah started in on her. She accused momma of committing adultery and she tried to make her feel horrible. I defended her and told Kaleah that she had it confused. Her father was the one who was guilty not our mother. I pointed out that her father left us without a way to provide for ourselves. Momma told her if Kalani and I hadn't pitched in we would be homeless. Kaleah didn't want to hear it, or believe it. I told my momma to stop trying to convince her. I told her everything could be solved and returned to normal if she could do one thing. Everyone looked at me, I told her to call her father and tell him to come home. I said if she couldn't do that then she really needed to shut up. Kaleah exploded in anger.

****

"KB!" I heard someone call out to me.

I wasn't overly excited to see him, but I wasn't mad either. "Hey Darryl." I said as I hugged him when he got close.

"You don't know how to call nobody?"

"You're never home, plus I mostly work after school."

"DAVID?" A woman called out from his Aunt's house. She was looking at him.

"Oh man! I'll be right back!" He said as he ran back across the street.

"DAVID I NEED YOU!" She said calling him back to the house. Darryl helped her back inside, then Ahjanae came outside. She asked me why I was standing around. I told her I just saw Darryl but some woman was calling him David. I asked her if his name was Darryl or David? She said she's always known him as Darryl. She said it could've been a middle name or something. I told her I had to tell him I was leaving. I walked across the street and knocked on the door. Ms. Lorraine came to the door while I heard the other woman in the background crying and carrying on. I introduced myself and then I asked her if she could tell Darryl I'd see him later. D-Rick told me to come in and tell him myself. Ms. Lorraine stepped to the side so I could enter. Then D-Rick called out that I was there. Darryl's face was serious and it held no comedy like it normally did. He looked a little upset. I told him we were leaving to take Ahjanae to the doctors. That woman started calling him David again and every time she said it, it looked like she wounded him. Then D-Rick said hi to her and then she smiled at him and started calling him David. I was relieved to know he had at least given me his real name. He didn't look like he wanted to talk about it so I hugged him and told him it was good seeing him. It was weird seeing Darryl upset. Normally he was full of jokes and laughter, but today he was quiet and serious. As I started to walk away, he said, "oh! There it is! I've missed that booty! Hold on, let me walk you back across the street." He told his Auntie he'd be right back. "KB! I've missed you."

"No you haven't," I said teasing.

"Un huh! Every time I hear music I think of you. You backing that thang up, you know the good times." He smiled.

"Why did she call you David?"

"Long story. How's your summer shaping up?"

"It's shaping up to be about the same as last year's."

"Are you going to leave Thursdays open for me?"

"I will take at least one day off a week, but I can't guarantee it will be Thursday. Besides if things continue like they should I'll have a boyfriend this summer."

"As opposed to now?" His seriousness was back.

"I didn't know that I'd ever see you again."

He stopped us and put his hands, on my shoulders, "I will always come back for that booty! Don't give my booty away! Don't you dare back that thang up for anyone but me. You understand? Promise me! Promise me!" When I didn't respond cause I was laughing he shook me by my shoulders. "I'm serious! Don't give my booty away, hold his hand or something. Promise me!" When I didn't say anything cause I was still laughing, he kissed me. He caught me off guard and I had to tell myself I had a boyfriend and to get away from him.

When he looked at me, I crossed my eyes, and he laughed. "Well dang! Get me in trouble why don't you!"
"I got something else for you, when you're ready of course."

Chapter 7

Nellie

As if he didn't act like he hated me before, now Nathan acts like I'm not even worthy of acknowledging. But at least I'm not alone in this; he has been giving our daddy the cold shoulder as well. They even came to blows one time and Junior struggled to break them up. Poor Nassya has been an emotional wreck seeing all of this fighting. Lately she sleeps in my bed because that's the only way she can stop crying at night. I just wish she wasn't such a wild sleeper. She kicks, slaps, one time she plopped on top of me like she was doing some wrestling move. I thought for sure she was awake but she was knocked out.

Although my parents were grateful that Ahjani made me come back. My daddy did not like the idea of me having a boyfriend. Without coming out and saying it, he made it impossible for me to see Ahjani. He had me take the bus to his office after school and then he had me work around there. Everyone says how big I've gotten. But all I can think about is the last time I saw them. When my daddy is stuck on calls I call Ahjani and try not to cry when I hear his voice. He tells me how much he misses me and I tell him I miss him too. It seems like whenever we come up with a plan to see each other it's spoiled.

Ahjani says he needs to see me so bad. It sounds like it's burning inside of him. I tell him I need to see him cause I do, but... If I try to ignore the craving it drives me crazy. If I don't give in to the craving my mind wanders to things I don't want to remember. I can't function until that stuff is off my mind. I feel horrible, but I can't wait for Ahjani. My grades have finally picked up again, and my parents take that as a sign that things are getting better for me.

****

I blinked my eyes! Could it be real? Was I really looking at D? He was with a girl but ask me if I cared. I started shaking my leg, cause I needed my mind to focus. I touched my pocket to make sure I had at least one condom. I told Bonnie and Cricket I'd be right back. I told Cricket to make sure nothing landed on my yogurt. I crossed the street in front of Darryl's group. Everyone was laughing at something he said. He looked at me and I shook my head yes at him. As I kept walking towards the garage. I didn't know where I was going but I pressed the button on the elevator to go up. "What do you want Noel?" He had no smile on his face, but that made me want him more. When the elevator doors opened I stepped inside and wiggled my finger to tell him to come. "No Noel! This ain't right!" He said like he was fighting with himself. I unbuttoned my pants and flashed my underwear at him. "Kendra!" He growled like he was trying to be strong. I turned around and started to pull my pants down just a bit. "Am I really this sexy? You gotta control yourself!" I looked back at him and shook my head. I could see the fight in his body as he stepped on the elevator. I turned around and kissed his lips. "Don't kiss me!" He said pushing me back. That hurt, but not enough to stop me. We stepped off the elevator on the top level. There were no cars up there. He pulled me to the not so visible side outside of the elevator. I quickly unfastened his pants, he put on his condom, as I was about to take him in my mouth he said there was no time for that. I couldn't see straight, this was better than I remembered. I screamed to the top of my lungs as I exploded! D finished then he picked up his pants. My body was still going. "Noel! If you don't leave me alone!" He rubbed his head as he looked around. "Now that I see you're strung out." He smiled, "I will end you if Kendra ever finds out!" He stopped smiling.

"She said you guys barely talk." I said trying to calm down.

"Don't matter, that's my future, you were a minute ago." Then he pressed the elevator button.

"I love you!" I said

"You don't know what love is!" Then he got on the elevator.

****

He was right; I didn't know what love is. I know that what I feel for him I've never felt for anyone. Not even Ahjani, I hated to hurt him. But I had to break up with him. We never saw each other and I hated feeling bad for cheating. Plus I'm going away to camp for six weeks. I've been trying to decide whether I want to break in a new guy or see if Aldo's learned anything new. Thinking about how much I hurt Ahjani only made my cravings stronger. Now the cravings kind of hurt, and if I don't do anything I feel sick. This can't be good, but I guess other people have to deal with worse so I'll suck it up.

"Nathaniel Tyree Parker" they announced as Nathan walked across the stage and received his diploma. Everyone stood up and cheered while I sat and politely clapped. Nathan ditched us after his ceremony to go party. Which turned out to be great for me. My parents asked me questions about my future and what I wanted to do. Even though I woke up that morning with really bad cravings, spending quality time with my family made them lessen though. That was interesting. We had dinner and then we went to the movies as a family just like Kendra's family used to.

I got a big lump in my throat the moment I thought of her. She's going to hate me just like my momma. The thought of it made the cravings come back.

"Leasha!" Clap! "It's so good!" Clap! "To see! You back!" Clap! Clap!

Same ole cheerleader style.

Then the camp director came over. "Mr. And Mrs. Parker, Dexter Strong Camp Director. I probably should've called but I wanted to speak to you in person about your oldest." My heart sank, did Aldo tell on me? "We received letters from the parents of the children assigned to Leasha's cabin. Everyone was so happy to have her. She was a wonderful addition to our team." Then he looked at me, "we're so happy you decided to come back." Is this man hitting on me?

My parents looked so proud and Nassya and I sighed in relief. My campers were excited about my return. Aldo cheesed really big when he spotted me. Once again, I had six weeks of fun. Dexter was nice to me and he watched me a lot. But he didn't say or do anything; he would smile and then tell me I was doing a great job. I did like hearing good things about myself every day. And to make matters even better, when I came home Nathan already left for school.

Kendra

"That is so gross!" Aunrey said frowning at Ahjanae's moving belly.

"It's not gross! It's beautiful!" Audra said

Aunrey looked like he was going to be sick. "There's a creature moving around in your guts! I don't care what ya'll say that's gross!"

"Go ahead and embrace the miracle of life." Kalani said

"No!" Then he looked at me, "so you've got a little boyfriend?"

I smiled, "who told you that?"

"So you know that guy you like is a Mason or did you forget?" Aunrey said sarcastically.

"What does that mean?"

"His arms are long! Anyone who gets in his way will bow down. He's nice to you. But he's crazy, you think I'm crazy..." He shook his head. "Didn't you see when he took that man down in front of this house? He wasn't even mad. He'll get mad about you, he likes you." He smiled.

"But we're not together, we've never been together. I can like someone if I want."

Aunrey shook his head, "you go ahead and believe that if you want to." Then the door opened, Ahjani walked in the door with Darryl right behind him. "Speaking of the devil!"

"KB! Come give me love girl!" I hugged him, and then he jumped. "Whoa girl! What happened to you?" He said to Ahjanae.

"Play with fire and you will get burned!" Ahjanae said matter of factly.

"What kind of fire was that? You don't look burned, you look swollen!" Then he looked at Kaleah, "isn't that stuff contagious? You better be careful!"

I looked at Kaleah, "careful about what?"

Everybody moved away from Kaleah to say she was on her own. "Don't make a big deal out of it!" She said trying to quiet me down.

I looked at Darryl, "how do you know what my sister does?"

"She messes with one of my cousins." He said putting his hands out. "I thought you knew."

I looked around the room, "everybody knew but me?" Everybody put their heads down and didn't look at me. "I hate all of you guys!" I spit. Darryl slowly moved away from me and then he sat quietly at the table. "You're telling momma tonight."

Everyone gasped, "SNITCH!" Darryl yelled.

"Whatever! If you're gonna be doing it you need to protect yourself." I said feeling confident in my resolve.

Darryl put his finger up to his chin, "good point. So when you gonna talk to your momma about us?"

Everyone including me gasped, "what?" Then I started laughing. "You remember. You were wearing that dress I like, while you were doing that thing I like." He raised his eyebrows.

Everybody started laughing, "me in a dress? You might've fooled everybody until you said that." He snapped his fingers. "Can I talk to you for a minute?" I said walking towards the door.

"We can't do it out there let's go back there." He said pointing to the back of the house.

"Stop clowning and come on." I sat on the trunk of Aunt Quilla's bucket. He leaned against it next to me. As if it were possible he's gotten even taller. "Did you put a hit out on my boyfriend?"

He stood up straight, "who told? It was supposed to be a surprise! You were gonna be all broken hearted and running to me. I'd have to rub that booty to make it all better." He said idealistically. I eyed him, "I was just doing my homework. Asking questions, I'm always gonna check up on you. I got your back!"

"My back or are you making sure I don't get too deep?"

He stood in front of me, parted my legs, and then stood between them. He put his hands on either side of my face then he kissed me deeply. "I'm gonna be your first when you're ready."

"I could fall in love tomorrow." I said breathlessly.

"Yep, with me." Then he kissed me again.

Then I heard a car pull up, "Kendra!" A very familiar voice yelled. I looked in disbelief; it was Kaleah and Kalani's father. "WHAT?" I yelled at him.

"Get down! Come here!" He commanded.

"You must have me confused with someone else! Your children are inside!" I said with attitude.

He stood on the gas, he ran up on the curb. Then he got out the car all angry. "What's wrong with you! Go away! This is my daughter!" He said to Darryl who turned to face him.

I put my arms around Darryl's waist, "she said she didn't have a daddy!" I could hear Darryl's smile.

"Well she lied to you, now move!" He said shooing him.

I squeezed Darryl tight, he laughed. "She won't let go. Looks like I'm stuck." Then he looked at me, "should we give him the news?" I shook my head yes.

"WHAT NEWS?"

"Father of the other girls. Mr. Hutchins?" He looked at me to confirm. I shook my head yes. "Ok, Mr. Hutchins it's a pleasure to finally meet you. I'm your new son in-law!" Jerry looked like Darryl punched him. "Don't look like that. I'm gonna be an excellent son in-law! And when the baby comes...."

"BABY?" He said bending over to catch his breath.

Darryl tried not to laugh. I buried my face in his back and took in his wonderful smell. "You see what had happened was...." Darryl swallowed, and then he put his hands up to paint the scene. "My parents kicked me out cause I dropped out of school."

"You're still in school?"

"Not any more, keep up. I had this wonderful idea...." He looked at Jerry; he was all sweaty and trying to catch his breath. "You ok? It's only like seventy, maybe seventy-two degrees you're sweating pretty hard my friend."

"I'm fine! I can't believe this!" He said

Darryl smiled, "we just playing. I bet our kissing seems like the lesser of two evils now!" He laughed.

"You kids play too much! Kendra get inside!" He said huffing towards me.

"You better stay back! You remember what my momma did to you the last time you put your hands on me!"

"Ooh! What she do?"

Jerry huffed and walked towards Aunt Quilla's house. I told Darryl that we needed to go cause my Aunt Quilla didn't play and I didn't want to go in the house with him. He asked me where I wanted to go, and I said I didn't care. He asked me if I wanted to go to Oakland. I said I didn't care. I asked him what his dad was like, and he said he was nothing like mine. He said there was no way a child or anyone for that matter could punk his dad. He said if I was his dad's daughter, his dad wouldn't have said anything. He would've parked, walked over and shot him, and then calmly told me to get in the car. When I laughed he said he was serious. That made me laugh harder. He shrugged like he tried to convince me. When Darryl handed me my Bart ticket I took him in, he didn't really look like he was in high school. It wasn't that he looked old either, but he carried himself way more mature than his age. Until you got him going of course. He is so silly! Everyone on our side of the train was cracking up at him, and he wasn't trying to be funny.

He took me to his grandfather's house. The light bulb went off when I saw him. That's why he got so mad at Nellie. This older nice looking white man said hello to me. "Granddad tell her I'm your favorite!" Darryl said blushing.

"Of all the Darryl's I know, you are my favorite."

"Mr.?" I asked

He smiled, "Tim is fine sweetheart what do you need?"

"Mr. Tim can I use your phone to call home?"

He laughed sounding a lot like Darryl, "Just call me Tim. And yes you can."

I used the phone in the living room. I left a message on the house phone. "Momma your ex showed up at Aunt Quilla's so I left with Darryl. I'll be home later, I'm ok. I love you!"

"So what are you kids up to?" Tim asked.

"Well I told her father we're married. So I guess this is our reception, Kendra I think it's time to get to the honeymoon." He raised his eyebrows.

"What is wrong with you son? This is a lady!" Tim said pointing at me.

"Thank you!" I said

"You're right. Honeymoon tomorrow!"

"Or honeymoon now?"

Darryl's mouth dropped open, "KB! Don't play with me!" I couldn't breathe I was laughing so hard. Darryl rolled his eyes at me. "You play too much!"

We had a good time laughing and joking with his grandfather, who was funny in his own, laid back and calm way.

"Granddad you know how I'm your favorite, can I drive your car?" I laughed cause I knew he'd say no.

"Sure, bring it back full." Tim said handing him keys.

"You're going to let him drive your car?" I asked in disbelief.

"Darryl's an excellent driver. I trust my grandson."

Darryl gave me a toothy grin. "I told you I'm the favorite.

"You better go before Tina comes home looking for my car."

I got in the car slowly. I told him my momma will kill him if he gets us arrested. He assured me that he knew what he was doing. He said as soon as he gets his car he'll take me wherever I wanted to go. "So, your grandfather is white. That's why you got mad at Nellie?"

"Who is Nellie?" He frowned.

"You never remember her. My friend that said she couldn't dance."

"Oh the stupid bird girl. Yea, she's dumb! People shouldn't make comments like that. One of my closest cousins is white. Only time I remember is when people point it out. To me he's just Ryder.

Shoot I'm white, it doesn't matter." Then he cut his eyes at me.
"You come straight from the mother land!"
He showed me where he lived, he said we couldn't go in cause his
neighbors would tell his momma and the rule was no girls in the
house while she wasn't there. Instead he took me up a hill to an
open lot that he parked in. He told me to come look down on The
Bay with him. The weather was perfect, just enough crispness on
the air to enjoy him holding me. We could see straight out across
the Bay to the city. It was beautiful up here. He said he comes up
here a lot when he needs to get away. I asked him what would he
need to get away from. He exhaled; he said his family can get
pretty stressful at times. He said what gets to him the most is he
can see how much pain everybody is in and they always try to act
like they're ok. He said he'd rather acknowledge the pain so he can
find a way to laugh at it. Then he admitted that he has a horrible
temper. I told him that the funniest people normally do. The most
giving people can be the meanest, the funniest people can be the
saddest, and so on. He smiled at me. He said he doesn't let people
close to him cause they tend to let you down and disappoint. Then
I asked why he let me in. He said I'm in just about as much pain as
he is. I knew he was talking about Jerry. I sucked my teeth and he
smiled, and said there was the pain. I started yelling, "HE LEFT
US KNOWING WE COULDN'T SURVIVE WITHOUT HIM
AND HE DIDN'T CARE! HE HIT ME FOR CALLING HIM ON
HIS CRAP!" That's when the tears came. "He never hit me before
that."
Darryl rubbed my shoulders, "since we're sharing traumas." He
tried to laugh, but nothing came out. "My last name is Mason, my
granddad is Wallace, and my dad's name is Latour. My
grandmother who lives across the street is a Mason." I gave him a
confused look. "It's says David Mason on my birth certificate, but
the only dad and father I've ever accepted is my dad. I have very
vague memories of David. I was little when he left. But the one
clear memory I have is of him grabbing my momma. The look on
his face, the look on my momma's face. They didn't realize I was
right there watching the whole thing. My momma has always been
good about keeping us connected to David's side. David's father
was just like him but my momma got out before she ended up like
my Grandmomma. When I go see my Grandmomma she's only
existing in pain, it's hard to see. But she'll have like three minutes

of clarity and I love that. If I can make her laugh when all she does is hurt, I've accomplished something with my day." He tried to smile.

"Why is it your job to make her laugh?"

"I'm the peacekeeper of the family. Even when things get crazy, I bring a measure of laughter to the table. If I didn't laugh people would die a lot more than they do."

"I take care of everybody; my momma, my sisters, and my cousins."

"I know, that's why I told you about your sister. She's a little misguided, probably hanging out with the bird too much. But she needs some help."

"How do you know that about Nellie?"

"Who?"

"You called her the bird girl."

"You can see it all over her."

"I've got some choice words for her when I see her. She broke Ahjani's heart."

"That's who he was whining about? Why would he take her serious?"

"Nellie can be really sweet. My momma says she's misguided. If it wasn't for my momma we wouldn't be friends now. She's like a sister to me, I don't like that Kaleah mimics her. I think one in each family is enough." Darryl was quiet for a long time. No jokes in his face, he was thinking hard. "Penny for your thoughts."

"How long are you staying with your boyfriend?"

I sighed, "I barely see you in the summer. You travel a lot and you've got your whole life. Once school starts we're both gonna be focused."

"So.... I'm your secret summer fling?"

"You're not a secret and you're not a fling." I got nervous but I told myself to do it. "I like you Darryl."

He smiled, "you like me? Or you LIKE me like me?"

"I LIKE you like you!" I said pushing past my embarrassment.

He squinted his eyes at me. "You're in love with me aren't you?"

I gasped, "In love would have to be mutual. I have a strong like for you. Even though I have a boyfriend." I smiled.

"I guess that will do for now."

"You like me?"

"You're alright," then he smiled at me. "I mean I brought you up here. You met my granddad. I punked your father, I like you. It's just hard to trust you."

"Trust me?"

"Every time I turn around you got a boyfriend. Doesn't stop you from letting me kiss you. I'm trying to digest how someone like you present yourself to be could truly be friends with someone like the bird girl. She's not your friend, but I can see you're going to have to learn that the hard way. I just hope I don't lose you as a result of it."

"Why do you kiss me if my having a boyfriend bothers you?"

"It's not my fault if the motherland is alive and well in you. I can't resist you."

"But that's not really fair, you can't be faulted for your weakness for me. But you hold mine for you against me. Take me home then."

"Ok, ok! I mean I know I'm sexy too. So let's call a truce."

"What about you? Don't you have girlfriends?"

He shook his head, "I don't love these hoes. No girlfriend for me, friends and hoes. That's all a brotha knows."

The breeze of the evening swept in. "I guess we should get going."

"KB! Now you know the whole point of coming up here with daddy issues is to let me feel on that booty!" He smiled

"I didn't ask to come up here. If I knew this was a setup I would've said take me home right away."

"But we're here now." He raised his eyebrows. "Think of the pain KB! Think of how good it will feel to have my hands all over your body."

I smiled, "yea but you're right. I shouldn't be here with you when I have a boyfriend. It's not right, and I don't want you looking at me as anything other than the Queen that I am." I smiled, "thank you for focusing me." I patted his hand.

"You gonna play a brotha for being honest?"

"Look at it this way, when we're finally together it will make everything sweeter."

"We don't have to wait for that. We could be together now. What's his name, I'll have somebody shoot him right now."

"I'm not ready to have sex. You saw Ahjanae; I've got too much going on to be worried about ending up like that. I plan to graduate with my hymen intact."

"Just because you have sex doesn't mean you get pregnant."

"If I don't have sex at all I don't have to worry about it. I don't get the hype any ways." I said

He smiled, "that's because you're a virgin."

"And proud of it! Nothing is sacred anymore. I want to be in love, I want a beautiful experience. I don't want to feel like I'm sneaking."

"Sex doesn't have to be about love. Sometimes it's just sex."

"I guess, but these days it's like people forgot that love has anything to do with it. I'll wait for love." I smiled

"Fine!" He stood up, he took my hands. He took two long exaggerated deep breaths. "Kendra, when you rolled your eyes you reminded me of my momma. When you walk past me I've got to watch. Girl your booty is magnificent! I've never seen anything like it before. You're smart, you're funny. I...." He looked around, "I love you ok!" He said like it was hard to admit. "Now can we please get in this car so I can feel you up?"

I laughed, "no. But nice try."

"No? See! I just poured my heart out."

"You were playing." I laughed.

"You're right. Ha! Ha! Ha!" He said sarcastically.

I looked at him, "I think I missed something."

"I know, let me take you home." He said dropping my hands.

"You're mad at me because I won't make out with you?"

"No, because I was serious. You can't look at me and tell the difference so that's fine."

"You love me?" I said looking him in his eyes.

He rolled his eyes, "no I don't! I don't love anybody! I just want your booty just like everybody else. Let's go!"

When we got in the car, I tried to ask him about it. He wouldn't talk about it. He talked about other stuff, laughed a little. But I could see irritation in his face. When we pulled up to my house Jerry's car was in front I was instantly irritated. I started screaming immediately. Darryl sat there looking but not saying anything. I don't even remember all that I said but I was going off. Then he started shaking his head. He apologized for taking my lack of faith in him personal. I frowned at him; I told him I don't have daddy issues. He smiled at me and said ok. When I playfully pushed him, he grabbed my arm and pulled me in for a kiss. This kiss was the best one yet. Darryl pushed me away and told me to get out of the car before he drove us somewhere. I reluctantly got out of the car. I exhaled a little when Darryl got out to walk me to the door. When I opened the door Jerry was talking to my momma and sisters. He tried to ask me where I've been. I asked my momma to come to the door. When she did I introduced her to Darryl. Her eyes were red and she was too sad to respond properly. Darryl gave her a hug, then he told her to give him the word and it would be lights out for Jerry. Jerry stood in the middle of the floor tapping his foot, as if he deserved our time. Darryl turned to walk away when he smiled. "Jay-man what's up?" He said shaking Jason's hand.

"What are you doing here?" Jason said

Darryl pointed at me, "what are you doing here?"

"This is my woman's spot." Then he looked at my momma. "What's wrong?"

"Jerry's here." She said sadly.

"He's acting up?" Jason asked

"He's talking about he wants to come back." She said sadly.

"What did you say?" He asked at the bottom of his voice.

"He hasn't asked me anything. He's talking, he's been talking for a long time."

"Excuse me," Jason said walking past us.

"Aw sookie! Sookie now! Ms. Hutchins can I please stay?" Darryl pleaded like he was excited to see this go down.

My momma nodded then we went inside. Jason strolled in looking Jerry up and down. Jerry was a little taller than Jason but I doubt that mattered. Jerry couldn't handle my momma, there's no way he could handle a man. Jerry frowned at his new audience. "Kharee this is personal!"

"I guess you didn't know that she's not single so you can continue to make your little pitch to me. Or you could be about your daughters and roll up out of here!"

"My daddy doesn't have to leave! He came back just like I said he would. Now you can leave our family alone, and we can get back to normal!" Kaleah said

"Le-le baby your daddy and I are not getting back together. I could never forgive him for all that he's done to our family."

"What I've done? You got all these thugs around our daughters like this is normal!"

"Aw! You noticed! Kendra you said he wouldn't notice. Thank you Jerry!" Darryl smiled

Jerry looked at Darryl with angry eyes. "You know I will fight a kid! You need to learn some respect!"

"NOOOO!" Kaleah screamed probably remembering what he did to Juju.

"But you won't fight a man? Figures! You look like the type! Let me tell you how this is going to go. You can come pick up your girls whenever. But you can't come inside anymore. Kharee is no longer your concern, she's with me now." Jason said like there was no negotiation to be made.

"Kharee?" Jerry said like he knew she would check Jason.

"Jerry you have to leave." My momma said through clinched teeth.

"WHAT? Why? No! Make him leave! I want my daddy!" Kaleah said running to Jerry. "Please don't leave again. Take me with you!"

"Kaleah!" My momma said like she was hurt.

Jason looked at Jerry like he was reading him. "Kharee if she wants to go with her father, let her go."

Jerry told Kaleah she couldn't come with him. He said he was going back to Aunt Quilla's if she needed to see him. Kaleah asked if she could go there with him. He reluctantly told her she could come. Jason put his arms around my momma as she cried watching her daughter walk out the door. Jason told her that Kaleah was going to be back, but she needed to see her dad for who he is. That was the first night that Jason slept over.

****

Ahjanae sat down catching her breath. "Uncle Jerry gets on my nerves! Got me walking all this way to come see you cause you won't come to the house no more! I mean he sees how big this belly is, he could at least offer to drive me." She blew air, and then Kalani brought a glass of water. "He keeps crying, and following my momma around the house whining about his life. Whoever that woman was she did a number on him. She emptied their account. Packed all her stuff and left. Oh and did I mention she did all this after she got him fired?" Kalani and I gasped. "Yep, came to his job. Acted a complete fool! The next day he goes in, he's fired. Comes home, she's gone! He's been applying all over the place, but he's got nothing."

"That's too bad," Kalani said shaking her head.

Ahjanae smiled then she told us about last night. She said it had been building for a while. But Kaleah was trying to hang in there with her dad. Waiting on him hand and foot, and listening to him whine about our momma's happiness. Through all of that he hadn't said thank you once. She was sleeping on the floor just to be near him when she has a bed. Uncle Jerry and Aunt Quilla got into it because he was talking about your momma and she was defending her. You could tell Kaleah was getting fed up. But then he came yelling at her, nobody knows why. Then he slapped her. Ahjanae said her momma went off on him; slapping him around, and then she said Kaleah cursed him out so badly. She told him she was the only one of his kids that still loved him and he did that to her. She said that's when Kaleah asked her momma to bring her home. Ahjanae asked what it was like having Jason in the house. We told her he's nice, and a lot of fun. If he comes home and momma isn't home yet, he makes dinner. He did share with us that he's been in prison before, but he didn't say what for. He said he met Darryl's dad in there. He said Darryl's dad owns the barbershop that he works at. We think he really loves our momma cause he's always all about her. Mrs. McCall said she really likes Jason too. He told her to call him whenever he needs anything. I told her that Jason acts so sprung off of momma, I wouldn't be surprised if they got married.

Chapter 8

Nellie

"Hello?" Nassya said, "Who's calling please?" She smiled, "oh hi Kendra. Nellie's not home, but I'll tell her you called." Then she laughed, "yes. I will. Ok bye." She put the phone down. "Why don't you want to talk to Kendra?"

"She's going to be mad at me. I don't want her to be mad." I said

"Not Kendra, she's too nice." She said confidently.

"How you know she's nice?"

"Because she's always nice to me. Even when I spilled her drink and she had to buy a new one. She didn't get mad at me. See!" She said like that could convince me.

The way I see it I've got two choices. I can come clean, face the music, and deal with the repercussions of my actions or I can let the friendship go altogether, and focus on making D my man! My mind still swishes when I think about sex with him. I don't even care; I can change my name to Noel if he wants me to. I don't even have to be his girlfriend. I don't care; I just want to do it again. My leg starts shaking whenever I think about him. I know he's going to Oakland high this year. I will search high and low until I find him, if it's the last thing I do. I've got to have him any way I can.

"What you two doing?" Junior said knocking on our door as he opened it.

"She's making me tell Kendra she's not here." Nassya tattled.

"Why?" Junior asked

"Because I can't even deal with her right now." I said shaking my head.

"She wasn't the aggressor in any of that. Nathan was on her." What is he saying to me? I tried to play it off like I knew. "She could've told me."

"You know Nathan, he wouldn't let her tell you. Shoot, the only reason I knew is because he begged me to tell you to bring her to my graduation."

I cursed! "You mean to tell me all that loving support that night from her was because of her guilty conscience!" Junior and Nassya's eyes got big. I thought it was so special and kind of her to carry me on her back across the parking lot when I cut my foot on glass, and here she was feeling guilty the whole time. "Here I am feeling guilty about stuff and she was sneaking around doing my brother!"

"Whoa! Whoa! They didn't have sex, she wouldn't do it. That's all he was trying to do though." Junior said in Kendra's defense.

I deflated a little, "oh. But still! How she going to talk to my own brother behind my back. A real friend would've told me."

"Come on. You know Nathan's a jerk. You're really going to fault her for this? Kendra's a good girl."

"Why does everybody ride her nuts like she's so great? She's not better than me!"

"Princess? Who's ever said she was better than you? No one said that."

"But everybody acts like it. Oh Kendra this! And oh Kendra that! She's not smarter than me, and she's never prettier than me! I don't get it!" I growled.

"I don't get what you're mad about. All I was saying is that none of that was her fault. However, I do know this! If you waste your time comparing yourself to other people you'll never be content with yourself. Who cares who's prettier or smarter. Just be the best you that you can be."

I clapped my hands. "Cool speech bro!"

Junior stared at me for a minute. "You make my butt hurt!"

Nassya started laughing. "Anyways, who's down to ride with me? I gotta go to Sacramento."

"Me!" Nassya said excitedly as she put her dolls away.

"What about you?" He asked me.

"No thanks. You're just going to see that girl. I'm gonna call Bonnie and see what she's doing."

"Ok, but you know you can't go to Richmond by yourself!"

"I don't have a reason to go to Richmond anymore. Besides, I would think the police have found Bobby by now."

"Dad checks regularly, he's not letting it go. He's still out there."

"Whatever! He's not going to find me." I said trying not to reflect my fear.

****

I can't sleep! D is all over my thoughts, which is fine. But then the guilt of Kendra comes right after. I'm so mad at her! How could she give Nathan another look when D is right there? They're not even in the same league. D is strong, powerful, and feels like a man! Nathan is a little brat of a boy! When he calls home, if I answer the phone he hangs up. So I make it a point to keep answering the phone. One night he kept calling and hanging up. I took the phone to bed with me and when he called in the middle of the night, I still answered. He's such a punk! So what if we have the same mother, she's not with either of us. I asked Junior if he knew Nathan had a different momma and he said he didn't. He was too young to remember any of that. He did say that my momma would look at Nathan differently than she did him.

Ok and so maybe at one point she wanted me and showed me love. But then her high roller boyfriend pays me attention and she treated me badly because of it. Sometimes I wonder if she knew. My heart tells me she didn't because she would've made his life horrible if she did. But every once in a while there's a little voice in the back of my head that says she knew something was up. I can remember her screams at the police station. But then, I remember the policewoman having my daddy's back telling him to basically take me and there would be nothing she could do about it. Did they think she knew? I hate wondering about this stuff, it literally makes me sick to my stomach. My cravings have changed some, I need D! That's what I want, that's who I need! Ahjani would be a suitable consolation, but I can't figure out how to get to him without risking running into Kendra or D finding out. I've come up with a plan, with Bonnie's help. I've figured out my bus route and everything to get me to and from D's school. I don't care where we do it, I just need it. Bonnie is my friend because she wants to be me so bad. She's alright looking, however whenever I do something she has to follow my lead. The exchange student Cricket was just like her, but she went home. I thought Bonnie only followed me in hair and fashion, but then I peeped that she was having a conversation with... I can't even remember his name. He provided me relief the week before and then she hooked up with him. When I asked her about it she thought I was going to be mad. I told her I didn't care as long as it wasn't D. Then she asked me who D was. I struggled to find the words to relay how delicious he is. She sat there like she was in a trance listening to me talk about him. I didn't tell her about Kendra of course and I told her he's so busy it's hard to nail him down. That's how I explained that we lost touch. She promised to help me find him. Then she asked me if I thought Junior would go for her. I didn't think so because he was acting all sprung off that girl. But I told her to go for it.

Junior was nice about it, but he told her in no uncertain terms that he was not interested and that it would never happen. When I asked him later why he turned her down he said she was a little girl and he couldn't look at himself in the mirror if he took advantage of her. When Junior said it, I surprised myself when I started crying. I didn't mean to and I didn't want to. But these tears forced their way out. Junior rubbed my back and told me it was going to be ok and that I was safe now. I asked him why this had to be my life? Why did this have to happen to me? He kept rubbing my back as he told me he didn't know the answer to my question. He said sometimes bad things happen to good people. That's when I asked myself if I was a good person.

Kendra

Jason picked us up from Mr. & Mrs. Pritchett's house. We were so tired we almost crawled into his nice car. He didn't pull off; he asked us how our day went. We said it was fine in unison. That's when I noticed that he was nervous. I asked him what was wrong. He sat there for like forever as if he was trying to find the words. I looked at Kalani with horror in my eyes. Was he going to break up with our momma. She has been so happy with him and even happier since he started spending the night. He couldn't find the words so he reached into his pocket and pulled out a ring box. He asked us if we would be cool with him sticking around. Kalani and I screamed and we told him yes over and over again. He looked so relieved. Then he asked us if we thought our momma would like the ring. We told him she was going to love it! He smiled then he asked us if we had any suggestions about how he should ask her. Suddenly we weren't tired anymore. Kalani suggested that we go out to dinner to celebrate something else. Somewhere we'd have to dress nicely, and then he could pop the question before we had dessert. Jason laughed, "somewhere we have to dress nicely, and we're staying for dessert?" Kalani laughed and said it was only a suggestion. He said he liked it.

The next day he told us he had a reservation for that Saturday at a restaurant in San Francisco. Friday night we went shopping for dresses with our momma. Since Jason now paid all of our bills for the house and everything, Kalani and I had a nice savings that I told her we should use for college. We used our side money to buy our outfits for Saturday even though Jason offered to pay for everything.

Kaleah seemed like she was torn, and the moment she didn't like something Jason said or did she was throwing a fit. We knew she was going to hate this but we didn't care, she was out numbered three to one.

Jason said he would come at five. So Kalani and I hurried through our appointments in the morning and then hurried home to get ready. When Kaleah heard we were going out to dinner, she begged momma to let her go over Aunt Quilla's. Kalani and I fixed our braids up real cute. And by three we were ready. Momma seemed nervous like she had an idea of what was about to happen. And I guess our giggles didn't convince her otherwise. Mrs. McCall came over to see us off because Kalani and I told her about the special night tonight. Mrs. McCall got so happy for momma she said she really liked Jason. She said he got an A plus plus in her book when he didn't run from a single mother with three girls. We were chatting in the living room all full of butterflies; it was a little after four when there was a knock at the door. I figured like everyone else that Jason was super early instead of his normal early. When I opened the door and saw Jerry standing there I rolled my eyes and slammed the door. I told everybody I didn't know they moved trash day to Saturday. And how dare someone put it on our doorstep. Jerry started banging on the door. I stood up straight and with all the attitude I could muster I opened the door ready to tell him how unwelcomed he was. But Jerry had a gun, I couldn't speak. He was sweating really hard and his eyes were red from crying no doubt. He told me to move so I backed up like he told me to. "Daddy?" Kalani yelled when she saw the gun.

"Oh now I'm daddy! Now you remember who I am! SHUT UP!" He pointed the gun from person to person. He went on a whole soliloquy of randomness. Talking about how wrong we've done him and how no matter what he never gets no love. Then he called my momma all kinds of whores and tramps for replacing him with a little man. My heart was pounding out of my chest and I wished I knew some move like on TV that made him drop the gun and then we'd beat him up. Jason used his key to open the door. Jerry pointed the gun at my momma while his hand was shaking. My momma closed her eyes like she was waiting for him to pull the trigger.

When Jason walked in the door Jerry pointed it at him. Jason's smile evaporated, then he slammed the door, so hard that it slowly reopened just a bit. Jason was beyond angry. "See baby I told you this is how cowards come back!" He said to my momma, in a calm angry voice. He looked at the gun; "all you're going to do is make me angry with that little thing!"

"You gotta be this tall to be scary!" Jerry said holding his hand out.

"Says the punk holding the gun cause he can't come like a man! Kendra sweetheart call 911, they may be able to revive him when I'm done."

Jerry's hand was shaking too hard like he was mustering the courage to pull the trigger. I know he hates me the most, so I would be the easy target. I was scared. Jerry called Jason all kinds of names while Jason took off his nice jacket and prepared himself for what was about to come next. Jason told Jerry he wasn't gonna shoot nobody then he hit Jerry so hard you heard it. Jerry's hand flew up and he shot the ceiling, as we ducked his hand came down and he squeezed again. My momma flew backwards on the couch. We screamed, Mrs. McCall ran to the phone to call 911! Kalani and I ran to my momma, her feet were kicking from the pain.

"Kharee!" I heard Jason's voice yell. Jerry pointed the gun at Jason and pulled the trigger but he had nothing. Jason's eyes turned evil. Mrs. McCall gave me a towel from the kitchen. She told me to hold it on momma's shoulder to stop the bleeding. The police came in the door with guns drawn. Jason was still beating Jerry even though they told him to stop. They handcuffed Jason then set him in a chair and cuffed him to the chair. He was still coming after Jerry; it took two officers to almost hold Jason back. Jason may have been a little bit shorter than Jerry, but he was a beast! His size did not matter. They told me I couldn't ride with my momma even though Kalani and I tried with all our might to get in the ambulance. Aunt Quilla came before they pulled off and she rode with momma. Ahjanae drove her momma's car and we followed the paramedics to Brookside hospital in Richmond. Everybody was crying and Kaleah kept asking us what happened. Kalani screamed at her and told her that her daddy shot our momma. Kaleah screamed and said she was sorry and she didn't know.

Ahjanae told us to go ahead cause it was going to take her a minute to walk to the emergency room on account of her almost being at the end of her pregnancy. We ran inside and Aunt Quilla was talking to someone. She was crying really hard but she said momma was gonna be ok. They were taking her into surgery, and things should be ok. The police came to the hospital to question all of us. Then this scary looking man came into the emergency room. His voice was real deep almost like Vader's. He asked the officers if they were here regarding Kharee Hutchins and Jason Palmer. I couldn't hear what he was saying but he spoke real calm and seriously. We asked each other who he was. I had never seen him a day in my life. He looked at us then he continued talking to the officers. Finally the doctor came out and said everything looked good. He said they were able to stop the bleeding and she had a clean break on her collarbone. He told us he'd come get us once she was out of recovery. The man was listening then he said something to the officers then they left. He looked at us, but didn't say anything.

Jason came in with red eyes. He shook the man's hand and thanked him. He agreed to something and then the man left. Jason hugged all of us as we cried. When they wheeled our momma to her room the nurse told us we could stay as long as we stayed out of the way. A woman knocked on the door. She only came as far as the door and she had bags and bags of food for us. Jason thanked her, and then he gave us the bags. I knew I was hungry but I couldn't feel it. I didn't want any of the food, I just kept staring at my momma, and thinking about all the what ifs. One by one everyone fell asleep, except Jason and I. Jason kept switching emotions in a matter of seconds, he'd be sad, mad, and then thankful. He reached in his pocket and took out momma's ring. He put it on her finger, and said she'd have something worth looking forward to when she woke up. Momma woke up at dawn, and at first she looked a little panicked. Jason assured her she was safe, she looked at him and cried. She said she was scared; he kissed her and told her he was too. I sat there quietly watching them, taking in the moment. At eight o'clock there was a knock at the door. And then Darryl popped his head in. His face was serious as he surveyed the room. Momma smiled at him and told him to come inside. He locked his eyes on me as he walked in the room. Then he told Jason it was all cleaned up. He gave my momma half a hug, and then he asked her how she was feeling. She said she was ok, and as she reached out for Jason's hand she finally noticed her ring. Her eyes got big and she asked Jason what it meant. He tearfully asked her to be his wife, she tearfully said yes. And then he kissed her and rubbed her hand. Darryl smiled at him, "I'm gonna tell my dad you were crying!"

"Shut up fool!"

"Women be making men soft!" Darryl said teasing Jason.

Aunt Quilla said she needed to get home and throw out all of Jerry's stuff! Plus Ahjanae really needed to sleep in a bed, she was a trooper though. Kalani and Kaleah went with Aunt Quilla because they were nervous about going home. The nurse said if everything went well with momma today she could go home tomorrow. Jason said he would take me to get what momma needed. Her dress was cut up in the whole process of getting her here. They cut off her bra and everything. Darryl volunteered to take me so that Jason and momma could have some alone time. I told Jason I'd bring him back something to eat. He tried to protest but I wouldn't take no for an answer. As we walked towards the door, "A!" We looked at him, "Darryl that's my daughter. Control yourself!" He said seriously.

Darryl put his hands up and then he followed me out. He was driving a different car. I asked who's car it was and he said it was his cousin JoJo's car. He said JoJo lives in Southern California, but he left his car out here for when he comes home. He said JoJo has another car for out there. I asked Darryl how he knew we were at the hospital, and he said it was on the news. I gasped because that meant everyone was going to know my business and that irritated me. When we walked in the door, all of the living room furniture was gone. I was stuck for a minute thinking on top of everything else, somebody robbed us too. Darryl said Jason had a cleaning service come and clean the room and remove the furniture, and now we get to go shopping. I tried to smile but my heart was still heavy, I couldn't hold back my tears any longer. I started crying and Darryl put his arms around me and he rubbed my back. I buried my head in his chest as I cried my eyes out. He kept rubbing my back telling me it was ok. I had been up for twenty-four hours straight. I was delirious. I called the hospital and I asked my momma if it was ok with her if I took a nap before I came back to the hospital. She said it was ok, and then Jason told me to put Darryl on the phone. "Hello?.... Whoa! Jayman! Whoa!....... But I didn't........ I didn't... I ain't even....... Why you gotta... but just let me… AW! Jayman!……. Ok!…. Ok!….. I love you too!….." Then he made kissy noises.

My momma told me to get some rest and to come back when I was rested. I invited Darryl into my room. Our house was three bedrooms, my room was the smallest, but I had my own room so I didn't care. Darryl smiled looking around my room. His smile got bigger when he saw my seashell and our group picture on my nightstand next to my bed. I gave him the remote to my TV, I needed a shower but I wanted to sleep. I couldn't decide which one to do first so I cried. Darryl laughed at me when I told him my dilemma. "KB! You cannot get naked while I'm in this house. I might just have to take that bullet that Jason promised if you do!" "You'll be fine Darryl, but I really think I need to take a shower. I'll sleep better."

"You're right, but lock the door when you go in there. I'm just a man!" He pleaded.

I grabbed my things then I got in the shower. While I was in the shower he knocked on the door and told me he couldn't believe that I locked the door. I laughed and tried to stay awake. I put on my most comfortable and unsexy moo-moo and sweat pants underneath. Darryl was sitting on my bed shirtless when I walked in the room. His mouth fell completely open. "I never thought an outfit could be that hideous! Baby you are not sexy in that get up!" He said putting his shirt back on.

I laughed, "good then it's served its purpose. I'm truly tired." "I know, cause why else would you…." he gasped. "And now you're putting on the ugly scarf!" He shook his head at me. "If you ever want to know how to turn a man off, remember this get up. I can't believe you KB!"

I laughed, "please! I'm sexy no matter what I'm wearing. You better recognize!" I said with my hand on my hip.

He smiled while frowning and shaking his head, "nope. I'm not gonna lie to you. No you're not!"

I laughed again, "If you say so. I'm so sleepy!"

Every time I would fall asleep good the sound of the gun going off would slap me from my sleep and I'd wake up crying. I was tired, but I couldn't sleep longer than ten minutes to save my life. Darryl rubbed my back and I kissed him. I was kissing him and then I woke up cause the gun woke me up. Darryl cut his eyes at me when I came in for another kiss. "No!" He said shaking his head.

"What's wrong?" I said confused.

"Do you have any idea what it's like to kiss someone and then realize their sleep. I'm all into the kiss, laying down some serious tongue action and YOU FELL ASLEEP! NO!" He folded his arms.

"Aw! D! I'm sorry!" I said

He looked at me, "don't call me D. That's what people who don't know me call me." He said tensing.

"Sorrrrry! Darryl! I didn't mean to fall asleep. I didn't even know I was sleep." I said rubbing his arm.

"You know what?"

"What?"

He smiled, "this moo-moo is kind of sexy! It's like the big fake out! It's like the pretend like you don't have a body outfit and then BAM! You're naked and I'm drooling." He laughed, "This could make a great stripper costume! You'd freak all the men out and then BAM! You drop that KB on them! Wait! No on me! You only strip for me, ok! You'll be my private dancer."

"Whatever you say." I said laying down again.

"I know why you can't sleep." I looked at him. He laid down and put his arms out. "Come on, you need to feel safe." I put my head on his chest and he rubbed my back with his arms securely around me. What do you know, that worked.

Chapter 9

Nellie

I exhaled looking at my class schedule, everything was advanced. BORING! I knew I was going to be in class with a bunch of nerds and geeks. I wondered if Albany high even had one suitable "in the meantime to take the edge off" kind of guy. Everybody here seemed so happy to be back at school. I was surrounded by nice kids, UGH! In a nice school, UGH! With nice teachers, UGH! Bonnie on the other hand was making a list of all the guys she wanted to give it to. Some of them were ok, for her, but small fish if you ask me. Ahjani was the big man on campus at his school. When I went to his game everyone knew who I was and they saved a front spot on the bleachers for me to watch his games. I couldn't go from that to a nobody here. He at least needed to be on the football, basketball, or baseball team. Heck he could play soccer, but he had to be somebody. And so yea I know I wasn't that picky before, but like I said after D, things changed.

****

First Attempt

My leg started shaking as the bus approached the school. I hadn't even seen him yet and my insides were going crazy. Bonnie and I blended in with the other students and we strolled around the campus making eye contact with a few people but really trying our best to lay low. We went all over that school and nothing.

Second Attempt

This time we got there just as the bell rang for lunch. Kids spilled out of everywhere, I knew this was a long shot. But I was hoping it would pan out any ways. I wasn't as disappointed, cause I didn't think it would actually work.

Third Attempt

I am so disgusted, he's nowhere to be found. This time we came to the school right before it let out. When the school was cleared out, I hung my head in defeat. Maybe I misunderstood what school he was actually going to. As Bonnie and I waited at the crosswalk for the light to change, Bonnie turned around to look at the school. "Oh Mylanta! I think I'm in love!" She exclaimed.

When I turned around it was D! He was standing on the steps in front of the school looking at me. He didn't look happy to see me, but he knew why I was here. "That's him!" I said walking towards him.

"What do you want Noel?" He sounded irritated.

Bonnie looked at me to ask who Noel was. "You know what I want!"

"Why can't you just let a nigga be? You keep coming up here messing with my head."

"D! I need you! I need you real bad!" I said shaking my leg as I pleaded.

"It's that serious? You're really that strung out?"

"I wasn't exaggerating!" I said rolling my eyes at the memory.

He smiled, "who are you?" He asked Bonnie.

"She's nobody! Can I talk to you for a minute?" I said wanting this dialog to be over.

"Nobody, you come stand watch." He told us to come. We walked through the school to the huge library. We went to the far corner. "Nobody, if somebody comes knock them over. Got it?"

"Got it!" Bonnie said turning her back to us and pretending like she was looking at books.

I felt like the explosion was waiting just because it was him. As soon as he made contact I covered my own mouth. I was in heaven! I saw Bonnie looking and I couldn't blame her, I would've been looking if the shoe was on the other foot. But it made me angry when she started looking at him with stars in her eyes. I grabbed his shirt as he pulled his pants up. "Stop making me look for you, call me!"

"Noël, I'm not gonna call you. This is bad enough."

"Can I call you then?" He hesitated, "I'm not friends with Kendra any more if that's what you're worried about."

He thought about it for a minute, and then he shrugged and said he was hardly home anyways, he gave me his number and I felt like he gave me the key to his heart. "Good looking out Nobody, I hope you learned something along the way."

He was gone and I was still trying to calm myself down. My mind kept replaying his touch over and over and my body was going crazy. Bonnie stood there watching me with the biggest smile on her face. Then she asked me why he called me Noel? I told her that was just the nickname he gave me. She asked me if it was as good as it looked and I told her it was better.

****

"Got it?" I asked him. He was too busy staring at me to listen to what I was saying. I smiled through my frustration. "How are you in this class if you need this much help?"

"Do you like Asian guys?" He said staring at me.

"I've never thought about it outside of Russell Wong, but who are we kidding he's that gorgeous!"

"So you've never thought of me?" He said with his eyes locked on me.

"I never thought you'd look at me. Besides I know you've heard about me. You don't have to do all of this just to hook up." I said

"All of what?"

"The long stares, pretending like you need tutoring, all of this."

"I like you!" He said directly.

"Whoa!" No one has told me they liked me since Ahjani. "Are you serious?"

"Very! I don't care about what other people say. I like you."

Saved by the bell, I picked up my things and hurried out. All these guys only come for one thing, and I don't even care. If I'm in the mood ok, but if I don't feel like being bothered then I turn them down. He sounds like he was rallying for more than I understood.

Bonnie and I have added a few more girls to our clique. Sheila has been showing me how to dance. She said it's like sex with your clothes on. Once she said that everything made more sense. I still haven't mastered the fancy footwork, but at least now I'm not embarrassed to go on the dance floor. Sheila is the oldest in our clique and she's a junior. She said she remembers my brother and he was always preying on the innocent girls who didn't know no better. Even though they hooked up a few times she didn't really like him.

I shared with them what Marquez said to me. Sheila warned us to be careful. She said some of these boys were only looking to have us sprung off of them so they could brag about it to their friends. Then she asked me what was I supposed to do with a Filipino guy anyways. I shrugged and said the same thing I would do with any other guy. Everyone else was quiet while Sheila stood there thinking. She told me to give her one-week, she bet me ten dollars that he would be telling her he loved her and not paying me any attention.

She was beyond irritated when he firmly turned her down in front of everybody.

107

****

"Hello?"

"D?"

"Yea, who dis?"

"Nellie," I said.

"Who?"

I blew air, "Noel." I said sadly.

"Oh! What?" He said not changing his tone.

"You know what, let's get to it." I said asserting myself.

"Naw! I'll pass, next time though." Then he hung up.

"Hello? Hello?" I growled in frustration.

I waited ten minutes, and then I dialed his number again. "Mushi! Mushi!" He said. I laughed hard, he laughed a little as well. "Who dis?"

"Noël!"

"Oh, what's up?" As if he didn't just hang up in my face.

I was confused, didn't I just talk to him. "I wanna see you. Please!" I could hear the smile in his voice, "why?"

"Because my body craves you! I need you!"

"Like that? Hhhhmmmm. What time is it? I'm going out tonight, I could use a little jump start to my night."

"Does that mean yes?" I asked trying to contain myself.

"I'm feeling generous, why not. Where are you?"

"I'm at home, but I can catch the bus to meet you wherever." I said completely excited.

"The bus will take too long. I'll pick you up. Where am I going?" He couldn't come to my house. "El Cerrito Plaza Bart station."

"What are you wearing so I'll know which one is you?"

"Grey skirt, black jacket, red scarf." I said

"Ok see you in thirty."

I told my parents I was going over Bonnie's as I ran out the door. That thirty minutes was more like an hour. I was starting to think he blew me off, but I heard him call me. He was driving and I started bubbling over. Is there anything he couldn't do? When I got in the car he looked at me and said oh yeah, right! Noel. I remember now. He took us up the hill to this dark street right next to Tilden Park. It was even better as if that was possible and we did it three times! "I love you!" I said feeling like I should say it even though I know how he's going to respond.

"You've said that before." He said reaching for his pants.

"Because I mean it."

"What does that mean? You don't care about what we're doing to Kendra."

"I don't talk to Kendra anymore. I mean I felt bad at first. But I can't fight what I feel. Besides she seemed to think it was ok to date my brother behind my back."

He stopped moving, "who's your brother?"

"Nathan," I said

"Oh, right. Why do you care if she dated your brother?"

"Because she hid it from me!"

"So what is this? Pay back?"

"No! I love you, I'll be your mistress when you guys get married."

"Married? I'm not getting married!"

That made me smile, "so how is she your future?"

"She'll be my woman, we'll be together. But no marriage."

"Kendra wants to get married."

"She'll be fine." He said not giving it a thought. Then he smiled at me, "Noel... This was fun! Now I don't have to hook up tonight."

"Tonight?"

"Yep, I'm hitting the club."

"You're not even eighteen."

"Doesn't matter, those rules don't apply to me."

"I've never been to a club."

"I'm sure you will go to one once you're old enough." He said ignoring my fishing for an invitation. "Where am I dropping you off?" I directed him to the corner by my house. "Later," he said waiting for me to get out.

"I really can't kiss you?"

He looked at me with no emotion for what we just shared. "Is your name Kendra?" Then he unlocked the doors again.

****

I don't understand Marquez, he watches me all the time. He gave me his jacket one time when I said I was cold. He goes out of his way to be nice to me. One time I left school early cause I was sick, he cut his class to walk me home even though I told him it wasn't necessary. My stepmom pulled up to the house as we were walking down the street. She thanked Marquez for walking me home. When we got inside I was in need of medicine and she wanted to ask me fifty million questions about him. I told her he was just a silly boy from school. She was the one who pointed out that he was cute.

Kendra

"Hello?" I said stirring the pot of chili I was making.

"Ahjanae's in labor can't get in touch with Jabbar. I left a message with his little sister. She's asking for you. Can you come?"

I started jumping up and down! "I'm on my way! I'm coming! Tell her to wait for me! Don't push!"

Jason leaned around the arm of the couch, "what's going on?"

I ran to him too excited! "Ahjanae's in labor! Can you finish my chili? Can you give me a ride to the hospital?"

"Whoa! Sure," he said jumping up to take me. "Ask your mom," he went to the kitchen to turn off the fire under my chili.

My momma and Kaleah were laying down and talking. Kaleah blames herself for the shooting. She said if she never would've said anything her daddy wouldn't have come. Momma tried to explain that it wasn't her fault; Jerry was responsible for Jerry's actions. That doesn't stop her from getting really depressed.

She hasn't been the same since, but then again none of us have. Jason has rearranged his schedule to be around the house more. Momma is so attached to him now. Kalani seems so jumpy about every noise we hear. Jason is the only one who answers the door now. He wanted us to move to his house in Oakland, but we didn't want to switch schools. Darryl was excited about it until I told him we weren't coming. Jason's mom comes by weekly to check on everyone. She's really nice and she refers to us as her grandchildren already.

I apologized for interrupting them, and then I asked my momma if it was ok for me to go to the hospital with Ahjanae. Momma smiled real big and said yes. She said I needed to see the unhappy part of having a baby. Kalani heard me and asked if she could come too. We asked Kaleah if she wanted to come and she said no. She wanted to stay up under momma.

Ahjanae was in pain and she said it hurt so bad she couldn't cry. Kalani and I sat with Audra and Ahjani. Aunt Quilla looked at us and started laughing. "Let this be a lesson to all of you. Sex leads you here." She pointed to Ahjanae who was in undeniable pain all-alone.

This was really happening to Ahjanae and it looked horrible! The pain would calm down and as soon as she caught her breath there it was again. I felt so bad for my cousin, Ahjani kept calling Jabbar. Every time they said he wasn't there Ahjani got madder and madder. It was bad enough that rumors were spreading about Jabbar moving on. Which was shocking cause I thought he and Ahjanae were in love. But I guess when the school year started and she wasn't there he forgot about the love they shared. He told his sister Ahjanae was his wife. She thought he was worthy of this risk. I felt horrible for her, and I wanted nothing to do with this kind of drama.

When it was time to push Ahjani quickly exited the room as Ahjanae got in a position that was most comfortable to push in. I was trying not to squirm as I saw the baby's head painfully crowning. The door opened and I saw Aunrey's hand throw Jabbar in the room. His clothes were all twisted as if he could've tried to fight not to be here. Jabbar looked terrified as he watched Ahjanae squat and push. Ahjanae looked so hurt as she gave one final push and the baby gushed out. They gave her to Ahjanae who was still squatting, then they took her and had Ahjanae lay down then they gave the baby to Jabbar who was speechless. When they gave the baby back to Ahjanae, Aunt Quilla went off on Jabbar who had nothing to say in his defense. Audra and Kalani quietly sat to the side holding each other, no doubt trying to erase the trauma they just witnessed as well. I know the birth of a child is supposed to be this beautiful thing. But I think we all were traumatized by what we just witnessed. Nothing about it was cute or ideal, like some people try to make it seem. Jabbar's mom and little sister came in and his mom cried when she held the baby. Aunrey kept threatening Jabbar when he thought no one was looking. Normally I try to tell Aunrey that violence isn't necessary. However, today Jabbar needed to be reminded of what laid waiting for him on the other side if he left Ahjanae hanging like he was trying to do.

****

"Kendra I really like you, and I think we're good together. I can see us married with a couple of kids." Omar said with his arms around me.

"After college right?"

"We could be married in school. I'll wait for you for as long as you need me to. But I want to give you something." Then he reached in

111

his pocket. He pulled out a little ring with a little heart in it. Last weekend when we went to Berkeley I tried on this ring. But I put it back and kept moving. I couldn't believe he went back and got it. He put it on my right hand. "I'm not kidding when I tell you how much I care." I hugged him.

"Wait a minute!" Tanaka said out loud. "What is that?"

"A promise ring." He said blushing.

"A promise to what?" She asked

He sucked his teeth, "a promise to upgrade it to an engagement ring when the time is right."

Now that the summer is over I don't see Darryl all that much. He calls when he can, but with school, my business, helping my momma and Jason plan their wedding. I barely have time for Omar, and Darryl and I barely catch each other home. If it wasn't for Darryl, I know I would be head over hills for Omar. Omar plays basketball with Ahjani and he's good too. Omar says that basketball is his ticket to college. He gets good grades, and he works after school too. He's a good egg, however I'm not stupid. I know all these little girls like him too. I wasn't going to take him seriously because of them. But he kept pushing the issue. He doesn't exactly pressure me about sex either, but he's probably messing with someone on the side. I'm not stupid enough to believe he's given up sex cold turkey just to be with me. And so I don't feel bad about kissing Darryl on the side. "I love it Omar, thank you." I said kissing him.

Tanaka made such a big deal about my ring that I'm sure all if Kennedy heard about it. There were quite a few girls looking at me crazy, no doubt because of my ring, but then Aunrey's Baker cousins would tell them to keep on walking and so no one was crazy enough to step to me.

****

"May I sample your vanilla?" A familiar little voice said.

I turned around to see Nellie walking into the frozen yogurt shop behind her little sister. Nellie's face flushed while her little sister's face lit up when she saw me. Nassya and I gave each other excited hugs. "How are you?"

"I'm good! Princess look who it is!"

"Hi," she said dryly putting her hands in her pockets. "Are you really going to get vanilla?"

"Nellie?" I said feeling my good mood leave me.

"Kendra," she said dryly. Her friend's face lit up when she heard my name. Have they been talking about me? She looked at Omar, "who's this?"

"This is my boyfriend Omar, Omar this is Nellie."

She looked him up and down. "He's cute, he break you in yet?"

I frowned, "what? Why would you ask me that?"

"Still a goodie goodie! I see!" She was not happy to see me at all.

"What's happened to you? What happened to my friend?"

Nellie looked at me with no emotion in her face. She shrugged, "fine. I guess I've changed. But we aren't friends anymore, I guess I figured you'd understand that by now." Her friend started laughing, and telling her that she was cold. She stood there looking at me with no expression. Nassya looked like she wanted to cry.

"Why?" I had to ask.

"Even she asked me for permission before she went after my brother." She pointed at her friend. "You snuck behind my back. If you were my friend you would've told me about it, no matter what he said to you. We were friends first!"

"I don't know why he told you but we weren't serious. He...."

"You should've come to me!" She said with hatred in her eyes.

"Kendra, let's go." Omar said taking my hand.

When I got home I told my sisters and my momma about Nellie. Momma was not happy to hear that I was sneaking around with a boy that much older than me, but she was relieved that nothing happened. She said sometimes friends grow apart and I needed to let Nellie go. If she was ever my friend she'd come back to me, either way I needed to move on for the better.

That night my momma came in my room and shut the door. She sat on my bed. She looked me in my eyes with sad eyes. "Kendra you know there's nothing you couldn't talk to me about?"

"Yes..." I said wondering where she was going with this.

"I've been postponing this conversation out of fear on my end. I really appreciate that you came to me and you told me about Nellie's brother, but I'm disappointed that you came to me after the fact." She said gently.

"I'm sorry momma. I thought you'd be mad at me."

"How are things going with you and Omar?"

"Fine." I said not knowing what she was getting at.

"Do you think you'll be having sex soon?"

I gagged, "seriously momma? After everything Ahjanae is going through?"

My momma laughed, "that was kind of the point of letting you go. Everything doesn't end up like a fairy tale. But it would be unrealistic and really unfair to think that you're always going to be this responsible young lady. One day Omar might get your engine going and the next thing you know, you've forgotten yourself. I don't want any of my girls having babies until they're ready for them. And you have plans for your future that a baby won't allow you to execute."

"Momma I have no desire to…."

Momma put her finger up to my mouth, "hush child. When the desire hits you it's too late. I want to put you on birth control."

"What?" I looked at her in disbelief.

"Consider it a protection for your future. This does not mean that I'm giving you permission to go out and be a hoe. You are always a lady first! Remember that! It's an honor and a privilege for any man to hold your hand, and anything further than that you guard that as sacred. But I have a confession." She swallowed. "Jerry and I got married so young because we were pregnant. I lost the baby though. But I don't want any of my girls marrying someone because they feel like they have to. You marry who you love."

"How did you lose the baby?" I asked with wide eyes.

"Wasn't the right time I guess. But that's why we waited to have you. There were so many times I didn't want to be married to Jerry. I kept saying it's easier to walk away if I don't have any babies. He found a way to make me love him and love him enough to have three of the most gorgeous and wonderful babies! I can't imagine my life without any of you. But I want you in a place where you can't imagine life without your kids and not in a place where you wish you had anything but your child. You choose when you're going to be a mother. Don't let your body choose for you. Make sure Omar protects himself and you by always wearing a condom. Don't tell him you're on the pill. You tell men you're on the pill and even when they love you they get lazy. Protect yourself. You hear me?"

"Yes momma."

Then she kissed my forehead. "I love you baby. Good night."

Chapter 10

Nellie

I am so happy! I see D regularly now! I call him, he picks me up, and we park. I'm happy he's happy. He's even starting to recognize my voice when I call.

So this also means that I don't mess round with these losers at my school anymore. Why mess with these little boys when D is a man! To maintain my cover I've had to bring Bonnie with me a couple times. She said she's tired of watching and she wants to get some as well.

"D, you got somebody for Bonnie?"

"Who is that?" He said

"My friend, you remember I called her nobody."

"Oh yeah, hold on." I could hear him talking to somebody in the background talking about chicken. "I'm with my cousin. He's down to roll. You guys wanna go to the drive-in?"

I said yes before I checked with her. I told him I'd call him back with instructions on where to pick us up. I told Bonnie I was spending the night at her house. Her momma was gone for the night before we got to her house. Her sister was expecting company so we had the night. I was too excited, D and I hadn't gone anywhere together before. I felt like he was coming around. At first I thought we had the wrong car, cause there was a white guy in the driver's seat. He started laughing hard at my reaction when I saw him. Then I heard D's voice tell me to come on. "Do you own any pants? Every time I see you, you've got a skirt on." D said.

"I wear skirts and dresses for you." I smiled as I got in the back.

"Oh, makes sense. Carry on." He said, "This is my cousin Ryder."

"But he's white?" Bonnie said.

Ryder stood on the breaks. I AM? D? SAY IT AIN'T SO! YOU SAID YOU'D PROTECT ME SO THIS WOULDN'T HAPPEN! YOU LIED!" He faked paranoia.

"Calm down, you're not white. I told you. Anyone who says that needs their eyes checked." He cut his eyes at Bonnie.

"But she's not the first one to say it, and you know what? I think my momma is white too!"

D gasped! "No! Don't say that about your momma. That's my cousin, let's just say she's American."

"Ok! Ok! I think I can handle that. We're an American family right?"

"Right! Ignore ignorant comments from people like nobody back there." D said.

"Nobody?" Ryder said looking at Bonnie through his rear view mirror. "Do I really look white?" Bonnie had her mouth open like she didn't know how to respond. He started laughing. "D! She look scared."

D took his seatbelt off and turned to face Bonnie. "You scared?" He asked with a smile.

Her eyes bounced between them. "You guys are crazy!"

They started laughing and D turned around. "That's so sweet! She noticed!"

"I know, I think I like her." Ryder said.

"Serious? Don't play with me! You like her man?"

"Well you know.... For tonight!" They laughed again. "Tomorrow is another story!"

"I'm already working on that line up. Don't even trip." When we got to the concord drive-in Ryder asked if we wanted anything from the snack-bar. "Noel wants chocolate covered nuts, don't you?"

"Be nice!" Ryder said, "other girl what's your name again?"

"Bonnie."

"Bonnie why don't you come with me so you can pick something out. The least I could do is feed you."

"Yeah, yeah you just trying to make me look bad. Come on Noel."

I got a soda, I hadn't eaten dinner but I was too excited about seeing D to remember to eat. Ryder got a big tub of popcorn. I guess this is why D got mad at me all those years ago. How was I supposed to know he had white people in his immediate family? Ryder was checking Bonnie out in the snack bar, I heard him tell D she was cute.

"D?" I heard a female voice say.

He smiled, "oh hey girl, how you doing?" He gave her a hug.

"Who's this?" She asked nodding at me.

"Noel," he said matter of factly.

"Where's your brother been? He hasn't called me in a minute."

"He's living that college life. But call Pearla cause we 'bout to take a trip out East on Winter break. See if you can go."

"Ryder you going?" She asked him.

"Of course!"

She gave him an evil smile, "ok then I'll call Pearla." Then she hugged both of them and walked away.

They excitedly talked amongst their selves for a minute then they remembered us.

As D paid for my soda someone called his name again. "Darryl?" It was another girl. "Who's this?" She said looking me up and down like she hated me.

"Uh!" He said smiling.

"Uh? You mean she's just a hoe! What happened to the girl from the park? The one we twisted those girls up in the bathroom for."

"She's at home being a good girl, this is Noel."

"Whatever! You got so many what's the point of learning the name of a irrelevant female?" She said like she was daring me to respond.

"Who are you here with?" He asked firmly.

She smiled, "Dorian and his parents."

D cracked up, "ha! Ha! That's what you get!" He slapped the counter, "you've gotta be on best behavior."

She didn't laugh, she just stared at him. "Your point?"

D stood up straight, "nothing. Cause you wasn't doing nothing anyways."

"What's up Darryl?" A very CUTE guy said to D.

"Dorian, my man! So you guys are here with your parents?"

Dorian looked embarrassed, "it makes the parents feel good when we interact with them." He looked at me, "who's this?"

"She's nobody just one of Darryl's hoes." The girl said.

Dorian's mouth fell open as he looked at the girl, "Lanie. I swear sometimes you have no manners."

"I call them like I see them." She said looking me in my eyes.

"Be nice cousin." D smiled, "Ryder's over there."

"Ok, see you later." She hugged D, "come on Dorian." She went over to Ryder and gave Bonnie the same attitude she gave me. I wished D would've said something to defend me, but I let it go cause I didn't want it to ruin the night.

Bonnie and I excused ourselves to the bathroom. I asked her if she liked Ryder, and she said he was cute. That was all she needed was cute, and he bought her a soda. She was good. Bonnie and Ryder got in the back. I sat on D's lap in the front. I saw the opening credits of the movie and then it was on. I got a little jealous when I saw Bonnie kissing Ryder and he was ok with it. But I closed my eyes. After the movie Ryder said he was hungry and so they took us out to National Burgers in San Pablo since they're open twenty-four hours. I couldn't pretend I wasn't hungry. We were sitting by the window laughing and talking when they walked in. It was my momma and Bobby. They looked like they had been out at a club. I sunk in my seat and did my best to go unnoticed. D looked at me then he looked around the room. His eyes landed on them and he watched the scene, and I was thankful that he didn't say anything until they left. Bobby looked in our direction, but he didn't see me. D asked who they were and my hands wouldn't stop shaking. I was screaming at myself to get it together. I didn't want to lose D behind them, but it was hitting me fast and hard. My momma knew, she just didn't care!

Kendra

"Kendra you can't keep spending your money on my baby like this." Ahjanae said overwhelmed by everything I brought over. "Nonsense! What is the sixty dollars Jabbar gives you every two weeks supposed to do?"
"Buy diapers," she said sadly.
"And that's about it. I got all this stuff on clearance. Besides she has to look fantastic for the wedding." I smiled.
Ahjanae tearfully thanked me. Jabbar got a job after school at the burger joint up the street from his house. His momma makes him give Ahjanae most of his money. She keeps him so busy; he doesn't have time for a girlfriend. And she tells him his grades better not drop either. So I buy the fun stuff. The pretty dresses and outfits that I piece together off of the clearance racks. Jason bought the crib and changing table when Ahjanae's dad acted like it was Aunt Quilla's fault that Ahjanae got pregnant. And instead of stepping up as a father, he sat back and pointed his finger at my Aunt like she set the wrong example. Jason was the only one who could calm Aunrey down. Aunrey was upset because he felt Ahjanae's dad was talking about him. And we all knew he was, but

Aunrey isn't wrapped too tight we didn't know what he'd do if he got a hold of him. I wonder what that says about Jason that he could talk him down. Meanwhile, I'm trying to convince Ahjanae that she can go to continuation school and get her diploma at least. I know she feels bad because she thought she and Jabbar would be together forever, but it just isn't the case. Ahjanae is so depressed. Kaleah is depressed about her dad. Everybody is depressed. Kaleah's dad is trying to say that all of our statements are bogus because Jason threatened our lives. He said he was acting in self-defense and my momma getting shot was an accident. He's trying to use Jason's past against him. That mean looking man of little words has come to talk to Jason a few times. The last time the guy came Jason told momma it was ok to respond to Jerry's letters. He told her to go ahead and purge everything. Kaleah asked if she could write him a letter too. Jason said he thought it was a good idea. He asked Kalani and I if we wanted to write one. Kalani did, but I declined. Everything I had to say to him I already said to his face.

Jason collected the letters in their individual envelopes and he told us he'd mail them for us.

Meanwhile the wedding day gets closer and closer.

Nellie

It's been months and D hasn't called, or been home when I call. I'm hurting and nothing seems to dull the pain. I'm tired of hurting! I took my pills with some Kool-aide, and then I waited.

"What's wrong with you? And don't fix your lips to tell me nothing! You've been sulking and completely unlike yourself. Are you pregnant?" Junior asked me.

"No," I said dryly as I laid on the couch staring at the TV even though Junior turned it off.

"Then what?" He said shaking my foot.

"Nothing," I said as a unruly tear fell.

Junior huffed then he snatched my blanket off of me. He threw me over his shoulder, and walked out the door into the backyard. He laid me on the hammock then he started shaking me by my shoulders. His eyes turned red. "This is the way you were when I found you in the mall that day. What's happened to you?"

"I saw them!" I said just above a whimper.

"Them?"

"My momma and him. They looked like they were coming from a club." I looked at Junior, "she knew! She didn't care! Why would she knowingly let that happen to me? She must have never loved me. Maybe she loved me and then I did something to make her not love me? If your own momma doesn't love you, how will anyone else? Daddy didn't love me, he knew we were dependent on him for everything and by cutting her off he cut me off! He didn't care if I had food to eat, a place to lay my head. Of course we'd end up victim to someone like the Monster! Once he has confirmation that I'm hurt then he steps up. It makes all of this seem like a joke. Then to mess with my head more the only other person who could probably feel my pain in all of this hates me more because he knows we shared the same womb. Why is that my fault? It makes sense though, you and Nassya have big beautiful hearts! You guys don't look at people the same way that Nathan and I do." I sighed, "I don't want to live anymore. Life is nothing but pain. I'm over it! Your momma could finally have the life she wanted with me and Nathan gone. Her family with her husband."

Junior shot up and started stomping around and screaming. "YOU BETTER NEVER! DON'T YOU EVER HURT ME LIKE THAT! I CARE! I'VE ALWAYS CARED! YOU ARE MY SISTER AND I LOVE YOU! FORGET HER! FORGET HER! DAD IS WRONG! HE HEARD MY MOUTH ABOUT IT CONSTANTLY WHILE YOU WERE GONE! I DON'T MATTER TO YOU? YOU'RE MY SISTER! I LOVE YOU!" He bent over to grab air. "I CARE NEALESHA! I CARE!"

"Junior? What's wrong?" His mother said snatching the back door open.

"DID YOU DO SOMETHING?" He looked at my face. I shook my head yes as tears poured out of my eyes. "CALL 911!" Junior yelled at his mother. He sat me up, "what did you take?"

"Aspirin, the whole bottle."

"Momma! Tell them she took a bottle of aspirin!"

I started to get sleepy and then I closed my eyes. I could hear Junior screaming at me.

Kendra

My momma looks so pretty! Her dress is knee length cream and taupe. Aunt Quilla's dress was taupe, and our dresses were cream. Jason had the scary guy stand with him, but he said he standing in

for his best friend who died some years ago. I didn't get it, wouldn't that make him the best man? But it made sense to them so that's all that matters. It wasn't a big wedding cause my momma didn't invite a lot of family. Jason's momma and his uncle were there and a few other family members. Most importantly Darryl was there smiling a mile wide when he saw me. I didn't invite Omar because I knew Darryl would be here and well, I didn't want any drama. It's been a long school year and now it's time to start the summer off right with my parent's wedding and then getting some work in. My parents got married in a beautiful rose garden in Oakland, that I never paid attention to before. The ceremony was out in the garden and then the reception was inside. It was less than a hundred people here. I think my momma said it was around seventy people. When I saw Darryl talking to the mean guy I asked him who was that guy. I told him he's come by the house a few times and he came to the hospital that night. Darryl said that was his dad Malcolm. I could understand him being D-Rick's dad. But Darryl didn't act anything like him. He was so serious and about business, whereas Darryl. You know Darryl; if you weren't in stitches you were dead when you were around him. D-Rick stayed for a little while, he danced to a few songs. He danced with Ahjanae and Kalani, and then he said something to Jason. Jason smiled and then D-Rick left. "This is a nice wedding and all, shoot. I gotta head out to another one in a week." Darryl said
"Who's getting married?"
"My Uncle Mali, I guess his girlfriend finally wore him down." Then he got quiet like he was thinking about something.
"You ok?" I asked cause his face showed no happiness.
"Yeah, I guess she finally wore him down. My Uncle Mali is THE MAN! LONG TIME BACHELOR! NO KIDS! WOMEN!" His eyes rolled in his head like he was thinking about it.
"Your such a pig!" I said
"My Uncle has all the women and I'm the pig?" He chuckled while he shook his head.
"Did he just meet his fiancé?"
"Naw! They've been together forever, off and on."
"She must be real patient!" I said rolling my eyes.
"She knows there's nobody better than my Uncle." His voice trailed off, "she waited for him to grow up." He started looking serious again.

"What's up with you?" I asked him

"What do you mean?" He said with his hands around my waist as we danced.

"You're off today. Did this wedding make you sentimental?" I smiled.

"No, but my Uncle Mali's did." Then he let me go. He shook his whole body. "The DJ better pick the beat up, and FAST! I don't know how many more slow songs I can do." He said

We sat with Ahjanae for a bit, then Darryl made her get up and dance with him. I held little Erin then eventually she and I went on the dance floor. Darryl had Ahjanae twisting and turning so much, she was either going to be dizzy or smiling. He had her cracking up and I was glad she was finally smiling; she normally spends most of her time looking sad. Aunt Quilla was having a good time flirting with one of Jason's cousins. When my momma and Jason left in their very fancy chauffeured car, everyone started clearing out. Jason's cousin said he wanted to take Aunt Quilla to get a drink. All of us looked at Darryl to say whether he was cool or not, Darryl smiled and said he was cool, and he knew the spot he was going to take her to. "What are you guys about to do now?"

"I'm going home. My feet hurt and I'm tired. What you about to do?" I asked

There was that serious look again. "Oh I don't know. Maybe I'll go be the third wheel with your Aunt." He said kicking the ground.

"Darryl what's wrong? You're not your normal self."

"Will you take a ride with me?" He asked.

"Remember last time I rode with you, you got mad cause I wouldn't let you feel on my booty."

"I want to show you something."

"Let me take my sister's home, you mind following me?"

Kaleah didn't want to go home without momma there and Kalani didn't want to be there alone. So I took them to Aunt Quilla's house. Then I parked my little car that Jason helped me buy in front of my house. Darryl's car was big and old school. He said when his oldest brother drove it he put Hydraulics in it. And then D-Rick put the amazing sound system in it. He said he inherited this perfect car. The car was really nice and well taken care of. It floated down the highway. We went to the San Leandro Marina and he put his jacket down on the hood, so my cream dress wouldn't get dirty sitting on this sparkling clean car. Planes were landing and ascending from the Oakland airport.

I looked at him and I asked him what was up. Normally he has something hilarious to say or something, but right now his face was really serious. He told me they went out to breakfast, his parents, his brother, and his grandfather. "It was a normal Saturday. My momma was mad about the night before with D-Rick and some chick. My grandfather calmed her down like only he could." Then he looked around, he said before he could understand what was going on his grandfather grabbed his arm and he was having a hard time breathing. I was looking at him with big eyes. He said they got him to the hospital in time for his grandfather to have his last goodbyes with his kids and his dad. Then he had a heart attack early that next morning and died.

I gasped and threw my arms around him, "why didn't you call me? I would've come to the funeral."

"I didn't need you there making me weak!" He tried to smile. "My momma's been on autopilot, Malcolm's hurting and disappearing. My Uncle Mali wants a family. That's what made him change his tune." He swallowed and looked away. "It's hard to understand, you know?" I shook my head yes agreeing with him. Death is hard to understand. All of my grandparents passed away before I was born. I felt kind of robbed never having the grandparent experience. "I mean, I never thought… I can't comprehend…."

Darryl struggled to find the words; I rubbed his back trying to give him some comfort. He took a deep breath, "is the thought of dying alone that scary that my Uncle Mali would give up all those chicken heads?" He chuckled.

I sucked my teeth, "seriously Darryl? It's you and me right now. You don't have to make me laugh. It's ok if something hurts you every once in a while. I won't tell anyone that you bleed."

He stopped laughing, "I wanna call him. I can't! I've picked up the phone so many times out of habit and called him. It's not until someone answers the phone that I realize he's gone. Wallace's don't die, unless we're old like Poppa and Nana, my great grandparents. I can remember them, they were old, and they died. You met my grandfather, he wasn't old."

"He was quite handsome even."

"Yeah that's where I got all my smashing good looks from!"

"I can tell!" I said

"Show you right! The men in my family have to fight the ladies off. Even Malcolm!"

"Your dad's not ugly."

"I know, but he could use a smile lesson. He's always scaring someone with that serious mug."

"He didn't scare your momma away." I smiled

"Because she's crazy! As mean as he looks would you try to go upside his head?" I shook my head no. "Let her get mad at him and she got fist flying. She's crazy!"

"He doesn't hit her back?" I asked with wide eyes.

"Naw! If she goes there he did something to deserve it. I think he likes that she goes there with him. When she doesn't that means something's up."

"Like what?" I asked

"More family skeletons, another night." He exhaled, "well thank you KB! I feel better!" He said throwing on a smile. "Let me take you home."

In the car, he did his best to fake the funk. To act like his mood was lifted, but I wasn't buying it. When we got to my house, I suddenly realized I was at my house alone, and yeah I didn't want to be here alone either. So I invited him inside. He asked when we were moving to Oakland. I told him they'd probably move there after Kalani graduated. I turned on the TV in my room and then I went to the bathroom. I put on my tank top; sweat shirt, and pajama pants. When I walked in the room he stared at me. I asked him what was wrong with him; he said I didn't have a bra on. I giggled and asked him how he could tell. He rolled his eyes, "I know how they sit up just right when you wear bras like you wore today. When they're smoothed out and a little smashed in your sports bras. And those are unleashed perky breast begging for me to sample their nectar." He said licking his lips.

"No, actually I was getting comfortable for bed."

He stood up and tore his clothes off letting them fall wherever as he speed raced himself down to his boxers. "SLEEPOVER!" He announced. "I'll be the new kid and you can be Becky Big Booty!"

"SHUT UP DARRYL! You are too stupid!" I laughed. "You can sleep in my bed as long as you don't do anything to me that I don't want you to."

"DEAL!" He said diving into my bed.

"WAIT!" I said cracking up, "I cannot sleep with this mess surrounding me. I clean houses for a living, you gotta know I need order."

"Oh! My bad! A brotha got a little excited. You can't blame me. You never took your undies off before." He said running around the room grabbing his clothes. I admired his body as he moved quickly. "Please don't tell me you want me to fold and iron them as well." He said putting his things in a pile next to my bed.

"Not this time." I said

He smiled, "there's going to be a next time? I'm excited!" He laughed.

He picked me up with his strong hands and laid me on the bed. Then he gently kissed me. His hands went all over me squeezing me and feeling wonderful. "Wait! Darryl wait!" I said breathlessly. "You know sex can lead to babies."

Darryl shot up and banged his head on my headboard. "OUCH!" I laughed, "Why would you bring up something so horrible at a time like this?"

"I thought about Ahjanae and Erin. I don't want that."

He patted my hand. "All you have to say is condom? To verify whether I got them or you got them. I got condoms, my question is whether or not you really want to do this?"

"You said you were going to be my first, and tonight just seemed like our night."

Darryl opened his eyes wide, "Kendra don't play with me! I'll be perfectly fine rubbing on your booty!"

I laughed, "I guess."

"You guess?" He backed up, "things getting serious with that punk?"

I held up my hand, "he gave me a promise ring." I thought I would die saying this to Darryl, but it felt natural to tell him everything.

"He promises to do what?"

"Give me an engagement ring later. Be a part of my life forever."

"So then why are you here with me?"

"Because I want the memory of you forever."

"You don't want me forever?" He asked sounding jealous.

"You say you aren't ever getting married. My momma says you don't try to change a man's mind. If he says he doesn't want kids you don't give him any."

"Kids are different."

"Why would I want permanent kids but no permanent father? Besides, I know you're always out doing you. The fact that you care at all says a lot to me. I care about you a lot, but looking ahead I see heartache and pain if we ever tried to be anything other than we always have been to each other."

He put his head down, "what's that?"

"You're my heart, and I believe I'm yours. But you're a round peg and my life is a square peg. I'm not going to force you to be anything other than you." I kissed his lips, "let's have tonight." I kissed his lips again. "Ok?" He shook his head ok in defeat, as he let me kiss him. "You better not hurt me!" He tried to smile, but his face remained sad.

In the morning, there was a knock at the door. Darryl said it was a man. He stood close by when I opened it. It was Mr. Parker. "Mr. Parker?" I said opening the door in my robe.

"Kendra are your parents' home?" He looked frazzled.

"No, what's wrong?" Darryl walked into my bedroom.

"Nealesha tried to kill herself yesterday." He said with tears in his eyes.

"WHAT? WHY?"

"They were able to pump her stomach in time, but it was a rough night. I'm not sure, but she's been saying your name in her sleep. Do you know anything?"

"Come in," I said

"No, your parents are not home. You don't invite men into your home without your parents there. No matter how well you think you know them." He scolded me.

"Yes sir," I said putting my head down.

"We're trying to put this all together as well." He said

"Can she have visitors? I'll come to the hospital." I volunteered.

"No not right now, not even my wife and I can go in. When she comes home, I'll have her call you. I just thought you should know, and I was hoping you could shed some light on all of this."

"The only thing I know is that she had a lot of questions about her mother."

Mr. Parker looked like I hit him, he lowered his head. "Of course she does. Thank you Kendra, I'll be in touch." Then he left.

Darryl came out of the room dressed, he asked me what happened. I told him my friend tried to kill herself, he said he was sorry. Then I told him that he's met her before, I reminded him of the girl that couldn't dance. He got quiet and he told me he was sorry. He asked me if I was going to go to the hospital, and I repeated what her father said. Darryl seemed anxious to leave, but he waited for me to get dressed. He walked me out to my car; he picked me up and kissed me so powerfully that my toes curled. "I hope he's worth saying goodbye to me for."

"I wasn't saying goodbye. I was…"

He cut me off, "I won't let you turn yourself into a hoe overnight on my account. Thanks for letting me hit first! Later!" He threw up the peace sign and walked away. But that wasn't what I meant… But it did sound that way. Maybe I didn't know what I meant.

Chapter 11

Nellie

I cried so hard when I woke up. My stomach hurt, my throat hurt, and the taste of that charcoal mess lingered in my mouth. I was so upset they kept giving me stuff to calm me. Whatever they were giving me left me in a state of existing. It's hard to think with this stuff in my system and I'm so sleepy. I open my eyes and it's light in my room. I open them again and it's dark again. Every now and then a doctor comes in my room and tries to talk to me, I answer best I can. A couple nights I dreamed that D was in my room. He was trying to talk to me but I couldn't really understand him.

This morning I woke up feeling sad, so I guess they didn't give me meds like they had been before. I got in the shower and brushed my teeth then I sat on my bed. An orderly brought the breakfast cart in and asked me what I would like. Nothing looked good, so I told him to leave yogurt and a fruit cup. As he was walking out, someone was walking in. I was looking at my fingers for no particular reason. "I would think you'd want some French toast, maybe waffles, or pancakes. I don't care if I was a girl, those yogurt and fruit breakfasts would not satisfy me." D said smiling at me. He had a hospital jacket on and a stethoscope hanging around his neck.

I couldn't believe it! I jumped off my bed and threw my arms around his neck. "Are you really here? Or am I dreaming again?"

"I've been here off and on, but they've had you so doped up I doubt you remember."

"I thought I was dreaming."

"Sit down, sit down." He told me as we moved back to my bed. "Now I'm concerned." He looked me in my eyes. My heart started pounding, I didn't know what he was going to say. "Your charts say Nealesha Parker, but I thought your name was Noel. Why did you lie to me?"

I laughed, "I never told you my name was Noel. I don't know where you got that from. Most people call me Nellie."

He shook his head, "but you're Noel."

"I'll be Noel for you." I smiled.

"Good! Cause you're parents are out of line for giving you that name. What were they thinking?"

"They wanted to give me a unique version of my father's name."

"It's unique alright!" He laughed.

"How did you know I was here?" I asked him.

"Your dad came by Kendra's the morning after you got here. I figured I should come check on you. But you've been so doped up. So I had to read your file, to understand what I was dealing with."

"How did you do that? I thought that information was confidential?"

"Noel, I keep telling you those rules don't apply to me. Your parents can't even come back here, and here I am." He smiled. He rubbed my hand, "it's ok. We're all a little crazy." He stood up. "I even know who triggered your vacation here. I saw them remember?" I nodded, "but what I don't understand is. You've got a stepmom who loves you, a couple of brothers, and a sister. They didn't matter?"

"I thought they'd be better off without me. Even you moved on to hooking up with someone else." I put my head down.

"You're not the only person strung out over D's Deliciously Dynamite D!" He chuckled, "but I've been laying low. My grandfather died and it's been hard to deal with." He got quiet.

"I'm sorry I didn't know."

"How could you? I never share anything other than a good time with you."

"I know but death is hard to deal with."

"Right! Says the person who tried to cause her own." He looked at me.

I hadn't thought about it like that. I took a deep breath. "I didn't think of it like that."

He touched my chin, "I think you're gonna be ok. But don't let them dope you up like that anymore. If you need to cry, cry. Work through the emotions don't postpone it. Hurry up and get out of here so we can hang out."

My heart fluttered, "how do I stop them?"

He showed me how to put the pills in my cheeks so they'll think I took them. He told me to spit them out and hold on to them until I went to the bathroom. Then to wrap them in tissue and flush them. He said the only pill I needed to take was my birth control. He told me it's gonna hurt, but he wanted me to talk to my parents. He said they've been worried sick about me. He said they're at the hospital every day asking when they can see me. When I told him she was my stepmom, he said you wouldn't know it by her level of dedication to being here. He said she hasn't gone home since I got here. He said once they say I can have company he'd come visit me. That made me feel like I could do whatever they asked me. THEN he kissed me! I pinched myself to make sure I was awake. He told me he at least owed me that much. That kiss kept replaying in my mind, giving me calm when I felt like I was going to explode. They had a doctor meet with me and my parents the first few times they were allowed in my room. My stepmom admitted that she was just as much to blame as my daddy was for turning their backs on me. My stepmom was better at taking responsibility for her actions than my daddy. A few times he had to walk out of the room or my stepmom kicked him out because he was bucking at everybody. I never knew she had that much power over him. I knew she would flash him looks from time to time. But I didn't know he did what she told him. My momma didn't have that kind of control over him.

When Nassya cried I felt HORRIBLE! I definitely did not consider how all of this would affect her. For the first summer ever she didn't go away to camp. When I came home she followed me everywhere, even the bathroom. When I took naps she would quietly read books or play her hand held games right next to me. She was my shadow. Junior's girlfriend came over every day and she was a really good cook. She said she used to want to go to culinary school, but now she's in cosmetology school. She put the cutest curls in Nassya's hair. She gave us pedicures and manicures; we helped her convince Junior to let her give him a pedicure and manicure as well. She stayed with Nassya and I while Junior and daddy went to work, and our stepmom took care of her appointments. Nathan didn't come home for the summer, which worked out for the best.

Junior's girlfriend said it was ok for D to come by one morning. We were in stitches when the doorbell rang and Marquez came in with flowers. When Junior came home his eyes bounced back and forth between D and Marquez. Neither Marquez nor D seemed to care that the other was there. My stepmom recognized Marquez but she was trying her best to get a good read on D. My daddy wasn't happy about either one of them, so he gave both of them a hard time. Marquez came by every day after work. He'd sit with my family and eventually he blended in. I asked him how he knew about me, and he said he convinced my little sister to tell him. He told me he loved me and to never be that selfish again.

Because my daddy went over Kendra's, at first she was calling all of the time. I told them I didn't want to see her. So they kept telling her it wasn't a good time until she eventually stopped calling. D didn't say anything he would get quiet. Until the next funny thing popped in his brain.

Nassya had a very confused look on her face one night when she asked me, which one was my boyfriend. I told her they were both my friends. She asked if they were my friends like Bonnie and Sheila? That's when I realized none of my so-called friends called me all summer. They might've thought I was away at camp at first, but the summer is almost over.

Kendra

As soon as I walked in Ahjanae's room she smiled. I shut the door and locked it. I shook my head yes and we squealed. She wanted a play by play of every detail.

So I told her how we kissed and made out for a long time. I told her how amazing his mouth is. She scrunched her nose while she smiled. I watched him put the condom on the whole time wondering how all of that was supposed to go inside of me, and how I was supposed to think that was going to feel good. I froze up from thinking about it. But when he kissed me I melted again. I told her how he kept saying how tight I was. I asked him if that was a good thing. I had fifty million questions and at one point he stopped and asked me if I was studying for an exam or making love to him. The first time I thought he was trying to kill me. By the third time I realized he was being very gentle the first time. She asked me if he was rough, and I said no. But when he was working me from behind he told me to roll my hips like I was dancing. When I did it he said I did it perfectly and I was a fast learner. I rolled my eyes at the memory, I told her it was perfect and it felt great. Ahjanae smiled, then I told her how each time we finished he asked me if I was ok. He kept hugging me and kissing me, then he ask me if I could go again. After the third time I felt like I would regret going again, but I wanted to. It was amazing, I get it! I get it! I told her. I wanted him to stay and spend the day, but he seemed like he was upset. When she asked me how, she said she thought he would've been beyond happy to have finally connected with me. I shifted in my seat. She asked me what did I say. I exhaled and then I told her everything like I told him. Ahjanae was literally sitting there with her mouth open. "So let me get this right. Before you make love to Darryl, who's been waiting on you all this time, you tell him about the ring Omar gave you, and your future plans with another man? How in the WORLD do you think he was supposed to take that?"

I shrugged, "Darryl and I have never officially been together. I thought he would understand."

"Understand what? That you let him break you in for another man. Please don't tell me that you plan on telling Omar about this!" I frowned again. "Oh my God Kendra! To be so smart you can be so dumb! DO NOT TELL OMAR ABOUT THIS!"

"He's gonna know!"

"No! I promise you, he won't."

"How do you know?"

"It took my body a minute to respond like someone who's had sex before. You're not going to run out and sleep with Omar right away. Take lots of HOT, and I mean as HOT as you can stand them baths. Do your kegel exercises, and Omar won't know unless you tell him. Don't shoot yourself in the foot twice."

"Twice?" The thought of losing Darryl didn't cross my mind.

"You messed up big time with Darryl. I'm pretty sure he was thinking you guys would have more when you finally slept together. He was opening up to you and being serious. Come on! Darryl doesn't let people in. I can't even imagine him when the laughter stops. I'm afraid to know what that's even like."

"You think he's mad at me?"

"PISSED off! Heartbroken! You name it right now. He was already going through a lot."

I sat there feeling like I was sinking into nothingness. Then I told her about Mr. Parker popping up, she told me to let her know when everything was in the clear with Nellie before we told Ahjani about it. If we told him at all. Even though Ahjani had moved on you could kind of tell his heart hadn't completely healed from the whole thing.

****

"Leave a message!" Darryl's voice said

"Hi Darryl, it's Kendra. Again! Miss you! Hope you're well! Please call me when you can. I splurged and got my own line, so call me whenever...." I rambled on as I left my number.

Then I sat there staring at the phone trying to force him to call me. I kept telling the phone to ring, begging it to ring. When it finally did ring it was Ahjanae calling to talk. I asked her if she's seen Darryl around his aunt's house. She said no, she sees his brothers from time to time. I felt horrible and the more time that passed without a word from him, the more I realized how hurt he actually was.

When I got off the phone with Ahjanae I called him again. "Darryl! I'm sorry! I didn't mean to hurt you, or make you feel like you were less special to me. All of this has been crazy; PLEASE call me back so we can talk. I miss you terribly, and I want the chance to explain. I don't think I said anything right the last time we spoke." That night I fell asleep with my shell on my ear calming my nerves. When two days passed without a return call, I figured that was my answer. He didn't want to talk to me.

****

"Kendra, I love you so much! Please! Baby please! I've been patient and faithful." Omar said kissing me again.

Taking my cousin's advice I didn't tell Omar about Darryl, although sometimes I wanted to. Meanwhile, I've been waiting for Omar to get me going like Darryl had me that night. His touch isn't the same, nothing is the same. I can tell that Omar is smaller, but I don't know what that means yet. Tonight has been good though, and I guess now is as good as any. "Condom?"

Omar's face lit up, "he very clumsily got up and went to his dresser. He put the condom on and came back to his bed. Ok, this is it! Ugh! I don't have to act, I'm not ready. "Hold on! Hold on!" I said backing up.

"Baby it's going to be a little uncomfortable the first time. But it will get better. Trust me!"

"But you're hurting me!" I said still backing up.

Then he smiled, and disappeared under the covers. This I liked, just as he had me going he came up. I thought to kiss me and slowly work his way in the way Darryl did it. But instead he did one big thrust and sound escaped me! **OUCH!** Tears came to my eyes before I could register how much he hurt me. He was too busy working to notice how stiff and paralyzed I was. He came hard and then he started kissing me. When he realized I was crying he looked like he was about to cry. "I'm sorry!" He said completely heartbroken that he hurt me.

"WE WILL NEVER DO THIS AGAIN!" I said through sobs. "No Kendra! I'm sorry! I went too fast! I'm sorry! I got too eager! I'm sorry! The first time is always the worst. I promise it will get better."

If I didn't know better, I might've believed him. I slowly sat up, put my clothes on and left. When I came home, I got in the shower. Then I got in my bed and cried some more. Jason said Omar was on the phone. I told him to tell Omar I'd call him back later. Jason eyed me then he brought my momma in the room, while he stood in the doorway looking like he was going to break Omar into pieces. Momma asked me if I was ok. I told her I was, I was just really tired. Jason wasn't convinced, but I could hear my momma calming him down outside of my room. I cried some more, because that was awful, my stuff hurt. I calmed down when I listened to the ocean in my shell. Eventually I fell asleep.

In the morning, Kalani and I went over Mrs. Sutherland's house to do our normal cleaning. I was working on autopilot really; I don't know what I was thinking about. When Kalani and I came out to my car Omar was waiting. His eyes were red and puffy; he apologized for twenty minutes straight. I told him I didn't want to do that again. He said he'd wait on me; he'd never been with a virgin. I guess gentle was a new concept for him. When I finally let him in again, he waited for me and went at my pace. It was one hundred percent better, he was still no Darryl, but he was fine.

Nellie

"I need a favor," D looked at me. "Will you go to my junior prom with me?"

"What night is yours? Someone else asked me the same thing the other day." He said putting on his shirt.

"The first weekend in May."

"Fine whatever. Why wouldn't you go with Marquez? He's the one in love with you."

"Because I'm in love with you." It wasn't the first time I've told him this.

"One of these days you'll learn to love the one who loves you back. Marquez may not be me, but he's a good guy. He loves you with all your faults and you still run after me. You're gonna end up in a bad place if you keep this up."

"Just because my name isn't Kendra you can't see a future with me?"

He looked irritated, "of all the names to pull out of the hat you pick that one. Kendra's happy with her basketball star. Obviously you don't talk to her anymore."

"Who? That tall modestly alright looking guy?"

"Omar Gordon, you know him? He's pretty good on the courts."

"He's not better than you." I said firmly.

"You definitely swing hard from my nuts." He chuckled, "I'm good. He's different. Besides he has Kendra so what difference does it make?"

"What made her so special to you? I never understood it. She's not better than me!"

"She's a good girl and she does as she's told." He said smiling at the memory.

"Uh huh! Good, pure, and clean! Virgins know nothing!"

He smiled, "she's not a virgin."

"How would you know? Her boyfriend tell you?"

"Nope," he smiled like he was reminiscing.

My blood boiled! "I'd rather you tell me you slept with Bonnie!"

"Cool! Cause I did." He smiled.

I hit him with the pillow, "please tell me your joking." He started to say something. "NOPE! Never mind! I don't want to know! Guess that's why we aren't really friends any more. You ruin more friendships."

"Or maybe you need to be a better friend and have better friends around you."

"I guess. My dress is going to be Emerald Green, can you get a tux?"

"Go pick everything out, just tell me where to go to pick it up. See if we can have the night."

I got excited, "the whole night?"

He smiled, "the whole night."

Kendra

"How original is it that three different high schools would have their proms in the same area? I bet you they got some kind of discount for having them so close together." Omar complained.

135

"How many times are you going to say that?" I asked looking at him completely irritated.

"I'm sorry, nothing about tonight feels original. Look at all these limos…. they! WHOA! But look at that one!" Omar said drooling over the completely expensive car that drove up to the hotel.

"When I make my millions, we're riding around like that." He said completely admiring the car. "That's a Rolls! It's beautiful!"

I had to nod and watch cause I didn't know cars like he did. Anything expensive and Omar was all over it. The more these scouts come out trying to recruit him, the more his eye turns to expensive things. I like that he says we'll have… we, we, we! Basketball used to be his ticket into College, now it's all about making it into the NBA.

I ask him about a backup, cause a lot of those schools were after Ahjani last year as well, but Ahjani said it would be nice to make it all the way. But the odds are not stacked in his favor. So he's trying to make sure he has his game plan together. Ahjani was not being seduced by the things that Omar is as he tours these campuses.

Omar is feeling himself and honestly believes he's going to make it all the way. He's good enough to make it, but I would feel more comfortable if he had a backup plan just in case. Still I think lusting after a car like that is a complete waste of………. **Darryl**! I tried not to react when I saw him get out of the car. He looked like a million bucks. My mouth dropped open when I saw Nellie get out of the car. They were together, his tux matched her dress. I was so confused! Why was he with her? Omar said, not knowing who he was looking at, that they were a good-looking couple. I about wanted to die! Omar asked me if I was ready and I reluctantly said yes. I kept my eyes on them as they moved through the lobby and onto the elevator. The sign said Albany High on the 20th floor, and Kennedy High on the 22nd floor. I talked myself out of going down there. Obviously Nellie doesn't want to be bothered with me or else she would've come to the phone one of the thousands of times that I called last summer. I sat there unable to understand how I felt. When did they find each other? I guess they've been hanging out and that's why I couldn't catch him at home.

Omar spent a good portion of the night talking about basketball and the school he finally decided to go to. Tanaka was in the lobby by the elevators taking pictures. She convinced me to jump in the mix and pose for a few pictures myself. We were being completely silly and having a good time. I kept looking at the elevator doors hoping Darryl would suddenly appear. When Omar eventually came out looking for me, I sighed cause the scene I imagined in my head did not come true. A few teachers rallied around Omar as we walked in the door. They were so proud that our Kennedy alumni were making it out of here. So they always wanted to talk to him. Tanaka told me to come dance with her while Omar talked. I told him I was going out on the floor. He shook his head as he continued to talk. I was doing the "I'm cute and not about to mess up my hair" dance on the dance floor. Tanaka looked at me funny when someone started dancing up on me. I turned around and started screaming when it was Darryl. "Oh my God! Oh my God!" I hugged him. "What are you doing here?"

"The sign said your school was here so I came up to see if you were here. Who could miss this booty on the dance floor?" He smiled

"You're here with Nellie." I said trying not to convey disappointment in my eyes.

"We hang out." He said watching my eyes.

"I guess so," I said looking at Omar who was completely involved in his conversation.

"I see you're still with the star. So how's this going to work when he's gone next year?"

"I guess we'll be living for the holidays."

He moved his hands around, "this is a dance floor. Why aren't you dancing?"

I was holding back tears, "I miss you! I called you and called you! I'm happy you're here, but...."

He put his hand up! "Oh snap! This is my song! Stop playing girl!" He said moving around the floor. I forgot how good of a dancer he is.

I danced with him by default, but I really wanted to talk to him. He hugged me and told me it was good seeing me, and then he left. I wanted to scream and I would've followed him out if he didn't have to walk by Omar to go.

A group of us went out to eat afterwards. I did my best to seem interested in the night but it was over for me.

Nellie

D looked so good last night! Everyone was breaking their necks
trying to figure out whom I was with. I was there with an unknown
and then he was FINE! You could see people scratching their
heads when he was chatting with Marquez. It was no secret to
anyone that Marquez likes me. It was like people followed us
around all night trying to understand my story. I took pictures with
D! Pictures with Marquez, pictures with Marquez and D! The night
got interesting when Bonnie and I had words when she tried to
dance up on D! I slapped the mess out of her. D was cracking up
which made everyone else laugh. I told her D was off limits and
she didn't listen. I lost a lot of friends that night. Ask me if I cared.
****

"Hi!" Clap! "Leasha!" Clap! "We're so proud!" Clap! Clap! "To
have you back!" Clap! Clap! Clap!
Same old cheerleader routine! It doesn't even seem like I missed a
summer. Nassya's friends complained about the junior counselor
they had last year. They said she was mean. They got sad when I
told them this was my last year as a junior counselor. Next year
would be my last summer before college. Dexter was watching me
again. Yeah, this grown man wants me. There's a Bobby
everywhere! But he's seen my daddy. He knows my daddy is one
of the biggest and well-known Commodities Brokers in Northern
California. I don't even exactly know what it means other than he
makes stuff happen for other people. In turn they make stuff
happen for him. Dexter better watch himself.
****

Aldo said I was different this summer. I guess because I wasn't
spreading them. Now I sit here wondering how I even gave him a
taste, my barometer was very low at this camp.
"I hope you remember the camp after you graduate college. Come
back and say hello to the kids." Dexter said watching my eyes.
"I'll have to think about it. But this camp was always good to me."
"I have to say, this summer went without any entertainment." I
know we put on tons of shows, things like that, so I didn't know
what he was talking about. "I guess you have a boyfriend worth
being faithful to this summer. You and Aldo didn't put on a show
for me like you had in the years past." He gave me a knowing look.
"I guess I'll have to settle for the memories on video." He smiled,
"mental video."

I felt like I was going to be sick. He could've kept that to himself. Is it wrong that part of me wanted to see what I looked like blowing that little boy's mind?

Kendra

My phone was ringing, and the sun was not up. "Hello?" I said barely awake.

"You have to work today?" The voice asked.

"I work every day!" I said trying to wake up.

"We need to talk. Can you ask your sister to cover for you?" Omar pleaded.

"I can't. My clients depend on Kalani and I. I can meet up with you after."

He exhaled, "what time will that be?"

"I can push for noon."

"Fine!" He didn't sound happy. "Call me when you're ready."

I thought I wouldn't be able to fall back asleep, but I did.

I called Omar after my shower and told him I'd be ready in twenty minutes. Kalani and Kaleah left when Audra came to pick them up. Momma and Jason run around like love struck teenagers. She's so happy with Jason and I'm so happy for her. She jumped at the opportunity to quit her job when he asked her if she would consider it. He bought her a new fancy car, and anything she wants. She said she's never been so spoiled before in her life. I got in Omar's car, he was nervous. He drove us to his house. His momma made a big lunch for us and she took out all of her nice things. She kept looking at me and smiling. "As you know, I'm going to ASU next year." I nodded, "the good news is that it's only a car ride away. But I worry about my mom being out here by herself. She'd have you, but you work a lot. We talked it over and she's going to move to Arizona while I'm there."

"But what happens if you change schools?"

"Then she'll move with me. But the deal at ASU is so sweet, I think I'll stay there."

"Ok," I said wondering what this had to do with me.

"When your acceptance letters start coming in I want you to choose ASU too." When I was about to say something, "three years ago I promised to upgrade your promise ring." He opened a ring box. "This will be ready for you as soon as you step foot on campus."

Carey Anderson

It was beautiful! I looked at his momma to ask her if this was for real and she shook her head yes at me. "Wow! I don't know what to say."
"Tell me you love me!"
"I love you!" Then he kissed me.
"When I make it, we'll buy your parents and your sisters houses. You and my momma will never want for anything!"
He went on and on about how his career was going to change our lives. Then the argument started, all I asked was what was his backup plan. They accused me of killing the mood, but I didn't care. I told him he's not invincible and he could get hurt. He needed to be practical and have a backup plan just in case. Then his momma accused me of not supporting his dream. Then he's defending me telling his momma that's not what I meant. Everything turned ugly; his momma was in tears telling him he only needed her love and support. She's the only one who's ever truly been there for him. Since he didn't live far from Ahjanae's house I picked up my purse and walked out the door. I was half way to Ahjanae's when Omar pulled up. He was full of apologies. He said the day was supposed to end with both of us feeling loved and appreciated. I told him that ever since his graduation ceremony his momma has not been feeling us being together. I asked him if we should breakup temporarily while he's in school. He immediately got upset. I told him he's about to meet thousands of Kendra's and I didn't want to interfere. He said that I was the only one who was there from the beginning. He couldn't trust anyone new. I held to my guns, I told him I knew he was about to be tempted beyond belief. Last thing he needed was the guilt of the little girl he's leaving behind. I told him to take that ring back, and not to get another one until it was time to be truly engaged. He didn't want to, but he finally gave in. He told me he loved me, and I told him I loved him. We went back to his place and to his room. His momma left probably upset that he went after me. He told me to call him the moment I got my acceptance letter from ASU. I didn't have the heart to tell him I didn't apply.

Chapter 12

Nellie

Ok so Marquez is a good kisser, which makes me curious. We were in my backyard hanging out like we normally do and he kept watching me like he normally does. So I asked him if he wanted to kiss me. It seemed like he deserved that much from me. He didn't say yes or no, he moved quickly and laid it on me. His kiss was so good I sat there trying to stop spinning. D doesn't kiss me like that and that's only when he feels like kissing me. Marquez seems like he'll do anything for me, and only me. Girls at school will ask him for whatever and he responds quickly and firmly with a No. I don't know why he's chosen me to have a weakness for. I kind of like how he looks after me, and is kind to me. Junior is the only other guy to act like he cares like Marquez acts. I don't know why that makes me want to run from him just like Ahjani but it does. I even tried to have Marquez around D in hopes that he would see how much I love D and stop this foolishness. But in true D plays too much style, he started teasing Marquez about when he and I get married and have babies. Could you imagine me as someone's momma? I was even more surprised when Marquez seemed open to the idea. "Hold on!" I stood up next to our table. "Why would I marry him and not you?"

D exhaled, "I'm not gonna marry you. This fool is in love with you. Matter of fact," he looked at his watch. "I'm hooking up tonight. Marquez? You'll take her home?" He said standing up.

"Of course!" Marquez said

"Alright then! It's been real." D said walking away.

I looked at Marquez then I rolled my eyes, "you know you're excited to be alone with me." Marquez laughed at my surprised expression.

I was irritated; I thought I'd get alone time with D tonight. "Excited remains to be seen!" I said crossing my arms.

"You ready?" He said standing up.

"For?"

"Get up, and you will see!"

I looked at him; I don't know why I liked the sound of him talking to me like this. "No!"

"Suit yourself, I'll carry you. Doesn't matter to me."

"No you won't!" I dared him.

"Grab your purse," then he lifted me off the chair. He threw me over his shoulder, and then he walked out of my pizza spot. I was so surprised I couldn't stop laughing. I laughed harder when he smacked my butt. He put me in the car, and then he turned the music up so I couldn't ask him anything. I folded my arms and smiled out the window. We pulled up to the Allegra ballroom. I looked at him like I didn't understand. He told me he'd carry me inside if he had to. When we walked inside the door a girl checked our coats then I heard him say we were here for dance lessons and the party. I looked at him with pleading eyes but he pulled me inside. The room was full of people ready to learn a few salsa moves. I shook my head at Marquez; this was not going to end well. The instructors stood in front of the room of people standing side by side. They demonstrated the steps and my heart sank. NO! FANCY FOOT WORK! I looked around the room at the rainbow of different people and hoped that I'd blend in and that no one would look at me like I was supposed to automatically have this. Forward one-step, back cha-cha-cha, and back one step. Seemed simple enough right! UGH! The embarrassment! Marquez had it and was grinning at me as he watched me struggle. I wasn't the worse person in this class, but I'm not going to lie and say I was halfway good. Marquez tried to keep a straight face, but at one point he stood there looking at me shaking his head. He told me that I'm so good at everything else he couldn't believe he found my weakness. I frowned at him. When the classes were over, he danced around me and twirled me. And then we stuck with the dances I could do. Once I got over the embarrassment of my technical difficulties on the dance floor. I found myself having a wonderful time with Marquez. When it was close to nine, I showed Marquez my phone. My curfew was ten-thirty. When we stepped outside, the cool night air coming directly off of the Bay felt so good on my skin. I fanned myself as if that would make the breeze hit me faster. I pulled my hair up off of my neck. Marquez stood there smiling at me. It was a full moon and it lit up the sky so beautifully. When I couldn't stop staring at the beauty of the big cookie in the sky, Marquez had an idea. We got in his car and he drove us to the Richmond Marina. He took me to the side before the boat docks and there were a few office buildings over there. He told me to come on and then he took my hand and led me to the railing on the pier directly over the water. It looked like the moon was hovering over the city just across the Bay and its beautiful light entertained us with a dance that I couldn't perform on the bay water. "This is so pretty!" I said

"Yes you are!" Marquez said looking at me. I faked making myself gag as I laughed at him. "You'd accept anyone else telling you anything, but when I say it you always reject me." He said watching my eyes.

"Marquez! Come on, cut it out! We're just friends and you're my first male friend ever. Don't mess it up by being corny."

"That's all I am to you? Corny?"

"You're my friend."

"So what does that make D?" He asked me leaning on the rail.

"You know I love him."

"Does he love you?"

"Doesn't matter." I said looking at the ground.

"You don't love him, you just can't have him like you want him. That's why you put me in the friend's zone. You figure you already got me so there's no challenge."

I took a deep breath, "if you say so." I leaned against the rail and looked out at the water.

"What does it feel like?" He asked matching my lean and looking straight ahead.

"What does what feel like?"

"To know that you're standing next to your future, but you run from it."

"YOU DON'T MAKE ANY SENSE TO ME!" I said as a burst of anger came out of nowhere. "I'M IN LOVE WITH D! I WANT TO BE WITH D! I DON'T KNOW WHY YOU KEEP HANGING ON. LIKE THERE'S SOME CONVERSATION THAT'S GOING TO CHANGE HOW I FEEL!" He stood there looking unfazed by my anger. Like my words and love for D were not even real points. That made me madder! "WHAT WOULD YOU KNOW ABOUT LOVING A BLACK WOMAN ANY WAYS? WHEN A WOMAN TELLS YOU THAT SHE'S IN LOVE WITH SOMEONE ELSE YOU DON'T DO THIS! WHO DOES THIS? YOU HAVE TO BE THE WEAKEST AND MOST PATHETIC FOOL I KNOW! YOU HAVE TO KNOW I WOULD NEVER BE WITH SOMEONE LIKE YOU! YOU TAKE EVERYTHING I DISH AND IT'S LIKE YOU COME BACK

FOR MORE! WHO DOES THAT? YOU WILL NEVER BE MY MAN YOU'RE TOO WEAK!" I stopped to catch my breath, but I planned to say more.

He shook his head, "you're just mad cause you know I'm not weak. I am the smartest person you will ever know. I'm so smart in fact that I see around the little shield of ugliness you put up and around you. Regardless of whether you're black, white, Asian, or Latin you're a woman. I know how to love a woman from my heart, cause I was raised to see with my own eyes. Nobody's ever wanted you before and you don't know how to handle it. I understand that. So I'm waiting, patience does not make me weak. Seeing you does not make me weak. I know who I am, and I'm strong enough to be with you! I'm waiting on you to understand it. When you grow up and stop acting out, you're going to realize that I'm the only one who's ever loved you and wanted you beyond an erection." Then he walked away.

I stood there for a minute trying to replay his little speech in my head. Hearing his words frustrated me more. He was walking back to the car. I walked behind trying to think of how I was going to counter what he said. He was not going to have the upper hand on me. He opened his passenger side door to take me home. I sat there trying to think of what I was going to say to give myself the upper hand! When we were a block away from my house, I said. "I don't want to be your friend anymore!"

He chuckled, "imagine that reaction from all that I said." He shook his head.

"I'm not going to play this game with you."

"Right I know." He said still acting unaffected by me, which only made me madder.

"SHUT UP! JUST SHUT YOUR FACE UP!"

"Oh! Shut my face up? What about my hands? I think you're mad at my heart, why can't I shut that up instead?"

"Whatever it takes!" He parked in front of my house. "I'm not going to play this little game with you. All you want is some booty anyways, so let's just do it and get that out of the way so you can go on your merry little way. Cause I'm never going to be with you, love you, or feel anything more for you than I feel for a friend."

"I don't want to have sex with you." He said looking at me.

"I knew it! You've been castrated haven't you! Why in the world would you think I'd want to be with someone who couldn't even perform?" He didn't say anything he sat there looking at me. "Let me see it! It's small isn't it? What am I asking, of course it is." I said pulling at his pants. When he didn't stop me from unbuckling his belt, curiosity couldn't stop me from now having to see what was waiting on the other side of his draws. I unbuckled his belt and pants. I pulled his shirt out of the way and then I pulled down his boxers. He rose to salute me, OH! There it was! Bonnie and all of them told me that Asian men are small, all these horrible stories. But he was bigger than some black guys I've been with. He was definitely doable, and happily doable. Not small! Not small at all! I licked my lips as my leg started shaking cause now I wanted it inside of me. I gently picked him up and massaged him in my hand.

He put his head back grabbed air, and took my hand off of him. "You've seen what you needed to see." Then he started fixing his clothes.

"What? Why?"

"Get real! You need to go inside before you break curfew, and I don't want to screw you in a car."

"Take me somewhere, I'll take my punishment." I said still shaking my leg.

"No! I only let you see for my own prideful reasons. As you can see I'm not lacking, but if all you're offering me is what's between your legs I'll pass."

"You'll pass? You'll pass? Who does that?"

"Marquez Pelayo. Now go inside before your parents call!"

"What?" I was confused.

He looked me in my eyes, "GO INSIDE!"

I have never been so confused in my life. When I walked in the door, my stepmom was in the kitchen. She called out that I made curfew by the skin of my teeth. "Don't answer the phone if Marquez calls anymore. I don't want to be his friend."

Kendra

"I updated my Will last month, did I tell you?" Mrs. McCall said
"No, but congratulations!" Kalani said as she put the groceries away.

"Thanks baby. How come the other one never started working with you guys?" She asked

"She's taken all this stuff pretty badly with her dad." Kalani said matter of factly.

Mrs. McCall shook her head. "Poor thing! She had so much faith in her father too. Parents, not just fathers, cause I've seen mothers do it too. They take their children's loyalty for granted. They provide their children with their first heartbreak and they set them up for failure. It's a shame!" She said shaking her head. "I'm so happy you two were able to get beyond the pain. Your resilience is a real sign of your strengths. And the fact that you guys continued to work when your momma and that hunk of a man got serious and swept her off her feet impresses all of us. I know I did for sure, and a few others, we thought you'd up and quit on us."

"Why on earth would we do that? We know how much you all rely on us to help you. And you guys were there for us when we needed you the most. Because of you all we weren't homeless on the street." Kalani said getting emotional.

"I don't know how you're going to manage all of us when Kendra leaves for college next year."

Kalani shot me a look, I exhaled. "I'm not leaving Mrs. McCall."

"WHAT? A SMART GIRL LIKE YOU? WHY WOULDN'T YOU GO?" She looked angry.

"I can't see going into debt like that for something that only has a thirty percent chance of working in the direction I acquired the debt for. My plan is to take the necessary classes at Contra Costa Community College to manage my business properly. I don't need a big fancy life, and I don't want to be in debt trying to get there either."

"Oh honey, one day we're all gonna die. What are you going to do then?"

"That's why I'm going to go to Community College. If while I'm there I feel like the debt is worth the risk then I can always apply to a major University from there. But I'm not too keen on leaving right now."

"What do your parents say about all of this?"

"Jason offered to pay for everything since I was so worried about the money. But I feel like it's a waste almost. I'm good at taking care of people. I don't need a degree to know how to mop a floor, or clean a window sill."

"Kendra honey, you gotta think bigger. School will help you with that."

"I am Mrs. McCall."

She sighed, and then she told us about the place she's been going to for lunch with her friends in Piedmont. She said the food was so good there that I had to go check it out as soon as I had a chance.

****

I tickled Erin's hand as she reached for me. She didn't really want me, she wanted my cup. "I wish I knew what was so funny back there?" Ahjanae said looking back at the banquet room that kept spilling out cries of hilarious laughter whenever the door opened. Kalani grabbed my arm and squeezed! "He is SO fine!" She said about a guy who was quite fine as he walked into the room. "Get a grip girl!" I said snatching my arm. I put my hands on my forehead. "Explain this to me cause I don't understand it." Ahjanae shrugged, "I don't understand it either. All I know is somehow he found money for a lawyer, and he's being released." Jerry is being released, I don't know the details. Jason was concerned all of a day and a half. His calmness about it alarms me and I don't know why. Whether Jerry thought Jason would be there or not, he came to our house with a loaded gun. He was not happy when he heard about the wedding last year. I don't understand any of this.

A cute tall white guy came busting out of the room. He was cracking up then he looked at our table. He looked at us with recognition and I had no clue who he was.

He straightened up and approached us. "Ladies," he nodded to us.

"Hello," we said in unison.

"You're all more beautiful in person than your picture."

"Our picture?" Audra asked

"Where are my manners? Hello," he said shaking all of our hands. "I'm Ryder, Darryl's cousin. I was supposed to go to the park with you guys that day, but I got put on punishment at the last minute. Then he looked at me and smiled. "Darryl doesn't know you're here?" I shook my head no. "Oh! Oh! I just found a way to win my money back!" He started jumping around just like Darryl. "Don't move! I'll be right back!" He grabbed his composure, then he glided in the door and it shut behind him.

"What was that?" Kalani asked, I shrugged.

The door flew open and when Darryl saw me surprise was all over his face. He reached in his pocket and handed Ryder money. All the men started cracking up. Darryl and Ryder came to our table. "Woman! What you doing here?" Darryl said tapping his foot. "Eating!" I said with attitude. "Ooh! Did you hear what she said?" Ryder said instigating. "Uh huh! Yea, I heard her. Thank you!" Then he pointed his eyes at me. "This is my..." He cleared his voice cause it cracked. We all started smiling. "Stop acting like you don't miss me! Get up! Give me some love! What a nigga gotta do?" He picked me up by my shoulders and hugged me tightly.

"Huh?" I was laughing but I was honestly confused. He was the one who never returned my calls.

"It's been a, *missing the one who got away, kind of week!* And then you're here! It's like it was planned." Ryder said smiling. "You set me up man?" He asked Ryder who was laughing. "Did he set me up?" He asked Ahjanae.

"No, it's a coincidence." She said

Darryl looked at Erin, "baby, you will tell me the truth won't you?" He said lifting her out of her seat. "Did they set me up?" Erin shook her head yes and her little ponytails moved with her movement. "See! Out of the mouths of babes!"

"She just wants to tell you yes. Watch this, hey little baby. Is he ugly?" Erin shook her head yes. Everyone started laughing except Darryl. He was looking at his cousin like he couldn't stand him. "Baby am I the most handsome man you've ever seen?" Erin said yes, enjoying our reactions to her yes.

Darryl tenderly put his arms around the baby, "stop abusing her. She doesn't know what she's saying."

Ryder reached for Erin and she happily went to him. Then she started messing with his hair as she watched his face to see his reaction. "Who's baby?"

"Guilty." Ahjanae said

"She's such a little cutie. You going to have anymore?"

The whole table replied, "NO!"

He bucked his eyes, "it can't be that bad."

"Obviously you don't have a child." Ahjanae said shaking her head.

Ryder motioned for her to scoot over, and then he sat down next to her looking between Ahjanae and Erin. "Tell me about it." Darryl and I sat down on the opposite side of the booth. Ahjanae explained what her life has been like since she's had her daughter.

She said it took her little brother graduating last summer to give her the gumption to go back to school and get her diploma. She said she can't be carefree like her siblings; she has to consider her daughter in everything she does. She told him about Erin's constant ear infections and all of the late night runs to the emergency room when little Erin's fevers jump off the chart. Ryder and Darryl listened intently. Ryder asked where Erin's father was. Jabbar is around but he's not there in the middle of the night. He's not there in the middle of the day. He has a girlfriend, works, sends the little bit of money he makes, and he comes by when he can. But she has to raise her daughter. Ryder looked at Erin with sad eyes, he said she looks so happy though. Ahjanae said she does her best to keep her baby happy. "But you will have another one. Look at this girl, she's too perfect! You can't deny the world of more perfect people."

"And go through all of this alone again? NEVER!"

Ryder swallowed and looked at Darryl, "I think she's gonna use that word."

Darryl put his hands out, "we don't want no problems. Let's not spoil the vibe here."

"What's wrong with marriage?" Audra blurted.

"AH!" Darryl and Ryder said at the same time.

"Marriage ain't for everybody! And it for sure ain't for me!" Darryl said.

"You don't want a family?" I asked him.

"Um... HELLO? My parents weren't married when I was born! Doesn't make me any less here!"

"And mine were, and they're not anymore." Ryder said.

"So the family you grew up with is what you'd want for your child?"

"What's wrong with the family I grew up with? I've always had two parents who love me and would walk through fire for me." He looked at Ryder, "I'm the favorite!"

Ryder started laughing, "No you're not! D-Rick is!"

"How you figure? I'm the favorite!"

"Drew's the emotional brat! You're the spoiled baby! And D-Rick is the logical and less dramatic of the three."

"Forget you! You don't know! I'm the baby and I'm the favorite!"

"I'm saying that I want to live in the home with the father of my children going through the motions together." I said

"We don't have to be married to do that. AND!!!! Just because you're married doesn't mean that you aren't doing everything by yourself. It just looks good on paper." Darryl said.

"My momma was doing it all, so she said she might as well be free while she's doing it all. Just wish she would've squeezed out a brother for me while she was at it." Ryder said.

"You got me though!" Darryl said

"It should be against the law to have a child this perfect and stop at one! Next time you and your baby daddy fool around you getting pregnant." Ryder laughed

We all gasped, "So I'm really not having another baby. He hasn't touched me since we told our parents I was pregnant." Ahjanae laughed to cover up how much that hurt her.

"He's crazy!" Darryl said.

"Child birth ain't pretty," I said remembering what I saw.

"But he had this beautiful woman going through all that for him and he acts like that with her? Ain't right! I had more faith in Jabbar than that." Darryl said.

"You think you could watch child birth and then still get turned on by that same woman later?" I asked.

Darryl looked at me, "I love this woman! She's carrying my seed! We become one person through the life she's carrying for us. It would hurt me to see her go through it, and I'm sure five minutes later I'm not going to be thinking about it. But by the time six weeks rolls around and we've been appreciating our expression of life together I'm all over her!"

"Why wouldn't you complete that with marriage?"

"Cause one day when she decides to leave me, she's not taking my millions with her."

"Right!"

"She don't believe me! Oh well!" He shrugged me off.

"Ryder, who's baby?" A woman said.

"Hers," he said pointing to Ahjanae. "Sophia isn't she perfect?"

"She is perfect! How old is she?"

"Almost two." Ahjanae said

"Cherish these moments cause they grow up fast."

"Sophia, this is Kendra, her sister Kalani, her cousin Audra, her cousin Ahjanae, and the baby's name is Erin. You guys this is my cousin Sophia."

"Nice to meet you." I said.

"I thought you said it was a guy's hangout in that banquet room?"
"It is, Jeff's holding down the fort. Ryder brought me out here talking about they didn't set me up." Darryl pursed his lips, "right!"
"We didn't. Mrs. McCall told us we had to come check this place out. She came here the other day and she said it was delicious." Kalani said
"And the survey says?" Sophia asked
"EVERYTHING IS DELICIOUS!" Ahjanae said
Sophia smiled, "I'm glad you liked it. I have another spot in Walnut Creek. You guys should come and check that location out as well. It's easier to get to from the freeway than this one is." Then she looked at Ryder, "I'm gonna tell your momma how comfortable you look holding that baby!"
Ryder turned red, "don't be getting me in trouble. You know that woman's temper is outrageous!"
"Wait! First tell her to make me a red velvet cake. I'll eat that while I watch her whoop on you." Darryl smiled.
Audra raised her hand, "I hope I'm not being rude. I'm so sorry if it sounds that way. But how are you guys related? Darryl you don't look mixed."
"What is 'mixed' supposed to look like?" Darryl asked but he didn't look mad.
"Light skinned, curly hair, freckles maybe." She said thinking.
"Curly hair?" Darryl said pointing to his hair.
"Boy please that ain't nothing but a ultra curl!" Sophia laughed and they joined her.
"Nobody is mixed, I hate that term. We're an American Family. My grandfather, her daddy, and his grandfather were all brothers." He gestured towards Sophia, "she grew up out here. It gets no blacker than her!"
Sophia laughed, "boy you are stupid."
"And Ryder.... Well he's in the homeboy reconditioning program."
"Yeah, it's like I grew up in Concord, but Oakland is my home!" Ryder said
"People always stare when we're together, you should've seen the way they stared at me and my granddad. I look a lot like him, but all people ever see is color. It gets old."

151

"I hope I didn't offend you. Kendra said she met your grandfather before. She didn't tell me he was white. I was confused." Audra said.

"Naw girl it's all good. You weren't rude. I gotta go say hey. It was nice meeting all of you." She said, and then she went in the banquet room.

"Kendra you can't be coming up in here with no boyfriend. Only the single ladies are allowed in here." He pointed at Ahjanae and Kalani, "you guys can come back."

"I can't come back?" Audra asked.

"I said only the single ladies. I can tell you got a man, it's all over you."

"Oh," she smiled.

"But I'm single." I said

His eyes went to my promise ring, "not with that thing on your finger."

"Technicality!" I said taking off my ring and putting it in my pocket.

Darryl looked at me but he didn't say anything.

****

"Hello?"

"Come outside!" Darryl commanded.

"Ok," I said grabbing jeans and a shirt to pull on. I had just gotten out of the shower after getting home from work. I didn't know why he didn't come to the door.

I came out to his car as he sat on the hood. "I'm upset with you, and I don't invest emotions in females cause most of them are as goofy as you have proven to be!" He fired at me, no hello, no how are you doing.

"Ok, you're obviously on an agenda. Hi Darryl, how are you? Nice to see you again."

"I'm upset with you!" He said burning a hole in me with his eyes. I smiled at him. "Nothing's funny!"

"I know," I said still smiling.

"You let me walk out the door. You let me drive away. I came back you left! You took a couple of weeks to call me! ME!"

I shook my head while still smiling. "You're right! I'm so wrong. I treated you horribly, can you forgive me?"

He eyed my smile for a minute. "No!" He shook his head. "I'm gonna leave! I'm not the girl in this!"

I grabbed his arm, "no Darryl! Don't leave! If you leave me now I'll go crazy!"

"I can't stand you!" He spit at me. "You think you've got the upper hand don't you? Don't you?"

"Are you saying you want to be my boyfriend?" I teased.

"No! I ain't the settling down type! I've got oats! A fist full of them!"

I kissed his lips, "so why are you here?"

"Cause I'm mad?" He said weakly.

"You missed me, and you wanted to spend time with me. Say that." I kissed his lips again.

"Cause I..." He frowned at me. "You supposed to be a snake charmer? I feel confused!" He said pulling his head back.

"Missing me confuses you?" I licked his lip.

"KB! You've changed!" He said in defeat.

"Only for the better."

"If you say so."

****

We were supposed to be going over Aunt Quilla's after work. But she called and told us to go home. When we walked in the door Kaleah was stretched across my momma's lap with her head buried as she cried. My momma was crying rubbing her head. Kalani asked what happened, and Kaleah slowly lifted her head. Her nose was swollen, lip busted, and her eye was blackened. Kalani and I dropped everything and asked where we were going cause we were fighting somebody! Kaleah started crying harder as she said, "daddy." I knew I heard her wrong, she didn't say that this man put his hands on his little girl like this! Kalani and I asked her what happened but she kept crying in our momma's lap.

Jason walked in the door with a smile on his face until he noticed our faces. "What's wrong?" He said coming in the door. When no one answered his face became serious as he realized that Kaleah was crying. "What happened?" My momma swallowed, then she told Kaleah to look at Jason. The horror that flashed across his face. In a low grumble he asked if it was her boyfriend. My momma shook her head and said Jerry. Jason growled, my momma was trying to calm Jason down. Not to protect Jerry, but to protect her man. There was no calming him down. He wanted to know how this happened, and where. Kaleah said he showed up at Aunt Quilla's but Kaleah was across the street talking to her boyfriend

Milton. She said as soon as her boyfriend left he came charging out the house calling her names and going off. When she didn't take his crap he lost it. Ms. Lorraine came out and started hitting him with a 2x4 that was on her porch. Aunt Quilla heard the commotion and then she called the police and he left. Jason looked at Kalani and I, he told us to sit down. He paced for a minute as he tried to think past his temper. Then he looked at each of us, "are you with me or him?" My momma told him she was with him, and then we each followed suit. Jason took out his phone and growled into it. Before long a guy with long locs was at the door. He had a box and he handed Jason a brown paper bag. Jason gave the bag to my momma; it had stuff for Kaleah's face in it. Witch hazel, alcohol, peroxide, gauze, ibuprofen, and ice packs. Jason told us to stay inside while he went out with the guy with the box. They walked around the house looking at everything. Then the guy took out tools and started putting stuff up. Darryl's dad, the scary guy came over. He saw me looking out the window as he talked to Jason. They went in the back and talked with the guy working. The guy was explaining stuff to Jason, they were all so serious. When he was done, Jason gave them Aunt Quilla's address and then he said he'd call her. Jason came inside and told my momma to come to the room. They were in the room talking for a long time. Then Jason made dinner while my momma kept comforting Kaleah. All I knew is that Kaleah's depression was only going to get worse after this. Even with everything that happened before, Kaleah still loved her daddy. I knew it would be hard to process this. He only slapped me and you'd think he shot me as well.
When we sat down to eat dinner, Kaleah sat at the table staring down. Jason got up, I thought he was angry, he picked Kaleah up and kissed her forehead he told her he was sorry, and he'd never let Jerry hurt her again. Kaleah started crying again as she hugged him back. Jason's fried chicken, French fries, and corn looked and smelled great. None of us could really eat outside of putting a few fork fulls in our mouths. Jason and momma tucked Kaleah in and then she asked Kalani to sleep with her, so she did. Jason secured the window, and then they came to my room. Jason secured my window while my momma gave me a hug and kiss goodnight. I could hear Jason going around the house. Then he went next door to Mrs. McCall's house. He talked with her for a little bit then he came back. That night everything made me nervous, every sound

made me jump. I couldn't understand how Jerry could do this to the only child of his that wanted him in their life. Only the sound of my shell could calm my nerves enough for me to fall asleep. In the morning, Jason explained that there was going to be someone watching over us while we were at work. He told us to come straight home as soon as we were done. Kalani and I did as we were told, we went to work and then we came straight home. When we came home there were police everywhere, and there was an ambulance there but it looked like it had been sitting for a while. My heart dropped immediately I thought of Jerry. He came back to my house! I parked on the side street and then Kalani and I held hands as we held our breath approaching our house. All the neighbors were outside and looking like they were getting all the juicy details. An officer stopped us and asked us who we were. The scary guy told the officer this was our house. Then he told us to go inside. When we walked in the door Jason was holding my momma and she was crying. Kaleah was laying on the love seat staring at the ceiling. We ran to our momma and I cried the hardest cry of relief I've ever cried in my life. I asked my momma what was going on. Then an officer answered for her telling us that Jerry came here again. He shot and killed himself in the backyard. I looked at my momma and asked why he came here. The officer said it looks like he came to confront my momma and sisters about the letters they wrote him while he was in jail. "He probably got tired of waiting for Mr. Palmer to leave, and turned his gun on himself. We're having the scene analyzed." He shot himself in the backyard. My momma was crying and Jason was watching our faces for reactions.

The story didn't sound right, and my momma being upset was upsetting to me. Kaleah looked like she was going to lose it. She was staring up at the ceiling singing a song just above a whisper. There were people all over the house for a long time. I called my clients for tomorrow and I explained that I had a family emergency and I wouldn't be able to come tomorrow, and that I would give them discounts because of the inconvenience.

That night when everyone left, my momma told Kalani and I that Aunrey came over too upset because he heard about what happened with Kaleah and Jerry. When he saw Kaleah's face he went completely ballistic. As Jason was trying to calm Aunrey down to explain the plan Jerry seemed to have a plan of his own.

He was trying to open the back door. Jason told my momma and Kaleah to stay in the front of the house. She said they weren't out there long, she heard the gun shot and Kaleah started screaming. Jason came back inside and told my momma to call the police. When she hung up he told them Aunrey was never here and then he went back out to the backyard. When we asked Jason what happened back there he simply said we didn't need to worry about it, and it was over.

****

Omar was full of nervous energy as I drove him to the airport. He wanted to know when I was coming out to visit him. I told him with everything that has happened lately I honestly couldn't tell him when. I could see him trying not to be selfish and understand that my family was going through a lot right now. Omar kept telling me how much he loved me, and how much he couldn't wait for me to come to ASU with him. So I asked him what happens when I don't get in. He looked me in my eyes and told me I was getting in, he already had it set up. The money that would be provided to me through grants, etc. depended on my final GPA. I guess it pays to be a star athlete. I gripped the steering wheel and told myself I could wait to have the argument about me not applying to ASU. I didn't feel like having it today. I do love Omar; I don't know what it is. But something makes me drag my feet. I think I'm just scared of everything with him. I don't want to end up like my momma. She and Jerry were high school sweethearts and look how that whole thing ended up. I gave Omar the biggest kiss ever and then I drove off. I thought I would be ok to hang out with Darryl today, but I wasn't feeling up to it. When I called him there was a lot of noise in the background. He could tell by my tone that I was trying to back out and he wasn't going for it. He stayed on the phone with me until I got to his cousin's house. He met me at my car. "KB! It's good to see you girl!" He said pulling me out of the car.

"Hi Darryl," I said. I just didn't have the juice today. I told myself this was a mistake.

He eyed me, "so the star left. Did he take the best part of you with him?"

I sighed, "no. But I think it was a mistake to think I would be any fun today."

"KB! As long as you walk in front of me, you're a blast to hang out with on my barometer!" He smiled.

"All you want me to do is walk?"

He smirked, "I'm not touching you while you got the star on your brain. That would be beneath me! So for now…. MUSH!" He said pointing to the house.

"I'm not a dog!" I protested…

"Not like that, but MUSH!" He said again chuckling to himself. I rolled my eyes at him. "See! I told you, you do that just like my momma! Now I miss her. Hold on!" He took out his phone. "MOMMA!" He pretended like he was crying. "I MISS YOU MOMMA… WHEN YOU COMING HOME MOMMA… I NEED YOU MOMMA… CALL ME BACK MOMMA WHEN YOU GET THIS MESSAGE!" Then he hung up and wiped his fake tears. "Stop making me miss my momma!"

I remembered a lot of his cousins from the amusement park, and then there were a lot I didn't know. But everyone was funny and silly just like Darryl. They were a nice distraction. When I got in the car to go home Darryl called me cause he wanted to know that I made it home safely. We ended up talking until two in the morning when I couldn't take it anymore and I got seriously sleepy. Being with Darryl did make me feel a lot better. Better than coming home and being sad.

Nellie

All I can think about is getting out of this school. My senior year starts in a week, and I'm ready for it to be over. I still have no idea of what I want to do with my life. I'm not even really excited about college except for all the new guys. My momma would tell me that college is where I looked for the big fish and find the guy with the most money and make his money work for me. She may have not taught me much, but I do remember those words and I hold on to them. I only need a few credits and then I'll be ready to graduate! So for "FUN" my daddy told me to take all college prep classes. As if that wasn't what I've been doing. Marquez didn't blow up my phone like I thought he would've. He called a couple of times, and then he stopped calling. Shoot! Kendra tried harder than he did. If he loved me like he claimed he did why would he give up so easily? I knew he was all talk and not to be trusted.

Carey Anderson

Sigh! To make my home life even more interesting Nathan finally
came clean, he dropped out of school right after the beginning of
last year. He was living off someone and then he finally came
home when he had to. He's lost a lot of weight and he's always
high. He hangs out all day long and then comes home and eats up
all the food. I don't like Nassya seeing him like that, cause she
remembers him a certain way and it's just not ok for her to see him
like that. Seeing him high would make me think of Bobby. Bobby
would get my momma so high she'd be laughing and completely
wasted. Once she was passed out he'd come for me. Now that
Nathan comes home like that it doesn't sit well with me. I don't
know if my parents know about it or not, he does a good job about
laying low. But Nassya comes everywhere with me. I can't have
him there while I'm gone though. I have to decide how this is
going to play out.
"Look, look here comes the next unsuspecting victim." Nassya
said like we couldn't see them.
We were at the Wharf as a family plus Junior's girlfriend. We were
standing and watching like everyone else as the bushman
frightened the daylights out of unsuspecting tourist. The bushman
sat on a crate behind branches from a bush. People would be
walking and not paying attention to the crowd of people watching
them from across the street. As soon as they were up on him, he'd
yell Boo! Or something like that. One lady took off running
leaving her partner behind. The honest scared reactions were
priceless. After watching for over an hour we decided to finally go
eat. We sat down and ordered, and after Nathan placed his order he
disappeared. When he was gone for a while I asked my daddy
where Nathan went. He started to say the bathroom when he
realized it had been a minute. When another five minutes passed
and no Nathan my daddy excused himself and went to the
bathroom. When he came out the bathroom I saw him walk out of
the restaurant. When my daddy was now missing for a while, I
asked Junior what happened to the men. I told him daddy went
outside. Junior came back inside and asked our waitress to bag up
all of our food as she was laying it out on the table. He told us we
had to go. We packaged everything, my stepmom paid the bill, and
then we followed Junior out. There were four police officers, two
were talking to my daddy and two had Nathan down on the
ground. My daddy looked so embarrassed and Nathan was talking

mess the entire time. Nathan was being arrested for public intoxication, disturbing the peace, and resisting arrest. Daddy had been trying to calm the officers down, but Nathan's mouth kept running. He came out to get ready to eat; an officer smelled his weed before he saw him. Nathan tossed his stuff in the water, but got angry when the officer said he was going to site him for public intoxication. Nathan escalated the situation causing the officer to call for backup and now they were taking him in. Daddy apologized to us, and then he asked Junior's girlfriend to ride with us back to the house, and then daddy and Junior went to the police station to get Nathan. Nassya cried for her big brother, but I told her it was his own fault and to never be that dumb.

Nathan is such an idiot. I didn't have to say or do much. All I had to do is point out when he was missing or something to my parents and then they'd bust him doing something. And just like that, they kicked him out. All I could think was good riddance. All he did while he was here was call me out of my name, and mouth threats of beating me up as soon as he got me alone. He was still mad at me about what happened years ago, but whatever. And that wasn't even my fault.

Kendra

Everybody wants to know how Omar's doing. I can barely walk down the hall without all the questions. He sends me links to newspaper articles about his games all the time. He keeps saying he can't wait for me to come tour the campus with him. I normally don't respond to that or find a way to talk around it. We used to talk all the time when he first got to school. But as the year started to progress our conversations became less and less. As usual I don't tend to talk to Darryl all that much during the school year either.

Kaleah keeps having mental breakdowns and suicidal thoughts. My momma has put her in the hospital because she says Kaleah is a danger to herself. Thankfully Kaleah doesn't reject the help and she's receptive to it. Kalani and I talk about the whole thing with Jerry all of the time. In our extreme sister bonding moments we tell each other how thankful we are to have each other to go through this with.

As a morale booster, one evening Kalani and I decided to prepare dinner for our parents and buy them gifts just because we love them and appreciate everything they've done for us. Our gifts weren't extravagant or anything like that, but it was the thought that counts right. We had dinner and then we sat them on the couch and read our speeches of love and appreciation for them. When Kalani and I practiced our speeches together we did not consider the emotional factor. Kalani went first and when she got choked up during her speech for momma that was a wrap. When she got to Jason his eyes turned red, and he shook his head saying we weren't going to make him cry. He kept blowing air. Then I couldn't help it during my momma's speech I kept stopping on a count I was crying and telling her how much I always appreciated that she had my back and she did her best to protect me from idiots. I thanked her for empowering us to help her and how we all survived as a family. Then I thanked her for finding my real daddy. Jason held his breath. To add some humor I thanked him for being ready to beat up anybody who did anything other than make me smile. I told him that his friend is scary and that still did not stop him from threatening to shoot his son if he did anything to make me unhappy. "Remember when you made my momma come make sure I was ok? I knew you wanted to go beat Omar up and all you knew is that I wasn't happy." He smiled at the memory. I told him every girl needs a daddy who would throw caution to the wind and do damage on her behalf, and I was so thankful that he loved me enough to want to protect me like that. Then we hugged and kissed our parents.

Nellie

Marquez walked up to me yesterday, put me in a bear hug, kissed my neck, put me down and walked away. I stood there for a minute trying to figure out why he keeps doing that? All school year he's been popping up randomly hugging me and kissing on me. He doesn't even try to talk to me anymore. I kind of wish he would try cause he's my oldest friend at this school. I've made a few associates; I wouldn't call them friends per-say. Bonnie and her clique still run around sleeping with everybody. Getting pregnant, having abortions like it's cute, or even worse sometimes having the baby. Since my legs only spread for D these days I don't get to part them not nearly as much as I would like. He's so anti-babies even though he knows I'm on the pill the last thing I have to worry about is coming up knocked up.

Nassya watched with tearful eyes as I went over my acceptance letters. Whenever I said I got in, she asked how far away the school was. If I said anything further than a car ride away she wasn't having it. My parents and Junior sat there beaming with pride as they waited for me to tell them what my final choice was going to be. I didn't have the heart to tell them I didn't care one way or another. In my mind I randomly picked and I landed on ASU. Nassya asked as a confirmation that Arizona was only a car ride away if she needed to drive there. My daddy took me in his arms and he told me he was so proud of me. I sighed with happiness; I lived for moments when he would hold me like I was still his little Princess. My stepmom said I could come home as often as I needed, she said even if I only flew home for the day it was perfectly ok.

I told D I was going to ASU and he said he was proud of me for making a choice. When I asked him where he was going, he would change the subject or say it didn't matter. Then he'd say Marquez got into the University of Santa Barbara and ask how were we going to make it work. I'd cut my eyes at him, I hated when he did that. I asked D to go with me to my senior prom just like my junior and he told me no. He told me to ask Marquez. I got angry and started going off. D hung up in my face, when I called him back he told me he wouldn't see me again until I asked Marquez. I literally threw a fit and drug my feet about it at first. For all I knew Marquez could've asked that girl who appears to be in love with him. When I called he answered but he wasn't too conversational. When I asked him if he would go to the prom with me. He told me he'd call me back. The thought of him saying no, never occurred to me. Twenty minutes later he was at my house. We sat on the porch and he told me that I was too stubborn for my own good. Then he asked me if I would go to the prom with him.

Unlike D, Marquez was into all the planning for our night. He went dress shopping with me. When I found the perfect dress, we took it and made sure we matched a tux to it. He's been growing his hair out and its long, thick, and wavy. He asked me how I wanted him to wear his hair. As Nassya was having a blast combing and brushing it. Putting it in braids and then taking them down. I told him to wear it down as I watched him enjoy my sister's playtime in his head.

Kendra

"KB! When's your prom?"

"You want to take me?"

"I'm asking aren't I? I thought you knew it was me and you this year."

"I wasn't sure if you were going with Nellie or not."

He blew air, "when are you going dress shopping?"

"I honestly haven't thought about it."

I could hear the smile in his voice, "you want me to come?"

"If you want to."

"If I want to? KB! I get to watch you model different dresses for me. Of course I want to. The dress you wore last year was cool. But this year you need something that highlights your main assets."

"You've put a lot of thought into this I see."

"I've definitely got some ideas. But here's the thing you gotta trust me."

"What does that mean?"

"Ok so here's my plan." He cleared his throat, "for kicks and giggles we have you try on some styles and see what you like best. **THEN!!!!** My momma has this dress designer friend who can make your dress for you. That way your dress is original and you don't have to worry about anyone having your dress. Sound good?"

"Sounds expensive!"

"Don't worry about the cost. I got you!"

"You got me? What does that mean?"

"Means I'm paying for everything. I want your night out with me to be unlike any night you've ever known."

"Everything with you has been unlike anything I've ever known."

"KB! Don't go there with me right now! I'm trying to be strong." He cleared his throat, "sound like a plan?"

"Sounds like a plan."

After work on a Saturday Kalani, Ryder, Darryl, and I went all over the Bay Area looking at and trying on dresses. I asked Kalani to try on dresses for me as well as another reference point. But we really used that time to whisper about how silly Darryl and Ryder were. The dresses I liked I took pictures in. I told Darryl what I liked about each dress and then he asked me what color I wanted the dress to be. When I said black, he smiled. He asked me if I wanted to add silver to make it perfect. I told him that was fine. He told us he had reservations for us so we went to Point Richmond to the Mac Hotel. He had a banquet room reserved for our party of four. There was a piano in the room. He told me to come sit at the piano with him.

He held his hands just above the keys, "just so you guys know. I'm an artist, but Ryder has the pipes. So we're going to play a little melody for you. We hope you like it." Then he took a deep breath. He looked at Ryder and he nodded, Darryl started banging on the piano making a bunch of horrible noise. Then Ryder started singing calmly, but equally horribly. Kalani and I laughed so hard we couldn't keep it together. I don't know why this fool wasn't concerned about someone hearing us. Our waitress came in the room and she looked like she was sent to tell him to stop. "Mr. Wallace?"

"I'm sorry I don't take request yet." He said smiling at her as he continued banging.

"Ok but, Mr. Wallace…"

"I know! I know! Music has been known to soothe the average beast!"

"Yes, but Mr. Wallace…"

"You want me to sing directly to you. You got it," Ryder said. He pointed at Darryl, "Hit it!"

Ryder dramatically walked towards the waitress singing his horrible song while Darryl pounded on the keyboard with an evil grin. "Don't hurt her now!" He said to Ryder. Ryder took the waitress in his arms and spun her around. Then he slow danced with her while singing his song. It was so horrible, she couldn't help but laugh. "MR. WALLACE PLEASE!" She yelled in between laughs.

Darryl stopped pounding, "you can call me Darryl!" Then he went back to pounding.

"Darryl! Please! You're gonna get me fired!" She pleaded while laughing.

"Ok!! Ok! Point Richmond is not ready for our musical genius." He said to Ryder, "but waitress. You gotta admit, you have never heard musical styling's like ours before."

"I agree! I have never heard anything like that before." She said still laughing.

Nellie

Junior's girlfriend did my hair. She does an amazing job with it, it was down and basically straight with a slight bump to it. But I loved how shiny and healthy it looked. My stepmom took pictures of me along the way to totally ready. When I walked in the living room dressed and ready Marquez's reaction to me was priceless. He told me I looked so beautiful. He looked very handsome himself, and then they took tons of pictures of us. Marquez's uncle rented a car for him for the night. Marquez and I took pictures and talked with our associates, he danced with me. And then I asked him to come with me for a walk. Earlier that day Junior's girlfriend got a room for me in this hotel. I used my allowance to pay for it. When the elevator doors opened on the floor of our room Marquez stood there looking at me. I took him by the hand and I led him to our room. He didn't say anything; he kept frowning at me and looking like he didn't understand what we were doing here. I led him into our room. I took his jacket off and laid it on the chair. I moved his hair as I kissed his neck and unbuttoned his shirt. I asked him to unzip my dress and he did so very slowly. Every time he touched me it felt brand new, it wasn't anything like D's touch. D basically knew how to handle me, but Marquez was touching me. I tried to make tonight as beautiful as possible. He had been waiting for tonight since we were freshmen and it was the least I could do before we went our separate ways. PLUS! I wanted to know what this would feel like. It felt better than I imagined. No one will ever last longer than Ahjani, but tonight feels like love and not just sex.

Kendra

Darryl delivered my dress personally. He warned us that the dress was going to be extremely sexy, but when I tried it on I saw that I underestimated the sexy. The dress was black and long. It had a plunging V-neck in the front and a deep V in the back. The waist was sheer, and there was a thigh high split on the right thigh. The bottom of each V had silver beading. When I walked out the bathroom in the dress, Kaleah and Kalani gasped, my momma's eyes got big, and Darryl yelped. "That is some dress!" My momma said trying to find her words.

Kalani and Kaleah watched my momma before they said anything. "Mrs. P! I know my vote doesn't count, but she looks amazing." Darryl said like he was salivating.

"Turn around." My momma said. When I did, Darryl yelped again. My butt did look amazing in this dress if I do say so myself. "Do you like it?"

I smiled sheepishly at her, "yes! No one will have anything like this."

"It's so…. so… Mature!" She said looking at my dress. "You're going to be comfortable walking around like that?" I nodded my head yes. My momma threw her hands up in defeat.

"BLESS YOU MRS. P! BLESS YOU!" Darryl said running to my momma and kissing her cheek.

I got my hair done in a beautiful bun. I went to the makeup counter and got my makeup done. Darryl came at six-thirty. I could hear him and Jason talking in the living room. Kalani insisted on getting before pictures of Darryl and Jason talking, pictures of Jason when he saw me in my dress, and then she said she'd show me pictures of the argument him and momma had when I left cause he was going to be pissed. Kalani went ahead and then she told me to come out. Jason was smiling until he saw my dress. He turned completely red. He asked my momma what I was wearing. And she said a dress as if he couldn't see that. His eyes turned evil when he looked at Darryl. Kalani was snapping away on her camera. Kaleah was cracking up for the first time in forever. Her laughter distracted Jason while we slipped out of the door. There was another equally beautiful expensive limo car outside as the one he rode in with Nellie. "How do you get all these beautiful cars?"

"What do you mean?"

"I saw the car you rode in last year."

He smiled, "my brother owns the car service. They have exotic cars like this, regular limos, limo buses, party buses, you name it they got it." He said. Then he took my hand, "Kendra, you're stunning!" I smiled and said thank you. "I can't believe we made it out of that house with you dressed like this. I thought for sure Jayman was gonna rain on our parade!"

I couldn't help but think about how Omar said when he made it we would ride like this regularly and I mean it was nice and all. And I loved the feeling of arriving and leaving in this car. But in the end it was just a car. For special occasions ok. But I didn't want this to be a part of my everyday life.

When Darryl helped me out the car I took a good look at him, he was so FINE! Everything hung off him like it was meant for him. He held every door open, he pulled out my seat for me. And of course he kept everyone at our table in stitches all night. We took three sets of pictures, the ones for everyone. He said we had to use sexy smiles for those. The completely silly pictures that were for our wallets and to remember the good times. And then he said the last one we had to give the camera sexy looks. I had to practice for a couple of minutes and try not to laugh when he reacted to my stupid looks. I couldn't wait to see these pictures. After the prom we went out for dessert with Tanaka and her date. When Darryl walked me to the door, Jason turned on the light to let us know he was right there. Darryl laughed and asked if he could at least get a good night kiss? Then the light flickered. He said do it again for a no and two times for a yes. When the light only flickered one more time, Darryl shook his head laughing. He said he had to respect the Jayman otherwise he'd put Malcolm, Darryl's dad, on him. Darryl gave me a big hug and told me he had the best night with me.

Nellie

"Nealesha Makaya Parker!" I could hear my family and Marquez cheering for me. I did feel a sense of accomplishment as I crossed the stage in my honors garb.

"Marquez Nimuel Pelayo!" There was a loud roar of applause for him.

When he walked off the stage he hugged me and carried me the rest of the way back to our seats. There were only a few more honor students after us and then the ceremony was over. I kept feeling like someone was staring at me, so I kept looking around the room. I never found that person, but you know that feeling? Last night I had a dream that my momma came to my graduation full of apologies and congratulations. I guess I was wishing it were true. But I did have a surprise visitor. Nathan came and hugged me. I was so shocked. He looked rough and even skinnier than before. He looked like he's been through a lot. He kept putting his eyes on the floor and sticking to my daddy's side.

I looked at my phone expecting to see a missed call or something from D, but nothing. I guess he didn't even try to make it to my graduation.

Marquez came out to dinner with my family, my aunties and uncles and cousins on my dad's side all came to my surprise. Our family didn't get together too often, but when my daddy asked them to come they gladly came. After dinner, I went with Marquez to meet his family. Even though neither of us has agreed that we are a couple. It really does feel like it outside of when I hook up with D still, but even that isn't the same. I don't hide that from Marquez, just like I saw that girl still following him around the last few weeks of school after prom. Marquez's family is big and he has a lot of cousins and Aunties and Uncles. Most of his family was paired off with someone of a different background. His uncle that he lives with took me around introducing me to everyone while Marquez's family showered him with gifts and told him how proud they were of him. Everybody was nice just like Marquez and they kept congratulating him on me being so pretty.

****

In order to guarantee that D would come to my graduation party I had to promise to only stay for his ceremony. And I had to muscle my way in to his graduation at that. He told me his family is large and he barely had tickets for all of his family. I just wanted to see him walk across the stage even if he didn't make it to mine. I snuck in the back door while people were still setting up. As people started to fill in I found a seat closest to the stage. I spotted D-Rick sectioning off seats. It looked like they were expecting a big crowd just like D said. I don't know why I had to literally tell myself to calm down when I saw D-Rick talking to a very average looking chick. She was tall and thin, she definitely needs some Nellie flavor. I quickly came up with the perfect outfit to change her whole appearance. I got lost in the possibilities when I realized that the auditorium was filling up; and suddenly his section was swarming with people. I wondered if the lady on crutches was D's momma. She's brown just like him; I went over the other possibilities. I spotted his auntie as she sat down next to a girl with another woman. When the graduates came in the auditorium, I was looking for D amongst his huge class of people. I thought I missed him when his class entered and then the honor students started coming in. I couldn't believe it when I saw him with his honors garb. ALL THAT AND BRAINS TOO!!!! I was in love harder than I was before. D was smiling so big as he walked proudly with his fellow honor graduates. When they announced his name it seemed like the whole house roared to congratulate him on his success!

After the ceremony everyone crowded around D saying goodbye. Girls were foaming at the mouth rubbing their bodies all over him and stuffing their numbers in his pockets. Darryl was entertaining everyone when he looked up and saw me. He motioned for me to come forward and all those stinking heifers were so mad that he acknowledged me. One of the guys asked who I was as he drooled, D said I was a friend. The guys were all smiling at me like they were wishing I was here for them. When the crowd dissipated D looked at me and said thank you for coming. As he started to walk, "Um! Can I at least meet your mother?"

He stopped in his tracks. "My momma?" He came back, "why you wanna meet my momma? It's not like we're together or anything. You're about to go your way and I'm going mine." Then he thought about it, "what the heck? I'm feeling good today, it's my day." Then he told me to come with him. When we walked out of the auditorium a guy and a girl was waiting for D. "Nellie this is my momma, momma this Nellie." He said proudly.

My mouth fell open when he said it. "You look like you could be his sister." I guess it made sense for his momma to be light skinned, but she looked so young. I thought she was just some girl when I was looking at his family from across the room. "It's nice to finally meet you." I said still taking in every aspect of her face. "Finally?" She asked shaking my hand.

I looked at Darryl, "I see you've spent so much time talking about me."

Darryl looked at the guy. The guy jumped in, "it's nice to finally meet you, and I'm his big brother Drew." He said shaking my hand with both hands. His big brother was heck of cute! All the men in this family were delicious. The look on his momma's face was annoyed. She was looking at D to explain and he kept smiling and looking between his brother and his momma.

"Momma, what's in your hair?" Drew said. She frowned at him as she reached up to touch her hair. Like she didn't want to believe him, but she couldn't risk that he was telling the truth. She squinted her eyes at him. "Let me get it!" He said waving at us to escape.

"I'll see you tomorrow." D said to me waving me on.

Kendra

"Kendra Hutchins!" My family cheered for me! I was so happy this school year was over! After the ceremony we went out to dinner. Ahjani made it back just in time to be here for my graduation. He brought his girlfriend Olivia, she was really nice. Darryl kept confirming that I was coming to his graduation on Saturday and to the party afterwards, I told him I wouldn't miss it for the world. Darryl told me to bring my cousins to the party; he said there were going to be tons of people there and plenty of space. He reminded me that the party was going to be at his grandfather's house. He asked me if I remembered how to get there. I told him I did. At the ceremony I sat amongst the family and I sat there impressed that Darryl was an honors graduate. I wasn't, I missed the boat by a few points. But I sucked it up and made the best out of it. In the end, I was graduating with a beautiful GPA. When the ceremony was over, I hurried out to go get my cousins.

When I got to his house, he greeted us with big hugs and smiles. Ryder took Erin from Ahjanae then he told her to go have fun. Then he proceeded to make sure she ate so much that poor baby was stuffed. Ahjanae and I were reunited with Darryl's cousins. Lanie made a whole dramatic display about how much she missed me. I wasn't sure that she liked me before cause she was always quiet around me, turns out she's just as hilarious as Darryl. I guess that's another reason we got a long so well. I spotted the only one who could be Darryl's mother even though I wasn't quite sure cause she didn't look old enough. But she was the one I've seen in pictures, and she kept hopping on the dance floor with Darryl's dad. He didn't seem so scary in her presence which was nice. When Darryl introduced me to his mother, she smiled and it seemed like she released some tension. We chatted for a little bit and she was really nice. Darryl stood over to the side blushing. We had a good time; Darryl hugged me and thanked me for coming. Then he told me he'd call me.

Chapter 13

Nellie

My daddy sat on the other side of the table looking at us. His eyes turned red and then he put his hand over his mouth like he was giving himself a pep talk to just get it out. He took a deep breath. "Mary and I go way back." He put his hand over his mouth like he was searching for words. "Your mother wasn't some random female that I knocked up twice. I met my wife in college and I chose her because she was offering me something different. Because of my wife I got my stuff together and became the man that I am today. We had Junior and my business grew. Mary... She's like a drug, even when you think you've kicked the habit. Even the thought of her makes you weak and you do the unthinkable. Nathan you weren't planned, but I wanted you. That's why you're here, she had you for me. But she wasn't ready. When she brought you to me, I didn't question her. I took you home. I lied and told my wife you were the result of a one-time slip up. All the while knowing I was in love with your mother. When Mary wanted you back there was no way to make that happen. Nathan you had bonded with my wife, and you always looked at Mary with hurt feelings. We talked about it and the only way to give everyone what they needed was to have another child." My daddy shook his head. "I was young, dumb, and selfish. I never stopped to think about how my actions would affect anyone. I'm the biggest and the best, there's no one better than me. I deserved to have two beautiful women bending over backwards to make me happy. I worked hard to become me, I deserved it all. These are the stupid things I told myself. I felt like they had to deal with whatever I gave them because I was providing the best for them. I was providing very comfortable lives for everyone. Nothing excuses what I did to you Princess, nothing! I loved Mary! I didn't know how to stop things with her; I didn't know how to handle it. You two are suffering so much because of how full of myself I've been. I know you have questions, it's hard for me to talk on this level." He exhaled, "and I know just because I brought you here today doesn't mean you'd have questions on hand. I'm willing to work with you if you work with me."

My heart was pounding, "I want to say something." He nodded at me. "I appreciate you stepping up now. But it doesn't change how lost I feel. What you did was vicious and heartless. You replaced me and threw me away. When I see you guys again looking like a happy family I felt like the outsider. Junior has been the only consistent person in my life. The rest of you make me feel disposable. I appreciate you coming to get me and not letting me end up in the system. But I'm hurting!" Then I turned to Nathan. "And you! I don't know what I ever did to you to make you hate me so much. I can't control who's stomach I came out of or who put me there."

"You act too much like me. The difference is you would actually say the things I was thinking, and it made me angry. You act like you're entitled to all this attention. Attention that I wanted for me. I didn't even want you to be friends with that girl. I did my best to try to ruin your friendship, but she always defended you. I hurt her more than once because she would only focus on the good things about you and I wanted her to hate you." He said with his head down.

"What girl was this?" Daddy asked

"I don't remember her name."

"Kendra," I said as a tear fell.

"What ever happened to her?" Daddy asked

"I had to choose between her and someone else, I chose the other person."

It was quiet for a minute then my daddy looked around. "I can't do your mother. I can't! But I can offer someone else." He motioned for the person to come.

I looked up and my heart burst out of my chest. It was my grandmother. I screamed and ran to her. I buried my head in her chest and I squeezed like I was trying to break her. She had her arms around me as she kissed my head. "You are still beautiful child!" She said kissing me.

My daddy told us to come back to the table. People were looking at us but I didn't care. When she got close to the table she stopped walking as she looked at Nathan. "Neallan, who's this?"

"This is your grandson Nathan. Nathan this is your grandmother Johnny Mae."

My grandmother stumbled backwards a step. "Lord Jesus! The drama!" She yelled towards the ceiling. Then she looked at Nathan. "I didn't know." Then she put her arms out to hug him. Nathan hugged her then he sat next to daddy so my grandmother could sit next to me. "I met you before."

"Yes, you came by my house once. I was confused and looking at Mary to explain the situation, but of course she didn't." Then she put her arm around me. "You look good! I'm so proud of you! Graduating with honors, I'm so proud of you."

My eyes lit up, "you are?"

"Yes! Despite your parents you're still applying yourself. You've always been strong, I have no doubt that you will make it."

"I dropped out of school." Nathan said

"But you're going back aren't you?"

"Not right away. I've got to get healthy again, then we'll see."

"Healthy?" She looked concerned.

"I picked up some bad habits that I've got to kick." He said in a defeated tone.

"You can do it baby. If I can do it, you can do it."

"You had habits'?" I asked

"Yes," she exhaled. "When your momma was little. Drove her daddy away with my nonsense. Your momma had to provide for herself. When I got cleaned up, I tried to show her my life as how not to be. But the cycle continues." She exhaled, "I moved to Vegas. I had to get away from here. That thing your momma was dating shot up my house."

For the first time ever I got excited about going to school. "I'm going to ASU in the fall!"

"You won't be far, you'll have to come see me." She smiled, "and you need to come be with me."

Nathan's eyes got big, "you want me to come with you?"

"No one's going to understand what you need. Instead of helping you they may enable you." She looked at my daddy, "Neallan! Send him!"

Daddy looked at Nathan who was staring at my grandmother wide eyed. "Do you want to go?" Nathan shook his head yes.

I asked her if she knew where my momma was. She shook her head yes, but she didn't say anything further.

When we left the restaurant I felt like running. I didn't know where I was running to. I called D, but he sent me to voicemail. So I

drove to Marquez's house. He was in the kitchen cleaning when I
came. He looked at me with concern in his eyes and I fell on his
shoulder and I cried my eyes out. I couldn't explain how I felt, but
I didn't like it. I felt out of control and frustrated. Every time I'd
start to calm down my tears would start all over again. His uncle
asked Marquez if I was pregnant. Marquez looked at me asking
with his eyes. I shook my head no. He took me to his room and had
me lay down on his bed. He took my shoes off and pulled the
covers over me. He kissed my forehead and said he'd be back. I
heard his uncle ask him what was wrong with me and he told him
he didn't know. I cried myself to sleep smelling Marquez in his
pillow. When I woke up Marquez was spooning me. When I turned
to face him he was wide-awake. "My parents were in love. But he
chose my stepmother. I saw my grandmother; Nathan's going to go
stay with her until he gets better. What's the point of love if it
doesn't stop you from hurting people?"
"It depends on whether you love that person more than you love
yourself."
"I don't know if I'll ever be able to be good to anyone. Look at
what I know." I started crying.
Marquez kissed me. "I'll show you how."
"I don't want you to."
"Right, cause you're afraid. When your longing becomes greater
than your fear I'll be here."
"You're going to Santa Barbara."
"I'm coming back here after graduation. I have a job lined up
already."
"Doing what?" He got up and took a binder out of his closet. He
gave it to me. There were three sections separated by tabs. The last
section was the biggest. In the first section it was a beautiful
woman. Lots of pictures of her, and then some of her and a child.
The child was faceless but I could tell it was a boy. "This is your
mother?" He nodded yes. There was a picture of them being torn
apart with both of their arms and hands reaching out to each other.
Then next picture was of her lifeless hands. Then his pictures got
dark and painful. The faceless boy always had darkness around
him. The next section was full of landscapes, and beautiful nature
things. Like beaches, flowers, sunsets or dawn. They looked so real
I couldn't believe he drew them. The last section was full of
pictures of me. In most of them I look sad just like his mother. He

even drew me smiling at D. He had pictures of me naked, of us together. He said he was going to work at the animation studio in Emeryville. His pictures were so good they looked like photos of me. "Do I always look this sad?"

"Most times," then he turned to a picture. "Even though you can't dance you were happy." He kissed my cheek. Then he turned the picture. "Even though you said you didn't want to be my friend any more you looked for me. And your face would light up when you saw me until you reminded yourself that you hated me." He chuckled.

"I want you to meet a nice girl while you're in school. Someone who knows what to do with you."

He grabbed my hair and kissed me. "You're my nice girl! I want you!"

"I'm not nice, and I'm going to meet someone in school who knows it. If I come back, you better run away."

"I'll run to you, never away from you." He said kissing me again.

Kendra

"Kendra, baby come over here." Ms. Lorraine said as I got out of my car. I came over and I gave her a big squeeze while I hugged her.

"How's your family holding up?" She asked watching my eyes.

"Everybody's still kind of shaken up but we'll be ok."

"It's hard to believe his life turned out like this. I knew Jerry when he was a little boy. He and my nephew were friends." She exhaled, "now they're both gone." She swallowed air.

"Your nephew?"

"My nephew David and your dad were friends in Junior high school. Then David moved out here to stay with me. He and Jerry kept in contact over the years until David died."

"No one ever told me."

Ms. Lorraine twisted her face like she was fighting back emotion. "It wasn't right for him to go after your sister like that. No man has the right to treat any female like that. Give your sister a hug for me. Send your family my love." She said walking away and trying to shake off the bad feeling that was coming over her.

****

"You've been avoiding me!" Omar said

I exhaled, "Omar I'm not going to school out there."

"Kendra! The plan was for you to come out here with me. You never gave me the information for your graduation."

"It was last week." I felt horrible.

"Baby! I don't understand. You don't love me anymore?" He sound so hurt.

"I don't want the debt. I have people here who depend on me. I can't leave. You're so busy dreaming for us you haven't stopped to see my reality."

"Kendra, I am your reality! I'm out here working so that we can have something better. Something real! I don't understand why it's got to be all this?"

"You never asked me if I wanted to move away. You just assumed. With everything's that happened over the last few years I'm not comfortable leaving."

"Ever? Or for now?"

"I don't know Omar, and I don't want to hold you back. You've got a great life ahead of you. I don't want to be the reason you're stuck in Richmond trying to get along."

"So what am I supposed to do? I love you!" He said from his heart.

"Omar you know I love you. I'm sorry I didn't have this conversation with you sooner." I felt like garbage.

He was quiet for a minute, "Kendra I don't understand. Did I do something wrong?"

"No, you've been great. Do you want to hear my plan?"

He agreed in defeat, it's not like he could've changed anything if he didn't like what I said. "So you could still end up out here when and if you transfer to a major university? When am I going to see you? Can you come out to visit?"

"I need to focus on my business and try to grow it some more to pay for school."

"Your stepdad has offered to help you with school expenses, I don't understand why you don't just go?"

"Because I have two little sisters who are going to need the same offer. I'm not trying to milk him dry and leave nothing for them." Plus he was helping Ahjani out with the things his scholarship didn't cover. Audra was already set up for her journey when it's her time.

"You're always falling on the sword for your sisters, for your family. I want to give you what you're always passing up so that they can have. You deserve to be happy too you know."

I smiled, "thank you for seeing that about me. As long as my family is taken care of I am happy."

"Am I your family?"

I could feel the trick coming. "What do you mean?"

"I shouldn't ask I should just say that I am. We became family when you gave me your virginity. When do you fall on the sword for me?" I started laughing. "Get your mind out of the gutter! I'm trying to have a conversation with you." He said laughing.

"You haven't met your replacement Kendra yet?"

"There's only one you."

Nellie

Nassya looked around with sad eyes. "So this is where you're going to live? I wish you didn't have to leave me."

"We're going to see each other every school vacation, and I'm coming home once a month. You're going to get sick of me watch." I looked around, "baby girl you did such a wonderful job decorating this place. You should go to school for interior design. You have a gift."

She smiled, "I did do a good job huh." Then she laughed.

I wasn't kidding, it didn't look like I put this place together. Nassya picked out everything and it looked so nice. This was our third trip out here. First trip we found this apartment close to school. Second trip I got my keys. Third trip girl's trip, we setup my place. Daddy had my car shipped out here and it arrived this morning. We drove around getting familiar with the area. It was so hot; I started questioning why I chose this place. It did however create the perfect environment for tank tops, shorts, sandals, and Popsicles. We locked up my place and I flew home with my stepmom and sister for the end of my summer.

I kept calling D and he wasn't answering. I didn't know if he went away to school or what. Since I now know he values education, I don't doubt that he's going to school. I want to know where.

I went school shopping with Nassya. She loves when I style her clothes. I helped her pick out two weeks' worth of outfits (shoes, earrings, necklaces, etc.). Then she picked up little sidepieces to make that outfit into two or three. When we get home she hung everything up according to the entire outfits. My little fashionista always looks amazing.

I went out to dinner with Junior and his girlfriend. Junior spent the evening emotional about me leaving. I told my big brother how much I loved him and I thanked him for always taking care of me. When I got to Marquez's house he was sitting on the porch drinking and being real quiet. I asked him if he was ok, and then he stared at me for a long time without speaking. Then he told me to come. I followed him to his room, the moment he closed his door he was all over me. I kept looking at him cause he wasn't like his normal self. Whatever he commanded my body to do it did. I was speechless and light headed. When he told me he loved me I heard myself tell him I loved him too. Now why did I do that? My comment gave him a second wind and almost gave me repeated heart attacks. Marquez wrote down my address and he told me he was coming to visit me as soon as he could.

****

"D!"

"What's up?" He said nonchalantly

"I've been calling you all summer!"

"So, you should've call Marquez."

"So what happened? You and Marquez have a conversation and you passed me off?"

He sighed, "What do you want?"

"I'm leaving, you don't care?"

"Care?" He sounded irritated.

"D! I know you care about me stop trying to act like you don't." He exhaled and I could hear tapping in the background. "I want to see you before I leave." He didn't say anything, "D! Did you hear me?"

"I know you're sensitive so I'm trying to hold back. But you've got this whole thing confused. I'm not your man; you have no claim on me. If you want to feel like someone cares call Marquez with all that noise."

Anger turned in my stomach. "You must be sniffing around Kendra again." He didn't say anything. "Every time you're sniffing around her butt you're too good for me. I wonder how she would feel about you if she knew how long you've been digging me out!" I couldn't hear anything on his end. "Hello?"

"This is why you don't show chicken heads any kind of kindness! Listen here trick, I could waste my time threatening you or I can just come for you! Don't push me! You never wanna be on my bad side, you think you thought your life was worthless before; I'll make sure you finish the job! Let me find out you even thought about Kendra and it's lights out for you!" Then he hung up.

Nellie

"Gordon! My man!" One guy said making too much noise.
"What's going on T-bone! Glad to see you made it back!"
They did some stupid handshake. Already the fraternities on this campus were everywhere. It's been a couple of months and a few houses have approached me. I don't want to do it this year. But I'll think about it for next year.
I've been doing my best to lay low since I got here. I keep to myself and to my surprise I haven't hooked up with anyone. How does the saying go? Sticks and stones may break my bones but words will never hurt me! That is such a LIE! All I can think about are D's last words to me. How angry he sounded, there was no love in his tone. I guess he didn't care after all. But I'm so confused, cause I thought he did care. He came to the hospital to see me and he came to my house. He started kissing me, even though that wasn't all the time and very rare, he still did it. Whenever we were together I felt like he cared. Why would he have sex with me and as much as he did if he didn't care? We spent the night together; he's given me little gifts that I still have. I don't get it; he never told me he loved me or took me around any of his friends or family, but I had his time and his body. I don't get it. With all of this on my brain who has time to worry about these wanna be players on this campus. Since I don't have to work I study, I study my butt off. I'm on top of all of my classes and that gives me a sense of accomplishment.
"Excuse me miss, is this seat taken?" The skinny guy said. Another wanna be player, "it's open." I said returning to my book. He and his friend sat down. "What are you reading?" He asked me. I pointed to the cover and went back to reading. "You're a freshman aren't you?"
"I guess I need to go ahead and get that library card after all." I said very irritated. Then I looked at his friend, "you look familiar. Do I know you from somewhere?"
"You look familiar as well. Maybe we met when you toured campus." He said.
"I'm T-bone, and this is my man Gordon."

"Leasha." I said going through my mental Rolodex. "Where are you from?" I said to Gordon. His name did not ring a bell.

"California, but my team went to the championship last year. Maybe you've been to a game." He said smiling at me. "I don't think we've met cause I'm sure I'd remember you."

"What part of California? What city?"

"Richmond, you know it?" He asked.

"What do you play?"

"Basketball"

"My ex played basketball at Kennedy, where did you go to school?"

"Who's your ex? I played for Kennedy too."

"Ahjani Lubbock," I said as I remembered him from the games I went to. Then I remembered this is Kendra's man. Of all the places and all the people! This world is too small.

"Oh my man Ahjani! I guess that's why you look familiar. How's Ahjani doing?"

"We don't speak, you guys don't keep in contact?"

"We speak from time to time. But he's in Georgia." Then he sat back. "You don't speak at all? I find that hard to believe."

"Why?"

"You don't let the beautiful ones go forever."

"So that's what you do? You hold on to people forever?"

"Not people, just the beautiful ones."

"So then you're holding on to a lot. There are plenty of beautiful girls at this school."

"But I'm looking at you." He smiled.

"I'm T-bone."

I gagged, "that was weak." I got up and took my books to the counter. I checked them out, got in my car and went home.

I wonder why he and Kendra broke up?

Kendra

I was kissing Darryl and loving every moment of it. It's been a year of kissing and messing around, but no sex. I don't understand it, but I don't fight it either. If we aren't having sex then we aren't together. So I don't exactly question him when I don't see him all that often. "KB, when do you leave for school?"

"I'm not, when do you leave?"

"What do you mean you're not? You didn't get in anywhere?" His face was completely serious.

"I didn't apply."

"What? Why?" He sat up to look at me.

"I don't want to accumulate the debt." I said

He frowned, "the debt? I know Jayman's got you."

"My sisters will need his help, he can help them."

"That's garbage! I know for a fact he's got all three of you covered. Did he say he couldn't afford it?"

"No, but I can't assume on his pockets."

"Are you gonna be straight with me? Why aren't you going to school?"

"I don't want to go away to school! I need my family just as much as they need me. Everybody's so excited to go away, but I don't want to."

Darryl was quiet for a minute. "So why didn't you apply to a local school? There are universities and state schools right here. Drew went to Berkeley and D-Rick went to Stanford."

"Where are you going?"

"Berkeley just like Drew and my momma."

"Darryl that's a lot of money!"

"It's only money, but your education is yours forever! I can't believe Jayman let you get away with not going."

"I'm going to Contra Costa, I can get my associates there." I exhaled, "I can transfer after that."

"Don't act like you're doing me a favor. Your education is yours and yours alone. If you don't want it, then you don't want it."

"I do want it. But I'm scared."

"Of?"

I didn't want to say that going to school made me feel weird. Suddenly I didn't feel good enough. Plus how would I explain going to school and not going with Omar. What if I end up with Omar and then we end up like my parents. I'm afraid of loving someone that much. My momma gave my father her everything and what thanks did she get? I love Omar and there's no one like him. But I love Darryl as well. It's not the same kind of love though. Darryl is sweet and hilarious to be around. He has a mean streak, but it's never been pointed at me. I feel safe when I'm with him, and I think he cares about me. However, he holds back with me as if I can't see that. He's always traveling, moving around, going places. I still wonder how much of that time is spent with someone else. "Everything Darryl, more than I can put into words right now."

He looked me in my eyes, "you can't let fear rule you. If you allow fear to take over nothing will ever get done." His voice was deep and his eyes were burning me.

I smiled at him, "so that means we're getting married after I graduate?"

His body went limp and he fell backwards. "KB! KB! You ruined my serious moment! I had some more hard hitting and passionate," he sat up on his elbows. "Really deep stuff to say." Then he laughed. "That was a good one! You win this round my friend." He laughed again.

"Seriously, what do you have against marriage?"

"My parents! My momma keeps running around brokenhearted because Malcolm never married her. The last guy she was with wanted to marry her. Sometimes I could tell she wanted to marry him too. But how could she marry him if she's in love with Malcolm? She's the only person who didn't understand that. People don't stay in love anymore, I'm gonna take over where my Uncle Mali left off."

"Isn't he in love though?"

"You're missing the point!"

I looked at him, "please explain it."

He sat up and put his hands out like he was about to break everything down. Then paused, "well dang! I lost my point! KB did you slip me a Mickey?"

"Darryl you don't want to marry me?" I smiled.

He touched my cheek, "I love that booty. I do! But your heart doesn't belong to me. I'm not blind, I can see that. You still got love for the star. I thought you were about to run off to be with him. Had I known all year that booty's been waiting on me..." He shook his head. "Did he cry when you told him this booty wasn't coming for him?"

"No," I said laughing.

He looked me in my eyes with a serious face. "I guarantee you he did! I was gonna cry cause your booty was leaving. Where am I supposed to rest my hands if you take that booty away?"

"But you just got on me for not going away."

"No I didn't. I was on you about going to school, you don't ever have to take that booty away!" He said laughing.
"What if he comes back for me?"
"You better choose me or it sucks to be you!"
****

They came home with concerned looks on their faces. Jason called everyone into the living room. They said that Kaleah's doctor said that with everything going on it's too traumatic for her to stay here. So.... My family is moving to Jason's house in Oakland. His house was bigger anyways. They asked me to come as well, but I needed to stay. After a couple of days I came up with a game plan. Ahjanae would move in with me, and work with me. She got her G.E.D. and now I convinced her to take classes with me at Contra Costa County Community college. Kalani could come and work on the weekends. Kalani was not happy about switching schools, but she said she'd do it if it meant that Kaleah would get better. Meanwhile Kaleah's boyfriend Milton was having a fit that she was moving. Aunt Quilla said she had an excuse to be in Oakland now.
Our first night in the house without my parents.... HOUSE PARTY! Darryl brought a few cousins, and we invited a few people from school. Both of Darryl's brothers came, we had so much fun. Everyone kind of fell asleep where they landed. While Darryl landed in my bed. I had been dying to feel his touch again. But he didn't really do too much other than kiss me. He said there was a house full of people. When Erin pushed the door open when she woke up, I was glad Darryl had exercised control otherwise I would've been completely embarrassed. Ryder heard Erin's little voice and invited himself in my room. He sat on the floor and got comfortable singing the A, B, C's with her. Darryl and I stared at him like he needed to die! He smiled real big while he ignored us. Ahjanae came in next getting comfortable on the floor with them singing right along. Then Ahjani, his girlfriend Olivia, Kalani, Audra, Aunrey, Kaleah, Milton, Liz, Pearla, Lanie, and everyone else crowded in my room. Darryl nor I said anything to anyone, but they would look at our faces and crack up laughing. Throughout the course of the day people started going home slowly but surely. I kept getting butterflies the later it got and the more people that left and Darryl was still here. He volunteered to drive when it was time to take Kalani and Kaleah home. His cousin

Milton kept begging to ride with us. Darryl said no, and then he looked at him every time he asked after that. Milton and Kaleah turned their big brown puppy eyes to me. All I said was, "Darryl" he blew frustrated air as he gave in. Kaleah kissed me. Milton acted like he was going to touch me and the look on Darryl's face stopped him dead in his tracks.

When we got to my parent's house they were all smiles and anxious to get back to whatever they were doing. Darryl smirked at me and said my parents were being nasty and we interrupted them. I rolled down the window and hung my head out. I felt a little sick at the thought of it. When we got to the house Ryder was still there and everyone else had gone home. He was giving Erin a horsey back ride and she was eating it up. Ahjanae was cleaning up, and in her own world. Darryl smiled at me, and I smiled back asking him what it meant. Ahjanae never said anything about feeling Ryder, but Erin was loving him. I sat down at the table; Darryl was about to sit when someone knocked on the door. I heard Jabbar's voice asking for Ahjanae. I told Darryl to let him in. I smirked while I watched him take in his daughter enjoying the company of another man. Jabbar immediately looked annoyed. Erin was having so much fun with Ryder she didn't notice her daddy. Ahjanae walked in right, as I was about to call her.

"Jabbar? What are you doing here?"

Darryl quickly took his seat at the table next to me and then he smiled at them.

"I went to your house to bring you money and your mom said you moved here." He said looking around the room.

"Well maybe if one of the times I called, you actually tried calling me back, you would've known we were moving."

"Hi daddy!" Erin waved from across the room.

"You better come over here and give me a hug and a kiss." He commanded.

Erin smiled and got off Ryder's back. She ran over and quickly gave her daddy a peck then she tried to run back to Ryder but Jabbar caught her and picked her up. "Daddy!" Erin giggled as she tried to get down.

"Who's your friend?" He asked Erin as Ryder stood up.

"Ryder!" She said wiggling to get down.

"How you doing, I'm Ryder, friend of the family." Ryder stuck his hand out.

Jabbar tried to grip his hand as hard as he could. "Jabbar." He said mugging Ryder.

"Jabbar, that's an awfully powerful grip you got there little fella."

"What are you some type of comedian, you're Erin's clown?" Jabbar said with lots of attitude.

"Actually I was auditioning for the role of daddy. I heard there was a vacancy." Ryder said matching his tone.

I smiled at Ahjanae real big, her mouth was open. "Jen you're dating this guy?"

"It's none of your business who I date. Thank you for the money, now we'll see you in two weeks right? Next time call before you come over." Ahjanae said then she walked away.

Darryl sat there cheesing at Jabbar who looked completely pissed off. As soon as he stepped out of the door Darryl and Ryder started cracking up laughing at him. I told them they could've at least let the door close first. Ahjanae peeked her head back in the room she was grinning from ear to ear. "Well played Jen, well played." Darryl said putting his hand out to shake hers.

I could tell Ahjanae was confused by what she felt; it was only a matter of time before the anger came. "He hasn't paid attention to me since I got pregnant. Now because he sees Erin having a good time with someone else he wanna ask questions." Her breathing got heavy, "I didn't get myself pregnant! But yet I'm doing this all by myself. He better be happy you let him in the door! He's a sorry excuse for the one who used to carry my heart." Then Ahjanae stormed out of the room and into her bedroom, little Erin ran after her mommy all concerned. Darryl and Ryder actually looked like they felt sorry for her. I excused myself and then I went to her room. Ahjanae was laying on her bed crying. Erin climbed up on her bed and then she put her head on her mommy's back and rubbed it as she started crying. She looked at me and told me her mommy's tummy hurt.

Ryder knocked on the door and stood in the doorway. "Ahjanae, I wanna apologize for inserting myself like that. You never said whether you wanted him back or not."

"Thanks Ryder, I'm not mad about that. The situation is messed up. He forgot about me!"

"Can I come in?"

"Of course," She said sitting up.

Ryder sat next to her on her bed and he held Erin in his arms. "He lost sight of what's good. No man wants to walk in the door and see his family having a good time with another man and then acting like he ain't nothing. He's going to be back, what you gotta decide is whether you want him back. Does he deserve another chance?"

"I don't know, but I miss him. I never let anyone as close to me as I did him. But I don't want Erin to lose your friendship."

"Oh I'm not going anywhere. If you decide to get back with him, you're gonna have a long bumpy road ahead of you. My momma had my granddad as that constant male figure in my life cause my dad… well he was lacking to say the least. My heart goes out to single mothers," he looked at Erin. "NOTHING BUT DEATH COULD KEEP ME FROM HER!"

Ahjanae's mouth fell open and we were all cracking up. "What do you know about that movie?"

"That movie's a classic! I love it." He smiled.

"Tell them what character you relate to?" Darryl said from the doorway.

"Swain!" Ryder said with a smile.

"Swain? Who's Swain?" I said racking my brain trying to figure it out.

"Harpo's friend. He helped him build the juke joint, and he's the one that asked to have the gas pumped a little faster. He was trying to tell Ms. Sophia not to do it. But she did it anyways. He was always on the sideline. Next time you watch the movie pay attention to Swain. He was always there."

"We're going to have to have a movie day." Ahjanae said

"So you think you gonna get back with him when he comes around?"

I looked at Darryl and he told me to come out and to give them some privacy. I didn't want to leave, I wanted to be nosey all up in they business. But I walked out slowly so they could have some room to talk. Then I looked at Darryl and smiled. "Now what?"

"Let's go set the mood." He said walking into the living room. He turned on KBLX and smooth R&B played over the speakers. When I joined him we danced all of two seconds then he walked to the stereo and changed it to KMEL and hip-hop came on. "That's more like it. BACK THAT THANG UP!" He started cracking up. We had an old school dance off. "KB! My heart can't take one more run of the running man! Your booty is too beautiful!" He said cracking up.

"I need to change my shirt this is too hot." I said fanning myself as I walked back to my room. I peeked into Ahjanae's room and she and Ryder were still talking and on best behavior while Erin was knocked out across both of their laps. I went in my room and shut the door. I took my shirt off and put it in the hamper. I had my dresser drawer open when Darryl came in and shut the door behind him. He had a chair from the table with him and he put it up under the door to keep it shut. "Excuse you!" I said smiling.

"It's not weird sleeping in your parent's room?"

"It would be if I was sleeping on their furniture, it doesn't even look the same with all their stuff gone." I said turning to face him.

"Nice bra KB!"

"Thanks."

"I wanna see your panties." He smiled, I took my pants off. "They match! I LOVE IT! I LOVE black panties! They're my favorites."

"I'm glad you like them. I wanna see your draws."

He smiled, "I'm not wearing any."

"Freak!"

"Well it's not like I went home last night. I took them off this morning."

"Where are they?"

"Hanging in your shower with your delicates."

"Strip!"

"NO! I'm shy!" He said covering his mouth.

"You need to shower?" I said walking towards my bathroom.

"YES! I'm DIRTY!" He ran behind me.

Nellie

"How do you know Gordon?" This random chick asked.

"Know him? Who says I know him?"

"I've seen you two talking."

"Is he your man or something?"

"Everybody wants to land the star athlete don't they? If he keeps going like he's going he's going to make it all the way. If you're looking to have him or someone like him you really need to consider pledging next year. Not only will you have the network of sisterhood, but the right connections to socially provide the opportunity to meet more guys like Gordon. Think about it, you could have Gordon for a minute. Or you could have Gordon or a guy like Gordon putting a ring on that finger." Then she walked away.

When I got home Marquez called me. I asked him if he thought about pledging. He said they were trying to recruit him during pledge week, but he turned it down. He said pledging wasn't ideal for him. He said he understood why people did it and what it meant to them. However, he has always been his own person, and he planned to stay that way. I said it didn't make me unoriginal if I decided to pledge. He said he wasn't saying that, but he wasn't going to do it. I guess that's when I decided I would do it next year.

Marquez gave me his flight information for his flight this Thursday. I tried to act like I wasn't excited that he was coming but I was. For one I hadn't met anyone out here that made me even want to consider them, and "Gordon" appeared to be blocking. Clearly he doesn't remember me, and I doubt he's spoken to Ahjani. I'm waiting for it to all blow up.

When Marquez came I showed him around my campus. He met the few associates I had out here. He came with me to the football game. Gordon looked pissed off when he saw Marquez. Marquez asked me who he was. I told him Gordon was the star athlete on the basketball team. Marquez stared back at Gordon until he stopped watching us.

The rest of Marquez's visit was pleasant and we had a good time together. We made plans for my next visit home during break. Then the next time I ran into Gordon on campus he asked who Marquez was. I told him it was none of his business. Gordon frowned at me and kind of lingered. "Do you know who I am?"

"I know exactly who you are." I said, and then I walked away.

Kendra

Darryl hopped up cursing and screaming. I was knocked out and his sudden movement scared me, but as soon as I moved the room spun. My head was killing me.

Jabbar's momma wanted to keep Erin for the weekend. Ahjanae didn't want to let her go. So Ryder promised that if she let Erin go with her grandmother he would guarantee that she had a good time. He said whatever she wanted to do we would do. Ahjanae was still dragging her feet until Erin said she wanted to go to her grandmother's house. Ahjanae told her if she wanted to come home at any point all she had to do was call her. I didn't have the heart to point out that Erin would have to know how to do that in order for it to work. We got dressed to go out then Darryl and Ryder picked us up. They took us out to dinner to their Cousin Sophia's restaurant in Walnut Creek, she wasn't there but everyone was still super nice to us. When I ordered an iced tea, Darryl told our waiter to bring a Long Island version. When it came I was going to put sugar in it and Darryl told me to taste it first. It was perfectly sweetened already. It tasted different but I guess that's why it's Long Island. Ahjanae and I finished our drinks at the same time. Darryl asked me if I wanted another one, and I said yes. I was starting my second while Ahjanae sat there frowning at her glass. When Ryder asked her if she wanted another one. She asked him if there was alcohol in her drink and he said yes. I stopped drinking and looked at my glass. "That's why my lips feel funny?" Then I started laughing and continued drinking.

Ahjanae looked at Ryder, "we're friends right? I can trust you not to take advantage of me?"

He scooted closer to her. "Jen we're best friends. We have a daughter together." Ahjanae laughed, "I will not take advantage of you. You can drink as little or as much as you want. You're safe with me." Ahjanae smiled and said she'd have another.

When we finished dinner Darryl stopped at a liquor store and put alcohol in his trunk. Then they took us to a club. It was beautiful and amazing, he said since we were underage we couldn't drink in the club but we could go party. A lot of Darryl's cousins were there and they were really nice. I also noticed all the females who were calling out for D, and cutting their eyes at me. Darryl smiled at me "you're tore up!"

"I've never drank before, but no I'm not." I protested.

"Prove it! Do the running man." He said standing back to watch.

I could see myself dancing like I always do, but my execution and my mind weren't communicating. Darryl bent over holding his stomach he was laughing so hard. I told him to shut up as I tried again and I accidentally smacked his cousin JoJo in the back of his head. He turned around rubbing the back of his head; he told me I made the dance floor a war zone. I apologized and apologized; he kept saying it was ok. We closed the club down, it was so much fun.

When we got home Darryl mixed drinks for Ahjanae and I while he and Ryder drank straight liquor. Ahjanae threw herself on her bed. Ryder kept trying to convince her to come back out but she said she was sleepy. So I gave him blankets to sleep on the couch cause his best friend conked out on him. Darryl and I went in the room. Now I remember him taking a condom out, so I don't understand the fuss this morning. "Kendra! I didn't use a condom!" The horror in his voice.

"Yes you did, I saw you take one out." I said rolling over like he was being ridiculous.

His voice grumbled. "You mean that condom on the floor? And that's only one, we are a marathon couple we keep going."

I opened my eye and sure enough there was a condom on the floor out of the wrapper unused. I rolled my eyes, "as long as you don't have anything it's fine!" Then I rolled over.

Annoyed with my ambivalence he growled at me, "Kendra this is serious wake up!"

I huffed and sat up slowly cause my head was killing me. "I'm on the pill Darryl it's fine."

He squinted his eyes, "when do you take your pill? Cause I haven't seen you take it."

"I take them at night." I said

His eyes turned to fire. "I've been here for the past week and a half. You haven't taken anything!" He panicked.

"Yes I have!"

"No you haven't!" Irritated I got up to get my case to shut him up. The walk to my purse felt off and a little out of routine. I got a knot in the pit of my stomach. But I tried to play it off. Darryl sat in the middle of my bed and pulled his knees in. When I opened my case my mouth dropped. I hadn't been taking my pill. "Un huh! Join me in this freak out moment will you!" He yelled.

"IT'S ALL YOUR FAULT! YOU TOOK ME OFF MY ROUTINE!"

"MY FAULT? IT'S YOUR FAULT FOR BACKING UP INTO ME. YOU KNOW YOU'VE BEEN TRYING TO GET MY SEED THIS WHOLE TIME!"

"THE ONLY SEEDS I WANT ARE JOHNNY APPLE AND SUNFLOWER!"

"KENDRA! WHO IN THE HELL IS JOHNNY APPLE?"

I started laughing, "the candy. You never had Johnny Apple seed candy?"

He was trying to hold on to his anger. "No!"

"Oh well you should. It's real good. They're like lemonheads but they're apple flavored." I smiled.

He tried not to laugh, but he was losing. "Stop trying to make me laugh."

"I can go get some right now, Johnny Apple for you, and sunflower for me. That's the only seeds I want right now."

Darryl started laughing, "You get on my nerves." I snuggled next to him on the bed. "Kendra I don't want any babies right now."

"You think I do?" I said blowing air.

He looked at me and smiled, "it was good though huh?"

"If my head wasn't killing me right now I'd be all over you."

"They say orgasms cure headaches."

"I bet they do, but I need water. Thank God I don't have to work today." I tried to lay down.

"No, but seriously KB! I wanna do it again!" He said rubbing my butt.

"Sorry! My head is killing me!"

"I'll fix that!" He said kissing my neck.

"Stop playing! I need medicine, I need Gatorade!"

"Going to the store I'll be right back!" He said throwing his clothes on.

I heard him wake Ryder up and then they left. Ahjanae stumbled into my room holding her head. She landed on my bed on top of the covers. "You guys should not have sex when you're drunk!" Ahjanae blurted.

I put my covers over my head, "what?" I was so embarrassed.

She laughed, "sounds like he knows what he's doing." I laughed and kept my face covered. "Do you think there's like this school for thugs. How to put it on your woman? There's nothing like thug loving!" I kept laughing, and still embarrassed. "I bet Omar never had you calling out for God like that!"

I scooted further under the covers, "leave me alone! Omar was fine!"

"Just fine don't have you like that. Stop blushing and give me dirt, I gotta live through you."

I frowned at her, "Ryder is right there why aren't you taking advantage and finding out for yourself?"

"Ryder doesn't like me, we're just friends." She said

"I think he does! He's always here!"

"Yes for Erin."

"Erin's not here now!" I smiled at her.

"He does not, we're just friends. Besides what if I went there with him and it didn't work out. Erin would lose her stand-in dad. I could never forgive myself for costing her that." She said sounding defeated.

"What if there was a guarantee that it would workout. Would you go for him?" I asked daydreaming.

She thought about it for a minute. "Shut up! There's no guarantee, so there's no point in thinking about it and setting my heart up for failure like that."

I smiled at her, "you like Ryder! You like Ryder!" I sang.

She hit me with her pillow, "no I don't! Cut it out!" I hummed my tune, and she hit me again. "It was good huh?"

"You'll see!" I smiled at her.

"Nope not me! Sex leads to pregnancy! I'm cool!"

The room spun, I started to feel nauseous. I stumbled to the bathroom and rendered everything in my stomach. "Alcohol is the devil!" I put a cool towel on my head.

When Darryl and Ryder came back they had food and aspirin. When Ryder handed Ahjanae her breakfast exactly the way she likes even down to her eggs scrambled soft I smiled at her and started humming. She cut her eyes at me and told me to cut it out. Darryl said he was tired as he nodded for me to join him in my bedroom. I hummed the song at Ahjanae as I followed Darryl to my room. Three hours and countless mind blowing experiences later we came up for air. I told him they were quiet out there, Darryl told me to be quiet and walk like him. He crept in the living room with me behind. They were laying across each couch watching some show on TV both of them were focus on the screen. When the closing credits came up, they erupted into an argument about who called the ending first. Darryl and I frowned at them. Everyone got showered and then we got dressed. I thought we were going to a restaurant until we pulled up to a big house in Concord. I asked whose house we were at and Ryder said it was his grandparent's house. "Uncle Dale!" Darryl said when the man with eyes just like Darryl's grandfather opened the door. They hugged and then he smiled real big and asked who was who. I

flashed Ahjanae a smile. Ryder introduced Ahjanae, and then he
asked where was the little girl he's heard so much about. Ahjanae
said she was with her grandmother. You could smell food cooking
from the kitchen. Ryder very proudly told us to follow him. This
house was big and beautiful! There were lots of skylights and big
windows. I had never seen a house like this before. It was
amazing! The kitchen was huge and the women in there were
moving around very comfortably. Ryder introduced us to his
momma and his Grandmomma.
"Sharon! You love me!" Darryl said smiling from ear to ear.
"Of course I love my lil doodle man. I made one for you to take
with you." She smiled real big.
Darryl put his arm around her neck; "you know your cake is the
only thing that stopped me from shooting that girl!"
"I know baby, you can't let that idiot get to you like that." She said
looking at him with love.
"She came in there messing with my parents. I've never liked her!
But NOBODY messes with my parents!"
"I know baby, your heart was in the right place."
Ahjanae and I stood there frozen listening to him talking about
shooting someone like it was nothing. "KB! My cousin Sharon
makes the best red velvet cake! She knows whenever we get
together I'm looking for it! Nobody gets a piece until I get some or
else it sucks to be them."
"It's my momma's cake and she won't let me have none until he
gets some."
"That's right!" Darryl smiled.
"That's why I take it anyways!" Ryder said to Darryl.
"That's why we fight! Respect a man's love for cake!"
"You've got too many rules! That's why I like messing with you!"
Ryder teased.
Darryl frowned at his cousin. "So Ahjanae...."
"SHUT UP!" Ryder said turning red.
Sharon smiled at her son. Ahjanae and I volunteered to help with
dinner. Darryl and Ryder sat at the counter arguing and being silly.
I kept shooting Ahjanae looks especially when the grandmother
kept telling Ahjanae how pretty she was. Ahjanae told me to be
quiet! I was so tickled. I noticed Darryl's humor was a little
different. There were no N-Bombs, but he was still his hilarious

self. When we left Ryder's grandparent's house he was very quiet, but so was Ahjanae. "Ryder?"

"Shut up!"

"Man! How you know what I was going to ask?" Darryl laughed.

"I know you, and just do us all a favor and shut up!" Ryder laughed

"I was just gonna ask why you so quiet?"

"I told you to shut it!"

"I think it's a legittimate question, don't you KB?"

"Oh yes! It's so unlike you to be so quiet."

Ryder leaned forward, "you know what, Kendra all this time we've been hanging and I never did ask you what KB stands for. Your last name doesn't start with a B!"

I gasped, and started laughing. "I'm not in this!"

"I'm not ashamed of it, I'll tell him what it stands for."

"No! Darryl don't!" I pleaded.

"What he's the only one who doesn't know. Jen was there."

"You see what he did? He turned you on me to take the attention off of him." I turned around and looked at Ryder and shook my head. "You are cold blooded."

Ryder shook his head, "you're starting to act just like him!"

"Alright!" Darryl and I high-fived, "can you believe it?"

"I never doubted you KB! I knew you had it in you!"

"Does this mean that Ahjanae is going to start acting like Ryder? I mean they're together just as much as we are."

"No KB! They're together **more** than we are."

I thought about it, "that's true! They are together **more** than we are." I looked at Ahjanae who looked like she wanted to slap the mess out of me. "Uh oh! Ahjanae is giving me that look! I better shut up!" I said turning around. Ahjanae and Ryder were sitting on opposite sides of the backseat like they were afraid to touch. "It was nice meeting your family, thank you for taking us Ryder."

"Yes, thank you. I guess you really do care for Erin." Ahjanae said.

"Are you kidding? I love that little girl! She's an amazing kid, I tell you that all the time."

"She is pretty awesome isn't she?" Ahjanae sounded prideful.

When we got home Darryl warned us not to touch his cake. He said he hated to be a jerk, but he loved his cousin's cake. Ahjanae showered then she came out in her pj's. I told her that tonight was her last night of freedom. She told me to go away. So Darryl and I

went in my room and watched TV. After a couple of hours we went in the living room to see what they were doing. And just like last time they were on separate couches watching TV.
They were talking across the living room about the movie, and arguing about who called the outcome first. It was cute and I could see Darryl and I doing the same thing before I knew about the other side.

****

I could hear them whispering, asking each other if I was in fact me. I didn't know who the girls were. I looked at my sisters and Ahjanae to see if they were hearing the same thing. Maybe I thought these girls were talking about me and they weren't. The looks on their faces told me I wasn't mistaken. I tried walking away but now they're following me. Irritated I went through the rack of the clothing store as if anything on that rack interested me.
"Excuse me, don't you know D?" one girl asked.
"D? Can you be more specific?" I said giving a little attitude.
"I know that's her!" One of the girls said. "Weren't you at Elegant Affairs over a month ago with him?"
"That girl was cute this ain't her!" The other girl said.
"Who wants to know, and why?"
All of them looked at me like something stank. "Ooh! No she didn't?"
"Un huh! I think she just did! You gonna take that?" The other girl said.
"Kriszella wants to know, because he's my man!" The first girl said.
"You're Kriszella?" I asked she nodded. She was cute, but very hood. "I have a question. If D is your man, and you saw me with him why didn't you confront him then? Why are you coming to me, obviously I didn't know about you."
"Don't try to flip this! He's my man! You've been warned!" She said bumping into me as she walked away.
My blood boiled, this was not the first time this has happened either. Ever since that one lovely night, and that one appearance out in public all these females have come with their knives sharpened. Darryl and I's first of many fights have all been behind these females. I took out my phone and called Darryl, he said hello and I started going off about the latest addition to my list of doing too much females. I told him these are only the females bold

enough to approach me, I told him his list of hoes was too long. I was getting tired of this.

I finally convinced myself to buy a pregnancy test to make sure I wasn't sick and in fact there was something seriously wrong with me. No longer scared more irritated than anything, I marched over to the counter and grabbed the two pack for the test. I went to the front of the store paid for my test and then I waited for the rest of them to finish their shopping. As I waited I figure I might as well take the test in the store. That way I could get rid of the evidence when it showed a false alarm. I pee'd on the stick and it said to wait two minutes for the results. But the positive sign came up right away and the more time that past the more determined the stick was to show me that my sickness was not the flu. I broke out in a sweat as I started cursing. I DON'T WANT TO HAVE MISTER PLAYER PLAYA'S BABY! I cried so hard in that stall, I don't want any part of Ahjanae's life. I'm not ready to be a momma and he already told me he wasn't ready to be a daddy. I took deep breaths to calm myself. Ahjanae called me and asked where I was. I told her I was in the bathroom, I was wandering around the store then I had to pee.

We took our sisters home and then as soon as we walked in the door Ahjanae told me to stop faking and to tell her what's wrong. I told her I was still upset about those girls and how this has been happening since that night. She watched my eyes and let me go on a whole tangent about how I keep cursing Darryl out about all these girls. I mean I knew he was fine, but I didn't know there were this many. She let me go on and on. Then she looked me in my eyes, "you're pregnant aren't you?" I bucked my eyes at her like how did she know. "I told you sex leads to pregnancy, you didn't want to believe me! What does Darryl say?"

"I don't want to tell him." I said lowly

"Why not?"

"He's already said he doesn't want a baby. And I don't want to have a baby right now. Why should I tell him?"

"Because he's gonna notice when your body starts changing."

"I'm not keeping it!"

"Kendra! Come on! Don't take the easy road out. Yeah sure you messed up, but don't do this. At least talk to Darryl about it."

"He already told me he didn't want a baby. I don't want to end up hating him like you hate Jabbar. I'm not strong enough to be you and Erin. I'm not having it."

"He'll come around once you tell him. He cares a lot about you. You won't be alone like I am."

"And you thought Jabbar was going to be by your side. He'll come around to probably living with his baby momma while he still messes with all these females. Where does he find the energy? Darryl and I are over, and this is over! I don't want to talk about it. I'm not telling anyone else so if it gets out it's because you told someone." I threatened.

Chapter 14

Nellie

He stood there about to drop to his knees. I exhaled and gave in by default. He picked me up and danced with me in his arms. I had a feeling like this would not end well, but this fool would not let it go. He was constantly on me. I even said you know who my ex is; you said you knew him and you don't care? He said it had to be a long time ago and he was fine with it. He didn't care about my past. All he knew is today he wanted to date me more than ever. I guess playing hard to get does work for the greater good. It's not that I'm not interested in Gordon, but I feel horrible about all that I've done to Kendra as it stands. I've tried to steer clear of him, but this fool won't leave well enough alone. He knows Ahjani is Kendra's cousin and he doesn't care. Oh well.

I told him to meet me at the school; I didn't want him getting any ideas by coming to my place. Gordon had the biggest smile on his face as soon as he saw me. The sun was going down so it was cooling off here in the desert. We went miniature golfing, the whole time I was looking for him to do something wrong. When girls walked by or came by singing hello to him, he was polite but his focus was on me. Marquez and Ahjani were the only guys to ever act like this before and I have to admit that I like it. I guess there's something to this good girl act. I had a nice time with Gordon, he was nice and sweet. I could only imagine that he was this sweet to Kendra. I wondered if this is how D is with her? I doubt he thought about me or even missed me. I tried to push him out of my mind cause there was no point. But my body screamed for him.

When I took Gordon home, he told me to come inside and meet his mother. My insides screamed, this was definitely new behavior and I felt unequipped. His momma was nice enough; she kept watching me for my reaction when she said stuff. I guess she didn't know her son was after me not the other way around. Gordon walked me to my car, while he thanked me for finally going out with him. He asked me to come to his next game, I agreed. When he started moving closer like he might try for a kiss. I told him goodnight and I got in my car and left.

Kendra

There are no words! I've been crying and crying nonstop since Wednesday. Tuesday night I thought I'd back out. But when I had Ahjanae drive me to the doctor everything went silent. Ahjanae kept trying to talk me out of it, but I couldn't do it. Every time Darryl calls me I go off on him! I yell at him, pick a fight! I want him to stop calling me. Ahjanae swears she didn't tell Ryder but he keeps looking at me like he knows. Or maybe it's just my guilty conscience, but I can't even deal with him right now. I stay in my room mostly with the door shut. Little Erin comes in cause she does not respect doors. She climbs up on my bed, and then she rubs my back and tells me my tummy aches. She tells me it's going to be ok. Then she sings some song I don't recognize. I cry some more because I feel like she's telling me I made a mistake without knowing what I'm going through. I told Ahjanae I don't want to see Darryl and to not let him in if he pops up.

My bleeding has calmed down a lot and the cramping is barely there. I'm hoping to forget about this whole thing and move on. I washed my hands and looked at my face briefly. The sight of my face made me cry again, and I didn't turn on the light so it's not like I was looking at my face completely. When I came out of the bathroom someone was sitting on my bed in the dark. If I would've had to pee it would've been all over me. I backed up to the bathroom and turned on the light. It was Darryl and his eyes were fixed on me and unbothered by the light suddenly coming on.

"GET OUT!" I said through clinched teeth cause it was the middle of the night and I didn't want to wake Erin. "I TOLD AHJANAE NOT TO LET YOU IN!"

"She didn't." He said watching me.

"Then how did you get in here? I have an alarm system."

"There's no lock that can keep me out. What's wrong with you?"

"You are what's wrong with me!"

"Me?"

"Yes you! I knew you saw other people, but so many? We go out to the club ONE NIGHT! And now everywhere I go females wanna fight me, everyone seems to think they have some kind of claim on you! I had no idea you were such a hoe! I don't want that in my life."

"What's wrong Kendra?" He said watching my eyes.

"I just told you!"

He cocked his head to the side. "You're scared!"

"I didn't know you were such a hoe. I took an Aids test. But they said to come back in six months to be sure. You might not care about your health but I care about mine!"

"That's what you're worried about?" He said patting the bed next to him for me to sit down. I refused and stayed by the bathroom. He exhaled, "I'm clean. I get tested regularly, and until you, I've never had unprotected sex. I told you that."

"Still!"

"Still? Still? Still what? You want to break up with me because I had to kill time waiting for you to get your head out of the star's butt some kind of way? You're not making any sense!"

"As long as I make sense to me that's all that matters. Get out!"

"Kendra you're trying to hide something from me. I can see it all over you. Tell me now, don't make me investigate." His eyes turned evil.

"Investigate? You can investigate all you want! I don't want to be with a hoe!"

"Why because you're running for saint now. I may be the only other person you've been with, but the star doesn't know that. He stills thinks he was your first and only. I know every move you've made up until a point. But now you're making me regret closing my eyes. I know you're not crazy enough to cheat on me. So you can either tell me or I will find out on my own."

"How do you know what he thinks?"

"All you need to know is I've got eyes and ears everywhere. Kendra I'm warning you, you're breaking my heart. Tell me what's going on and then stop this! I've never been like this with anyone, don't make me regret it."

"I guess we're even. Because I already regret loving you! Get out!"

When Darryl stood up he seemed even taller. He kept flexing his hands and unflexing them. "This is what I get? I've loved you since we were kids. I moved slowly with you, turned a blind eye when you've hurt me the most, and this is the thanks I get? This is what happens when I put myself on the line? Then you wonder why I don't want to get married? This is what you get when you care about someone! All those girls were before you and I were ever official, but that doesn't matter to you. All you wanna do is be mad about my past like you have a right to judge me. I hope for your sake whatever I find doesn't make me come back here!

Something's wrong with you, and you're trying to cover it up. I
didn't shoot Tupac, so I don't understand why it has to be all this!"
He said with a straight face.

That was a tester joke; if I laughed or let the joke register he
wouldn't leave. I rolled my eyes, "get out Darryl!"

He scanned me up and down. He started towards the door and I
exhaled and a few tears fell. He looked back at me, when he saw
my tears. He rushed back to me and wrapped his arms around me.
"NO! You love me! This is nonsense! I don't care Kendra! I don't
care about any of it, don't do this to me! I've been good since we've
been together. Don't hurt me like this! It's not all for nothing!"

I let my tears fall, "this is too much Darryl! It's too much!"

"You want to kill them? I'll do it! They don't matter!"

"No," I said in defeat. He was almost out the door.

Nellie

"Leasha, I like you and I want us to be exclusive!"

"Gordon are you sure? You could have anyone else." I said feeling
a little uneasy.

"I'm sure! I want you!" Then he kissed me.

I liked kissing him. "I can't!" I heard myself say.

Gordon looked mad, "why because of the Mexican?"

"Marquez is not Mexican. Not that it matters. But he is very
special to me and I can't give him up."

"You're special to me, doesn't that count for something?"

"Gordon you are very sweet. I thank you for even noticing me. But
I can't give him up. I understand if you don't want to hang out any
more." I wasn't giving Marquez up for anyone.

Gordon was quiet for a minute, and then he pulled me in close.

"How about an agreement? We won't discuss him; I don't want to
see him. You can have him ONLY! And when I travel for games
you don't worry about what happens while I'm out?"

I smiled, "deal!" He was gonna be hooking up whether I agreed to
it or not.

"You are the coolest girlfriend EVER!" He shouted then he kissed
me. "Do I finally get to spend the night at your place?"

"Oh I see! You just want to get in my draws." I teased

"I'm dying to live in your space!" He smiled.

I exhaled even though the situation is different I still feel bad.
"Let's go." As we drove to my place I kept thinking of Kendra.
"Gordon, tell me something. Is there anyone special back home?"
"My momma?"
"Not your apartment Doo-Doo head! Back in The Bay."
I could see the thought of her spread over his face just like it used
to over D. Then he snapped out of it. "Um, well. Um!"
"Gordon, we can talk about this kind of stuff. We won't be that
couple keeping secrets from each other."
He exhaled and looked at me. "I think I love you more now!"
"Love me? You don't even know me."
"This right here has put you on top of the list." He exhaled, "there
was this girl. We were high school sweethearts."
"What happened to her? Why did you break up?"
"The best I can understand is she didn't want to go to school.
Whenever I'd talk about making it into the NBA, she wanted to
know what my backup plan was, like she didn't believe I could
make it."
"Sounds like she wanted to make sure you were covered."
"I guess, after my first year I saw a few people lose their dream. I
have a backup now, but I don't know if I see her as the woman on
my arm anymore."
"Oh?"
"Leasha, you're smart, beautiful, and sexy. You've changed the
way I see my life going."
"But what about her?"
"She wouldn't even come out to see me. We're over!"
"Don't be so sure. You can say that cause she's not here and well,
you're with me." I smiled. "But when you see her again, your heart
might lead you to feel another way."
He looked at me with his mouth open shaking his head. "I SWEAR
TO GOD YOU ARE THE COOLEST GIRLFRIEND EVER!"
Then he stuck his hand down my shirt, and kissed on my neck
while I drove.

Kendra
Darryl is being weird, sometimes I'll be knocked out and then he's
getting in my bed. Ahjanae says it's creepy when he's suddenly in
the house and no one let him in. He hasn't asked and I haven't
offered sex, but he's getting darker and darker in his mood. A

couple months ago he came over when he should've been in class. He said his brother had a baby the night before; he laughed a crazy laugh when he said he was an uncle. He's gone on more than a couple rants about how much he hates his brother's baby momma. He always says she's the devil.

Then a month later he brought his brother and the baby over. I cried as soon as I held him. Darryl and Drew held the same expression as they watched me. Ahjanae told me to get a grip. Ryder sat over to the side not saying a word.

I came home from a job and Ahjanae was at school. Ryder was in his last year of school and he was coming from class. "You notice how nobody laughs anymore? Remember how we used to laugh all the time?" Ryder asked

"Yep, I think too many people are hiding." I said

"I agree!" He said watching me.

"Why won't you tell my cousin you're in love with her? You're here every day, she won't assume you're here for her. She thinks you're here for Erin only."

"Why won't you tell my cousin you killed his baby? He thinks he did something wrong."

I Gasped! "Who told you that?"

"Nobody, I'm here every day. I told you I'm on the sidelines watching everything."

"He didn't want a baby with me anyways." I said in my defense.

"I'm not gonna sugar coat it. He's going to be devastated. He doesn't want a family right now... with them! You were the exception. And even if you guys would've come to the same conclusion together at least it would've been together. You underestimate how much he loves you! But he needs to know! I don't know if you guys can get past it. But clear the air so you can heal. One minute you're fine, the next minute you're going off. It's not right Kendra. I miss my cousin who was fun and silly."

"He hasn't been too silly or fun lately has he?"

"I was talking about you."

"Ok but what about you? I'll come clean after you do."

"Do you think she'll go for me?"

"Ryder you are the man in her life. She's going to say no at first because she's scared and she's been hurt before. Remain persistent, if she didn't care about you, you wouldn't be around her daughter."

"I keep waiting for the baby daddy to come back."

"Not gonna happen. He broke her heart and she doesn't pass out a lot of opportunities to hurt her like that. So with that, if you aren't ready you wait." I said

He smiled, "you want me to stall so you can."

"PLEASE RYDER! I'M SCARED!"

"I'm not gonna lie and say it's gonna be ok, cause I don't know. But you gotta tell him." I rolled my eyes at him. "You do, do that just like Amber." He laughed.

"Ryder can you do me a favor?"

"What's up?"

"Can you ask, no beg your momma to send over a cake?"

Ryder smiled, "good idea!"

Nellie

I looked at the clock! Crap! I'm late! I was lost in the world of studying, time flew by. Gordon was going to be upset if I missed another game. I took the fastest shower I think I've ever taken and I hurried out the door. When I got to the game I tried to blend in and look like I had been here the whole time. The way Gordon looked at me let me know he knew I was late. I tried to get my bearings when I saw a familiar form run by. I knew that method of playing. Swish! Ahjani was dominating this game. I felt like I wanted to run away! I should've missed it! I shot Gordon pleading eyes, but he was focused on trying to turn this game around. It seemed like everyone on the court disappeared and it was only Gordon and Lubbock on the court. This was bad and I wanted to run away. I haven't seen Ahjani since we were kids, but he could still be hurt behind it. Then I remembered how long Ahjani would last. I wondered if he was still like that. The only complaint that I had with him is that he wasn't D. Ahjani's team won and I moved right away. Gordon was upset about the loss so he was going to be in a mood. He motioned for me to meet him out front. I saw Ahjani's team load up on their bus to go back to their hotel. I relaxed as I waited for Gordon. When he came out he looked at me, he looked mad. He told me I better stay on the Dean's list with all the studying I do, and then he kissed me.

"Omar I told you, you could never beat...." Ahjani was coming over, rubbing in his victory until he noticed he already lost.

"NELLIE?"

I was embarrassed, "hi."

He stumbled backwards, "Nellie! You disappeared! I...."
"I know, I'm sorry. There was a lot going on back then."
Gordon put his arm around me with a big smile. "How do you know my girlfriend?"
Ahjani bucked his eyes, "girlfriend? This is wrong on so many levels!"
"Wrong?" Gordon said
"Nellie is my ex."
"Puppy love though. You weren't serious about anyone until Olivia." Gordon said like he knew what he was talking about.
I shook my head no, "I was serious about her. She disappeared. Where did you go?" Ahjani asked me.
"My father made me come to his office after school. They kept me so busy, I couldn't hurt you like that." I said looking at the ground.
"You guys were together together?" Gordon asked looking like he was uneasy.
"Yes!" We said unison.
"You knew Kendra?"
"Kendra was her best friend, that's how we met." Ahjani said not taking his eyes off me.
"Son of a! You've got to be kidding me!" Gordon threw a fit.
"How did you two end up together?" Ahjani asked.
"I went after her, I wore her down. I wouldn't take no for an answer." Gordon sounded like he was going to be sick. "What have I done?"
Ahjani and I stood there staring at each other. I never thought I would see him again. He was the first guy to show me intimate kindness. I wanted him! I wanted him right now. "You missed your bus, you need a ride?"
Ahjani looked at me like he could read my mind. "Yes." Then he looked at Gordon. "This is what you get for trying to be a show off!" Then he laughed.
I moved my backpack to the back seat of my car and then Ahjani climbed in. Gordon couldn't get comfortable in the front seat. He was extremely huffy.
Ahjani thanked me for the ride then he asked me if I wanted my notebook to stay on the seat. When I put my backpack back there it was in my bag. I told him on the seat was fine. Gordon kept asking me question after question about Ahjani. I answered each question honestly. Gordon got out of the car slamming the door. I couldn't

feel bad for him. He was trying to show off and it blew up in his face. Then the explosion, Ahjani wrote his room number in my notebook. Even though I wasn't worried about Gordon popping up since he didn't have a car, I still parked in the back of the hotel out of sight from everyone. When I knocked on Ahjani's door my heart kept fluttering. He snatched open the door and pulled me in. He gave me the biggest kiss and all I could remember was how much Ahjani loved me. I melted in his arms. No words were spoken; everything with him was just as I remembered. We tore up that room. I asked him if Olivia was his current girlfriend and he said yes. I expected that to be the case. I asked him if he was still going to be a dentist, and he said that was his backup plan. He said so far he's proving to be really good at the game. Then he shrugged, and started kissing me. He said he couldn't believe he was touching me again. He told me he still loved me and he thanked me for coming. I told him I still loved him too. Then I told him about Marquez. He said Marquez sounds like a better fit for me than Omar. He said Omar was going to end up crashing and burning if he didn't get it together.

****

"WHERE HAVE YOU BEEN?" Gordon yelled into my phone.
"Sleep! I forgot to turn my ringer on. What's wrong?" I said completely groggy.
"Seems like you keep doing that a lot lately!" Gordon barked
I rolled my eyes; ever since Ahjani's visit Gordon has become this insecure ball of emotions. If he can't get in touch with me when he feels he needs to be able to reach me he freaks out. "I'm sleepy! What do you need?"
"I'm coming over, don't go anywhere!"
"I'm staying in the bed." I said rolling over. When he got to my house, I opened the door and then I got back in the bed. He undressed and got in the bed, then he started rubbing on me. "I'm sleep! Stop!"
"Oh so you see Ahjani and all of a sudden I'm not good enough?"
I could smell weed on his breath, "are you high?" I asked looking back at his face.
He smiled, "a little bit."
"I told you I don't like that, you can't come over here like that!" I said feeling panic spread all over my body as flashbacks started

205

entering my mind. I shook my head trying not to remember them, not to think of them. But this situation felt too familiar.

"Oh my bad I forgot, and I'm here now." He said rubbing all over my body. I only had my nightshirt on, and he was already starting to strong-arm me.

"No! Gordon, please stop!" I pleaded, but he wasn't listening to me. He already had his condom on and he was forcing me on my stomach so he could enter me. I buried my face in my pillow as I screamed and cried. He was in his own world not paying me any attention, suddenly I was in middle school and terrified cause I didn't understand what was happening to me. I told myself to go numb and relax and it wouldn't hurt as much. I was grateful that Gordon wasn't as big as Bobby otherwise this would hurt as much physically as it does mentally. When he finished he collapsed on top of me. He started kissing on me, and acting like he missed that this was not a shared experience. He was like Bobby! He rolled over like he just did something great, and I kept my back to him as I cried. He patted my leg then he went to the bathroom to flush the condom. I kept opening and closing my eyes. I'm at my apartment; I'm not at Bobby's place. That's my boyfriend Gordon, that's not Bobby. Gordon doesn't know what he just did. He missed that I wasn't into it. When he got back in the bed he cuddled up next to me and spooned me. Then he fell asleep.

****

"I'm gonna miss you. You sure you have to go home for the whole summer?" Gordon asked looking sad.

"Yes," I said quietly.

"Leasha what's wrong? You've been acting funny for the past few months. I don't like you going home with us feeling so off and disconnected."

I kept my eyes on the ceiling, "I told you I don't like when you smoke."

"HERE WE GO! I told you I need to smoke to relax! You have no idea how much pressure is on me out there on the court. Smoking helps me relax."

"Then don't come around me when you're like that. I don't like it."

"When would I see you then?" He smiled, I didn't. "I don't want to spend our last night together arguing about this. If I gotta accept you creeping around on me, you can accept my smoking."

"I wasn't creeping around on you, we were just talking." I said. T-Bone was trying to get at me, but I wasn't going for it. By Gordon's reaction you would've thought he walked up on us having sex. That was the first time he grabbed me in front of people. Normally when he's high in addition to using my body any way he feels like it, he always grabs me or pushes me. I guess because he doesn't technically hit me he feels like he's not doing anything wrong. He may not know for sure, but I know what happened with Ahjani. I guess he can feel that something happened so all of this has happened. I don't want to come back here next year, but my parents already renewed my lease without asking me first. I guess they figured everything is going well so why mess up a good thing. I am so happy to get away for the summer. I'm hoping to have a nice and peaceful summer away from all of this noise and drama. Maybe Gordon will meet someone over the summer and dump me. I'm hoping cause I don't want to come back here.

"T-Bone looked too comfortable in my woman's face." He sat up, "when I go pro, you wanna have a baby?"

"I never saw myself as the mothering type."

He frowned, "who wouldn't want to have my baby?"

"Obviously there's a lot you don't know about me."

"Like what? You can't have babies?"

"I guess," I said in a defeated voice.

"I can't marry you if you can't have babies. I gotta have kids and pass on my legacy. Boy or girl they can grow up and play professionally. The Gordon's will dominate the courts."

"What if your child doesn't like basketball or can't play?"

"Then they couldn't possibly be my child. My kids will dominate just like their father."

"So why wait, break up with me now."

Anger flashed across his face, "You can't wait to go lay up under the Mexican, huh? You gonna run home and try to forget about me?"

"No," I said plainly listening to him pumping himself up. "Make love to me!"

"Gordon, I'm not feeling well." I said even though I knew that wouldn't save me.

"What's wrong with you? You can't be pregnant so what else could be wrong with you?"

"I'm tired and I feel sad."

"Making love to me will fix that." He said pulling me on top of him.

"No," I said shaking my head. "It won't."

"Yes it will." He said rolling us over.

"I don't want to, I don't feel like it." I said without fighting him.

"I'll get you there," then he went under the covers. His tongue felt like sand paper, it did nothing for me. But he drooled all over me so much that he mistook his saliva for my excitement. He climbed on top of me and started working me, I was still somewhat dry but he didn't act like he noticed. If I close my eyes and imagine I'm somewhere else, this will be another memory that will barely exist in my mind.

Kendra

"It smells delicious in here!" Darryl said coming in the door.

I gave him a nervous smile. "We're having tacos, I hope you like it."

He smiled real big, "I love tacos!" He exclaimed

I smiled, "I know." Then I went back to my shells.

He walked in the kitchen and put his arms around me. "KB! Look at you getting all domesticated for me." He kissed my neck. "We've been off haven't we?" I shook my head, "we can fix it though."

"Darryl, can we talk about it tonight? I don't want to do it right now though."

"What's wrong with now?"

"Everybody can come in and out at any point. Ryder will be here any minute. I don't want to start and then stop." Darryl said ok, but I knew he was reading me.

When Ryder and Erin walked in the door, they both were smiling really big. Ryder had a big bouquet of flowers and he was dressed really nice. Darryl immediately started teasing him. I guess he could tell that today was the day that he was going to go for it. He looked nervous but excited; Ahjanae came in the door a few minutes later. She asked Erin how the movie was, I saw her notice Ryder's clothes but she didn't say anything. Ryder opened the wine he brought for dinner. Darryl kept smiling at Ryder and telling him he was proud of him. Ryder told him to shut up as he turned on music. When we sat down to dinner Ryder lit candles and then dimmed the lights. He explained that the candles were hot to Erin and that she shouldn't touch them. "Ryder? I mean I know I'm sexy and all, but you aren't my type." Darryl said smiling at him from across the table.

"I love this little girl, even though I didn't know you when you were pregnant she feels like she's my child. There isn't anything I wouldn't do for her," Ahjanae smiled as she listened. This isn't his first time saying something like this so, it wasn't odd or out of place. "I love her so much, she's a great kid!" Ryder said

"She loves you very much as well, don't you baby?" Ahjanae said to Erin who blushed.

"What about you? Do you love me?"

"Of course! You're my best friend!" She said as she realized what she had been set up for. She looked at Darryl and I as we smiled really big back at her. "What's going on?"

Ryder looked embarrassed and like he was going to back out. "Jen, I…" He blew air! "I don't want to be just your friend anymore." Ahjanae gasped and then she covered her mouth, "I love you, but more than just a friend."

"Ryder! Why are you doing this in front of everybody?"

"Jen don't worry. We're not everybody, and we would know about it later anyways." Darryl smiled, "this way is more direct. Carry on…"

"Can I talk to you in the other room?" Ahjanae said getting up and going to her room.

Ryder looked nervous then he followed her then they shut the door. Darryl and I looked at Erin, "what they doing in there?" Darryl asked Erin, she smiled and covered her mouth.

They were in there for a long time, we could hear their voices but we couldn't hear what they were saying. Then Ryder came out of the room he had no expression on his face. He walked right out the door. He came back in the door with two containers. He set one in the middle of the table and then he got forks and took Erin with him back into Ahjanae's room. Darryl's face lit up for half a second then he eyed me. "What's up?"

My heart dropped, "I asked Ryder to ask his momma for a cake for you."

Darryl smiled, "sounds suspicious KB! A Mexican feast and then my favorite. You pregnant or something?" Then he laughed, and I didn't. He looked me in my eyes, "what is it?"

Tears immediately fell out of my eyes. "I messed up!" My sudden tears alarmed him but he didn't say anything. It was like he was frozen as he waited for me to explain. I started talking fast, "remember when we forgot the condoms and I messed up on my birth control?" He nodded his head while watching me. "We both said we didn't want a baby, so I took care of it." Darryl rolled his eyes real slow like he was chewing his initial reaction. "I thought we were gonna be over anyways, so I figured there was no point in discussing it."

His eyes were red; "it's your body so it's your choice right?"

"You said you didn't want a baby." I said wiping my tears.

"I dont, but you didn't even try to talk to me like a person who may have some kind of feeling invested in this! I'm not ready to be anybody's parent, but I would've stepped up for us. You should've told me." His voice was real calm and angry. "So what happened, why did you tell me?"

"My guilty conscience."

"I knew it was something, yes you were mad about the females but now it all makes sense. I think I've bent over backwards not to be treated like some guy with you. I love you despite your daddy and trust issues. You've got a big heart and you're always looking out for other people, I guess I'm not other people cause you weren't looking out for me."

"I was looking out for you. Do you know how much money it takes to raise a baby? We'd both have to drop out of school just to make it work. Then what? We become roommates so that our child would have both parents? I don't want that struggle for either of us."

"Kendra!" His eyes were angry, "money is a cop out. I've got money! I've got so many millions that I could never work and that would be fine. This isn't about money, you were thinking about yourself. Your whole fantasy of marriage and a family. I say I'm never getting married, just like I say I don't want kids. What a man says and what a man does depends on the woman in front of him." He exhaled, "you hurt me Kendra! I thought no matter what I'd be safe with you. I thought you'd protect me like you do for everybody else. I guess I was wrong."

"Where are you going? I'm sorry!"

"I need to go be around my family for a while. Take in some chicken heads because at least with them I know they're only out to serve their best interest."

"But!" I stood up and threw my arms around him like he did me. "I'm sorry please don't go! I love you! I'll always protect you. I messed up! Please don't go!"

He stood there letting me hug him, "I gotta go. I'm angry!" He said calmly.

"Ok, but don't leave, stay. Let's talk it out."

"No, I gotta leave. I could really hurt you right now. David's blood is alive and well in me right now. Kendra let me go!"

"What does that mean?" I said letting him go.

"It means I have to leave." Then he walked out the door.

Chapter 15

Nellie

I felt like I was on a covert mission. I parked in the garage and walked inside the airport. When I saw Marquez walk off the ramp my heart fluttered and I was excited. Marquez flew out here to drive home with me. I told Gordon that I left two days ago. I parked my car in my garage and quietly laid low waiting for Marquez to come and save me.

The thought of Marquez coming was my only happy thought. I felt like I was going to slip into that dark place if I couldn't hold on to the fact that he was coming. Marquez gave me a huge hug and kiss; he told me I was a sight for sore eyes. I told him there were no words to describe how happy I was to see him. We got food and then we went to my place. He was telling me about school, we even talked about the girl he was dating out there. He showed me a picture and she was cute, I look better of course. But I could see the attraction.

When we got in the bed his hands started roaming, my heart started pounding. I held his hands and asked him to be patient with me. He looked at me for a long time. Like he was taking in everything that I wasn't saying. He held me all night, in the morning when I woke up he was knocked out and his hair was loose and wild. It smelled great and I asked myself how I ever became friends with such a person. Marquez is too good for me; he's smart, sweet, kind, and patient. I don't deserve to have anyone like him in my life. Kendra was like him, and well... I know what I did to her. Dealing with Gordon is payback for what I've done to her. I don't deserve to have Marquez in my life at all. I was trying to be quiet as I laid there crying, but Marquez opened his eyes and looked at me. Before he could ask me what was wrong I kissed him. I kept kissing him, and then I gave him everything I had to give. Every time he looked like he was going to ask me what was wrong I was all over him again. We got on the road four hours later than we planned because I was all over him.

Of course Marquez asked me what was wrong once we were out on the road. I told him I was dealing with a lot of reality and it was system overload. I told him that I would be completely crazy right now if it wasn't for him. He smiled and soaked up all my words of appreciation for him. He told me to get his sketchpad out of his bag while he drove. He said in his spare time he made a little cartoon featuring me. I couldn't believe it. The first one was of me walking away from darkness, my face was always sad. A lot of the pictures would have darkness surrounding me constantly. I laughed when he drew light around him in his first picture. He was surrounded by bright light and I was running away from it cause I was used to the darkness. I laughed then I cried, his pictures were so accurate it was scary. Marquez didn't say anything he let me work through everything and process how I was feeling.

I asked him what his plan was for this summer, and he said following me around. That made me smile; I told him Nassya was leaving a couple of days after we got there for six weeks to her camp. Then when she came back she'd be glued to my hip. He said that was fine and he would glue himself to the other hip. I liked the idea of him wanting to be around me all that much. He asked me if Nassya would appreciate all the hair he grew for her to play with? I told him I loved it even if she didn't. His hair was now longer than mine. That Arizona heat made my hair so dry, it seemed like I was trimming split ends more rapidly. So my hair seemed like it stayed the same length. Being with Marquez was so refreshing I could feel the cloud lift and my soul felt renewed. We had so much fun driving and stopping along the way. Marquez noticed my mood change, he smiled at me and then he kept talking. Nassya screamed with excitement when we walked in the door. Even though she saw me a month ago she did not hold back her excitement about seeing me. She hadn't seen Marquez since last summer so she was excited to see him as well. She talked our ears off, and when it was time to take Marquez home, she grabbed her purse because she automatically knew she was coming. She was too cute and growing up so fast.

That night she got in my bed like she has done since I came home from the hospital. She talked until she fell asleep. I inhaled deeply and slowly let it out. I was home, where I was loved, and where I was appreciated.

****

I know I shouldn't have. But my curiosity wouldn't let it go. So I took a deep breath and I dialed the number, on the third ring I thought it was going to voicemail. "Hello?" He answered.
"D?"

"Who dis?"

"Nellie," when he didn't respond right away. "Noel... Nellie."

"Oh yea, what's up?" He said recognizing me.

"Listen, I wanna apologize for the way I acted the last time we spoke. I was out of line, I was too desperate to see you."

"What happened?"

"You don't remember?"

I could hear the smile in his voice, "no I remember. I'm asking what happened, why would you think it was ever ok to go there with me?"

"I don't know, I was desperate. I don't understand it all still to this day."

"The lines got blurred there for a little bit huh." He said like he understood.

"I guess, I'm always coming from a place of love for you."

"Noel, you don't love me. You can't have me, so that makes you want me more. I told you from the beginning that I liked and wanted Kendra. No matter how good the sex is, you don't win a man's heart like you were trying with me. You gotta learn to love yourself, you're so lost." Then his voice smiled, "how's my man Marquez?"

"He's good, he drove home with me last week."

"I wanna see my man. What's his number?"

I could feel my bratty ways coming forward, "you don't want to see me?"

"Can't trust you, you're all sentimental sounding. You're probably thinking that this conversation shows love on my part. When I'm just a friendly and outgoing person."

"Doesn't change how I feel about you."

"Noel, I'm trying to take you off the chicken head list, but it's like you fight to stay there. I'm going to do you a favor and explain this one time to you. No matter what you say or do, I will never see you as a girlfriend or anything more than that. I could spend time with you. Drop a couple dollars on you, chump change. But all the love you're looking for comes from my man Marquez. He loves you like, like shoot! I don't even understand his love for you. What man knows you're sleeping with someone who doesn't love you, and still wants to give you his heart? I'd never deal with the stuff he deals with, with you." Then his voice trailed off, "I don't wanna deal with the stuff I deal with."

"How's Kendra?" It pained me to ask.

"I don't know." He said letting attitude, anger, and hurt enter his voice.

"What happened?"

"When have I ever sat back and discussed Kendra with you?"

"You sound upset."

"I am!"

"You sound like you need to talk about it."

"I'm a popular guy! The ladies love D! Some of them are aggressive, ok. She don't want me to kill the ones who were stupid enough to step to her so then what? I don't know why other females acting dumb equal her shutting me out. Females are a TRIP!" He said with the angry tone he had the last time we spoke.

"She probably doesn't know that you hold her to a higher standard than everyone else. She probably doesn't want to feel like other people have had with you what she thinks is reserved for her."

"But I don't give you guys what I give her."

It hurt that I was lumped in the group. "But does she know that?"

"Other people have explained that to her, but she don't get it."

"Have you explained it?"

He was quiet for a minute, "kind of." Then I heard movement, "I'm on the ground! I've fallen and I can't get up! She hurt me! She hurt me bad! I never thought she would or could hurt me like this."

I knew it was useless to ask what she did; there was no way he was going to tell me what happened. "When you love someone they're going to hurt you. I love you, and it hurts me that you will never love me back."

"But don't...."

I cut him off, "and it hurts that every time I tell you that I love you, you try to down grade what I feel. Let me have my feelings, you don't feel the same. Fine, but don't try to tell me how I feel." I said standing up for myself.

His smile was back, "you're just trying to get in my pants. Nope! I'm not falling for it." He said laughing.

"Oh come on! We never had goodbye sex! It's only fair, one last time. PLEASE! Then I'll try not to ask any more."

He smiled, "you'll try? Meaning you're still going to be craving my sexiness until the end of time?"

"Forever more!"

"Noel, you're sweet. I appreciate this conversation and all, but…"

"DON'T SAY BUT! PLEASE D! You can't honestly expect me to go cold turkey."

He exhaled, "I know it has to be tough. I mean I'm me, and you're you. You want me, and I'm telling you no. Probably makes you want me more. But…."

I started crying, "Please D! You have no idea what I've been through. I'm begging you."

"UGH! I like that! Begging is good! This is the last time Noel aka Nellie!"

I smiled through my tears, "really?"

"You have to come now, I'm at my brother's place in Albany."

"I'M ON MY WAY!"

Kendra

I keep calling Darryl and he won't answer my calls. I've even driven to his momma's house and sat outside hoping to catch him coming or going. D-Rick has appeared at my car window out of thin air so many times that it doesn't even scare me anymore. A couple of times he's invited me inside with him and Drew. I'd hold the baby and hang out, but no Darryl.

Desperate I asked Ryder what I should do. He told me to let Darryl work it out, but he couldn't tell me if Darryl would ever forgive me. Ahjanae let me cry on her shoulder and she never said I told you so. I beat her to the punch, I told her I should've listened to her. The worst part is thinking that I moved too fast and I could've kept my baby. I didn't have to go through all that pain. Seeing Ryder and Ahjanae kiss is a bit of system overload, so I try to spend my down time from school and work with my family.

Kaleah and I sit in silence a lot. One day she looked at me for a long time like she was trying to understand me. Then she said Darryl would be back I just needed to be patient. I didn't tell her he was gone so of course her comment made me cry some more.

Kalani came in the room and said she had enough of me moping around.

The three of us went to the movies and out to dinner in Richmond. We decided to eat at the restaurant next to the theater. The girls said they were missing Richmond. Kalani and I went over our summer schedule. Since Kaleah basically tapped out the year before, she and Kalani were now set to graduate together. So they were planning a lot of their Senior activities together. Kaleah said she was doing good to graduate from high school she hadn't thought much beyond it. Then she said that she and Milton broke up, he's got a baby on the way, yadda, yadda, yadda. My stomach knotted up when she said he was having a baby, but I talked through it. I asked her if she was ok. She said she's trying to be. We were talking and laughing when a couple walked past us. I don't know why the back of their heads caught my attention but they did. The woman had labels on head to toe. It's sad when people my momma's age feel the need to walk around like that in my opinion. I watched them walk across the restaurant and disappear in their booth. We went back to our conversation and then Kaleah called out to Aunrey. I hadn't seen him since last summer when we had that house party at my house. Ahjanae said Aunt Quilla said he doesn't come home too often. Since Audra is going away to college this Fall, Aunt Quilla said she's going to give up her house that she's been renting for years and get a smaller place. Aunrey gave us all hugs and asked what we were up to. We said we were hanging out and we invited him to join us. He said he had some business to tend to and if we were still here when he was done he'd come hang out with us. Then we watched him disappear into the same booth as the label couple.

We were running our mouths so much that it was taking a while to get through our meal but we were having a good time. Aunrey slid into our booth with a big smile. Then the label couple walked towards us to leave. The guy was walking in front and he looked big and mean, not friendly at all. When he passed I noticed her right as she saw me. "Kendra?"

"Ms. Mary?" I got up and gave her a hug. The scary guy stopped walking and came back to us. Kalani and Kaleah got up to hug her as well.

"How's Nellie doing?" Kaleah asked

"She's good, she graduated with honors you know?" She bragged, then she darted her eyes at the scary guy who looked like he was hearing this information for the first time.

"Wait a minute! You talking about the Nellie Ahjani used to go with?" Aunrey asked

"Yep," Kalani said

"Who is that?" The scary man asked.

"My brother," Aunrey said eyeing the guy like he didn't like his tone.

"You knew about this?" He asked the woman.

She put her hands out. "I didn't know he knew Nellie, of course I didn't."

"How is Nellie?" I asked

Ms. Mary looked uncomfortable, "my momma said she's in school and doing well."

"What school is she in?" The guy asked.

"I don't know." She said looking sad.

"What's it to you?" Aunrey asked the guy.

He shot crazy eyes at Aunrey, "not that it's any of your business. But I love that little girl, and I know my little girl misses me." Something about him didn't sit right with me. When I looked at everybody at the table, it looked like we were all on the same page.

"Alright then, you can go now." Aunrey said dismissing them.

"I take it you don't talk to Nellie anymore?" Ms. Mary asked with sad eyes.

"No, I called and called after she got out of the hospital, but she doesn't want to talk to me. I don't know why."

Both of their faces froze, "why was she in the hospital?"

Why did I say that? Everybody was looking at me, waiting for me to respond. I took a deep breath. "She tried to kill herself."

"WHAT?" Everybody said at once. People in the restaurant looked in our direction. "I tried to call her for a while after that but she wouldn't take my calls."

"When was this?" Ms. Mary asked.

"A few years ago. I did see her from a distance later that year and she looked like she was doing better."

Ms. Mary looked at the scary guy with tears in her eyes. "You don't talk to her now?" The scary guy asked.

"She already said she doesn't." Aunrey said annoyed.

He looked at Aunrey then back at me, "can you tell her to call me when you do hear from her?" He said handing me a card.

"Nope! No! My cousin isn't calling you for nothing. I'll think about calling you, but this whole thing don't sit well with me." Aunrey said giving crazy eyes back.

"You'll think about calling me?" He said, "I'll cancel your whole distribution if you don't bring her to me. How about that?"

"Nigga you ain't the only supplier in The Bay! What fool ruins business over a female? You wanna be petty, fine by me. See who moves your supply without me. I don't need you, you need me." Aunrey said relaxing in his seat.

"You're not the only mover in Richmond." He said

Aunrey sat back in his seat, "no I'm not. However, my distribution is bigger and heavier. My guys aren't getting locked up every five seconds. You know what, I don't have to explain why you came to me. You know why. If you feel this is worth ruining our deal for be my guest. No sweat off my back, I have other options."

"Little boy I will squash you!"

"You could try, but without me you sit like a sitting duck holding, waiting for someone to pick you off. My team doesn't move without me!" Then he leaned forward, "and so that we're clear. My entire family and me are off limits. If anyone close to me even breaks a finger nail it sucks to be you!"

The scary man stood there brewing, Ms. Mary looked sad and a little scared. "Bring Nellie to me!"

"Go get her yourself! I don't play fetch for nobody." Aunrey said.

"Do you know where she is?"

"No, and I don't care."

"What about you?" He asked the rest of us. We shook our heads no. "When you see her let your cousin know and I will take it from there." Then he turned and walked away. Ms. Mary hesitated then she followed him out.

"He's scary!" Kaleah said.

"Makes me appreciate Jason so much more." Kalani said.

Aunrey was quiet, "Jason is a good guy. I need to come see him, after everything he's done for me." He said looking at his hands.

"What did he do for you?" Kalani asked.

Aunrey shifted in his chair. "We'll talk about it another time." Aunrey drummed his fingers on the table. "How's my niece?"

"She's getting big, you've gotta come see her." I said handing him my phone with a picture of Erin on the front.

"Whoa. She's growing up fast. Jabbar still bringing money?" His face was serious.

"Yes, he's gotten a better job so he brings more every paycheck. He's having a hard time dealing with Ryder though."

"After all this time he's still acting funny about that?"

"They're together now." I said watching Aunrey.

Aunrey frowned like something tasted nasty. "My sister let the white boy in?"

"He is white isn't he? I keep forgetting. He seems like any other light skinned guy to me." Kalani said.

"He's D's cousin so I guess that's cool. But you'll let me know if anything goes wrong won't you!"

"After the time he spent patiently waiting on Ahjanae to give him a chance. The only person I see messing that up is her."

"Still, people get bold when they think no one is watching."

A woman ran in the lobby, "SOMEONE PLEASE CALL 911 THERE'S A WOMAN BEING BEATEN!" She screamed.

I looked at Aunrey and he shook his head. People were running to the windows and out the door. I could hear the scary guy's voice. Kalani and Kaleah ran to the door. Then they came back, they said Ms. Mary and the guy got in his car and drove away. They said his car was black with black tinted windows, and the dealer plate was still on the car. They said he burned rubber when he left.

Nellie

"Marquez for two?" The hostess called out.

We followed her to our table and then we sat. Marquez and I noticed the cutest little girl who was being a little kid and moving around in her seat looking at everyone in the restaurant. She waved hello at us, then her father told her to sit down. He turned around to see who she was waving at, his face lit up with recognition when he saw me. He waved and I waved back, but I was trying to remember where I knew him. Then it came back to me. "He used to go with that girl I was friends with cousin. I can't remember his name though." The guy must've been telling the girl he was with the same story cause she was looking at us.

When the girl took their baby to the bathroom he came over to our table. "Hey Nellie how you doing?"

I felt bad that he remembered my name, but I couldn't remember his. "Hello I'm good, this is Marquez."

"How you doing, I'm Jabbar." He said shaking Marquez's hand. "I haven't seen you in forever, where did you go?"

"Long story. So I see you've got a little girl. She's cute." I said changing the subject.

He smiled proudly, "thanks. That's my heart. Her momma's supposed to be meeting us here." Then he looked up, "speaking of the devil."

She walked up to him, it was Ahjanae. "We're going to have breakfast here. So just bring her to our table before you leave." She said focusing on him.

His eyes looked out to the lobby and he looked irritated. "Fine." He said in defeat.

"Where's Erin?" She asked looking around him.

"In the bathroom with my girl. Look who it is." He said gesturing towards me. I wanted to run and hide.

She glanced at me, then she did a double take. "Nellie?"

I waved, "hi. This is Marquez."

"Hi, I'm Ahjanae," she shook Marquez's hand. "Where did you go? How have you been? You disappeared." She said focusing on my eyes.

"Things got a little crazy for a while." I said

"Baby, we're right over here." Ryder said following the hostess who was seating them. He looked at me, but he turned his attention back to Ahjanae.

"Ok, I'll be right there." She said

"That little girl is your daughter?" I asked pointing between the two of them. "And now you're not together?"

Ahjanae shot Jabbar evil eyes, "who would've thought right?" Then she looked at her table. "Baby, come over I want you to meet an old friend." She said waving Ryder over. He reluctantly came over. "Ryder, this is an old friend." She said

He stuck his hand out to shake mine, "nice to meet you Ryder."

"Noel," I said. Then he shook Marquez's hand.

"Noel?" Ahjanae frowned.

I slipped up, crap! "Nellie! I meant to say Nellie. I've got too many names."

"Nice to meet you." Ryder said then he turned his attention to Jabbar, "where's Erin?"

Jabbar looked at Ahjanae, "I'll bring her to you when we're done." Then he looked at me, "it was good seeing you." Then he walked away.

Ryder went back to their table, he picked up his menu but I know his ears were extended in our direction. Ahjanae took out a pen. She wrote Kendra's name and number on a napkin. "Call her when you can. I'm pretty sure she could use a conversation with an old friend right about now."

"Thank you," I said as I stared at the seven deadly digits that seemed like they glowed on the napkin. Then Ahjanae went to the bathroom, probably to check on her daughter. Ryder walked over to our table, looked at the napkin. Then he took it and smiled at me as he said I won't be using it. Then he put the napkin face down in the dirty dishes on the table next to us. He went and sat back at his table, Jabbar was watching the whole thing and he was frowning. Marquez asked for the story, so I told him.

****

I was sleep, and someone nudged me hard. Since Nassya was away at camp, it scared me because it wasn't her wild sleeping and anyone else would've been gentler trying to wake me up. I opened my eyes and D was standing over me. He looked angry. "What are you doing here?" I said trying to focus my eyes.

"Get dressed and come outside." He commanded.

I did as I was told, and then I went out the front door. I closed it very softly hoping not to wake anyone up. D was leaning up against his car and he looked angry. "What's wrong?"

"What kind of game are you playing? Why would you get Kendra's number?" He said flexing and unflexing his hands.

I put my hands up, "I didn't ask for Kendra's number. Ahjanae wrote it on a napkin without asking if I wanted it. "Did Ryder tell you he took the napkin and made sure it was thrown away?"

He looked at me like he didn't want to believe me. "How did Kendra come up?"

"She didn't, I saw Jabbar. He came over to my table. Then Ahjanae and Ryder came in. Ryder wasn't acting like he recognized me so I didn't say anything. Ahjanae wrote down Kendra's number and told me to call her. I was looking at the napkin when Ryder came over and took it."

"Why were you in Richmond?"

"That was Hilltop."

"That's still Richmond, you play too much! Noel, I don't want to have to hurt you!"

"I wouldn't cross you. That would jeopardize me seeing you again." I searched his eyes.

"You said last time was the last time." He looked irritated.

"Yes, but if there's a next time I'll take it." I smiled, "how did you get in my house?"

"There's no lock that can keep me out."

"We've got an alarm system."

"Technology has flaws."

I put my arms out and when he didn't reject me I came in for a hug. I started kissing his neck. "This could be the last time."

"You said last time was the last time." He said not moving.

"Yes, but this time could be the last time. You're so sexy when you're scary in the dark."

"I am sexy aren't I!"

"Un huh! And you're adrenaline is going; you need to release that anxiousness. Why call someone else when I'm right here? This could be our sweetest goodbye yet." I said still kissing his neck.

"Get in the back!"

****

Marquez went fishing for the weekend with his uncle. We were in the backyard enjoying time together.

"Nellie! Telephone!" Junior called out from the kitchen. He set the phone on the counter as he went out back to tend to his barbecue.

"Hello?" I said wondering who would be calling me on the house phone instead of my cell.

"YOU CAN'T CALL ANYBODY?" Gordon yelled into the phone.

I immediately dropped my head. "I'm sorry, I was so happy to see my family everything else kind of fell by the waste side."

"I AM YOUR FAMILY! OR DID YOU GET OUT THERE AND FORGET ALL ABOUT ME?"

"No, I didn't forget you." I said feeling sad.

"I think you should come back early."

"Why?"

"BECAUSE YOU'RE PROBABLY OUT THERE LAYING UP UNDER AHJANI AND THE MEXICAN WHEN I NEED YOU HERE!"

"I'm not doing anything like that. I'm just spending time with my family."

"Have you seen Ahjani?"

"No! I went years without seeing him and now suddenly I'm supposed to see him?"

He was quiet for a minute, "I'm sorry. I didn't realize things were serious between you two. You never let on that it was anything more than a little crush."
I knew better than to fall for this trick. "It was a long time ago. I've moved on, he's moved on. I can't be caught up in what I felt when I was a child. Gordon I have to go, my daddy is looking for me."
"Why should I care about your father?"
"For one, if he doesn't write the check I can't come back, for two he's not someone you wanna mess with."
"Ok but I wanted to tell you. I've got meetings all next week with agents who want to work with me."
"You're not going to finish school?" I said trying to hold back my excitement about him possibly being away.
"It depends on what's happening. I'll let you know more when I hear. I love you!"
I didn't want to say it back, but he was going to act ugly if I didn't. "I love you too."
When I walked out into the yard Junior and Ahjani were cracking up laughing at some story Junior's girlfriend was telling. Ahjani looked at me, "you ok?"
"Yea, that was Gordon. It's like he could feel that you were here or something."
"Who's Gordon?" Junior asked.
"Her boyfriend back at school. Did you tell him I'm here?"
"NO! There's no way he'd understand that you happened to drop by today, and that none of this was planned."
"What am I missing?" Junior said all up in our conversation.
"Gordon is from out here. He and Ahjani played for the same school. I told him when I met him that he looked familiar to me, then I told him that he played ball with my ex. I wouldn't talk to him for the longest time because of that, but he was persistent. Things were fine between us until they had a game against each other. Ever since then he's been emotional and clingy."
"Because he could never beat me. I don't know why he has to compete against me. But I'm not mad though, his stupidity brought you back to my life."
"I've got too many balls in the air though. Gordon at school, Marquez when I'm home. I don't have anywhere to put you."
Ahjani smiled, "I'm fine with being the man of your dreams."
"You are so corny!" Junior blurted and we all laughed.

"And you may have been the first guy to tell me he loved me and mean it." Junior cleared his throat, "that isn't related to me of course."

"Ok, well make sure you make that clear." Junior said walking back to his pit.

"Stop messing with it, it's fine. Let those slabs smoke." His girlfriend said.

"Like I said, I just wanted to come and say hi, make sure you were ok after that night. I'm meeting up with Olivia later."

I smiled and patted his hand, "tell me something. Gordon said agents are meeting with him next week. You think he's going to sign with someone?"

"Probably. He's good and could definitely go pro." Ahjani said "What about you?"

There's a few coming out to meet with me over the summer. But I want to at least get my BA before I decide to do anything. That way I can continue on my career path if the deal doesn't work out. Ball isn't the only thing I got going for me like some people." He smiled, I smiled back. If my dad didn't mess things up I could've been his Olivia and everything would've been perfect. "Tell me something." I looked at him, "you gonna reconnect with Kendra this summer?"

I shook my head no. "I can't."

"She needs to know about Omar. Cause I'm sure he probably still tries to blow smoke up her butt about forever. Does he talk about forever with you too?"

"Yes, I used to like it. He's changed so much since that game. I can't see forever with him."

"So if he can't have forever why does he get to have you right now?" Ahjani was staring at my eyes.

I put my eyes on the floor. "It doesn't matter."

"Nellie it matters." He said firmly.

"You don't even know me."

"I know you, and I know you deserve better. If I wasn't with Olivia you'd have better."

"Great! That makes me feel good."

"Nellie, I never stopped loving you!" I knew he meant it.

"Why would you tell me this when there's nothing you can do about it?" I exhaled.

"I know it's selfish, I'm sorry."

"This is my parents all over again, history repeating itself."
"How?"
"My dad, my stepmom, and my momma. The mistress gets screwed. I can't be that dumb especially when I'm living the outcome of their story."
"I don't know what to do. I can't help what I feel! I didn't break up with you. I never thought I'd see you again."
I didn't say anything, I could see this whole thing blowing up in my face.

Kendra

I looked at my caller ID in disbelief. Omar was calling after all these months, "hel-lo?" I said slowly.
"Hey beautiful, how's your summer treating you?"
"Good and yours?"
"Wonderful! It would turn into a spectacular summer if you told me you were coming out in the Fall."
"Nope, I get my AA shortly, and then I'll decide. But if I transfer it will be local. I've got to keep growing my client base.
Immaculately Tidy Cleaning Service is growing."
"That's the name of your little business? Cute." Then he chuckled, "I've been meeting with Agents to discuss possibly going pro next season."
"Wow!"
"So my question to you is what kind of ring do you want?" His voice smiled.
"You can't be serious."
"Very! I've always told you what my plans were for you. They haven't changed."
"Surely you've met someone by now?"
"I meet females all day every day, there's even one that's a close contender, but she's not you."
"Oh so I have competition?"
"I wouldn't call her competition but she wants your spot."
We talked for a couple hours. He was so excited that everything was coming together for him. He asked how things were going for Ahjani, and he said he was happy to hear it. He asked if I was going to be hanging around Ahjani this summer. I told him that Ahjani was spending most of his time with Olivia and I doubted that I would see him more than a couple times this summer. He

asked if there was any way I could come out to see him before the summer was over, and I told him I couldn't see how. He sighed in defeat. By the time we got off the phone I felt loved and appreciated, my conversation with Omar was the little pick me up that I needed to help me focus on my job and getting ready for the school year.

Nellie

He smiled at me when he saw me. What a difference a year makes. Nathan looked like his old self again, healthy and full of life. I shifted my weight from leg to leg to hide my nervousness. Nathan gave me a big hug, and a kiss on my cheek. "Where is everybody?" He said looking around.
"I asked to have time alone with you."
He smiled bigger, "you did? You drove out here by yourself just for me?"
"Oh well, Marquez is with me. But it's about the same as being alone. He won't say anything if I don't want him to."
"So what's your plan?"
"I feel like we need to talk. I know I'm a brat, but I'm trying to grow."
Nathan laughed, "me too."
We got his bags and put them in the car. Marquez took us to a place in San Bruno to eat. Nathan was so excited to share his experience with our grandmother. He said she filled in all the blanks for him. Things he didn't understand about himself she helped him understand. We drooled over all the food she made for him. It had been years since I had her cooking but I could taste it all as he talked about them. He looked at me probably for the first time ever, then he said I do look like him. Then he apologized for hating me and how he treated me. He even told me everything about him and Kendra. He told me that both times he broke up with her for not putting out and for defending me. I shifted in my seat, I felt even worse about the way I've betrayed her. Nathan asked me if I wanted to see my momma, he still called her my mother. I had an immediate heat flash and I broke out in a sweat. Marquez grabbed my hand and asked me if I was ok. I told Nathan I can't see her, as far as I know she's still with Bobby. I didn't know how he was still out but I remember his crazy, and I did not want to chance being in his clutches again. I shook my head no at

Nathan real fast. Nathan and Marquez watched me as I tried to get a grip on my emotions. I buried my head into Marquez's chest when I couldn't pull it back. Marquez rubbed my back as he held me.

****

My phone rang in my ear, I got excited when the caller ID said D was calling me. I made myself wake up then I answered. He told me to come outside. I brushed my teeth real quick then I put on my jacket and I went outside. I got in his car, he looked angry.

"Ahjani?"

"Yes?"

"Why was he here?" D barked.

"He came by to see me." I said not grabbing his point. "How did you know he came here?"

D shook his head, "this is bad! That's too close to home. I'll never get her back when this blows up." He said shaking his head.

"I'm not gonna tell!" I said fearing that this was it.

"You're not looking at the board properly! Everything's lining up against me. You won't have to say nothing."

"What board?"

"The chess board! CHESS!"

I was quiet for a minute while D tried to get a grip. "I can lie, we both could. It could be our word against there's. The only ones who know for a fact are Bonnie and Ryder. I don't know her anymore and Ryder wouldn't tell."

"Lying would only make things worse. I might be a lot of things, but I am not a liar."

"Tell me what you want me to do."

"Stop calling me, stop begging, leave me alone!" He said painfully.

"D!" I said as tears came to my eyes.

"It should've never happened in the first place. You caught me off guard and I've been stuck on stupid ever since." He said

"I'm your weakness?" I looked at him in disbelief. I didn't think he cared.

He blew air, "come on now!" He said fidgeting in his seat.

"You always said you didn't care." I said with my eyes wide.

"Cause I don't." He said unconvincingly.

It was bitter sweet. "Let me say my peace and then I will try to leave you alone." He kept staring at his steering wheel. "It's not

fair! I knew you were worth all of this from the moment I laid eyes on you. She plays hard to get and your nose is open. I was sprung before that first contact and I will never be the same having known you. But you choose her over me! I would never leave you! I would give up everyone for you! You know I'm telling the truth."
D shook his head, "that's only true for now. Eventually you'd choose yourself over me. You walked all over Kendra to be with me. You're too high risk." He took a deep breath, he sat up straight and looked ahead then he looked at me. "Besides, Marquez loves you with all your flaws and you still come after me. Why wouldn't you let love in your life? Stop running from him, he deserves everything you have to give."
I exhaled, "I love Marquez. I know it sounds crazy, but I love all three of you. You were my first man, Ahjani was the first to love me, and Marquez knows everything and still loves me and is good to me." I exhaled, "I can't promise to stop coming for you. I just can't! You don't see yourself from where I sit!"
"I know I'm irresistible! I got a chicken coop full of chicken heads all clucking at me. You are going to have to control yourself woman. I mean I'm smiling now, but it will piss me off later. This has to stop."
"Ok...." I said watching his face.
"Don't look at me like that either. Giving in starts the clock over. No!"
"D! A few days makes that much of a difference? After tonight when will I be able to touch you? This is it for real.... Unless you change your mind, pretty please!"
He smiled, "with a cherry on the top?"
"We can put whatever you want up there, just say yes."
He started the car and my heart fluttered.

Kendra
"Kendra?" Ryder was knocking on my door.
"Come in," I called out. I was on my way to Jason's house for a barbecue with his family and friends. I was sitting on the bed putting my sandals on.
Erin ran around Ryder and to me before he was in the doorway good. Little missy was learning to respect closed doors. We set up my old room, the smallest room for Erin, so that Ryder and Ahjanae could occupy her room in peace. Ryder's eyes were

serious. "Do you know who's black car has been parked outside lately?"

"Black car?" I said looking at him.

"Yeah, it's not every day, but it's pretty often. I never see anyone get in or out. I don't see the car pull up or leave, but it doesn't sit well with me that it sits out there like that either."

"I guess I need to pay better attention when I'm out there huh?"

"You should pay attention always. You never know who's watching you, who's following you. You never know."

"Who's going to be getting in my bed in the middle of the night and I didn't know they were in my house…" I smiled.

He smiled, "some things can't be helped but make sure you stay on top of everything else."

"Ryder, how long is he going to be mad at me? I messed up! Ok, I get that. Is he done with me?" Ryder looked away. "Come on tell me. Tell me if I should be sitting here waiting for him to come around or if I should move on with my life."

He exhaled, "I don't know what to tell you. You hurt him pretty badly. In my honest opinion, I think he'll come around. But I don't know. He spends so much time giving me a hard time about being sprung off Ahjanae, he doesn't want to talk about anything else. I can't tell you if he'll come around. I can't tell you to wait on him. You're going to have to listen to your heart and decide for yourself."

"FINE! He doesn't want to talk to me! I don't want to talk to him! I was honest with him and I put myself on the line. I get punished for telling the truth! We'll see when that happens again. Everything was crazy! I'm over this! I don't want him back!"

"You're just saying that, you don't mean it."

"Look at me! Ryder, I'm over this! It's been months. He doesn't forgive me, then I don't forgive him."

"What did he do?"

"He's a hoe! Got females wanting to fight me because they saw me with him. I don't need that in my life. I'm not out there hoeing myself around, nor would that be acceptable if I did. If I can't be a hoe, the man I'm with can't be one either! HIV and Aids is real! I don't need that frustration in my life." I said standing up with Erin in my arms.

Ahjanae walked in the door and put her arms around Ryder's waist. "Baby, what are we going to do with our cousins?" He asked her.

"Nothing, let them find their own way. Neither one of them listens no how."

I rolled my eyes at both of them and then I grabbed my purse. I said bye to Erin and then I walked out the door. I felt like a deer caught in headlights, as soon as I saw the car, I recognized it. It was the scary guy's car. I stood still for a moment not knowing what to do. Ryder came out the door, as he was coming the scary guy got out of his car. Ryder walked a couple of steps ahead of me, "can I help you with something?"

The scary guy looked Ryder up and down, then he looked at me. "I didn't mean to scare you. I was wondering if you've heard from Nellie? If you've seen her, or anything?"

I shook my head, "I haven't seen her or talked to her in years. I told you that, that night."

He held out a hundred dollar bill and a paper, "if you happen to run into her can you call me? I miss my little girl, I'll make it worth your while if you do."

"What is that supposed to be?" Ryder said holding up a fat wad of bills and I saw hundreds all through the roll. My mouth opened when I saw Ryder's stash.

"What is it going to take?" He said folding his arms. "Everybody has a price. What's yours?" He looked between Ryder and me.

"Mister! I told you I haven't spoken to her in years. Nellie's a smart girl, she has to be away in college right now. She doesn't want to talk to me."

"Why?" He asked watching my face.

"I don't know. My point is that I don't see her, talk to her, or even know where she is."

He handed me the money and number. "Just in case she happens to pop up."

I looked at Ryder, "he's not listening."

"Go to your car." Ryder said sternly, as he walked behind me.

"Call the house when you're on your way home. I don't want you out here by yourself."

I agreed. When I got to Jason's I was telling Kaleah and Kalani what happened when Jason's ears extended across his yard and he came over. He made me tell him the story all over from the beginning. As I was talking my momma and Aunt Quilla came over to listen. Aunt Quilla told us that Nellie has been through a lot. She said she had a conversation with her parents once while She and Ahjani were dating. She said it was like her parents needed to purge and Nellie had so many issues, she got scared for Ahjani. So she asked them to keep Nellie away from Ahjani. We looked at Aunt Quilla in shock, she said she should've been more careful about Ahjanae.

Jason was not happy about the scary guy sitting outside my house on a regular basis. He went over to his friend Malcolm, and I could tell by his mannerisms that Jason was pissed. Malcolm's eyes darted towards me then back to Jason. They sat over on the side talking for a long time. Later Jason told me to follow him inside, we sat in the living room with Malcolm. He was definitely D-Rick's dad no joke in his bones at all. He asked me to describe the car, then he told me to describe the scary guy. When I mentioned that Aunrey knew him, Jason and Malcolm exchanged looks. Aunt Quilla gave me her phone to call Aunrey. Jason was describing Aunrey to Malcolm, he used words like smart, strategic, etc. to describe him. I hadn't thought of Aunrey like that but I guess he could be all those things. Malcolm asked if Aunrey was the same one? And Jason said yes, so I asked Jason what he meant. Jason shook his head at me and told me Aunrey would tell me when he was ready. When Aunrey answered Jason asked him to come over his house as soon as he could. Aunrey got there in twenty minutes, I was surprised. Jason told him to sit down, then he told him about the scary guy. Aunrey said his name was Bobby. Malcolm watched Aunrey the entire time Jason was talking. Aunrey was upset, he said he warned Bobby not to mess with us. Aunrey was livid! Jason got him to calm down, and then Malcolm told him as long as Ryder was in the house he didn't have to worry about us inside. I didn't know what that meant, but I sat there quietly listening. Malcolm assured Aunrey and Jason that Ahjanae and I would be safe. Malcolm told him they would plan everything and Aunrey had to be patient and not impulsive. He told him only a fool makes a move without a plan.

Chapter 16

Nellie

Nassya came home full of reports from the camp. She said that she and her friends miss me so much. I did miss the camp and I couldn't believe I liked working with the kids. I never thought of myself as a kid friendly kind of person, but Nassya and her friends made it seem easy.

The other day a guy I didn't know came over to talk to my parents. They went in my dad's office for a long time. I could tell my parents were upset about something when he left. My parents talked for a while after he left then they called all four of us into the living room. My parents decided to take us on a family vacation, they asked for suggestions on where to go. My daddy said the sky was the limit. We sat there not saying anything kind of looking around. Junior asked how long we'd be gone, cause he had a job and a girlfriend to consider. My dad said at least two weeks but he was hoping to spend a month away. Then we'd come home in time for school shopping and preparing for the next year. Junior said he couldn't take a month off from work. My daddy told him to put the request in and he'd make sure he got the time off. He'd cover his wages if he has to take the time off without pay. Junior asked about his girlfriend, my daddy looked at his wife. Then she sighed and told Junior he could bring her. Then she told us not to think about it. I snapped my fingers cause it would've been nice to bring Marquez along. It wasn't exactly fair that Junior got to bring booty with him, and the rest of us would have to suffer through the month. We went into my father's office and he called a travel agent. He asked for suggestions for family locations for a month. After a series of questions the agent suggested the Bahamas, everyone got excited. My father booked three rooms and our flight left next week. Then my parents asked everyone to step out of the room except me. My stepmother sat next to me and held my hand. My father was trying to hold back emotion.

He said the guy who came by was Kendra's stepfather. I didn't know her parents divorced or that her mother remarried but ok. He said Kendra ran into my momma and her boyfriend. I felt like I was going to be sick. My father's face was angry as he said he didn't know why they hadn't found him and locked him up yet. I asked him if Bobby hurt Kendra? He said he didn't hurt her, but he's almost insisting that she knows where you are. My father said a smart person would've left or something. But he's right there and very persistently looking for me. Tears came to my eyes, my daddy said I can't go to Richmond for any reason. He said it would be best if I stayed home for the most part until we left. I told him I had to go see Marquez. When he asked me why he couldn't come here, I shot my stepmother a look to ask her to help me out. She was clueless for a minute and then she said, "honey they need to be alone for a little bit." My father growled at us and went off. When he finally stopped going off she told him to get over it. I could tell he was really upset and probably wanting to run interference some more. He said to have Marquez pick me up, then he huffed and stormed out of the room slamming every door he went through. I asked my stepmom why he was so upset. She said no father likes to think of his daughter having sex. I asked him why he was bringing Junior's girlfriend if that was the case. He said Junior's girlfriend is not his daughter.

****

Our trip was amazing! Every day we woke up excited to wake up. Nathan, Nassya, and I were the three amigos a lot of the time. We did almost everything together. My father and Junior's room were pretty standard King sized bedrooms, but our room was a one bedroom. Nathan slept on the pullout bed in the living room and Nassya and I occupied the bedroom. However, that was only during the time we actually spent in our room. We had breakfast and dinner together every day and night as a family. Most days Junior and his girlfriend came with us, but sometimes they needed alone time. Nathan hooked up a few times and that was the only time he disappeared really. As long as we stayed busy I didn't think about the fact that the real reason we were out here was to fill our time this summer. When my dad had confirmation that Bobby was still in Richmond and looking for me, he freaked. He was on the phone one evening asking in a very angry tone why Bobby was still out on the streets. I heard him asking what he paid his taxes for if they couldn't do their job, I assumed he was talking to the police.

When we got home I was greeted by a ton of voicemails from Gordon. He went from cutesy messages like thinking of me and excited to see me, to going off because I hadn't returned his calls. I called him as soon as I was alone in Nassya and I's room. I explained that my parents surprised us with a family vacation in the Bahamas for a month. I emailed some pictures of me on our trip so he would calm down. He apologized a lot for biting my head off, he told me he couldn't wait to see me. I told me we needed to talk and it sound like he stopped breathing. I told him that it really bothered me when he was high in my presence. I told him I didn't care if he smoked, I didn't want him around me when he was high. I told him if he had to be high around me then he didn't need to see me anymore. I felt really good about asserting myself. Gordon said he didn't realize it bothered me so much, I don't know how he didn't know. Then he apologized and said he wouldn't come around me like that anymore. I was relieved, and after that conversation I was now ready to go back to school.

Kendra

Aunrey followed me home, and then he came in to see his sister and niece. Although Erin vaguely remembered Aunrey she fell in love with him right away. Aunrey told Ahjanae she looked happy and she told him she was very happy. Aunrey and Ryder stood there staring each other down for a long time. "You look kind of white!" Aunrey said
"Your sister likes it!"
"I don't!"
"I didn't ask you what you liked!"
Aunrey walked up on Ryder and Ryder didn't budge. I looked at Ahjanae like I didn't understand what was going on. "It really doesn't matter what color you are. You make my sister cry, I'll make you bleed!"
"Only tears I have planned for her are tears of joy. I'm not concerned with your threats. Save your breath for someone who cares."
Aunrey started smiling, "ok. He's cool! Don't mess over my sister though, I'm not playing."
"Please tell me why you're still talking like I should care?"
Aunrey looked at Erin, "you like him?"
She was hugging Ryder's leg and giving Aunrey evil eyes. "YES!"
Aunrey started laughing, "that settles it!"
****

I put up postings for Immaculately Tidy on the student board. The next day I got a call from Anton a fellow student. He wanted to talk to me about collaborating on landscaping projects. He said he has a landscaping business that he's trying to get off the ground. He asked me to refer my landscaping customers to him and he would refer housekeeping customers to me. I told him that I could manage simple landscaping projects, and I'd keep him in mind for larger project needs. He asked me to trade the simple jobs with him for the jobs he has for me. He said the simple jobs from me will make his business visible and word of mouth will help him. He said he doesn't book any housekeeping projects and he had a list of people in need. Anton was basically begging me to help him. I asked him to show me the list.

Nellie

Nathan drove back to Arizona with me. Marquez flew out of Oakland. Nathan asked a bunch of questions about my momma. He told me he knows all her faults, but he didn't know anything good. He said it was hard for our grandmother to say anything good about her right now, she's so angry with her. He said she's mad about everything that happened with me. And even after Bobby shot up my grandmother's house my momma was still with him. I told Nathan how Bobby made my momma quit her job. And he was paying for everything. I always knew money was important to her, but I didn't know she'd do anything for it. I told him how she gave up her lunch for two weeks to buy an outfit for me for Junior's graduation. I emphasized the point that she gave up meals to provide a want for me. I told him she's not like our stepmom, but she tried to be good within what she knew. He said he could remember her always looking at our father with so much love in her eyes. He said daddy would always be so happy to see her and happy about the time they spent together. He said now that he thought about it they did love each other. He said the years that I was away were hard because our father wasn't happy anymore. He said he would drink more and sometimes he'd sit in his office and work not wanting to be bothered. Nathan said Junior and our father would get into really heated arguments about me the whole time I was missing. Nathan felt like I took attention away from him whenever I was around and my attitude was always like I didn't care if I hurt him or not. I told him he always made me feel like the outsider, so my attitude would get worse with him because I knew he didn't want me around.

We talked like adults and it was nice. He stayed at my place for a week, he even met Gordon. He said Gordon was a show off and he wasn't impressed. Then he flew back to Vegas to our grandmother. Gordon was on best behavior, it was nice having my good boyfriend back. He was very supportive during my pledging, every time I wanted to give up and throw in the towel he encouraged me to stick it out. In the end, I was now a part of a sisterhood and I had connections all over the place.

Kendra

I was next door tidying up at Mrs. McCall's. Little Erin was my cleaning partner as her parents weren't ready to be up when I was leaving so I brought her with me. She's so cute, and an excellent duster. She's very careful, I am so proud of her. Mrs. McCall loves the things that come out of her little mouth. So she was very happy to see Erin this morning. "I've been telling everyone about your ad in the newspaper. Have you gotten any inquiries?"

"Some, slow and steady wins the race." I was reminding myself.

"Kendra baby look at me." So I did, "I know that boy loves you. He'll be back, but you've got to get it together. Put on a dress sometimes. Get out and enjoy yourself. Stop waiting on him. If you want him back you've got to move past him. Sounds weird I know, but it's true."

"Do you remember my ex? Omar."

"The basketball guy."

"Yes, he's been calling me. He says he still wants to marry me. Isn't that weird?"

"Why is that weird to you?"

"He's away in college and I'm sure females are throwing their selves at him all the time. Why would he want me?"

"Because you still hold his heart. You love who you love." Then she started coughing. Her cough was hard and lasted a long time. I asked her if she was ok. She said she was but then her breathing seemed real labored. I asked her if she was ok again and she said yes. But I kept watching her. She had been sick off and on a lot lately. As Erin and I were finishing up, I noticed that Mrs. McCall's lips were turning blue. I called 911 and asked them to send an ambulance. As calmly as I could I walked Erin back home.

Ahjanae saw the horror on my face immediately. We left Erin with Ryder and then we ran back to Mrs. McCall. She thanked me and then she told me to go in the cabinet next to her headboard. She told me to bring the folders to the hospital with her. When the paramedics came I rode with her. Ahjanae followed in her car. They gave her oxygen and assured her she was going to be ok. Mrs. McCall said she was tired and old. When the paramedics asked who I was she told them I was her granddaughter. She told me to stay while they examined her. The doctor said he wanted an ex ray of her lungs. I called my momma and she said she was on her way. The doctor said that she has pneumonia, but he saw another mass that concerned him. Mrs. McCall said she was old and tired and he could investigate if he wanted to but she didn't want any treatments she wanted to sleep. Ahjanae looked at her in disbelief. When the doctor left the room I begged her to do whatever she needed to do to get better. She hugged me big and strong then she refused. When my momma, Jason, and my sisters walked in the door she told us to stop fussing over her. She tried to perk up and act like she was fine. I told my momma what she told the doctor and everybody started crying just like I did. When she got tired of telling us no, she turned her head and looked out the window. She refused to even talk to us anymore. After a while all you heard were tears. Then there was a knock at the door as it slowly opened. Darryl poked his head around the corner with a big smile on his face. "Mrs. McCall you miss me?"
Her whole face lit up as she quickly turned to him and then prepared to sit up and talk to him. "Hi baby! Come in! Come in!"
"Your favorite is here!" He said going in for a hug.
"Yes you are baby! How are you?"
Darryl focused on Mrs. McCall like she was the only person in the room. "Why are we here? You don't look sick." He teased.
"The doctor said I have pneumonia. I thought it was my asthma acting up."
"That's not all he said." Ahjanae said
Mrs. McCall rolled her eyes, "Darryl baby they just wanna be sad about something. I'm old, if they want to find something wrong with me they will. Sit down baby." She patted her bed for him to sit. He did as he was told. "I've got two of the most ungrateful kids ever! Do either of them come check on they momma, see how she's getting along?" Darryl shook his head no. "No! Kharee has

always been more like a child of mine than they could've ever been. Kendra, baby, let me have those folders I told you to get." I handed them to her. Then she gave them to Darryl. His face was very serious as he looked at her documents. "All of my directions are in there. I have my plot next to my husband up in Rolling Hills Memorial Park."

Darryl interrupted as he looked at the papers. "Do your kids know you're here? You should at least let them have a chance to say goodbye." Mrs. McCall frowned at Darryl just like she did at us earlier. I thought she was going to shut down again. Then Darryl nudged her, "come on sexy. Do it for me, do it for the good times." She started laughing, "you are so silly. Sure, but they're not coming. If they come they'll only wanna know about my money." She exhaled, "Kharee baby can you call my kids for me? Their numbers are in the folder, Darryl baby give her the yellow paper." Darryl looked around the room and said hello to everyone. My hello was no different than anyone else's. My momma called from the room phone while Darryl and Mrs. McCall went over her folder. Darryl kept bouncing between serious and hilarious. Everyone was laughing except me. I couldn't laugh, my emptiness is the source of his pain. The orderly came and wheeled Mrs. McCall's bed away to take her for testing. Kaleah asked someone to take her back to my house because she couldn't take being in this hospital. She said there was too much history with our momma being in here and then her. Ahjanae took Kaleah and Kalani with her. My momma and Jason walked out the room without an explanation. Darryl looked at me, "doesn't this feel like a setup?" "I've called you, I've gone over your house, why are you ignoring me?"

"Hello Kendra how are you? See this is how you start a conversation." He tried to smile.

"Bump that! Answer my question!" I said feeling anger stir in me. He shrugged, "I don't know what to tell you." He said looking unaffected by my anger.

"You don't know what to tell me?" I stood up.

His face held no smile. "No! I actually gave you my heart. You know me on a level nobody else knows me. I even gave you the raw dog! The WHOLE RAW DOG! I gave you my seed! You let some jealous females change everything. Acting like I'm a mistake, like I'm some no good nigga you got caught up with. I'm hurt which makes me angry. I don't wanna hurt you just because you hurt me, so I'm stepping back. I need to clear my head." He watched my face for a minute. "Why is someone watching your house?"

"Some guy came looking for Nellie, Jason talked to your dad and then they told us this is how it's going down."

"What guy? Why would he come to your house?"

"I don't know. I really don't care! You won't talk to me why should I care about some scary looking fool showing up at my house? Darryl, I'm begging you. Please come back!"

He squinted his eyes, "you're begging?"

I walked to him slowly. "I am so sorry! Haven't you ever been so scared that you've done something horrible and stupid? I'll get pregnant right now if that's what you need to fix this. You're right, you've always been honest with me. You've given me everything! I betrayed you, and I'm sorry. Words cannot express how sorry I am." He sat there watching me not saying a word. "Please forgive me!" I said, then I kissed him with everything in me.

He pushed me a little by my shoulders trying to gather himself. "Wait a minute Kendra."

"No! I'm sorry!" I said going in for another kiss.

"But...." He said trying to push me away.

I shook my head, I put his hands on my butt. "Butt!"

He gasped, "KB!" He said squeezing my butt.

"Darryl I'm so sorry!"

"Ok!" He said pushing me back as he gasped for air. "KB! I think you mean it! You're sorry! I'm sorry!" I kissed him again. "Wait! Wait!" He said pushing me back. Then he frowned, "why you always breaking me down like I'm the female? I'm a man! Stop this!"

"Don't ever leave me again! If you do I'll be forced to take Omar seriously."

"The star? What he want?"

"He said he still wants to marry me."

Darryl blew air, "then maybe you should marry him."

"I want to marry you."

He got up, "married! KB! I don't like or want marriage!"

I exhaled, "what's the point of us being together if we're not working towards the same goal?"

"We're too young for all of this." He said coming for me.

"I don't want to waste my youth on something that goes nowhere."
"We can have whatever you want but I don't want the paper." He
put his arms around me. "I love you KB, I'll give you whatever you
want. You want to drop out of school have a house full of babies. I
could use some minions, let's do it. Let's not be defined by other
people's ideas of what is right."
I didn't want to argue, he just told me he loved me without me
fishing for it. "I love you, without the paper I can't give you
everything. We can do this for now, cause I can't stand being
without you. But this won't work forever." I went in for another
kiss.
He held me back, "KB! HOLD ON! BACK UP!" He said standing
up and grabbing his composure. "You want to get back together
just to break up again? I can't do this! My heart can't take that!
Nothing's changed with me. Chicken Heads still fill my days and
nights when you're not around. You couldn't handle that before,
for this moment cause you're thirsty for Sunny-D you'll drink it?
KB nothing's changed and we're going to be at each other's
throats as soon as the euphoria of our reunion is over." He took a
deep breath, "if we're not on the same page we can't." His voice
cracked.
"So then hurry up and propose already!"
"Kendra, I'm serious. I don't want to get married. If you need
marriage in your life, then you and me are a time bomb waiting to
happen." He said giving me sad eyes.
"Seriously Darryl? You want me to marry someone else?"
"NO! I don't!"
"Then what?"
"I want you to understand how much you love me. Understand that
there isn't anything I wouldn't give you. But I'm not budging on
the marriage thing. It's a stupid piece of paper!"
"If it's so stupid why can't I have it?"
"You can't even buy a drink, but you worried about the rest of
your life? You may not want to be with me for the rest of your life.
What if I lose my funny bone? You gonna love me when I can't
make you laugh anymore? I could become very serious like D-
Rick. Only Chantel can tolerate that kind of dry flavorless life."
"Who is Chantel?"
"My point is, people change."

"Your point is, one day you're gonna wanna trade up and you don't want to have to do right by me. You're planning your escape before we begin!"

He exhaled, "no I'm not."

"YES YOU ARE! Fine Darryl! Thank you for letting me know what the truth is before I put my everything into you."

He shook his head from side to side real fast, "nope, I'm not! You don't get it!"

I shook my head up and down, "yes you are. And I get it! You're meaner than you let on."

"How could I be done with you if we have babies? Malcolm never left us regardless of whether he and my momma were together or not."

I put my hands on my hips. "Now you know being there for your children is not the same as being with the person. Stop trying to play dumb, it doesn't suit you."

"KB! I'm not old enough to get married!"

"Ok, but that's not what you're saying. You're saying you never want to get married." I took a deep breath, "why even argue about this? We don't want the same things, stick a fork in this whole thing, it's done. You're not going to rent me for my best years, put stretch marks on my body having your babies and you never marry me. I'm sure one of your chicken heads would be more than happy to receive your seed. I don't want to be with someone who shows more loyalty to our children than they do to me."

"More loyalty?"

"You'll always be there for your children. But for me, it's temporary. AND THEN! To torture me you'll come around for our kids."

Darryl stared at me, "KB! You're making me tired. When I walked in here I felt pretty good about everything I was going to say to you. I was going to say…" He cleared his throat. "Hey KB! Looking Good! Can I smack your booty? You know something to take the edge off. But you come out guns blazing. I can't even deal with this, system overload. You're not even playing the game, you threw all the pieces on the floor. I can't pick that up, my back hurts!"

I frowned at him, "what?"

He smiled, and chuckled. "Can we agree to be friends or something?"

"I don't want to be your friend!" I spit.

"Like that KB? That's cold!"

"If I can't have all of you, I don't want none of you!"

"KB! You want me, you want all of me. Ok, you've given me a lot to think about. But for today, I would like to take you home and put it on you."

I rolled my eyes, "get real!"

"KB! Don't make me turn you on, you'll be screaming at yourself later. You can't resist me! I guess you forgot! I try to use my powers for good, but you're not leaving me with a choice."

"Darryl, this is not funny! I'm serious." I said

"I'm not playing, you're going to be calling out my name like you always do. I love it when I make your eyes roll back in your head. Makes me feel like a man."

My body did a silent celebration as I tried to pretend I'm stronger then he was giving me credit for. "Darryl, I'm not some hoe, you can't….."

"I don't care if the chicken heads get theirs or not. For you I pull out all the stops. Yep, today it's going down. Prepare yourself for the passion KB, I gotta have you. You sitting over there all concerned for Mrs. McCall, wanting me forever! I never thought of a hospital as sexy, but you know what? You make it work!"

"Darryl!"

"Yes, say my name again." He walked up on me, "your breathing is now heavy, and your heart rate has increased. I can smell your pheromones, you want me! And I'm going to give you what you want. We'll work out all that other stuff later." He stood in my face.

I was now on fire and aching for his touch. I wanted to feel like he forgave me, that he wanted me. "Darryl!"

"I love you too KB!"

****

It's like Darryl has put me on some new kind of drug where he looks at me and I'm ready. Whenever I try to talk about what we're doing he goes in deeper. I've finally stopped fighting it. I'm open, and I hate it while loving it at the same time. I was messed up for a week when my due date came around. Darryl even looked hurt; one time he asked me whether I thought that baby was a girl or a boy. I started crying so hard; Darryl asked me how I went through with it if I'm this mess up over the whole thing. I honestly don't know either, but if there was ever a regret in my life this would always be the worst one. Darryl normally gets quiet when the topic comes up. I can tell it hurts him like it does me, and then I feel worse. Then I don't see him for a few days.

Jason and my momma told me to come over. They told me I had to finish school at an state institution or university. Jason insisted on paying for everything, and he got mad when I tried to say that Kaleah and Kalani needed his help more. "Baby girl, you're always looking out for your sisters. That's admirable, but I'm looking out for you. I'm doing this for you because you have always been an excellent daughter. You deserve this now stop fighting it cause it's happening." I applied to Berkeley, San Francisco, Hayward, all of the local schools I could think of to finish school. In the end I decided to transfer to SF State.

Nellie

"Leasha your body is amazing!" My sorority sister said as she admired me in my bikini.

"Thank you!" I said feeling good about my hot pink number.

We were wearing bikinis, sarongs, and high heels. Our brother fraternity was having a party and we were hosting. I got a kick out of seeing all the heads turning and doing a double take at me. Brice always looks at me, but he doesn't say anything. I know he wants me, it's written all over his face. But he tries to act like he's in control. "Brice, would you like a Berry?" I said holding my tray in front of him.

"What are you offering?" He asked looking at me and not the tray.

"Try the strawberries they're delicious!" I smiled.

"Pick one for me." He said watching me. I picked the juiciest looking one, then I put it in his mouth. He chewed it with his eyes locked on me. "Isn't it delicious?"

"It's good!" He said still staring.

"Um Leasha? People over there need cantaloupe too." His girlfriend said breaking up our flirt Fest.

I don't know where she came from but ok. I continued around the party with all eyes on me. Gordon at first was beaming with pride as I paraded around. Once he disappeared for a while and came back the good times were over. He was high and paranoid. T-Bone had to run interference and convince him that I was only doing my job. That didn't stop Gordon from getting in Brice's face. Brice told him to back up, Gordon did for a minute and then.... He was running up on Brice. Now Gordon was bigger and more solid than Brice. But Brice busted out some ninja like karate moves. Not only did he beat Gordon up, then he thumped his banged up body in the pool. I chewed back my smile cause Gordon was always over powering me. It felt good to know someone could get him. T-Bone jumped in the pool to save Gordon who looked like his hand was broken, etc. One of the frat brothers brought his SUV around and we got in. We needed to make sure his hand wasn't broken. I wondered if Gordon's head was going to spin around he was going off so badly. Gordon's frat brother gave me sweats and a jacket to put on over my bikini. I called Gordon's mom who took a cab and got to the hospital quickly. She went off when she found out Gordon was fighting. T-Bone tried to tell her that Gordon was overreacting because he was high. But all she knew was it was my fault. She said I was jeopardizing his career, then she kicked me out. The Frat brother took me back to the house, because my car was there. I gave him back his clothes, then I walked slowly to my car. Brice jogged over; he asked me if I was ok. I looked at him but I didn't say anything. He took my keys and told me he'd drive me home and get a cab back to the party. I didn't say anything, I got in the passenger seat. He asked me where he was going and I shrugged. So he drove, we ended up at his dorm room. I felt like I was back in high school doing things just because. When Brice tried to kiss me afterwards I turned my face. I picked up my stuff and went home. I got in the bathtub and I laid there thinking of how everyone's lives would be simpler if I was gone. All I ever do is hurt people even when I'm not trying. Then I thought about Nassya, I couldn't hurt her like that. She'd never understand and I don't want her hurting on account of me. Then I thought about Junior and how much it would hurt him too. I'm just one person, what difference does it make if I hurt? I couldn't hurt them like that.

Gordon came over the next morning his hand was sprained badly but not broken. He said when he was high he could see Brice flirting with me. I told him Brice was with his girlfriend and he wasn't flirting. When I moved away from Gordon when he started kissing on me he got mad. The only way to get him to shut up was to go back to him. I didn't feel like having sex with Gordon but he was expecting it. I did everything technically right, but my heart wasn't in it.

Kendra

Ahjanae came in my room and got in my bed. She inhaled and then she exhaled, I looked at her with annoyance in my face cause I wanted to sleep. "Be honest, do you really think he loves me?"
I rolled my eyes, "you woke me up for nonsense?"
"I have a confession," I sat up for something good. "I've had a crush on him since we met him at the restaurant. I liked how he kept saying Erin was perfect."
I threw my head back on my pillow. "I thought you were going to tell me something I didn't know. Even Stevie Wonder could see your crush on him."
"WHAT?" She laughed an embarrassed laugh.
"Both of you morons make me sick. Both of you liked each other from day one, and you're the worst actress ever. I know you liked him which is why I told him to come clean."
"If you're so smart tell me this, should we have a baby?"
Something exploded inside of me. I tried to keep my smile, "what?"
"He's so good with Erin, I love him so much. I don't want Erin to be an only child, I think we should do it." She said like she was analyzing everything.
"What about school?" I said trying to take my sadness out of my voice, but it didn't work.
She rubbed my back, "I love him!"
"I think you should wait, you haven't been together for a year yet. Give it some time."
"I love him now, I want to be with him now. I want another baby now. I want the horrible experience of what happened with Jabbar out of my brain. He's like Audra's dad to me. Her dad was good to all of us, and they were so happy together. I can't believe my life is working out just like my mom's. Except it only took one child for Jabbar to run, and Ryder's not going to die over some nonsense."
"What does Ryder say about all of this?"
"We haven't talked about it completely yet. He has to be on board before anything happens, but I think he'll want it as well. He's almost done with school, and then he'll be an architect just like his grandfather, momma, and Darryl's uncle. I'll continue to work

with you, everything will be fine. Kendra I love him so much! I
want this!"
"What about marriage?"
"We can get married if he wants to, but I don't need it."
"I guess I'm old fashioned?"
"It doesn't make you old fashioned to need it. There's nothing
wrong with needing to be the legal wife. I love Ryder with
everything in me. What he needs I need, and if he doesn't need the
paper neither do I."

Nellie

I was at the sorority house with my sisters watching the NBA draft.
Everyone was cheering for Gordon to make it so that they could
say they knew a star. I wanted him to go away, make some money,
and hopefully come back a better person. We exploded with
excitement when the Los Angeles team picked Gordon. He was
really going away, it was really happening. I kept looking at my
phone expecting him to call, but it took him hours to finally call
me. I was sleep and over it! When I saw his name on my caller ID
I let it roll over to voicemail. I got up early around four a.m.
packed a few things and then I got on the road. I arrived in Las
Vegas by ten. Nathan buzzed me into their community and told me
where to park. It was really nice everything looked new. My
grandmother's house was a one-story house, but it was nice sized
and she had a pool. Even though I didn't recognize any of the
furniture, it still felt like I was in her house in Richmond. She said
she was so happy I FINALLY came out to see her. Gordon kept
calling me and I kept sending him to voicemail. Finally Nathan
asked who was blowing up my phone. I told him it was nobody.
We hung around the house talking and enjoying each other's
company. Nathan called in sick to work so he could spend the day
with us. For dinner we decided to go on the strip and see wherever
we landed.
My grandmother said there were more people than usual out here
because there was a boxing match in a couple of days. We kept
seeing celebrity after celebrity. Some were nice and others were
too good to be bothered. I was stuck and drooling as I watched
Dwayne what's his face signing autographs. I kept going over
possible ways to approach him in my mind. I had my ID and proof
that I was legal. I didn't want to date him; I just wanted to know

what he felt like. I wasn't even opposed to going in the bathroom if that was the way this had to happen. When Dwayne smiled at me I almost melted in the sun. I could tell he was smiling at my recognition of him; he had no idea of how I was about to be on him.

As if Nathan read my mind he stood in my path and asked me to pick out a shirt for him in the store he was in. Fire shot out of my ears. I told him I'd be right there, and when I looked back, Dwayne what's his face was gone. I could've stabbed Nathan; he smiled an evil smile at me. Our grandmother knew someone on the staff at this fancy hotel so she said we could have dinner like the rich and famous. I was looking at my menu and closely at the descriptions of the foods because most of the dishes I never heard of. Something told me to look up, and when I did I saw D walking with two girls. They were gorgeous probably twins. He had one on each arm and they were all smiling. Even though our table was in the back D's eyes swept the restaurant swiftly and he saw me. He smiled at me and kept going. I couldn't stop watching them, they were loud and having a good time. I wondered what was so doggone funny? I wanted to go over but I had no right. I kept drumming my fingers trying to think of what to do. One of the girls walked away and I told myself the other one wouldn't jump bad by herself. I excused myself from the table and then I walked towards D's table. He smiled a normal smile so I kept coming. "Hey!" I said to D.

The girl's eyes locked on me, she didn't smile. "Who's this?"

"Noel," he said nonchalantly.

She looked at D like she was waiting for more of an explanation. When he smiled she looked at me again, "you're here because?" She rolled her hands.

D grinned like he was enjoying this. "D, you are the last person I expected to see out here. What are you doing here?"

"The fight," now he's a man of little words. "What are you doing here?"

"I'm here with my brother and grandmother."

D looked around me, "that's the other brother?" I couldn't decide for the look on his face.

"Yes."

He kept looking at Nathan. "I'll come over and introduce myself in a bit." Then he cut his eyes at me.

I didn't know what the look was for, but I said ok, then I went back to my table. When the other girl came back they both looked at my table when D said something. After we placed our orders D came over and sat in the fourth seat. "Grandmomma and Nathan this is my friend D."

D was looking Nathan up and down, "how are you all doing this evening?"

The girls were openly looking at our table.

"We're good, how do you know my grand baby?"

He kept his eyes on Nathan. "Kendra!" Guilt flashed across Nathan's face. I silently rolled my eyes cause I didn't know where he was going to go with this. "She's how we met."

Nathan shook his head, "I owe so many people apologies." Nathan said which surprised me seeing all the remorse on his face. "I did her so wrong, I know a simple apology wouldn't cut it." D was locked on Nathan's eyes. "She hates me?" He asked D.

"Yes!" He said without an apology.

Nathan shook his head like he understood, "I deserve that. I've never met anyone like her, a messed up kid can't handle that kind of goodness." Nathan said in defeat.

"Right, cause she's too good for the type of person you tried to change her into being." D spit watching his face.

My grandmother kept looking between the both of them. Nathan bowed his head cause he knew he was wrong and D was looking for him to step out of line. "Sounds like you care about this girl very much." she said

"I love her! But I have to deal with the baggage that people like him gave her!"

I sunk a little in my seat, it naturally rolled off his tongue that he loved her and that stabbed me. "I'm sorry." Nathan said

I could tell D wanted an excuse to hit Nathan. I guess Nathan wasn't stupid. Then a hand patted D's shoulder, "you alright?" It was the Dwayne guy. His face was serious looking at D, and the girls were still looking.

"Of course! I was hoping he'd buck up at me so I'd have an excuse to break him down. He ain't stupid I see." D said still watching Nathan.

"Aren't you that guy?" My grandmother said with a smile.

Dwayne was focused on D he didn't see the rest of us. He smiled, "yes. And you are?"

"Johnnie Mae Richardson, can I have your autograph?"
"Of course! Whom should I make it out to?" He said taking the napkin and pen from my grandmother.
"To my suga momma Johnnie Mae!" She smiled real big.
"Got it," he said signing her napkin.
He gave the signed napkin to my grandmother and then D stood up slowly. They went back to his table. One of the girls said something and D was cracking up. My grandmother was too excited about her autograph. My grandmother pulled out her phone to call someone. I looked at Nathan and I asked him if he was ok. He asked me how Kendra was. I exhaled and told him I didn't know and we weren't friends anymore. I told him I gave her a hard time when I found out about them. He said he wanted to apologize to her personally. I told him that wasn't a good idea, then we looked at D's table and he was watching like he could read lips.

Kendra

I talked to Ahjani, I told him that Omar entered the draft. Ahjani said he has a little to go before he earns his Bachelor's. He said he's going to enter the draft next year, even though his potential agents wanted him to do it this year. He said Omar lacks patience and it was sad cause if he gets hurt or anything happens. He'll have to try to pick up where he left off in his career.
"Los Angeles wants Omar Gordon!" Kalani screamed as she ran in the room full of excitement. My momma, Jason, and I were watching a movie in the family room.
"Are you sure?" I said sitting up.
"YES!"
"I can't believe he did it!" Then my cell phone rang. "Hello?" I said with a smile.
"I'm going to ask you again, what kind of engagement ring do you want?"
My momma and Jason were smiling at me. "Congratulations, Kalani just told us the news."
"Congratulations to us! I'm going to come see you as soon as I can. I love you so much Kendra!"
"Whoa! Whoa! Omar, I'm not the same person you left behind three years ago. You're about to be in a totally different league."

He chuckled, "Kendra. I know you, I'm going to marry you. I'm coming out there to propose properly to you and then we'll make arrangements to set a date."

"Omar, you didn't even ask me if I was dating someone. I have a whole life here."

"Even if you are dating someone they're irrelevant to me. I'm Omar, your first love, your first real boyfriend, your first everything. Anyone after me doesn't matter to who we are and what we mean to each other."

"Omar!"

"If you don't tell me what kind of ring you want I will be forced to wing it. I think I can pick out a pretty good one on my own."

My momma was smiling at me, Jason wasn't. "We need to talk before you do anything that drastic."

"Fine, then let's talk." He said getting comfortable on the phone.

I couldn't bring myself to tell him about Darryl, so I talked around it. We talked for hours, and then I started to remember why I cared about him so much back in the day. Omar was always good to me and looking out for me. Yea so in the end he started thinking big, but that's because he believed in his self when no one else did. I can't fault him for that.

When we finally got off the phone I went back in the room with my parents who still had our movie paused and were now talking about something. Jason asked me what Omar was talking about. So I told him that Omar claims he's coming out here to propose to me. Jason asked me if that's what I wanted. I shrugged, his life is a lot more fancier than I wanted to live. However, he is offering me more than baby momma status. Jason said there was something he didn't like about Omar but he couldn't put his finger on it. He said whenever Omar shows his face to make sure to bring him by before I gave him a yes or no.

Nellie

"LEASHA!" Someone barked from behind me and made me drop my keys. I have been on a covert mission since I came back from Vegas. I didn't want to see or deal with Gordon. Let whomever he called after he was chosen deal with him. I'm over it! I snatched my keys off the ground while I gave him an evil look. "Why are you avoiding me?"

"I'm done!" I said with all the attitude in the world.

"What?"

"I didn't stutter! Go be with whomever you called right away when you got the news. I'm done!"

He grabbed my arm before I sat in my car, "wait a minute Leasha! I don't understand this. What's going on? What are you talking about?"

"You talk all this game about us being together, and all your plans. Then when something happens you left me hanging. It's ok Gordon, you go your way and I'll go mine. No love lost."

"I was talking to my mom. You're going to punish me for talking to my mom?"

"For all that time?"

"Yes, her dream came true that night. Do you think that was a quick conversation?" He watched my eyes. "I can't believe we lost all this celebration time over an assumption." Then he kissed me, "you know you're beautiful when you try to punish me." Then he kissed me again. "Now that that's out of the way, go home and put on something nice! I'm taking you out to celebrate."

"Like what?"

"Something sexy! I've got some serious love making to do to you if you think you could walk away from me like that," He smiled.

I gave him a courtesy smile then I got in my car. There was a little voice saying he was lying but I had no real way of proving it.

So I went home, showered, curled my hair, put on a little makeup, got dressed then I waited. Gordon looked nice and he loved my dress. He was driving a nice brand new car with all the bells and whistles. No more bumming rides from me. He took me to a nice restaurant in Scottsdale. He enjoyed a couple drinks from the bar since he could, while I sipped my soda. I could tell he was tipsy so I asked him for his keys. I wanted to see if he was going to be stingy. He quickly passed them to me. On the car ride to my place I was enjoying driving his car. If you tapped the gas it flew. This car had so much power I could see it getting him in trouble. He told me he wanted me to transfer to a school in Los Angeles to be with him. He said he's going to rent until he finds a house out there. Maybe a townhouse to start off. When I asked where his momma was going to be, he's sucked his teeth. He said she'd only be with us at first. I declined, I told him no thanks. I'd wait for him to get more established first. He didn't like that answer.

Even though he was slightly drunk he did a good job of getting me involved in this adventure. This was more like our sex in the beginning when he put some effort into it. Never mind blowing sex, but at least I got a release.

****

I helped Gordon and his momma pack up their apartment. His momma could've cared less that Gordon said it wasn't my fault, she was still mad at me for the whole incident.

We went out to lunch, in a nearby cafe as part of our last day together in Arizona. I told him to focus on his career and I'd be around later. Then Brice walked in and everything in Gordon changed. We were holding hands across the table and now he was squeezing my hands. "Ouch Gordon! Ouch!" I said trying to get my hands away from him.

"Stay away from him! You hear me!" He said squeezing my hands harder.

"You're hurting me!"

"Let's go!" He said grabbing me by the collar of my shirt and dragging me out of my chair.

He wasn't high or had anything to drink. I couldn't believe he was doing this in front of everybody. "Gordon let me go!" I said trying to remove his hand off my shirt.

He pulled me outside, "I turned a blind eye to the Mexican. Do you think that means I can't see?"

"I don't know what you're talking about!" I said getting my shirt free.

He picked me up by my shoulders and threw my back against his car, then he grabbed my face. "You think I don't know what you did, what you do? You're out trying to make me look like a fool!" Then he pressed my body into the car. I screamed from the pressure of him pressing in on me like he was ramming me against the car without lifting me. "Why would you purposely humiliate me like this?" He watched my face for an answer. "I'll tell you what you're going to do! You're going to transfer to LA to be with me! I'm the only fool stupid enough to love your tramp self! You're gonna stop giving my pussy away! Everybody knows you're a hoe, and I'm a celebrity now! You can go to the police if you want but no one will believe you. I'll be the poor athlete taken in by your womanly charms! I could kill you and I'd get away with it! Tell your daddy or whomever you're transferring next year. Don't make me have to come out here to get you!"

He was still pressing in on me and I heard a pop, then I couldn't move my arm, the pain was excruciating. "Gordon stop!" All those people were looking but no one did or said anything.

He looked at my limp arm, as I cried. "You dislocated your shoulder. Let me help you fix it." Then he grabbed my arm with one hand while putting the other in my armpit. He stretched my arm out to pop it back in place, all while I screamed in pain. Once my shoulder went back in, the pain wasn't as bad. He grabbed my shirt then he kissed me. I was scared and felt helpless. Then he told me to get in the car. He took me to the drugstore and he got a sling for my shoulder. He was being so kind to all the people in the store, explaining that he knew what to do cause this always happened to him when he was younger. He told me to take ibuprofen and to wear my sling for a week and that I'd be fine. My whole body hurt as I walked up the stairs to my place. Gordon followed me like nothing just happened. He ran a bath and put the Epsom salt and bubble bath he just bought in the water. As he undressed me he told me to shut up, and stop crying. He asked where my tears were when I was letting Brice or any of the others in. He told me to get in the bath, I did as I was told cause he looked crazier than I had ever seen him. He went down the short list, but list of men that I've cheated on him with. All he needed was to add Ahjani and D to the list and then it would've been complete. He said he wouldn't tolerate it anymore. "Tell your father you're coming to LA, don't make me have to show up out here and drag you out there personally."

I existed in a place of numbness until Gordon left. I waited an hour after he left then I called home. I told them I wanted to come home. I told them I wasn't coming back out here next year. My stepmom didn't ask a bunch of questions. She said she was coming first thing tomorrow to pack me up.

Kendra

"KB! What you doing girl?" Darryl's voice came blasting over my phone.

"Just got out the shower, I'm done with work."

"Cool, Ryder and Ahjanae are about to meet me for dinner. You should ride with them, I've got somebody I want you to meet."

"Who?"

"You'll see, just come on." I threw on jeans, a top, and heels. Ryder drove us to Gonzalez's a Mexican food restaurant in Oakland. Darryl's car was in the parking lot when we pulled up. When we walked in the door, the staff greeted Ryder and then we followed him to a booth on the side. Darryl was sitting across from two light skinned gorgeous girls. "KB! Come meet my sisters!" Both of the girls smiled, "this is Crystal and that's Tiffany, you guys this is Kendra." I waved and they waved.

"Nice to meet you." I felt relieved that they were family.

"This is Ahjanae, and our daughter Erin." Ryder said

"Ryder's got a girlfriend!" They sang together, teasing him. Ryder turned red and told them to cut it out.

Then the hilariousness of the evening began, they started telling us stories about when they were younger. Even their story about when Darryl found my seashell on their family trip. When they started talking about their weekend in Vegas the week before I told Darryl he gets around too much. Darryl smiled and said he's always making moves.

"Ahjanae and Ryder are technically the only ones old enough to get in. KB got jeans on." Darryl said trying to kill the thought of going to Elegant Affairs.

"Will Drew be there?" Tiffany asked

"I doubt it, he's been acting like an old man lately with his girlfriend. Drew don't fight no more, he ain't out all that much anymore, he's changed."

"He's maturing, you can't expect to be at the club your entire life." Crystal said.

"I can die trying can't I?"

"Please promise me you won't be that nasty old guy that we make fun of and run from at the club. He thinks he's doing good cause he normally hooks up. But he's only hooking up with the little girl with severe daddy issues. I want more for your life than that." Crystal said

"Naw, by the time I'm old I'll be hanging out at lounges, wine rooms, places that old people go. You know like places your dad goes to."

Tiffany huffed, "my daddy ain't old!"

Darryl faked surprised, "girl hush! You know your daddy is old!" Crystal shook her head, "no he's not! You're just a hater!"

"KB, tell them they daddy is old." Darryl said like he knew I'd have his back.

"I can't, I've never met him or seen him."

"Do you know who Dwayne Reed is?" Tiffany asked.

"Who doesn't know who he is." Ahjanae said

"That's our daddy, please tell him that our father is not old." Tiffany said

"SHUT UP! That's your dad?" Ahjanae said looking between both of their faces the same way I was. "Sorry Darryl, he ain't old!" Darryl smirked at Ahjanae, "good thing your name ain't KB! Go ahead KB tell them!"

I looked at the girls, "Ladies," Darryl sat up straight ready to say something like "see!" or something. "Your daddy is not old and he's FINE as heck!" I said giving Ahjanae a high five.

"KB!" Darryl looked at me in disbelief, "how you gonna act like this? Not in front of the kids!" He said pointing to his sisters. They were cracking up, "whatever! The point, our daddy ain't old."

Instead of going to the club Darryl talked them down to coming back to his brother Drew's place in Emeryville. He said since Drew got with his girlfriend he barely comes home, and the place basically sits empty so he comes here from time to time. I didn't say anything but I wondered if he ever came here alone.

Tiffany and Crystal were sweet and a lot of fun. I thought it was nice that even though their parents aren't together they remained a blended family.

Chapter 17

Nellie

I didn't sleep much at all last night. Everything felt like it was closing in on me. I thought about calling my sorority sisters to ask for help packing, then I thought about it. The sisters who were in the restaurant did nothing to help me. No one even called me to check on me. When I heard my front door opening my heart dropped. Although I never gave Gordon a key, I didn't know what was happening. "Princess?" I heard my father's voice call out. I ran to the living room with my arm in the stupid sling. Both of my parent's eyes went to my arm. My daddy wanted to know what happened to my arm before he'd even hug me. I told him I fell. My stepmom watched me but didn't say anything. I told them I didn't want to come back out here next year. I wanted to transfer to a school close to home. We went to a moving truck company. We reserved a truck for tomorrow to haul all of my things back to California. We got tons of boxes and supplies to pack my things. When my dad left to go put in my notice at the leasing office and then go get food, the door barely closed before my stepmom was on me. She wanted to know the guy's name that hurt me. Where he was, and why was I protecting him. When I tried to act like I didn't know what she was talking about she got mad and said I was insulting her. So I broke down and told her that his name didn't matter cause he moved out of state. I told her that he was demanding that I move with him and he threatened to come back for me if I didn't follow him. My stepmom said history was repeating itself and I needed help. I needed to stop dealing with predators, but I had to learn how to value myself so that I stopped standing out as prey. When I argued that I did value myself, she countered with asking me why I would protect someone who hurt me then. Her question made me angry so I stopped talking. I thought she understood, but her question showed she didn't. I don't walk around looking like a bum, or let myself go. If I didn't value myself I would look very plain and homely like most of these females around here. My stepmom kept trying to make me understand, but she lost me a long time ago. When my father came with food from the local taqueria, my stepmom informed us that she made a doctor's appointment for me that my father needed to take me to, to make sure my arm was ok.

My father asked why I had a sudden urgency to transfer close to home. I told him I was tired of this ridiculous heat, and I missed living in the Bay Area. He asked if Marquez was coming back early and that's why I wanted to move back. I told him no.

The next day my dad hired some guys to help him load up the truck with all my things. We did a final walk through with the leasing staff and then they put my car on the trailer, and we got in the truck. I called and changed my number, when they gave me the new number I felt like a weight had been lifted. Goodbye Gordon!

Kendra

My sisters looked so proud as the graduates. Milton brought his baby with him to support Kaleah at her graduation. My momma told me that they were ridiculous and she couldn't stand to watch them. She said Milton has another baby on the way, but he's constantly telling Kaleah how much he loves her. My momma said it was only a matter of time before Kaleah was pregnant too.

When Kalani walked over proudly holding the hand of some guy, Jason, Darryl, Ryder, Aunrey, and Ahjani looked like a wall of men ready to pounce. "Sis, who's this?" Darryl asked

"A friend." She said all smiles.

"What do you want?" Jason said folding his arms.

The guy started stammering, "he's coming with us!" Kalani said like she didn't understand what the big deal was.

Darryl shook his head, "this guy is weak. Application DENIED!"

"What?" Kalani asked squinting her eyes.

"We don't want no tag alongs tonight." Jason said

Kalani looked at her friend, "oh I see. One moment." She walked over to her friend and took his gown off. She pushed his pants to a slight sag, she turned his cap around backwards. Then she told him to mimic her stance as she stood like Aunrey. He did it, then she looked at the men. "Application resubmission!"

Darryl started cracking up laughing, which made everyone else laugh. "Why his pants gotta sag though? I don't sag, Malcolm would have a fit if I walked around with my draws showing."

"None of you even gave him a chance. Judging a book by its cover. I figured you'd have a better reaction to this cover." She smiled.

Darryl looked at Jason who was not amused. "Aw come on Jayman. If he knows what's good for him he'll remain harmless." Darryl flashed him a look.

"Not my baby girl! I don't even like you!" He said looking at Milton.

"I know! D told me you want to shoot me." Milton said like he understood.

"And I will!" Jason promised.

****

Anton's referrals were coming in left and right. I couldn't believe how much business we were generating just from him. So I did my part and started talking up his landscaping business, Tafoya Landscaping, which was making our partnership a win win situation. Anton thanked me for seeing things his way. He said we needed to go out to celebrate both of our successes. I told him that was fine as long as he wasn't hitting on me. Anton wasn't ugly, but he wasn't stop the presses this man is so fine either. Not that any of that mattered, no one could be finer than Darryl to me, my Hershey's kiss. Anton was handsome, but it didn't matter.
I had Kalani, Ahjanae, and Ryder come; Darryl was missing in action as usual. Aunt Quilla came and kidnapped Erin earlier that day. We met Anton and his crew at this restaurant in El Sobrante. Everyone was all smiles and full of appreciation for our collaboration. I did see Anton kind of get that look and I felt squeamish about it. I hope he understands this is a business relationship and nothing more.

Nellie

Marquez said it seemed so weird to think of me being at home without him. He went with me to transfer my information to SF State for the Fall. Being close to home was going to feel nice. Junior lowered the boom that he and his girlfriend were engaged and moving in together. That meant that I got to have Junior and Nathan's old room. Nassya wasn't happy that we wouldn't be sharing a room. Once I told her she could sleep in my bed still she lightened up about the whole thing. Nassya talked our dad into taking the carpets out of our rooms and putting hardwood flooring in both. We took my bedroom furniture out of storage and put my old furniture from Nassya's room in my storage. Nassya decorated both rooms, then we talked my dad into letting us do the whole house. Once we got my stepmom on board he didn't have a choice. Remodeling filled our summer with a task that kept us pretty busy.

****

Nassya and I were in the middle of getting measurements for each room when the house number rang. "Hello?"

"YOU CHANGED YOUR NUMBER!" Gordon's voice blasted me through the phone. "Guess you forgot to call me with the new number!"

I completely forgot that he had the number to the house. My head started pounding, "you know how it is when I'm with my family. I was going to call you."

"You're a liar!"

"Why would I lie?"

"You told them about me?"

"No."

"Good girl, now..." I could hear the smile in his voice. "When are you coming out?"

"I don't know." I said feeling helpless.

"Leasha baby, I need you. I'm stressed out, out here without you. I need you to come work your magic on me. I need you to bring the catnip."

I knew he was going to be mad. "Gordon, baby I'm kind of in the middle of a project here with my parents. I need to finish it before I talk to them about leaving."

He was breathing hard for a minute like he was thinking. "Fine." He said in defeat. His voice sounded sad, "Leasha. I'm sorry about the way we left each other. I wanted to come back, but my mom wouldn't let me. I didn't blame you for not answering when I called. When you changed your number I thought you were trying to passively breakup with me. But I remembered how much you love me. I know I have to earn your trust back, but that's why I need you to come out here so you can see me coming home to you every night. Taking you with me when I go out. I love you so much and my jealousy has gotten out of hand I'm man enough to admit that. I am so sorry for hurting you like that. It won't happen again."

"Ok," I heard myself say.

"Why would you cheat on me? What's wrong with me that you aren't satisfied with me?"

"Gordon I don't know what happened. I don't do anything to hurt you intentionally. You deserve better than someone who takes you out of yourself. I know I make you angry and I'm so sorry. Maybe you're better off without me."

"What? No! I can't be without you! I'll kill myself!"

"Gordon! Your mother would be so hurt."

"So what! She has her life and I have mine! She could live without me. I can't live without you! I haven't slept well without you. I've got to smoke just to sleep. When you come I won't need it anymore. I need you to make love to me. I need to feel your love. You're out there giving the Mexican all of my love."

"No," I said feeling guilty. I make love to Marquez, I've resorted to giving Gordon what he wants so he'll go away for a while. If I thought D would see me, he'd be on my love list. But he doesn't answer my calls. "Gordon, I gotta go. I'll call you back." I said then I hung up. I asked my stepmom to change our home number.

****

As usual Marquez came over every day. My father tried to give him a hard time at first, eventually you could tell his heart softened towards him. So we learned to escape to be alone before my father came home to spare his heart the agony. Junior and his girlfriend got a place in Berkeley not too far from the salon that she worked at. My stepmom, Nassya, and I went to her to get our hair done regularly.

We were always her last clients of the day then we'd walk back to her place with her and hang out with her and Junior. They were so cute together.

As I was talking about how cute they were Marquez asked me if I wanted to get a place with him after he graduated. I don't know why that instantly made me feel bad. Marquez put his arms around me and kissed my forehead.

****

Marquez and I decided to celebrate being 21 by going out with Junior and his girlfriend. They always go to this club called Elegant Affairs. Junior loves it here cause this club is nice and they play live music. He was extremely excited that I was finally old enough to come. We got here early so that we wouldn't wait in the line long. When I saw how long the line was behind us, I was happy we came early too. We got a table on the side, then Junior and Marquez went to the bar to order drinks and food. I loved the vibe in this place I felt so mature and grown up. We had been here for a while when the band started setting up the stage for a performance. I was on my fourth drink and feeling good when a hand plops on Marquez's shoulder. "My man!" D said with a big smile. "What's up? What you doing in my house?"

Marquez smiled big, got up and gave D a hug. "What's up? We came to check things out."

D said hi to everyone, I was disappointed that he didn't assign anything more to my hello than anyone else's. Marquez and D talked for a minute then D left. Junior's girlfriend and I went to the bathroom. This girl got in line behind us and openly looked us up and down. "How you two know D?" She asked boldly.

"Who are you?" I asked returning the scan of her from head to toe. She was nicely built, long black hair, deep chocolate skin. She was very pretty, but not prettier than me!

"Toya, he hasn't told you about me?" She said watching my eyes with evilness in hers.

I chuckled to myself, "whoever you are you're pathetic!" Then I turned around.

She moved closer to talk in my ear. "Clearly you have no idea who I am. You will regret turning your back on me."

I turned around fast. "You don't know who I am and you got the nerve to threaten me! You need to watch out!"

She smiled, "if you were going to do something you would've done it already." Then she walked past us and went into the next open stall.

"What was that?" Junior's girlfriend asked.

I shook my head, does alcohol make you hallucinate? When we got back to the table D sent more food and bottles of the good stuff. I looked around and a lot of females were watching our table. D was on the dance floor with some girl freaking the daylights out of her. I looked around and I didn't see that girl anywhere. I tried not to stare at D while he was dancing, but I couldn't help it. Everything he did was like poetry in motion. Marquez pulled me on the dance floor when the guy performing sang a slow song. D said "hey" to me then he went back to his partner who looked annoyed by his break in concentration. I told Marquez I wanted to ask him who the girl was. Marquez told me to wait until he came back to our table.

When Marquez and I sat down to drink some more, D came over. He kept directing his conversation to Marquez, which irritated me. "D!" Both of them shot me the same look. "Who is Toya?"

"The devil in a dress, why?"

"She threatened me in the bathroom!"

"Why didn't you handle her?" He asked like that should've been my natural response.

"I didn't get dressed up to come to the club to fight."

"But I'm supposed to fight for you? Why are you telling me?" He said sounding annoyed.

"She approached me on account of you. I thought you should know."

D looked at Marquez, "your Queen Cluck is a trip sometimes." Marquez started cracking up. "We'll talk later. I'll call you." Then he walked away.

"You talk to D?"

"All the time," Marquez said giving me a look that said drop it.

Kendra

I knocked on the door as I opened it. "Mrs. McCall? I'm here!" When she didn't respond I got a sinking feeling. I hurried to her room and she was laying in her bed with tears streaming down her face. I could tell she was in pain, but she was stubborn about taking her pain meds. She looked at me and shook her head. I called the hospital and they sent paramedics out to transport her to the hospital. My parents and sisters met us there. They gave her medicine to make her comfortable and then they said it wouldn't be long. We said our goodbyes and she passed away that night. My momma kept calling her kids from the time she came in here the first time. She never got a callback. When my momma called and left messages that Mrs. McCall passed away then they responded just like Mrs. McCall said they would. Mrs. McCall's friends came to the hospital grieving and going off on her no good kids who had the nerve to show up now. Both of her boys were older than my momma; their demeanors were cold and uninviting. They started asking about her will right away. When my momma started going off, they didn't care. Jason was pissed; he told them they would hear from Mrs. McCall's lawyer regarding the reading of her will. Jason told them we'd call with the arrangements for the funeral.

When Darryl came I cried on his shoulder. I told him how she saved us from homelessness. How much she helped and saved our family. He held me and let me cry it out on his shoulder. He told me he was going to miss her too. Darryl had to move his schedule around for the summer to be there with me at the funeral. Most of Mrs. McCall's friends cried their eyes out, including my momma. You would've sworn it was her mother that passed away by how hurt she was.

I was watching Darryl's routine before he got in the bed with me. He took off his clothes, folded them neatly. Brushed his teeth and washed his face. Then he'd do some silly kind of dance to the bed. I'd leave the big blanket at the bottom of the bed cause halfway through the night he'd have all the covers kicked off the bed. It never failed, if I waited until the middle of the night, the chances were higher that I'd have covering in the morning. Then we'd have a silly debate about the covers until he had me laughing so hard it didn't matter anymore. Today has been so sad I looked forward to him making me smile. He kissed me when he got in the bed. "Has Ryder told you their news?"

He cut his eyes at me, "about them going domestic? Yeah, he told me. Why?"

"I was just thinking. The older you are when you have babies, the less time you have with them."

He thought about it for a minute. "Yes, but the younger you are the goofier you are as parents. My parents tried to be good, but we were all right there going through the motions with them. They still don't make any sense!"

"So you don't want to have children now?"

"Not when I'm running around like a little Malcolm."

"What does that mean?"

He exhaled, "KB. I love you. But I'm not ready."

"Ok," I said then I turned my back to him cause I was crying. He was quiet, when he heard me inhale like I was crying he jumped. "KB! Are you crying?" He grabbed my head, and made me look at him. "What did I do? Why?" He looked concerned.

"You're going to keep punishing me!" I said feeling like a baby.

"I'm not punishing you, I just don't think now is a good time." I cried harder, he exhaled. "Kendra I don't understand why you're crying. Help me."

"Really.... Doesn't....... Matter....... Cause..... If...... I.......
Hadn't....... Messed up...... We'd be parents........ Right....... NOW!"
I could tell he didn't consider that. He put his arms around me. "I
know, but it's for the best and we can't change what happened."
"I...... I........ I....... I want...... My........ Baby......... Back!......" I
cried
"Kendra..." His voice sound hurt.
Then Ahjanae knocked on the door, "Kendra?"
"Hold on Jen," Darryl called out. I guess she thought he said come
in cause she slowly pushed the door open. Darryl covered me with
the covers and put the blanket up to his neck. "Jen!"
Ahjanae was focused on me, "Kendra are you ok?" She said
walking into the room.
I shook my head yes even though I couldn't stop crying. Ryder
knocked on the door. "Darryl what did you do now?"
"Nothing man! I'm laying here in my sexy suit and it was too much
for her." Darryl tisked.
Ahjanae and I started laughing, "your what?"
"My sexy suit! I had to quickly pull the covers up to my neck so
that you wouldn't be blinded by all my beauty!"
"She sees beauty daily! She ain't worried about your nibblets!"
Ryder said.
"Nibblets? Nibblets? Ryder I taught you everything you know, and
you still couldn't handle the lesson!" Darryl said putting his arms
outside of the covers.
"Apparently Kendra couldn't handle the lesson either. You finally
left the light on and she cried from the disappointment." Ryder
cracked up.
Darryl stared at Ryder with irritation, "you brought this on yourself
Ryder! I didn't want to have to show you up in front of your girl,
but you leave me no choice." He threw back the covers to reveal
his chest. "Look at these perfectly sculpted arms, chest, and
stomach. If I got on the floor and did pushups both of their heads
would pop off! POP OFF I SAY!" Darryl said rubbing his
stomach.
Ryder laughed, "well we don't want that to happen." Then he
tapped my foot. "You ok kiddo?"
"Long day," then I laid my head on Darryl's chest.

****

"To my son Ernest the second I leave my Sunday hat collection. To my youngest son Earl I leave my fan collection." The lawyer read. "WHAT?" Ernest stood up, "this doesn't make any sense. What did she leave them?" He pointed at us.

I was curious myself. I didn't want to come here, but Mrs. McCall's lawyer insisted that we were all present. She left her clothes, antique furniture, and cars to her friends. She left all her jewelry to my momma, the estimated value was about eighty thousand. My momma cried so hard. She left company stocks, bonds, and money to Kaleah, Kalani, and I. Then I thought I was going to pass out when he said she left her house to Kalani and I. Both of Mrs. McCall's sons hopped up screaming and hollering. The lawyer said that if they contested the Will they wouldn't get anything cause her Will was iron clad. Ernest was still going off when Earl told him two kids would only end up losing the house any ways. When Ernest continued to go off, Jason looked at the ceiling then he counted backwards from five out loud. Ernest and Earl looked at Jason in surprise. "Sonny is there any reason why they need to still be here?"

"No, I have your boxes right here gentlemen." The lawyer said handing a box to each son. "I've met with your mother over the past years, and she kept changing her mind about her Will. But one thing never changed." He looked at them, "one of you was getting the hats, and the other was getting the fans. It was always up for grabs which one got which."

"What am I supposed to do with some old lady hats?" Ernest said

"This is what your mother wanted. At least look at the hats, there's always more to a gift than you know." The lawyer said.

"No thank you!" Ernest said declining the box.

"And you can keep those fans! She used to bop me with those fans on Sundays during service. Your momma got jokes up until the very end I see!" Earl said standing.

"Gentlemen, so that we're clear. If ANYTHING and I do mean ANYTHING happens to that house or anyone in that house, I'm coming for you. You don't want me to come for you!"

"Ain't nobody worried about that house! I got my own house!" Earl said walking out the door.

"Gentlemen if you don't want the boxes, I need you to sign saying you're waiving your rights to them." The lawyer said.

They came back and signed the waivers and left. The lawyer shook his head. "Just like she said!" Jason said angry.
"I know, a mother knows her children. Girls." The lawyer said looking at us. "You want these boxes!" Then he gave us a form to say we were taking the boxes. In each box there were three boxes each one had one of our names on it. We sat there in disbelief about how well Mrs. McCall knew her boys. She knew they weren't going to take the boxes. On the top of our hats were letters to each of us from her. She was telling us how much she loved us and how proud of us she was. Then she told us to pay attention to each detail in our hats and the letter said the same thing in the fan boxes. Inside the hats were cash. The paper around the money said, "mad money". And the handles on the fans screwed off and there was more money rolled up in them. All hundreds!
"Sonny, what's with the cash?" Jason asked the lawyer.
"Mrs. McCall kept cash around the house as part of her in case of emergency money. As part of her last revision to her Will she decided that the girls would get the money. She knew her sons."
We signed more papers and then we left the fancy San Francisco Lawyer's office. Jason said it was a small world and it figures that Mrs. McCall would entrust her arrangements to someone he knew.

Nellie

Seeing Nassya all dressed and leave with my stepmom for her first day of school made me think about my momma. I wonder if she ever thought about me, if she regretted letting Bobby come after me. If she even cared about me anymore. My dad was about to leave for work when he saw me lost in my thoughts. He asked me if I was ok. I said an unconvincing yes. He told me to get dressed cause I was coming with him. In the car he kept looking at me and smiling. He asked me if I was missing Marquez already cause he just left. I shrugged. We went to his office. He made a few phone calls, answered a few emails. Then we got in his car, I didn't say anything. I watched the surroundings become familiar and I couldn't explain why. There was a park and a pond with ducks. Then a fountain in the middle of the other pond. "Do you remember this place?"
"It looks familiar but I don't know why."
"I used to bring you here all the time when you were little."

It all started coming back to me. "This is where you told me about Nassya."

He tried to smile, "yes."

"I don't mean to keep beating a dead horse but how could you leave us like that?"

"There is no excuse for what I did to you or Mary. I always told her I loved her and she could trust me. Then I chose your stepmom, Princess you don't ever have to forgive me. I understand if you don't, I never thought she would let someone harm you."

"Just you!" I spit.

My daddy swallowed, "ok. Point taken, I'll stop pointing my finger at Mary."

"I love my momma very much! There's a lot I don't understand, but she was all I had at one point in my life. You don't even know me or what I go through."

He looked at me, "you're just like Mary. I know you." He exhaled and rubbed his head. "I don't know how to help you. I want you to be better than Mary. If you continue like this you'll end up just like her."

"What's wrong with being like my momma? She loved me and showed me love. She gave up a lot for me."

"She also taught you to go after a man with money instead of working for your own. You don't have to be limited by what someone allows you to have. You can build your own. When are you going to pick a major?"

"I'm not Junior, I haven't loved computers since I was three."

"I'm not asking you to be a computer wizard. I'm asking you to have your own."

Kendra

Mrs. McCall's house was four and a half bedrooms with two and a half bathrooms. Once we got the house completely cleared out, Kalani and I took up the carpet and to our surprise. The original flooring was wood. We polished them and made them sparkle. The half sized room would be our home office. Kalani and I picked our rooms. I picked the room in the very back next to the bathroom, and Kalani picked the one in the front close to the other full bathroom. Jason was making a list of all the upgrades the house needed, and he arranged to have the security system installed. The house had an attached two-car garage around the back that Jason told us to always park in. Kaleah wanted momma's house, but she has no way to pay for it. So Ahjanae talked Ryder into staying although he wanted his own place for them. She said it was easier to stay then leave just yet. Now that Ryder is finished with school she said they'll start trying soon, both of them are scared but excited. I chewed back my jealousy and I was happy for them. As we painted the house I was thinking to myself. I really wanted a baby, and now I have the space to have one. With Kalani and Ahjanae's help our business would be fine and I could probably focus more on making it grow while I was pregnant. I didn't have Darryl's permission to get pregnant the first time. Like I'd need it to make it happen again. I made a deal with myself that I was getting pregnant as soon as he slipped up again.

****

Anton looked around as he complimented us on the look of the house. We thanked him, then we took him into our office. He showed us sketches of his plans for our front and backyard. They were beautiful, and we knew Mrs. McCall would've loved the new look. Anton said he'd have to work on our yard on Sundays so that he didn't interfere with other projects. I told him he could show us what he needed done in between time and we could work on getting it done. Anton refused, he said he was going to make our yards part of his showcase. He took a bunch of pictures all over. Then he came back inside and he asked for our preference on something's. Kalani got a phone call so she excused herself. Anton looked a little nervous about being alone with me, but talked through it. I didn't hear him coming or anything, suddenly Darryl was in the doorway applauding us. I smiled, "Darryl this is my landscaping partner Anton that I told you about." Neither one of them smiled, they kind of blank stared at each other. "Hello?"

"Why is he so close to you?" Darryl said leaning against the doorway.

"We were going over his pictures." I said not understanding his point.

"KB, you know that was ten minutes ago." Then he looked at Anton. "I know what you're trying to do. It ain't gonna work. That one is mine!"

"It ain't gonna?" Anton mocked him.

Darryl flexed his hands, "is it cracking time? You need to move before I break you down in front of my woman!"

Carey Anderson

Anton blew irritated air, "Kendra I'll call you later with more details." Then he grabbed his stuff to walk out the door. Darryl was a little taller than Anton. "Don't ever let me catch you in my woman's personal space like that ever again!"
"Whatever!" Anton said walking past him.
"Darryl!" I called him cause he was about to follow Anton out. "I didn't know you were coming over?" I smiled.
"So that's why you're flirting with the Gardner, cause you thought you'd get away with it?"
I frowned, "I wasn't flirting with him."
"I saw you bbbbbbeeeeennnnnddddd ova in front of him!" If I wouldn't have seen his face I would've thought he was kidding.
"I did not!"
"Oh so now I'm a liar?" He waited for a response.
"What's wrong with you?"
"I don't understand why you gotta try to play me. ME!"
"Nobody's playing you." Then I looked at him, "you're acting very guilty. What have you done?" I eyed him.
He was about to say something until my question made him think. He put his finger down then he was quiet for a minute. Then he shot me evil eyes, "I'll be back!" He marched out the door to Ahjanae's. He was banging on the door asking Ryder to open up.
****
I couldn't stop staring at her, she was still beautiful! You know how someone will be a cute kid and then you see him or her after high school and they look tore down? Nellie's still beautiful not that I wished anything bad on her. I know she doesn't want to talk to me so there's no point in saying anything.
She got off the Bart train at my stop, so I walked so many people behind her. I swallowed when she entered my school. I wonder if she's been here the whole time. When she went to the right I went to the left. I kept seeing that hot pink jacket everywhere, even in a couple of classes. Nellie's always been such a girl, dresses, accessories, long hair. Where I'm always in pants, shirts, and short hair. I have girlie moments, but Nellie is always on and always beautiful! Oh well, maybe if I wouldn't have wasted so much time trying to be her friend I would've made a bus load of other friends. Friends that I'd still have today.

When I got home I was telling Ahjanae who I saw when Ryder came home. "She looked exactly the same when I saw her too." She said

"When did you see her?"

"At the pancake house, it was right before that crazy guy started hanging around out front."

"Who are we talking about?" Ryder asked.

"Do you remember that girl at the pancake house that I introduced you to? Light skinned, real pretty, Filipino boyfriend."

Ryder shrugged, "not really. Should I?"

"No you shouldn't. But she used to be Kendra's best friend. They're going to the same school now."

Ryder bucked his eyes, "you don't say. So did you guys sit down and have a reunion?"

"Naw! She's done with me cause I used to like her brother. I tried to call her after that and she was still mad."

"I gave her your number, I guess she never called you." Ahjanae said

I shrugged, "I guess not. Eventually she's going to realize I'm there, I know she's been through a lot. So I won't make her talk to me if she doesn't want to."

Nellie

"NOEL! WHAT GAME ARE YOU PLAYING?" D yelled into my phone.

"How did you get this number?" I said rubbing the sleep from my eyes.

"If you don't stop playing, I'm coming in your house and waking everybody up!"

"What are you talking about? I didn't do anything!"

"SF State! How in the world did you end up there?"

"I fell out with my boyfriend at ASU, he threatened me so I bounced. What's wrong with me going to SF State? You go there?" I hoped he said yes.

"NO! I'm gonna tell you this once and once only, behave yourself. You bring me drama and we're going to have problems you hear me?"

"At least we'd have something, I didn't see you all summer!"

"You aren't supposed to see me ever again. Why don't you respect that?"

"D! I love you! I will agree to anything to make you happy."

"Then agree to stop begging for my goodies, it makes me feel weird when you beg."

I smiled, "cause you like it?"

"I'll choke you!" He said through clinched teeth.

"D you know I love it when you do that. Choke me, pull my hair, spank me! I love it all!"

"CUT IT OUT NOEL! You're on your period and I don't walk through mud!"

I gasped, "how do you know that?"

D chuckled at my surprise, "bye Noel!"

I was happy to know he saved my number. See! I do matter!

****

I don't want a boyfriend, I'm cool! All I want is D, so I'm waiting for him to breakdown and call me. Every once in a while I randomly call him. I'm patiently waiting for that moment of weakness when he gives in to me. It's going to be so good! I can taste it already!

Since I'm back in the Bay there's only so many places I can go by myself. I go to school, study and come straight home. I try to keep my head down and keep to myself. I wouldn't be me without my fashion flare and love for everything pink. But I try to keep everything as muted as I can personally be.

The other day I noticed this girl looking at me, she wasn't frowning but she was blatantly watching me. I don't know where I could possibly know this girl from, I assume we went to school together. She doesn't come after me with anything so I doubt we went to school together. I hope she's not crushing on me, cause I don't need that right now. But then this morning my question was answered. I saw her on the Bart train, she was watching me like she normally does and then her friend bumped her to show her something in a magazine. It was Kendra! The girl watched me as I recognized Kendra and then I moved behind a few people in the train. The girl shook her head and grinned like she liked my reaction. It was then that I noticed the girl and Kendra everywhere. Kendra and I had two classes together. This is why D was yelling on my phone. Does he still see her? I did my best to ignore her presence.

****

Gordon's name is everywhere, he's rookie of the year. Part of me smiled for him and the other part didn't know how to feel.
I've spoken with Ahjani a few times and he's slotted to go first round pick for the draft this year. I love talking to him and hearing how he's doing, but its torture at the same time. I know he has a girlfriend who should be me. She'd be a fool to break up with him now. He's about to go pro, I hate being the other woman, when I was the only woman and first! Ahjani tells me he loves me and that never changed. It hurts because I know he means it.

Kendra

"Hello?"
"Did you see me on TV? I didn't expect to get off the bench so soon. LA is loving me! Everyone is screaming my name just like I always dreamed they would."
"I'm happy for you Omar."
"Happy for us! End of this season I'm picking up your ring and I'm coming out there."
"Jason wants to talk to you before you do anything drastic."
"What do you mean by drastic?"
"Before you go picking out a ring or anything you should talk to my father," I said proudly.
He blew air, "he's not your father. He's your stepdad." He mumbled.
OH NO HE DIDN'T! "Oh no you didn't! Did you really just go there with me?"
"I'm just saying I don't understand how he's supposed to matter to me and you."
"JASON IS MY FATHER! THE ONLY REAL FATHER I'VE EVER HAD! AND IF HE SAYS HE DOESN'T LIKE SOMEONE WHETHER I UNDERSTAND IT OR NOT I WILL ALWAYS SIDE WITH THE ONLY MAN TO EVER HAVE MY BACK COMPLETELY AND TOTALLY! JUST BECAUSE YOU NEVER HAD A REAL DAD DOESN'T EVER GIVE YOU THE RIGHT TO DOWN TALK MINE!"
"Whoa! Kendra, I'm sorry calm down!"
"I WILL NOT CALM DOWN! I CAN'T BELIEVE YOU EVEN CAME AT ME LIKE THAT! YOU OF ALL PEOPLE SHOULD KNOW WHAT MY FATHER MEANS TO ME! I'M DONE WITH THIS CONVERSATION! DON'T CALL ME

ANYMORE!" Then I hung up. I was so mad my chest was moving up and down so fast.

Kalani walked in the living room. "Who were you yelling at?"

"Omar!" I told her what happened and what he said.

She shook her head, "he should know better." Then she twirled in front of me. "How do I look?"

"Great! Where are you going?"

"With Darryl's cousins, Lanie said she invited you on your way home from school the other day."

"I need to study, don't you?" I said turning off the ringer on the phone cause Omar was on my nerves already as he tried to call me back.

"I'm good for tonight. Don't wait up." She called out walking towards the back to go in the garage.

I dozed off when Darryl's touch woke me. "A! Yo! Bookworm! I've been blowing you up, why did you turn your ringer off?"

"Omar pissed me off and I didn't want to talk to him anymore."

"What did the Star want?" He sat on my bed.

"He was asking if I saw his game, I didn't but I talked around it. He said he's going to buy an engagement ring when the seasons over and then he's coming for me. I told him he needed to talk to Jason before he does anything drastic. He got mad and then he's gonna tell me Jason isn't my father! I went off! Then I hung up in his face."

Darryl shook his head and whistled. "I wish someone would try to tell me Malcolm isn't my natural father. Sucks to be them!" Darryl said completely understanding where I was coming from.

"OK! EXACTLY! Just because his father is cracked out in North Richmond somewhere doesn't mean he has to hate on the fact that I have one." I said angry.

"Did you ever meet him?"

"The crack-head? I saw him once, tore Omar up! But we were never properly introduced."

"He wants to propose to you? Does he even know about me?"

"What's to know? You come over, we carefully have sex. You disappear!"

Darryl frowned at me, "somebody's in a mood." I rolled my eyes at him. "I LOVE it when you do that! Nobody else can do that as good as my momma but you. Do it again!"

"Where have you been? Is that what I need to do to see you, ignore your calls?"

"KB! You're hurting my feelings." He faked insulted.

"You don't care…"

"OK! This is about to get real and I didn't come over here to argue."

"What did you come for? I see your cousin more than I see you."

"You and Lanie go to the same school, that's not my fault."

"What did you come for?" I barked at him.

He looked at me for a minute like he was reading me. Then he got up and walked out the door. I heard him setting the alarm and then he came back in my room and shut the door. He ignored me and took off all of his clothes. He folded them neatly, then he walked up to me and kissed me deeply. I thought I was getting ready to tell him to get out, but the warmth of his mouth intoxicated me immediately! Ok, so maybe I was a little hard up and I definitely needed this to take the edge off. BUT! Then I found myself irritated cause I hadn't found a way around that condom yet. Darryl always brings his own, my entire stash has been sabotaged and the day we need mine I know it's on!

Darryl told me to stop being so mean; I shook my head in agreement as I laid on his chest.

Carey Anderson

Chapter 18

Nellie

I convinced Junior and his fiancé that they wanted to go out tonight. I needed a D fix in the worst way. It's been over a year since I felt him, I needed to feel him. Junior hated my dress, but somehow we convinced him it was ok for me to go out with them like this. I found the perfect hot pink spandex dress. My dress was short and left nothing to the imagination. I spotted that girl Toya who spoke in my ear the last time I was here. She didn't look evil like she did last time, but I knew it was her. She was with a guy who looked so proud to be with her. I noticed I wasn't the only female watching that girl looking pissed. One girl was going on and on about how she wanted to fight Toya cause she thinks she's all that!

When I came out the bathroom D was standing there looking annoyed. "What are you doing here Noel?"

"I miss you!"

"You are like a rash that won't go away!"

"It's ok if you scratch me." I smiled, he wasn't amused.

D bought me a drink and then we sat in the lounge area talking. Then a girl walked up full of attitude. "D! Who's this?"

"Did I ask you to come over here?" He barked at her.

"You told me to meet you here. It couldn't have been to watch you talk to this hoe!" She said full of attitude.

Darryl frowned, "go sit your mighty midget self over in the corner or go dance. I'll get to you when I get to you." The girl stood there staring, "or you could go home. You have choices!"

She sucked her teeth. "No! I've been waiting, you're not going home with this thing by default."

"Then go! I got enough love for many. You can't keep up any ways." He said dismissing her.

"I can keep up," I said watching his eyes.

"Yea, but you're going to school with Kendra now. I don't know how you're missing that this is about to blow up. I will not lose Kendra for you."

"She's not better than me!"

He blank stared at me, "I already told you she is. You can't have me so you chase me." He grabbed my thigh. "You kept wrapping those legs around me thinking that the next nutt I bust is going to change my mind." He exhaled, "my heart belongs to Kendra. I could get the same sensation with my hand that I get from you. Barely memorable and something to do to pass the time while she works out her daddy issues." He opened my legs, "you purring for me already?" He put his hand under my dress. He flicked me with his finger and smiled. "You're addicted! What is my man Marquez gonna do with you?"

Immediate guilt hit me, "he loves me?"

"Very much, he turns a blind eye to stuff like this because he loves you. I'd have snatched you up a long time ago." He rubbed me, "I'm not gonna do this Noel. I'll hit you up for a dance but you gotta stop." Then he walked away. A few of the girls in the lounge were shooting me daggers with their eyes. I guess they watched that whole scene. I crossed my legs to calm myself then I went back to our table. Junior was on the dance floor and D was in the VIP talking to a guy and a girl. The guy pointed out Toya and D approached her table with an evil smile. She shook her head no as he walked over and he shook his head yes. I wasn't close enough to know what they were saying. But that same short girl marched over to the table full of attitude. She exchanged words with Toya and Toya's man got mad. D opened his jacket and told the guy to be cool smiling the whole time.

I danced with a few guys as I watched D work the room. All the females were watching him and hoping that he picked them. Two girls even broke out in an argument over him, which rapidly turned into a fight.

When the guy and his girl left D took me to the middle of the dance floor. The music was bumping and so were we. If I had any shame about my love for D, I might've felt bad about working him in the middle of the dance floor. But when I looked around everyone was doing it, or looked like they were. I climbed up on D and wrapped my legs around him as I exploded. He backed up; fixed his pants, "leave me alone!" He said walking away from me like he felt bad about what just happened.

Kendra

Anton was telling me that I should've accepted his invitation out last night. The way he kept putting emphasis on last night was hanging on the air.

"What do you think?" Anton asked holding up beautiful flowers.
"Pretty, but I thought I asked for something easy to maintain. I'm not a Gardner."
Anton smiled, "I'm not trusting this yard to you. I'm going to maintain it myself as part of my business card."
"Oh," I smiled. "Carry on then."
Anton sat on the porch, "can I ask you something? You can say it's none of my business."
"What?"
"I mean I've been wrestling with myself over it even up until now." He looked at me, and I waited for him to say, "What's the deal between you and the thug? When I met him, he's calling you his woman."
"You saw him somewhere?"
"Is he your boyfriend?"
"It's complicated," I said not knowing how else to explain us.
"It shouldn't be, it should be a yes or no. You love him?"
"Yes, very much!"
"Do you think he loves you?"
"Yes."
"Then that's all that matters right?"
"Did you see him last night?"
"Yes," he watched my eyes.
"Was he alone?"
"No."
I exhaled, "ok. Now you see the complications." I felt like I was about to burst into flames.
"You ok?" Anton asked still watching me.
"What did she look like?"
"Does it matter?"
"Yes!"
"Why? I don't understand how he could be with someone else when he has you."
"I'm no picnic. I have my ways."
Anton exhaled, "I like you Kendra. I think you deserve better."
"You're cool Anton, but I don't know that it gets better than Darryl." I said in defeat.
"If you say so. Kendra please open your ears and hear me." I looked at him. "I like you, I think you deserve better, if you get tired of the game one day please call me first."

I smiled at him, "don't you have a girlfriend?"

"No."

"What about that girl we saw you with?"

"We're not together, we don't even talk anymore." Then he exhaled, "I just wanted you to know how I feel."

Ryder and Erin pulled up. Erin was all smiles as she got out of the car with her balloon and present. She ran towards us, "guess what! We got mommy something just because we love her! Do you think she will be happy?" Erin yelled as she ran with the present and balloon.

"Of course she will munchkin." I said putting my hands out to catch her.

Ryder walked over. "Good morning," he said to Anton.

"Good morning, how are you?"

"I'm good." Ryder looked at me, "what cha doing?"

"Discussing the yard, do you like the flowers he's going to plant?" I pointed to the pot in Anton's hand.

"Right, come on Erin. Let's go get breakfast ready for your momma." Ryder flashed me a look and then he and Erin walked away.

Anton went to his truck and then he started working on the yard. I was sitting on the porch studying when Jabbar's car pulled up. I knew Ahjanae wasn't expecting him so I watched. He noticed me on the porch and he came over. "Hey Kendra, is Ahjanae home?" He looked horrible.

Jabbar wasn't all the way to the porch when a guy walked up, "can I help you with something?"

I've never seen this guy before a day in my life. He looked mean and about business. Jabbar looked at me to say who the guy was but I didn't know. Anton stopped working and looked at him too.

"You talking to me?"

"Duh!"

"I'm talking to her." Jabbar pointed at me.

He looked at me, "Kendra who is he?"

I was surprised he knew my name. "Jabbar."

The guy put his phone on his ear. He gave a complete description of Jabbar. "Jabbar Carver, your baby momma is over there. Leave Kendra to her studying." He said firmly.

"Who are you?" Jabbar asked

"I'm your worst nightmare if you don't get moving." The guy said with no jokes in his face.

My phone rang, it was Jason. "Baby girl, tell Jabbar to keep moving."

I looked at Jabbar. "You better go."

"I was coming to tell you that my little sister was shot and killed last night."

"Jabbar! I'm sorry! What happened?"

"Thank you," he said as tears escaped his eyes. "We're trying to figure it all out right now."

"Baby girl!" Jason said into the phone.

"Yes?"

"Tell Ahjanae that Erin cannot go with him. That's why he's there."

"My man!" The guy on the sidewalk said. "You gonna have to take all that crying and what not somewhere else. If I have to say it one more time." The guy showed no empathy.

"Ok, I'll call you back." I said then I hung up. I ran ahead of Jabbar and I knocked on the door.

Ryder opened the door, then he looked at Jabbar. "You know you're supposed to call before you come here." He said moving slightly so I could get past him.

Ahjanae was in the bathroom with Erin washing her hair. I told her what Jason said, she frowned like she didn't understand. I told her there was another piece to the story but Jabbar needed to tell her that part. Ryder came to the door and told her that Jabbar was here. Ahjanae asked me to rinse Erin's hair and then put a plastic cap on it so it wouldn't dry out. I heard Jabbar's voice then Ahjanae screamed and I could hear her crying. Erin's eyes got big; I told her that her momma was ok. When I put the clothes her momma had sitting out for her on, she ran in the living room. Ahjanae was hitting Jabbar with question after question. He was crying and trying to answer. Aunrey walked in the door and he had no sympathy for Jabbar. He went in on him. Erin's tears snapped me out of the trance of hearing all the things Aunrey was going off about. Jabbar was working for Aunrey indirectly. Then something happened with a side deal with someone that all exploded last night. Ryder took Erin out of the room; it was only a matter of time before Aunrey fired on Jabbar. Jabbar was trying to explain that he was only looking for someone for the guy. Aunrey was telling him it didn't matter, he said Bobby wasn't stable as he could see.

Aunrey told him if any of his family was hurt behind this not only was it lights out for him but his momma and family. Jabbar pleaded saying that they already took his sister. Aunrey told him that was only a warning! Ahjanae asked who they're looking for. Aunrey said it's the same girl. I asked him if it was the same Bobby that was coming around here? Aunrey looked at me like he was telling me to shut up. Jabbar desperately looked at me, "do you know where Nellie is?"
I looked at Aunrey whose face was beyond pissed, I shook my head no.

Nellie

When my alarm went off I sighed. I don't know why I signed up for an early morning Monday class.
I spent yesterday in bed. Seeing D so tore up about being with me hurt. If he'd only realize that he needed to choose me maybe this wouldn't be so bad. I decided to call him and ask him to meet me somewhere. I debated whether to wait to call, but I called anyways.
To my surprise he answered but he didn't sound happy. We agreed to meet at Yogurt Park right off Telegraph, a block over from Berkeley. Talking to D, even though he wasn't happy to hear from me put a little pep in my step. Seeing Kendra walk into my class with her plain olive green shirt and caramel colored jeans annoyed me. She should've coordinated her whole outfit, it could've been really cute even though it was muted in color. But she's determined to stay on the plain side. By now I know she knows I'm here, but she doesn't speak and I'm glad. I wrote down my info to finish my last class assignment and then I couldn't move fast enough out. I power walked to the Bart station, I tried to move the train faster with my mind. I got butterflies when my downtown Berkeley stop came up. I power walked to the yogurt shop then I waited. D called and asked if I was there, then he said he was on his way.
He looked defeated and unhappy when he walked into the frozen yogurt shop. I tried to hug him, but he told me not to. I bought yogurt for us and then we stood outside. "I've never touched you while I'm making love to her." He looked at his yogurt, "I can't! I can't do this anymore!" He shook his head. "I know she's a good girl and my guilty conscience has me accusing her of cheating. I mean she's got a big butt. Walking for her seems like she's taunting

any man. I need to chill out! If I'm going to be with her I gotta suck it up and be with her. I gotta tell her everything." He looked at me, "everything!" Then he exhaled, "I'm telling the truth! How you've always come after me and wouldn't leave me alone. I'M TELLING **EVERYTHING**!"

Tears ran down my face, "ok so when she breaks up with you. Are you coming back to me?"

He exhaled, "anybody but you!"

Kendra

"What you doing?" Omar asked

"Just leaving class, about to go to the library to work on my final."

"Guess what!" He was excited.

"What?" I faked excitement.

"I'm here!"

"Where?"

"In the Bay," I could hear his smile through the phone.

"No you're not."

"Yes I am." He smiled harder through the phone. "Let's go to our old spot for lunch like we used to."

"Omar! I need to study!"

"Come on! You know you want some Blawndee's Pizza!"

I waved at Lanie. "Ok. Meet me at the Bart station in thirty." I said, not even understanding why I agreed to meet him. I walked over to Lanie. "Change of plans, can I get a rain check?"

"Ok so where we going?" She smiled.

I exhaled, I knew I wasn't gonna be able to shake her that easily. Plus if she was with me I knew Darryl would hear about it. I'm tired of hearing about him and other females. I could pull someone else as well. "My ex wants to meet me for lunch." I tried to smile.

"I'm coming! He paying?"

"He will, you won't feel uncomfortable?"

"Girl naw! Everybody knows you're in love with my cousin. I'm coming for the entertainment and free meal!" She said smiling like Darryl would.

When we walked out of the downtown Berkeley Bart station Omar was waiting by the curb in a fancy car. I thought the officer he was talking to was giving him a ticket. When we got close I realized he was signing an autograph. "This is my friend Lanie." I said, Omar smiled. "She's coming with us."

His smile dropped, "I really wanted a moment alone with you."
"We don't need to be alone, you haven't talked to my father." I cut
my eyes at him.
He looked at the sky and blew air. Lanie started openly laughing at
him. "What's so funny?"
"Your insecurities! But we'll get to that later. Continue on, this is
an entertaining play."
I smiled at her, Omar didn't. She already annoyed him. We drove
over to the parking garage off of Durant and Telegraph. As we
walked out of the garage my heart dropped. Darryl was leaning
against the Yogurt Park building talking to Nellie. I told myself to
calm down it could've been a coincidence. If Omar was talking to
me I didn't hear him. Darryl locked his eyes on us as we
approached. Nellie was crying, I doubt this was a coincidence.
"LEASHA!" The evilness in Omar's voice jarred all of us.
Nellie looked like she was about to run but Darryl put his hand out
to her to tell her to stand still. "Who you barking at like you got
rights over here?"
Omar walked up to Nellie and grabbed her by her neck. "Well
dang!" Lanie said moving out the way.
"Omar let her go!" I yelled.
"You think you can leave me! Change all your numbers and I
wouldn't find you!" He looked crazy.
"OMAR! Let her go!" I yelled again.
Nellie cried but she didn't say anything. "Ok, ok you've proven
your point. You're stronger than a female! Let her go!" Darryl said,
when Omar ignored him. Darryl's face turned evil and he hit Omar
in the kidney, he went down. "What is wrong with you? Walk
away! Get a grip!"
I hugged Nellie as she cried; I could see his hand print on her neck.
"Why is he calling you Leasha?" I asked her.
"Everyone at ASU calls me that." She said through tears.
"Personally cousin, I think you're losing your touch. One hit
though? No bones cracking, black eyes, or broken eye sockets?"
Lanie shook her head.
"You dated Omar?" I asked feeling a little sick at the thought.
"Yes, he beat me up right before he left Arizona threatening to do
more if I didn't follow him to LA." She said through tears.
I looked down at him, "so you wanted both of us in LA with you?"
"She's lying!" Omar said trying to get himself together.

"He started acting out once he realized that Ahjani and I used to be in love."

"Ahjani too?" Darryl said looking angry.

"You beat her up!" I said angry for my friend.

"No I didn't!" He said getting up slowly.

"You just grabbed her by the neck with no warning. Why would I believe you didn't?" I asked

"Kendra, can we go talk about this somewhere else?"

Darryl blew air then he looked at me. "No Omar! If you'd hit Nellie, one day you'd hit me! Don't call me no more!" I said

"Not over a lying hoe Kendra! Don't do this!" Omar pleaded.

"A hoe you caught feelings for!" Darryl chimed in.

"And you didn't? What were you two talking about?"

"Told you, you should've cracked his jaw." Lanie said shaking her head.

"Nigga don't worry about what we were talking about! You need to hobble your way back to your car and don't worry about me and mines!" Darryl said.

I looked at Nellie who hadn't stopped crying. "You were at the club Saturday night?" Both of their faces held a busted expression. I stumbled backwards. "Wait a minute! Wait a minute! You guys went out in public together like I wouldn't find out about it?"

"Ok, see, we need to sit down and talk away from this crowd!" Darryl said looking guilty.

He reached for me, "DON'T TOUCH ME! Did you sleep with her?"

"Cousin say no!" Lanie said with her head down.

"KB! We need to go....." I hit him in his mouth.

"It's a yes or no question!" I screamed.

Darryl touched his mouth, "that's your one! Don't touch me again!"

"Or else what? You gonna hit me? Or worse sleep with my best friend?"

"Personally, I don't understand why you're not beating her up! She's just as guilty!" Lanie said looking at Nellie.

"Cause he claims to love me!" I screamed.

"What about him? He's the woman beater! He is psychotically in love with her. I just made a mistake." Darryl said.

"Was Saturday the first time?" Darryl deflated, I swung at him again and he moved out of the way. I punched Nellie in the face

First You Laugh, Then You Cry

with everything in me. She spun around and Lanie cheered saying
she was proud. I stormed away towards the Bart station.
Darryl told Lanie to bring his car to Del Norte Bart, then he ran
behind me. "KB!" He ran in front of me and put his hands out. "I
messed up! I was going to come to you even if this didn't happen."
I stopped walking, "what were you going to say? I'm sorry I've
been screwing your best friend!"
"Not those exact words!" I swung at him. "KB, please let me
apologize!"
"MY NAME IS KENDRA!"
"But you're my KB!"
"I'm not your NOTHING!"
"KB! I'm sorry!"
I walked into his face poking his chest with my finger. "You are
just like Jerry!"
"OUCH! KB, no I'm not!" He said trying to shake off my words.
"Yes you are! You're going to run around sleeping with everyone
while I'm sitting at home waiting on you. Then one day you won't
come home! You may be Jerry, but I'm not Kharee! I'm happy I
killed your baby! Who would want such a father!!"
Darryl stopped walking with me and he bent over like I punched
him. I kept walking! He better leave me alone! I could go in worse
on him.

Nellie

"Come on," the girl said grabbing my arm with her strong hands.
"Leasha you're going with me!" Gordon said looking at me like he
was crazy.
"Listen here fool! I don't know what your malfunction is, but if you
know what's good for you. You'd take that punch my cousin lightly
tapped you with as a warning and back up. She's coming with me!"
Gordon was bigger than her in every way. I was scared for her that
she wasn't afraid of him. He ignored her and looked at me.
"Leasha! You're coming with me!" Then he tried to walk around
her to grab me.
She yelled, "TAE-BO!" And kicked him in the face hard. Gordon
stumbled backwards then he fell, "come on!" Then she grabbed my
hand and we ran through the alley towards the Berkeley campus. I
didn't pay exact attention to which way we went. As we got to D's
car she told me to come on, then we got in the car. She started the

car and we were off. "He's a punk! How could you let him hit you?"

"Let him?" I said looking at my blood shot red eyes in the mirror, handprints on my neck, and my bruised cheek from where Kendra hit me.

"I didn't stutter!" She said full of attitude.

"Did you really yell TAE-BO when you kicked him?"

She started laughing. "The only reason to keep putting myself through that torture was to use it on somebody! I knocked that fool in the face!" She laughed to herself.

"Thank you," I said.

"Every guy who puts his hands on a female deserves a TAE-BO kick to the face. It wasn't personal." She exhaled, "so girl of many names. How could you do it?"

I felt like garbage. "I love D! He.... He's always chosen Kendra."

"So why go after him if he's never chosen you?"

"D is....... D is......" I was searching for the words.

"TAKEN!" Then she laughed a sarcastic laugh. "All you females kill me! My poor cousins got it so bad! All these ex females who won't leave them alone, and they're trying to secure love for their selves. Stop the madness! If he wanted you, he'd have you. He don't want you and he's still getting you. You can't tell me the life of a sidepiece is fulfilling and rewarding! How did it feel watching him run behind the female he actually loves?" I felt like she was beating me up. "Do you think if you wait long enough, she'll get tired of the drama and then he'll be forced to choose you?" She glanced at me. "As much as it gets on my nerves look at Malcolm and Amber. She had the sexiest man alive! And I'm not making that up, People magazine named him that. She had him, could have him right now if she wanted him. Is she with him? No!" She said like she was angry. "She's stuck on stupid over my cousin. Who ain't ever gonna get over her! All these sidepieces stepping all over each other thinking he needs time and then he'll choose them. When all he's really doing is killing time until Amber gives in. You're just a stand in. Malcolm and all his sons pick a girl, and that's it! It's a wrap! Sidepieces get extra miles on their coochie and knots on their heads. A few of them have gotten their faces rearranged. How your face feel?" Then she laughed.

As we got off the freeway my heart sank as I realized we were on the border of Richmond and El Cerrito. My dad told me not to come out here.

Kendra

There was no smile on Darryl's face; he didn't try to say anything else to me. He walked behind me in the Bart station and stood next to me, but didn't say anything. When we got to the station I saw Lanie waiting in his car and he walked with me to my car. I opened my door and he told me I better not even play as he stood there like he knew I was letting him in my car. Lanie drove up and Nellie was still in the car with her. I looked at his car and I backed out of my parking space. Nellie got out of the front and into the back as Lanie followed me. I could see Lanie's neck wiggling; I wondered what Darryl was trying to say like he could ever have a defense for any of this. It seemed like we were driving in a caravan to my house. There were two cars behind Darryl's. I parked in my garage and I heard Lanie park Darryl's car just outside of it. I turned off the alarm and walked inside as Darryl opened my back door and let them in. "WHY ARE YOU BRINGING HER TO MY HOUSE DARRYL? YOU NEED THE FINAL INSULT? YOU GONNA HAVE SEX WITH HER IN MY BED? OR HAVE YOU ALREADY?" I cut my eyes at him.

Lanie shook her head. "I thought you lived next door. That's where we had the party."

I stared at Darryl, there was no point in him being here. "Why are you here? You wanna see me fight her over you? Why would you bring her to my house?"

"There's a problem that's a little bigger than what we're going through right now." Darryl said looking at his phone and looking out the window.

"What are you talking about?" I said annoyed.

Darryl looked out the window, then he closed the blinds. "Stay away from the windows!" He warned.

There was a knock at the back door. He opened it and then Ahjanae came in the door holding Erin, Ryder was right behind her. "What's going on?" She asked me.

"I don't know."

Ryder walked in the living room, he cursed! "NOEL?"

Ahjanae looked at him, "why did you call her that?"

287

Darryl shook his head, "it exploded just a little while ago."

"That's how she was introduced to me." Ryder said plainly.

"Where did he get Noel from?" Ahjanae asked

"I couldn't remember her name I thought it was Noel, so I started calling her that."

I charged at him to hit him, "that was way back when we were kids! You've been sticking this tramp since then?"

Darryl grabbed my wrist, "STOP IT! NOT RIGHT NOW! YOU'LL HAVE YOUR CHANCE LATER TO CURSE ME AND VERBALLY BEAT ME UP!" Then he let me go. He dialed a number and put it on speaker, "go!"

"The celebrity is on his way." The guy said, Darryl's face remained serious. Everybody stared at the phone like it was a TV. "He's parking around the corner…… Now he's jogging to the house……… He's looking around….. Now he's knocking on the door looking for signs of life…….. He's listening to the door……… Now he's looking in the mailbox…….. Mister Big man is on his way….. the celebrity is still looking around….. Mister Big man is driving slowly he's almost in front of the house……… the celebrity is walking out towards the street………. check it out." The guy said then we could hear the voice.

"Looking for somebody?" The scary guys voice said, Nellie gasped and turned completely red. She broke out in a sweat just from the sound of the guy's voice. She sat down on the couch.

"Yeah, I'm looking for the Hutchins family. Do they still live here?" Omar asked

"They sure do, I'm looking for them myself. Let me park my car." The scary guy said, Nellie shook her head no and then she started rocking in her seat.

There was silence for a few minutes; we stared at the phone waiting to hear what was going to happen next. "Thanks man, I need to talk to Kendra."

"What's your name?"

"Omar, and you are?"

"Bobby, what you want with Kendra?"

"I need to explain the scene she saw earlier, that girl takes me outside of myself. I can't have Kendra thinking that how I deal with other females is at any time of a reflection of how I would deal with her."

"Oh one of those situations, well regardless. Every once in a while you gotta remind each female who's boss or else they try to jump bad with you." Bobby said

"Right, but you can't walk around saying stuff like that."

"Naw! You never talk about it, nor do you threaten it. When it's time you react, talking is just a waste of time." Bobby said

"Right, I'll need to remember that." Omar said like he was taking that life lesson to heart. "How do you know the Hutchins'?"

"My baby girl is a very close friend with the family. I'm meeting her here." Bobby said, then his phone rang. The person on the phone said we came home. Bobby was quiet for a minute. "Tell Jabbar to call his baby momma." The person on the phone said if no one was at our house to come next door to the old lady's house. Darryl told us to go sit on the floor in the kitchen and to remain quiet. When we moved towards the kitchen Nellie was sitting in the chair literally shaking like she was having a nervous breakdown. The lights were on but no one was home, that bad feeling about the scary guy Bobby was all over her. Lanie was trying to get her to snap out of it, but it wasn't until Darryl touched her that she seemed like she came back to the room. I wanted to thump her messed up body out the door and tell her to take this bad element away from my house. But I got the impression that Darryl was in all out protection mode. Instead, I took her in my arms and rocked her; she was shivering in fear as she cried. I didn't know what was so horrible about him, but I also knew I didn't want to find out. Ryder told everyone to turn off their phones.

Darryl hung up and then he called someone and asked who had Kalani. The guy took a minute to answer, then he said she was with Jason. The guy on the phone started cursing, he said no one called Aunrey to give him a heads up and he was heading our way with his brother in the car. I looked at Darryl with tears in my eyes. It didn't take a genius to know that it wasn't safe for Aunrey and Ahjani to be outside right now.

Darryl told Ryder they were going to have to do something they couldn't wait for Jason.

Darryl told Ryder to be casual, then they waited until Aunrey pulled up. Lanie and I crawled to the window laughing at our rebelliousness. Darryl and Ryder walked out casually talking about something and walking towards Aunrey's car. Aunrey parked in Ahjanae's driveway. Ahjanae said they were coming to hang out

and then they were going to pick Audra up from the airport later.
Ahjani got out the car mugging Omar. Omar walked towards
Ahjani and then Ahjani fired on him. Omar fights like a woman
beater, he can't. Ahjani told him to stand up and fight a man. Omar
stayed down, Bobby stood there laughing.
Aunrey asked Bobby why he killed that little girl. Bobby shrugged
and said he didn't know what he was talking about. Bobby said he
was waiting for me to come home, someone saw me with Nellie
today. Ahjani and Omar looked at Bobby with question marks.
Ahjani looked like he was calculating. Omar got up, "you're
looking for Leasha?"
"Nealesha, you know her?" Bobby said standing up straight.
Omar frowned, "go ahead! Tell that fool what you did to her
today!" Darryl blurted.
Ahjani looked at Darryl, "what happened today?"
Darryl laughed, "and you were trying to tell Kendra it never
happened before."
Bobby looked unglued as he held his gun pointed at Omar. Lanie
pointed at the guys creeping up on the scene she put her finger up
to tell me to be quiet or move if I couldn't be. I was stuck looking
at the scene though. "You put your hands on my baby girl? Nigga
you must wanna die!" Bobby said
Omar shook his head with his hands up. "I was coming to propose
to my girl!"
Bobby took a step closer, "who's your girl?"
"Kendra!"
"No she's not! Kendra is mine!" Darryl said, "Bobby!" Darryl
smiled at him. "This fool got all in Nellie's head. He beat her up
and was trying to force her to move to LA to be his concubine."
Bobby frowned, "his what?"
Darryl gave him an evil smile, "his sex slave!"
Bobby shot Omar, then he stood over him. "I'm gonna kill you
after you apologize to my baby girl!" Then Bobby started kicking
him. Ahjanae asked with tears in her voice who just got shot. I told
her it was Omar. "WHERE IS NELLIE?" Bobby screamed. Then
his phone chirped, the person told him the police were coming.
Bobby looked torn, "she's here isn't she?" Darryl smiled and said
yes. Ahjani looked surprised, he eagerly asked where. Bobby
looked at Ahjani, "why you wanna know?"
"Adobo don't tell him, he's crazy!" Darryl said.

"Tell me what?" Bobby asked as the person chirped in saying the police were almost there.

Darryl nodded for Ahjani to join them on the driver's side of the car. Ahjani jumped on the car and slid down with them. "You not gonna like this!" Bobby growled, Darryl smiled bigger. You could hear the sirens getting closer. "He's in love with Nellie, and I used to bang her!" Ahjani looked at Darryl in shock, Darryl threw him down as Bobby started shooting Aunrey's car up. The police came and they told Bobby to put his gun down. Bobby looked at each of the officers and when they realized it was him they put their guns away and approached him. Bobby was going off saying everyone here dies as soon as he gets his baby girl. He walked over to the other side of the car with his gun drawn. He yelled to the officers to find them. My phone started vibrating in my pocket although I had turned it off. I backed away from the window and looked at it. Jason was calling, I whispered, "hello?"

"Are you guys ok?" Jason's voice sound worried.

"Bobby shot Omar and the police aren't doing anything. We're in my house but it's only a matter of time before they come in here. I'm scared Jason." I said holding in my tears.

"I know baby. I'm on my way." He exhaled. "I have a bread box for you if you think you can handle it."

"I'm not hungry Jason!"

"Who's in the house with you?"

"Nellie, Ahjanae and the baby, and Lanie."

"Perfect! Tell Lanie the breadbox is in the garage behind the door. She'll know what to do."

I looked at Lanie, "Jason said the bread box is in the garage behind the door."

"Cool!" Lanie got up and went to the garage.

"I'm on my way, don't panic!"

"How did you call me? I turned my phone off."

"Technology........ I'm on my way."

"Ok," I said. When he hung up, my phone shut back down. I stared at my phone for a minute. Lanie came back inside with a gun and she told me to come away from the window.

"So you slept with my cousin, her cousin, and the basketball star?" Lanie asked Nellie. Nellie was sitting there holding herself and shaking.

"Did that man hurt you?" Ahjanae gently asked Nellie.

Nellie shook her head yes. "But why does that mean that you hurt me? You were always the center of attention. Darryl was the one guy I wanted for myself."

She looked at me with sad eyes. Her eyes were so red I expected her tears to turn into blood. "I love him!" She said lowly.

I kicked her as hard as I could. You heard it echoing off the walls, and she didn't respond like she was already numb. "I hate you! I will never forgive you for betraying me like this! I was always the one defending you. Now I know why Darryl always insisted that you were not my friend! I'm hiding like a prisoner in my house behind protecting you! If anything happens to my cousins and father behind this, forget about that creepy guy outside, I'm coming for you!"

Lanie smiled, "Ooh! I heard that!" Then she told us to go in my office since it was the only room with a window high on the wall so we could stand without being seen. We sat against the wall under the window. I quietly went off on Nellie telling her everything on my heart accompanied by the occasional kick. I was so happy little Erin was sleep and not listening to me go off. When my mouth was dry and there was nothing else to say then tears poured out of my eyes.

Nellie

Ahjanae asked me what Bobby wanted with me. I looked at her and her eyes filled with tears as she held on to her baby tighter. I told her he wanted to "*get me*" again. It was really nice that anyone thought they could protect me from him. But Bobby is crazy and I know it's only a matter of time before he kills everyone just to get to me. I can end this by going outside, anything he does to me now can't be worse than he's already done. My legs were weak and wobbly as I stood up. Everybody looked at me. "If I go outside he goes away! I've caused enough drama, I'm going to go." I said wiping my face.

"What?" Kendra stood up. "Everyone is risking their lives to save you and you're going to go out there?"

"He's only out there because of me. If I go out he goes away and no one is risking anything anymore." Icy coldness spread all over me. "I'm sorry Kendra. You don't deserve any of this, and you always were my one true friend. You and I both know I deserve this."

"Look! I'm not about to sit here and try to convince you that you need to stay. Wait! Stop! Don't! If you still go out there it's on you," the girl said.

I walked out the door. Bobby was looking around while he was talking to an officer. I stood on the porch and waited for him to see me. Surprise, shock, and hurt flashed across his face in a matter of seconds. "Baby girl come here!" He said like I was a hallucination. His breathing was heavy as he watched me. It didn't seem like I was moving even though Bobby was getting closer and closer to me. Omar was still laying on the ground. He was bleeding and it looked like he passed out. Bobby squeezed me tight in his arms as he kissed my forehead. Somebody yelled out, "what are you doing?" But we couldn't tell where the voice came from. Bobby kept kissing my face and he smelled like someone who smokes. "I'm going to take her home. Kill them!"

"WHAT? BOBBY NO!"

"They were trying to keep you from me! They all die!"

"No! It was me! I was scared! They told me to come out."

"Why would you ever be scared of me?" I pointed at Omar. "I wouldn't shoot you!" Then he opened his passenger sidecar door. I got in the car, Bobby excitedly ran around the car, and then I heard him repeat his order to kill everyone. Bobby got in the car and he put his disgusting tongue in my mouth. He stood on the gas as we pulled away.

Kendra

Lanie backed away from the window telling us to get down. Ahjanae covered Erin's ears and I dove on the floor as the sound of the gunshots and glass breaking came from my living room. Lanie crawled in the room. Then you heard pops and then it was quiet. Then the front door opened and I heard my name. I ran out to Jason, who's face relaxed when he saw me. Then he asked me if everyone was ok. I said we were, but Nellie left with Bobby. His serious face was back and he asked why I let her go. I put my head down, because I knew I shouldn't have let her go. I let my anger hold me back from doing the right thing. Darryl and Ryder came through the back door. Ryder hugged Ahjanae and then he touched her stomach and asked her if she was ok. I felt like my whole body turned green with jealousy. Darryl was watching them as well. Jason told Darryl if they were going to find Nellie they had to go now. "Why do you have to go? She left on her own." I knew it was my hurt feelings talking but I couldn't help it.

Jason hugged me, "it's the right thing to do. If we don't put him down he's going to keep coming after you guys." Then he looked at Darryl, "let's go!"

Darryl kissed me on the lips and then they left with Jason. We heard more sirens, Lanie hurried back to the garage. When she came back she was gunless. The officers came to make sure everyone was ok, then we had to give statements.

Nellie

Bobby kept looking at me and touching me saying he was happy to have found me. I kept my eyes on my feet until we were pulling into a garage. My momma was standing in the doorway smiling until she saw me in the car. Immediate horror flashed across her face. "What are you doing here?"

"They were holding her hostage, trying to keep my baby girl away from me." He said angrily.

She looked at my face, "you beat her up?"

"No, but that's why they're dying right now." Bobby said leading me past my momma.

"Where are you going?" She asked him.

"Um! Me and Nellie got some catching up to do! We'll be out in a few hours." He said pulling me by the hand.

"No! Bobby please don't!" I pleaded crying my eyes out.

"SSSHHHH! It's ok, we don't have to hide our love no more. Come on!"

"You're going to hurt me!" I yelled

"I never hurt you. They brainwashed you!"

"Bobby leave her alone!" My momma's face was angry.

Bobby looked crazy as he walked up on my momma he punched her in the face. "You shut up! I'm the only one who loves her! Your loyalty has been bought and paid for, five dollar hoe!"

When he hit her again I begged him to stop. I told him I'd do whatever he wanted as long as he didn't hurt her anymore. He looked at my momma, "you sit out here and deal with the fact that someone younger and finer is doing what you can't do for your man! Interrupt me one more time and I'm putting a bullet in your head!" He took his jacket off and threw it on the couch. Then he yanked me to his room and slammed the door. No matter how I tried to approach this in my head it hurt. Bobby wiped my tears and told me he missed me too. He took his clothes off then he took mine off.

He was about to do his thing when my momma banged on the door. He got up angry and snatched the door open. My momma pulled the trigger twice and Bobby flew backwards. She ran to me on the bed and covered me with a blanket. "I'm sorry baby!" She said crying on my shoulder.

Kendra

Around three in the morning all the bodies of the dirty cops were finally cleaned up, all the statements were taken, and all the cars were towed away. The insurance agent came out to file the claim to get my house fixed. Jason had some guy's board up my windows and Ahjanae's. I asked her why she didn't tell me she was pregnant, she said they just found out and they wanted to tell everyone together. Erin's just because gift and balloon made so much more sense now. I packed a bag for Kalani grabbing the things she instructed me to get and then I started packing mine. Darryl walked in my room with sad eyes. He asked when I was coming back. I told him it didn't matter cause I didn't want to see him. He exhaled and shook his head like he was expecting that response. He said we needed to talk and I told him there was nothing for us to talk about. He stared at me for a long time, then he said he would wait for me to say when.

Chapter 19

Nellie

I heard hurried footsteps into the Emergency Room. "Nealesha Parker?" I could hear the panic in my father's voice. I didn't have to guess I knew my stepmom was with him.

My momma held onto my hand as she watched the curtain where my daddy was going to appear. My parents paused when my daddy snatched the curtain back and they saw my momma. Surprise, shock, hurt, and anger flashed across my daddy's face in a matter of seconds. My daddy stood frozen while my stepmom rushed to me and kissed my forehead. She asked me if I was in pain, if I felt sick, etc.

My momma watched my stepmom who completely ignored her and tended to me like a mother would. My daddy's voice was low and angry as he asked my momma what happened. I spoke before she could and I told him about Gordon strangling me, and D making him stop. Then that girl kicking Gordon in the face to save me after D left with Kendra. That girl didn't know that I was supposed to stay out of Richmond and we went to the Bart station, one of the most visible places in Richmond. I told him how a guy looked at me when I got out of D's car to get in the back seat. Then a car started following us on the way to Kendra's house. I told him how Bobby showed up and ended up shooting Gordon when D told him what Gordon did to me. I felt bad for endangering everyone so I gave myself up. I started crying really hard when I said that Bobby still said he was going to kill everybody. I couldn't talk as I thought of each person. My momma told them how Bobby brought me to the house. My daddy stared at her bruised and swollen face as she explained that he hit her and then she took his gun out of his jacket that he left on the couch and she shot him. My daddy asked her if she was ok, and she shrugged then she looked at me.

An officer came in the area where my bed was. He asked some more questions then he left. The doctor said I was ok to go home, and that a grief counselor would be contacting me shortly. My parents stepped out of my area so I could put my clothes back on. My momma kept hugging me and kissing me and telling me she was sorry and that it was all her fault. As soon as we stepped out of the ER, two officers approached us to inform us that they needed to take my momma into custody. My momma didn't fight, she hung her head as they put cuffs on her. My stepmom asked if the handcuffs were necessary and they said yes. They said she was under arrest for aiding and abiding a criminal, and first-degree murder.

****

"Leasha?" Gordon said opening his eyes.
"It's me." I said looking at him all helpless looking in his bed. "How do you feel?"
"Ran over," he swallowed. "I really thought he was going to kill me."
"He was going to."
"Over you," he said dryly.
"No, over what you did to me." I couldn't believe he had no remorse for what he's done.
"My recovery time is going to be ridiculous, my career could be over. And what? You want me to feel something about you? What did you come here for?"
My irrational fear of his anger upset me. "I came here to tell you how sorry I was that this happened to you. And I was hoping maybe you had some remorse about what you did to me. But it's obvious that you don't. It was a waste of an emotional journey to come here. Unlike the others, when I leave this room you will be forgotten. You will be another scar that fades with time. However, as far as you're concerned, you will forever remember me. You will one day understand how your choice to bully someone weaker than you cost you everything. In a lot of ways we were so much alike, there was no way we were going to make it. Both of us competing with non-competitors to be the best. Kendra never wanted to compete with me, but I always had to try to prove that I was better than her, than anyone. Your competition with Ahjani is what cost you your career. And just so you know, he's better than you in every way. On the court, in school, looking, life, and oh yes ESPECIALLY sexually. That man has the gift of stamina. Ahjani gave me his heart, you were too busy competing to remember that's a required piece of a relationship."
"I wasn't going to give you my heart. My heart was given to Kendra."
"So then why? Why were you bullying me?"
"I fell in love with your fear of me." He said bluntly.

His statement made me angry but it didn't make any of it less true. "And now the tables have turned. Now you'll have to live in fear of me. Who I'll send after you, what could happen to you whenever I have a flash back of how badly you treated me." I stood over him, "one day I might send someone after you to finish what Bobby started."

Kendra

"Kendra it was before me and after me. I know it's messed up. But it changes nothing about what we had." Ahjani said trying to calm me. "I knew I wasn't her first, and I knew she wasn't waiting for me while we were apart." He put his arm around me. "Love isn't easy but what are you going to do?"

"Beat him in the face! Are you kidding? You can't claim you love someone and then you do this!"

"Your situation is different." Ahjani said.

My stomach was starting to hurt I was getting so angry. "You coming?" I asked as I touched the door.

"Now this fool!" He exhaled slowly. "No! Not yet! I'll come in, in a minute."

I slowly walked into Omar's room. He was watching TV looking depressed. He got the biggest smile when he saw me. "I knew you'd come." He said

His momma looked at me like she wanted to go off on me, but I could tell she was holding back. "How you feeling?"

"Fortunate to be alive. I can't complain." He said

"I won't stay long. I just wanted to come by at least once while you're here."

"No, you can stay. I'm so happy you're here. My momma didn't think you'd come at all."

"No! I said she better not come at all!" She chimed in with attitude.

"Ok?" I looked at Omar to explain.

"You know my mom," he said trying to down play her reaction.

"That's right! She knows me, and you know I don't play when it comes to my baby. How could you let this happen to him?"

"I didn't...."

She cut me off, "I had no idea you were surrounded by such a thug element. Otherwise I never would've let you two date in the first place." She went on to continue to blame this whole thing on me. I looked at Omar to tell her the truth but he didn't say anything. She knew nothing about the part he played in all of this.

The door opened and Ahjani walked in looking pissed off. "All I hear outside is your momma's voice squawking. How could you let her talk to Kendra like this? You know good and well that you and you alone are the reason you're in that bed. If I was Nellie I wouldn't care that you got shot. Your butt would be in jail where punks like you deserve to be!"

"What are you...."

Ahjani cut his mother off, "SHUT UP AND LISTEN! Your son! Your baby! He got shot because he decided to bully Nellie."

"Who?" She looked at her son.

"Leasha," he put his head down.

"Did you know you raised a woman beater?"

"You didn't?" She looked at Omar. He kept his head down. "Well I didn't see it so I don't believe it."

"I saw him grab her by her neck. He wouldn't let her go until someone made him. You may not want to believe it, but I saw it. Omar and I will never be together. I came by to wish you a speedy recovery, and to ask you to respect my wishes and leave me alone."

"And good riddance! Goodbye! Get out!"

"No! Wait! Kendra I'm sorry! Leasha made me crazy. She cheated on me constantly. She....."

"You cheated on her! You guys had an open relationship. You liked the idea of controlling her. It blew up in your face when you realized I hit it first, and that she still cared about me. You're always trying to compete with me, but you'll never be as good as me!"

"Kendra please! I was your first, please don't throw that away!" He pleaded.

I gently stroked his face, "I never told you that you were my first. You assumed. But second is still top five, don't beat yourself up too much about it."

Omar was in shock, he laid back on his bed digesting my words.

"See! She was gaming you the whole time. I knew it!"

"Whatever! If he keeps going like he's been going, he's gonna get you killed as well as himself. I'm officially off this crazy train. Have a good life Omar, I really wish you the best." I said walking towards the door, Ahjani was right behind me.

Nellie

"What did he say when you said that?" Ahjani asked

"He cried," I looked around the yard. "I thought it would make me feel better but it didn't."

"Right, stuff like that doesn't make anyone better." He exhaled, "so Darryl?"

I shook my head yes. "There's been so many I don't remember them all."

He made a wounded sound, "I don't understand it all."

"Me neither, but I didn't see him while I was with you. I couldn't." I smiled

He smiled back, "so what now?"

"You're in love with your girlfriend, go be with her. I'll always have love for you Ahjani, you were the first guy to be good to me. If our parents wouldn't have separated us I'm sure I would've made a mess of us and you'd hate me right now.

****

Ahjani Lubbock has been drafted to Miami! My heart fluttered, he did it! I know he's going to be great. Again I wanted to scream at my daddy for ruining my life, but it's done now.

****

Marquez held my hand. "The court finds Mary Lareese Richardson not guilty of first degree murder. In the case of aiding abetting the court finds Mary Lareese Richardson guilty." She wasn't charged with murder cause she was protecting me. But they threw the book at her, for knowingly staying with Bobby. Sentencing would be next week. Marquez helped me, no! Who am I kidding. He basically wrote my victim impact statement. He wrote everything exactly how I felt. Everything from the first time until the last. Like how wrong it felt when Bobby looked at me, but he gave me money. How scared I was the first time he touched me. How lost I felt, and how I've yet to value myself since this occurrence in my life. Seeing the words that expressed what I truly felt inside made me cry out from deep inside but it also felt like a release.

The grief counselor referred me to a therapist. I was terrified and refused to go at first. When Marquez said he'd take me, I finally agreed to go. In the lobby I was still unreasonably scared. I clung onto Marquez's arm for dear life. The therapist asked Marquez to come with me. We sat on the couch in her office. Babette was a tall brunette with eyes that constantly moved while you were with her. She took notes the entire time you spoke, as I explained my life, she asked if I felt like the different things that happened were my fault because they happened like they did. When things would get too painful Marquez would rub my hands and tell me I was doing really well and he was proud of me.

Today we were supposed to go eat afterwards but I wasn't hungry and I wasn't in the mood to be around people. Marquez got something to eat and then we went back to his room. I laid on the bed trying to focus on a thought. Marquez was finishing his Portumex burrito. Now that I could go to Richmond again I was overloading on my favorites. Portumex Mexican food, Andy's donuts, La Pearla Mexican food, Palace Golden Chinese food, etc. I looked at Marquez, and then I asked him how did he know? How did he understand? He knew I was talking about my impact statement. He said his momma had a boyfriend too. He said the boyfriend would put him in situations he had to fight his way out of. He said his momma died trying to protect him. Then he exhaled like that was hard to say even though he was trying to act like it didn't affect him. I looked at Marquez like I've never seen him before. He was now looking at the floor when he always looks me in my eyes. I touched his face like he always touches mine. I kissed his lips and all over his face. Then I pulled him on top of me. We fell asleep with his head buried in my chest.

When I woke up Marquez was awake but he hadn't moved. I asked him what he was going to do after he graduated. He reminded me that he had a job lined up. He said after graduation he was looking for a place. I told him Nassya would have a fit if he didn't let her decorate. He told me I had a whole school year to wrap things up. He said either I was coming with him, or he was moving on. I agreed with him, it wasn't fair to him to continue as we have been.

****

I hit D on my contacts list and then I listened. "Yes?" He said in a defeated tone.

"I'm sorry!"

"Thanks," he said dryly.

"Can we meet up somewhere?"

"No!" He said adamantly.

"Please!"

"What's wrong with the phone? The commercial said you could reach out and touch someone. But you act like that's not good enough."

"Commercial?"

He sighed, "AT&T that was their slogan for years!"

"D!"

He chuckled, "swoosh! The sound of my greatness going over your head. All you're going to do is give in to your weakness when you see all this raw chocolate sexiness staring you in the face! Then you'll start begging again, and you know where that goes."

"You don't leave me a choice, I have to beg for everything with you. Let's agree to meet, have a conversation and be done with it." I said

He was quiet for a minute. "Meet me at Homemade Cafe on the corner of Sacramento and Durant in Berkeley in thirty minutes." Then he hung up.

When I got to the restaurant D was walking behind the hostess in sweats and a T-shirt. When he sat down he didn't look happy.

"Thank you for coming." I said as I sat down. D nodded but didn't say anything. He looked like he wanted to be anywhere but here. "I need your opinion, should I reach out to Kendra?" D busted out laughing, he slapped the table. People looked at us and then away. "Why is that funny?"

"You forgot what she did to your face?" He laughed a little more. "She's still angry, and right now she's still trying to work out her feelings towards me." Then he sat up straight like he wasn't just laughing. "That's your plan? You're trying to make sure she's permanently done with me?"

"No, and if she hits me again it's not like I don't deserve it. I want a chance to explain."

"Explain?" He said rolling his hands.

"All the things I didn't tell her. To....." Someone walked in the door and they had D's complete attention.

I turned around to see this guy walking straight to our table. There was no smile on his face and he was as black as night. When he got to our table he sat next to me in the booth but he didn't acknowledge me. "Why are you here?" His voice was as deep as the hue of his skin. I looked at D to tell me who he was.

"She wanted to talk," Darryl said matter of factly.

"What could she possibly say that would be worth all of this?" The guy said like I wasn't there.

"I know!" Darryl said as he glanced at me and then went back to the guy.

"Are you even playing the game right now? You know what our situation is. You can't have someone who doesn't matter be the reason you're out the game. Son you're smarter than this. Think it through!" He said, "Jason is looking for you!"

Darryl exhaled, "right!" He shook his head then he grinned, "daddy save me!"

The guy gritted his teeth, "you don't mess with a man's daughter! And then you're here with her! You're asking for it!"

"But I don't want it daddy! I don't want it!" D laughed the guy didn't.

"This is serious Darryl!" He pounded his fist on the table. The table sound like it was going to collapse. "Is she pregnant or not?" I held my breath, is who pregnant? What are they talking about? Darryl's face was serious again, "don't know yet. Malcolm I got a question. How come it's ok when you played these for keeps games with my momma, but for me he wants my head?"

The guy squinted at Darryl, "Boy! In your wettest dreams you will NEVER be me! You can't do the stuff I've done, and I don't know why you would try." Then he shook his head, "besides. You don't think Tim came after me on account of his little girl? I was always on his yuck list every time your momma went flapping her gums to her daddy. You are not special, you need to go see Jason about his daughter!"

Darryl sat back, "ok, ok, ok!"

"I hear you talking but you're not walking!" The guy said

"Right now?" Then he whined, "but daddy we were about to eat!" He teased.

"Stop playing! Let's go!" Then the guy stood up. "Nealesha stop calling my son. Forget you knew him, you've done enough now move on." I was stunned he knew my name. "Neallan will be here in," he looked at his watch and then the door. "Now!" Then my daddy walked in the door.

My daddy looked angry as he walked towards us. "Malcolm," he stuck out his hand for a handshake. "Thank you for calling me."

"You called her daddy on her? Ooh! You in trouble!" Darryl sang then he laughed.

The guy and my daddy looked at Darryl who was laughing at his own joke. My daddy sat down and they left. "How do you know Malcolm Latour?" My daddy asked watching my eyes.

"I don't, who's that?"

"The guy who was standing here. You don't want to get mixed up in anything he's involved in."

"That's D's dad. I think, I mean that would explain why D's brown when his momma is so light." I said trying to remember her face to cross-reference.

My daddy asked me why I was here. So I unloaded everything on him. He rolled his eyes a lot like it was too much to hear but I kept going. In the end I told him I needed to go see my momma and I needed him to go with me. He reluctantly agreed.

****

I've never seen my mother with her hair all pulled back. When I looked at her face I saw my own. My dad looked like it was hard for him to look at her. "Nathan is your son?"

My momma looked at my daddy like he betrayed her. "He's your stepmother's son!" She said through clinched teeth.

"You gave birth to him?"

She exhaled, "yes." She said in defeat. "Neallan, you told them? I bet you were mad when you said it weren't you? You made an already bad situation worse, didn't you?"

"Your one job was to protect princess!"

"You left us to fend for ourselves! Your job was to love me! I trusted you! You told me you loved me! That you would never abandon me like my parents, and what did you do?"

"You didn't leave me with a choice, I told you to stop calling the house. You didn't listen!"

"Your daughter is crying and wondering where you are! I know how that feels to feel like your parents have abandoned you. You think I wasn't calling you? You didn't want me anymore fine, but our child didn't deserve what she got!" She spit.

"So you make a bad situation worse by bringing in the monster? Turning a blind eye to what was happening."

"That's what you think?" She looked between us. "Nellie, baby there's nothing I could say to change what happened. I thought I was crazy for thinking that's what was happening could be happening. I didn't know, I wondered if, but I was afraid to ask. That doesn't make it ok."

"But you stayed with him!" I said with tears streaming down my face.
"He wouldn't take no for an answer. Your grandmother kicked me out, and when I refused to come back he shot up my momma's house. He threatened to kill her if I didn't come back. I would send him on wild goose chases, he was looking for you all this time. I knew you wouldn't be safe with me. I was at your graduation. I was so proud to see my beautiful baby walk across that stage all proud."
"How long were you two actually together?"
"Too long!" My momma said quickly.
"Too long?" My daddy asked.
"Yes! I was there first! How did I end up as the sidepiece? Neallan you've always done me wrong and somehow it's my fault for reacting."
"Because you're selfish!" He said
"Being in love with you made me selfish? If I didn't advocate for myself who was going to? You never did!"
"I told you that you were making things too stressful! I told you to lay low just for a little bit and you couldn't do it!"
"I was in love and addicted to you! And you tell me to sit quietly on time out with no end in sight and you somehow expect me to be able to do that?"
"I was in love with you, but you were making everything too hard. You left me with no choice!"
"Neallan you broke my heart! You abandoned me! You left me and you didn't look back. I trusted you! I gave you everything!"
"Mary, I'm still in love with you. But I have to keep my distance. I love my wife and the home we built together."
"You said you were coming back to me when Junior graduated and then you let her have another baby! All your promises you never kept! Why would you put me through this pain? You know my life, you know everything and still this is where we stand."
I felt like I was looking at D and me, or Ahjani and me, or Gordon and me? No! This was Ahjani and I. Who was I kidding I knew I wasn't ending up with D no matter how much I wanted it. This was Ahjani and I, I can't do it. My parents kept going back and forth about their frustration with each other. They loved each other, but there was no way they could be together. Then the door opened and Nathan slowly walked in. His face held the same expression he

always had in regards to her, pain. My momma cried as she watched him walk in. Nathan sat next to me and stared at our momma. My momma said hi and he said hi back. It was quiet for a long time. Then my momma asked Nathan how he was doing. He shrugged as he watched her. Then he told her he could see himself in her face, which made her cry more. My brother and I sat there trying to understand our parents who were clearly not done with each other, but that wasn't our problem or issue. When we got in the car to leave my stepmom stared at my daddy but she didn't say anything.

****

Kendra came and sat out on her porch. She put a blanket over her lap, I couldn't see her stomach to know whether D was talking about her or not. She looked really sad, but I told myself to go over anyways. When I stepped into the street a car zoomed in front of me and two guys jumped out. Both of them looked at me with mean faces. "What do you want?" The guy closest to me asked. "I want to talk to Kendra." I said a little scared.

Kendra was looking, then the other guy called out to her telling her that I was here, he was looking for approval. When she told him to let me go, the guy closest to me said he had to search me. I put my hands up like he had a gun. He enjoyed his pat down more than he should have. I frowned at him and he smiled then he told his partner I was clean. They drove away and parked again. Kendra pulled her blanket up to her neck as if she felt vulnerable when I walked towards her. I put my hands out, "I come in peace." I tried to make a joke. She didn't laugh, she stared at me with fire in her eyes. "I came to apologize."

"Apologize to me? That would be a first." She said not taking her eyes off of me.

"Yes," I sat on the ground at her feet. "I don't know where to start."

"Whenever I got tired of your diva persona, my momma would tell me to be nice to you cause you didn't know any better! What thanks I got for being nice to a hoe! But you can't lay down with dogs and not expect to wake up with fleas!" I didn't say anything, "every guy I ever wanted you had to have and you did! What did I do to you to deserve all this?"

"You had a mother and father who loved you. No matter how pretty I am I didn't have that! You didn't have to do everything I did and guys still liked you. Your butt was bigger than mine, you're a better person than me." I exhaled, "my competition got me raped and ripped away from my momma. I went after him, D would tell me to leave him alone. I'd keep after him until I wore him down. He always made it clear that he was in love with you. The only time he came to me was when I was in the hospital, and when I went home."

Kendra looked so hurt, "you were my only friend outside of family! I can't even tell you how this feels!"

"I know, I'm...."

"YOU DON'T KNOW HOW THIS FEELS! HOW COULD YOU POSSIBLY KNOW HOW THIS FEELS?" She screamed at me. Ryder quickly opened the door and came out. When he saw me he squinted, "Noel? What do you want?" He said walking over his grass and carefully through the garden.

"I came to apologize to Kendra." I said

"Are you ok?" Ryder asked her.

She was crying really hard. "I need to go lay down. I can't deal with this. Just so we're clear Nealesha, I do not forgive you!" Then she stood up with her blanket still in front of her. I tried to watch for a sign of whether she was pregnant or not, but I couldn't tell. I went home in defeat.

Kendra

"I'm just saying that you have been real evil! You should at least throw some of your attitude on the person that a lot of it has to do with. I'm the pregnant one, aren't I supposed to be the witch right now?"

I sunk in my seat, "I don't want to see him Ahjanae!"

"Because you're afraid that you still have feelings for him."

"NO! I DON'T!"

"Calm down! See! You need to be yelling at him. Kendra I love you, but we about to fight if you keep acting like this!" She walked over to her house phone. "What's Darryl's number?"

"I deleted it from my phone!" I said folding my arms and wiggling my neck.

"Please! I know you know the number by heart."

"Even if I did, why would I give it to you to betray me."

"Look! Either you're going to give it to me, or I'll get it from Ryder and then he'll show up at your house in the middle of the night getting in your bed thinking you said it was all good."

"You wouldn't?" I asked in disbelief, but I knew she would. She raised an eyebrow at me. "Ok, ok…" I said in defeat. "Give me a few days to wrap my mind around the fact that you're making me do this." I said as run away tears escaped from my eyes. Ahjanae came and hugged me, she said I gotta let it all go so that I could heal and move on with my life. "Of all the people Ahjanae, it had to be Nellie? Every time I liked someone she took him! She always tried to make me feel like I was beneath her. Darryl was mine, I didn't even care about Omar. I mean I cared but not like Darryl." Ahjanae rubbed my back, "And then when it came down to it she had everyone who didn't matter. Darryl is in love with you. No matter what she did, she couldn't have his heart cause you already have it. I'm not saying that you need to forgive him, but you need closure for you. Do what you need for you to be ok. Do what you need to so that you can still love later. Don't end up bitter like my momma. You wanna end up alone?"

"No," I said tearfully.

"Then call him, not for him, for you, do it for you."

I couldn't sleep that night, I kept tossing and turning. I couldn't stop thinking about Darryl. When I gave up on sleep I sat up and wrote out a list of everything I wanted to say to him. It was four o'clock in the morning when I called. I expected him to be asleep, but his voice was clear without a lick of sleep in it. "I'm calling because I need closure."

"Closure?"

"Yes Darryl, closure."

"I guess you could try that, but I'm not agreeing to anything like that."

"Too bad it's not up to you. Now…."

"The sound of your voice is soothing I haven't been sleeping." He said yawning, "I think we should meet so that I don't risk falling asleep on you, and then you think I'm not serious about all of this. Can we meet tomorrow?"

"Meet?" I held my breath.

"Yes meet, this is a serious conversation."

"I have class in the morning."

"You mean in a few hours."

"Yes," I said now yawning myself.

"Ok, let's have lunch. There's a spot I wanna take you to. Lunch time rush, most come and get their lunch to go, so we should be able to eat in peace."

"Um," I said hesitating.

"Yes? Ok! I will be outside the Bart station waiting for you KB. I can't wait to see you! Thank you for calling me, now I can finally sleep. I love you so much! Thank you! Bye!" Then he hung up!

I let out a frustrated scream, then I peacefully fell asleep for a few hours.

I barely made it to class but I made it. Lanie got unnecessarily happy when I told her that Darryl and I were meeting for lunch so I couldn't hang out with her after class. I kept looking at my list on my way to the Bart station. I told myself to be strong and that I had this. When I walked up out of the Bart station subway and on to the street Darryl was standing there in a crisp white button up, blue pressed jeans, and shades. I melted a little then I told myself to get it together. He smiled really big and wrapped his arms around me, and of course he kissed my neck as he squeezed me. He smelled so good, if I could live in the moment of him wrapped around me and none of the other things ever happened, life would be good. When he chirped a new car, I asked what happened to his old school classic. He said he put it in the garage to save it for later. His new car was really nice and fancy but I couldn't tell what kind of car it is. When I asked where we were going, Darryl said one time his study group met at this restaurant and he liked it a lot. He asked me if I've ever had Ethiopian food, and I said no. He said this place was really good and he thought I would like it. I didn't think much of the outside decor. The building was tan with a simple sign that said "Addis" Ethiopian cuisine. When we walked in the door, like he said the place was basically empty and it was just after one so a lot of the lunch crowd had already disappeared. The waitresses smiled at us and told us we could sit wherever we liked. Darryl asked if I wanted to sit in the little hut looking section. The smile on his face told me he knew I was going to say no. I took one look at those low to the ground circular stump looking seats and said no. I didn't want to have plumber butt trying to balance my big butt on that little stump. We sat in the back far right corner. Our waitress brought our menus and she asked if we knew what we wanted to drink already as she passed us waters. Darryl asked for flax seed juice, and I asked him what was that. He said it so good and good for you. He told me to live on the wild side and try a glass. I agreed, then I looked at the menu. He sat there smiling at me as I tried to comprehend the menu. When I gave up he said he'd order for us. When the waitress came back with two glasses with brown liquid in it, my mouth dropped. Darryl started cracking up laughing. He told me to try it before I killed him. The waitress stood there proud as she waited for me to try it. I swallowed and then I tried it. It was actually really good, it tasted like roasted flax seeds and milk. Darryl ordered Kitfo special "COOKED", Lamb Aswaza Tibs, and a vegetarian platter. I asked him why he specified cooked and he said they normally served the Kitfo raw, but he didn't want me to run out of there.

I excused myself and went to the bathroom. When I looked back Darryl was watching me and smiling really big. I rolled my eyes at him, this definitely wasn't going to be easy. I washed my hands and then I came back to the table. "Now that you're back, I'm going to the bathroom to wash my hands." Then he got up and stuck his butt out while he pretended to switch as he walked away. "I do not walk like that!" I laughed. I took out my list and prepared myself for the things I had to say.

When he sat down he took my papers from me. "DANG! All of this?" He exhaled…. ok bring it.

He sat there patiently letting me go down my list of things to say to him. On item number forty-five our food came out on a grey platter. The ground beef looking meat was in a little black bowl and the waitress poured it in one spot on the platter . Then she gave us a basket with what appeared to be sponges. Darryl cracked up again, he asked me if I could come up for a breather so we could eat. I looked at him, "there's no forks?"

He put a napkin down and then he took a sponge out of the basket and laid it on his napkin, "bread." He tore a piece off and he picked up the salad with it. "It's a fork or spoon that you eat."

"What is everything that I'm looking at?"

He pointed at each item. "Chickpeas, lentils, greens, potatoes and carrots, Kitfo Special which is like really lean ground beef cooked with greens, Ethiopian cheese and their spices, Aswaza Tibs it's lamb and its cook in this special sauce with onions and seasonings. That powder is really spicy and that cheese is really good."

"What should I try first?" I asked tearing a piece of my spongy bread off.

"Start with the Kitfo and then work your way around."
I smelled the bread and it didn't smell any special kind of way. I followed his recommendation and it was delicious. The bread tasted like sourdough bread everything on the platter was delicious. Even the salad was tossed in probably olive oil and lemon juice but it was absolutely delicious. Darryl smiled watching me enjoy our meal. When I came back from the bathroom there were two wine glasses on the table. He told me I had to try the honey wine. As we finished our meal I felt one hundred times more relaxed than I felt before. I picked up my list and went back to where I left off. "So in conclusion, I'm saying all of this cause I want and need closure."
He frowned, "but I'm not offering you closure."
"Too late, I finished my list, I already got it."
He didn't say anything he got up and went to the bathroom. When he came back I thought he was going to sit down, but he rushed me and kissed me. "I don't want closure."
My head was spinning, I didn't mean to kiss him back. "Darryl I don't want to be with you. You broke my heart!"
"KB, I mean I know I'm wrong for what I did. I've thought of a thousand excuses and ways out of this whole thing. But I'm coming to you as a man, I messed up. I've always prided myself on being strong and teased my brothers for being weak, when the truth is I am just as weak as they are. Shoot, I'm probably the weakest, but I don't like how this comparison is going so I'm gonna bow out of that line of thought." He swallowed. "What kills me is how innocent you try to play in all of this. You always played hard to get but I was supposed to know that we'd end up together? If your cousin would've never busted you out about you liking me, would you have waited until you saw me with someone else to come clean? Even with that, I was still wrong I get that. But you gave me this whole moving speech about how you were going to graduate a virgin. THEN! You sleep with me in the middle of your relationship with the Star cause I guess I was supposed to understand that I deserved your virginity? I mean I know I deserved it cause I never did for anyone what I did for you. Arranging a fully paid adventure at the park. *DO YOU HAVE ANY IDEA OF HOW MUCH THAT COST?* Every time I opened my heart to you, show you something about me that I didn't show anyone else, you always made light of it and acted like you didn't believe me as if I ever lied to you." He leaned forward and I could

feel the heat from his body, "did you give me your virginity to try
to appease me during my grief? I didn't need you for sex. As you
know I have plenty of hoes for sex if that's all it was about. I didn't
need you for that. But that's what you reduced me and you to. I do
not make good choices when I'm in pain. I should've never let
Noel get me." He shook his head, "Nellie I mean. I was wrong for
that, but for you to sit up here and act like this is all on me, that
ain't right. I still love you! I still want you! But I see you're about
to play the denial game. I can see it all over you." I didn't say
anything I twisted in my chair. "KB! Will you please come make
love to me?"
"What?" I asked in complete shock.
"It's in your eyes, everything. You want me so bad! I want you!
I'm always going to want you, I know if I don't ask you'll let the
moment pass us by."
"You had sex with my friend! I don't want anything that touched
her touching me."
He smiled, "then you better get out of that chair."
I jumped out of the chair like it burned me. Darryl started cracking
up laughing with his hands in the air. He plays too much. I hit him
in the shoulder as he kept laughing at me. "You play too much!"
Once he stopped laughing he asked me if he could show me
something. I agreed in defeat. We drove to his momma's house.
When he opened my door, I asked him where his momma was. He
said she was at work in LA. I swallowed as he led me through the
house and up to his room. I was so pleased that everything in his
room was always neat even when I popped up unexpectedly back
in the day. Of course there were things I would do differently. He
told me to sit and I sat in the chair at his desk. He smiled and then
he brought out a shoebox. It was full of papers. He put it in my lap,
"I can't take back what I've done if I could I would. But these are
all the letters I wrote you when I didn't understand what was
happening. Now let me warn you, they can get pretty mean and
unsavory cause I was hurting. But I got a list too." Then he took
my purse and set it next to the bed. He turned his stereo on low and
a song came on. I looked at him and he said he's been listening to
this song on repeat waiting for the bridge to come true. "Before
you left me, I had it all. You were with me, and that was enough.
Then he came along, and I forgot all about you. I was the fool but
I'm wiser now!" Darryl sat there bobbing his head letting Shirley

sing for him. I squinted my eyes at him wondering how this song was supposed to help my mood. He lip-synced the bridge, "NEVER AGAIN! Will I let you go! NOW THAT YOU'RE HOME!...." When my expression showed no amusement, Darryl cleared his throat and turned the music down. He said the music has to move you, otherwise it was a waste of energy.

He watched me as I read the letters to myself. When I started the fourth letter he walked behind me and started massaging my shoulders. "KB! You need me to work this knot out for you. Move to the bed so I can work on it." I was so into the letter that I didn't think about what he was saying. As soon as I sat on the bed he moved the letter and kissed me. He put everything in that kiss, he went for every spot he knew would render me speechless. "You left, my world came to an end!..." played softly in the background. We fell asleep after round one with him lying there still connected to me. I woke up to him starting round two, and during round three I realized he didn't reach for one condom. "WAIT A MINUTE DARRYL! MOVE!"

He stopped moving but he didn't get up, "yes?"

"I'll love you forever...." Shirley kept singing in the background. "Condom?" I said as a tear rolled out of my eye.

He looked me in my eyes, "you are the only person I've had this with. If you never forgive me I will never have this again. I need to feel it one more time, then I can do whatever you want me to." Then he went back to working me over. "My world came to an end..." The problem with this is that I hadn't gotten back on the pill. Until Nellie's news I was scheming to get pregnant. He thinks I'm still on the pill, I don't know how to tell him I'm not. I closed my eyes and then fell into the biggest orgasm ever. "Then you came back AGAIN! NOW I KNOW! THERE IS NO WAY! I CAN GO ON WITHOUT YOU!"

"Take me to my car." I said just above a whisper. Darryl did as he was told, but he moved slowly. "Darryl, we're over! This will never happen again."

Darryl shook his head no at me. That made me angry, "I'm not agreeing to that. I love you, that will never change. And if you end up pregnant and you kill my baby again, it's gonna really suck to be you."

"What?"

313

"I know you're not on the pill anymore." He glanced at me, "you never refilled the prescription and your period started coming off schedule. Girls think they know everything and like men don't follow along. And don't get me started on the sabotaged condoms in your bedroom. Like I can't tell when a condom's been tampered with."

"If you knew why didn't you say anything?"

"Cause I was in shock for one that you would sink to such a chicken head level. And because I knew this day was coming."

"So you in turn sink to the chicken head level?"

He shrugged, "you're trying to leave me! Trying to bring my world to an end!"

"I'm not having your baby!" I yelled at him.

"The hell you're not! Don't tempt me, I'll tie you down for six months. I love you Kendra and our story doesn't end here. I need you to forgive me. I need us to be strong again."

I got out of the car slamming the door.

I was relieved when my period came three weeks later. I happily started taking my pill again although there was no way I was letting Darryl touch me again.

Nellie

I've been calling Marquez for a couple weeks and he hasn't called me back. At first I paid it no attention but then I thought about his on again off again girlfriend out there while he's in school. What if they've decided to make a go of things? HE CAN'T LEAVE ME!

Kendra

When I pulled up to my house Anton was pulling up behind me. I parked in my garage and then I walked out to the front. "You look tired."

"I don't know how Mr. Atchinson gets his place so dirty in one week's time! I told him how it cost him more but he doesn't seem to care." I shook my head.

"I guess you could never be with someone who's a little messy."

I ignored his comment. "Thank you for everything you've done here and next door. Erin has a real backyard to play in. I feel like you've gone above and beyond our deal."

"I did get a little carried away didn't I?" I smiled, "I wanted you to be able to come home and relax whether it was in your front yard or back yard."

"It's beautiful thank you." I said taking in my beautiful and exotic shrubbery. I walked over to this green bush that had these dramatically beautiful flowers growing from it. "This is beautiful, what's it called?"

"Bird of paradise," he said watching me.

"That's a fitting title!" I said taking in the beauty of this flower. I've never seen so many different colored Calla Lilies and lilies period. It was very relaxing and peaceful.

In my backyard he built a little fountain that looked like circular clay planter pots from the biggest to the smallest each one was slightly tilted. It splashed over the sides just enough to water the flowers around the base. Kalani has friends over all the time. They sit out in chairs around the fountain and review books they've read or are reading. "I haven't seen the thug around." I didn't say anything to that. "Can I take you out to dinner?"

"No," I said softly not wanting to be mean.

"Kendra, I'm hungry. You should be, I know you're tired. Let's let someone else do the cooking and worry about the cleanup. I promise to keep my hands to myself."

I exhaled cause I didn't feel like cooking or pressing the numbers on the microwave to heat something up. "I'm not ready to date." I said honestly.

"I'll wait for you, as for today we need to eat. Let's go eat."

"Fine! Let's go." I said, if it were a date I would've showered first. Since this was only about food, I walked to his truck.

Even though no one is funnier than Darryl, we had a nice meal. The whole time I was looking for him to say something wrong, to do something out of line. But Anton is good and well behaved.

****

"You and Anton are spending a lot of time together." Ahjanae smiled at me.

"We're just friends!" I said defensively.

She smiled, "YOU LIKE HIM!"

I gasped, "we're just friends!"

"You kiss him?" She asked looking at me sideways.

"No! Friends don't kiss." I said blushing.

"Yea, but you want to. I can tell." She said laughing at me while I sat there blushing.

Ryder's momma Sharon was too excited about her new grand baby. Ryder wants to legally adopt Erin, Jabbar is broken hearted about it. But I think he's learned his lesson about fast money. He's taking some classes at the college, but he's no financial support for Erin although she doesn't need it cause Ryder pays for everything. The sad part is that when Ryder's adoption goes through she will carry Ryder's last name, Wallace. I don't know how I feel about that, but it's not my business. I liked that Ryder's family adopted Erin as their own, especially since Jabbar's momma has clocked out behind losing her baby over some none sense. No one blames her for taking it so hard, and fortunately Erin has Sharon to pick up the pieces. Sharon spoils her rotten, and she promises to do the same with the new baby. Unlike Jabbar's family, Ryder's family is very hands on. Even Ryder's uncle Darren built a crib from scratch for the new baby. It's beautiful and better than anything I've seen in the stores.

Darryl walked in the door with his momma. He had a big gift in his hands, but his eyes searched the room until he found me. He smiled at me and I grinned slightly then I looked away. Ahjanae smiled at me cause she saw the exchange.

I stayed next to my momma during the games. Aunt Quilla keeps telling Ahjanae that this experience is so much better than Jabbar. For one Ahjanae and Ryder weren't kids, and she loves that Ryder's family is just as invested as we are. Aunt Quilla and Sharon were having too much fun having us do all kinds of fun ridiculous stuff. Changing baby diapers blindfolded, trying to identify the source of the poop in the diapers. Ryder and Darryl kept trying to get other people to taste the poop. They had all of us in stitches. When it was time to eat Darryl sat next to me. And when I didn't react he exhaled. He didn't eat cause he was asking me so many questions. His momma looked at us and smiled, but she didn't say anything. When the cake came out he deflated a little but then he put a fake smile on his face. Sharon gave him his own red velvet and he smiled and thanked her for it. I asked him what was wrong. He told me to follow him out the door. He exhaled, "I'm a mess! I miss you KB. So much has happened, is happening. It's a lot." He looked down at the cake. "I'm in therapy, I need help!" He leaned against the rail. "Did you ever stop to think, because we fell in love Ryder gets to live out his lifelong dream of being the father he never had?"

"I didn't think of that."

"Jen owes me EVERYTHING! If my auntie didn't live across the street from her she would not be here now."

"Ok...." I said looking around.

"KB I'm a mess!"

"Kendra," I corrected him.

He sucked his teeth, "nice try! I'm legally changing your name to KB! Or..... I can call you Kenny's Booty in front of everybody if you like."

"Kendra will do."

He rolled his eyes, "any who like I was saying KB! I'm a mess! These days I can't do nothing right. Even that cake, you know how much I love Sharon's red velvet."

I bucked my eyes at him, "what happened?"

He dramatically turned his body away from me. "Before I knew what was happening, I fell in love with another cake."

I gasped, "what?"

He shook his head. "I know! I know! It's my sister in law." He exhaled. "It's not her fault she didn't know what she was doing by making red velvet at her family dinner. One taste and I was hooked. Me and D-Rick got into the worst fight over the last piece the next day when we brought some home."

"Are you ok?"

"Yea he's fine, we always fight over food though. I told Drew he's gotta marry this girl, everything she makes is the bomb. But she's forever changed me. So check it," he turned to face me. "I was eating my cake that Sharon sent me not too long ago thinking about me and you. How nothing will ever be the same with Sharon's cake cause I had Tracy's. And how my chicken heads don't bring me joy any more since you. I miss you so much! KB I cry!"

"You do not!"

"I do KB! I do! Especially when I thought about how crazy you are. You're like my momma! I know I make light of it, but I kill people. I'll shoot, cut, stab, slice, torture. I could go on but why? None of that is an exaggeration. My therapist said I'm certifiably crazy. And with all of that," he looked at me and smiled. "You hit me! Then you kept coming back to hit me again! Warms my heart

KB! Warms my heart." Then he dropped his smile, "don't get me wrong. I don't like being hit. It makes me mad. But you aren't scared of me, I love that about you!"

I stared at him, "you are sick and twisted!"

"It's true." He shrugged. "So you're dating the Gardner I see."

"Who told you that?"

"I've got eyes, I can see." He exhaled, "I don't like it KB! But," he exhaled. "I decided to try something different this time. Actually try dating one person. When we were together that one time, that was the first time I ever lived like that. Until then, hoes at the club, I actually enjoyed it. So in my get KB back plan, I decided one hoe at a time." He exhaled, "it's exhausting cause none of them are worthy. They get sprung so fast, can't blame them for that. But it's not the same."

"Am I supposed to glean something from this?"

"Yes! I still love you! I'm trying to get better for you! We will be together again!" He smiled, "oh but here's the tricky part. I need a favor." I looked at him. "I need you to come to one of my therapy sessions." He clasped his hands in front of me pleading.

"Why?"

"I need to explain the whole Noel thing, and I can't do it without Joanne."

"Who says I want to hear it?"

He walked over to me. Kissed my lips, "please do it for your baby daddy!"

I gasped, tears started pouring out of my eyes. "You're evil!"

"Did I forget to mention evil on my long list of me?"

****

"Thank you for coming, my name is Joanne it's nice to finally meet you KB."

I shot Darryl a look, he started cracking up. "That's what's on my heart."

"Darryl! Why didn't you tell me her real name? What's your name sweetheart?"

"Kendra," I said sitting in the chair.

"Thank you for coming."

"Darryl says that you met when he hit you with a football."

"Yes, I was embarrassed."

"Joanne let me explain it again. I was going home. And then she walked past me. My life has never been the same since. That's when I named her KB."

"You name everybody!"

He shrugged, "it's a gift."

He made us laugh as he talked about the very beginning. I couldn't help it, I cried when he revealed how early things started between Nellie and him. He didn't think we'd end up where we did. He said he told her that he liked and wanted me, but he went for it. He said it made him angry every time she came for him. He said there was no emotional connection to her until she ended up in the hospital. I got angry cause I felt like he was using me as an excuse for what he did. He reminded me that his grandfather had just died, and he needed more than what I was offering. I told him I kept calling him, and he said that was only to apologize. It wasn't like I was going to change anything about the direction I was heading in. Which was true, although I loved Darryl and he was special to me, I had them confused. I was thinking Darryl was the unstable one even though I cared for him. Omar seemed more solid, sigh! Darryl said he was in pain and so was she, he didn't even talk to me while all of that was going on. He reminded me of our conversation at my junior prom. He said the Saturday before the blow up was the first time he ever touched Nellie while he was with me in some kind of way. He said as soon as he told her he was going to tell me everything I was approaching them. While he talked about Nellie was the first time he's ever not cracked even a sarcastic joke. Joanne asked him what he wanted me to get from all that he said. He said he can't take back what he did. It was important however that I understood he has trust issues, and I didn't make it easy for him to trust me. But one thing that would never change is how much he loves me. He said there would never be another KB in his life.

Then she asked him what he wanted to ask me. He looked at her like he was trying to remember. Then he slouched and said he was tired. She shot him a look then she said this may be his only chance. He took a deep breath, then he looked at me with tears in his eyes and he asked me how I did it? How did I have an abortion and keep it from him? Now I slouched in my chair. I told him that by the time I gave in to the possibility that I could be pregnant all those females were making my life miserable. I told him I was frustrated and scared. Scared that he wouldn't care, or worse. That he became a different person once he knew he successfully trapped me. He told me he didn't want a baby so I took it and ran with it. He said to be evil he tried to question whether it was really his baby. But he knew better. He said there was no guarantee that the final decision would've been any different if we would've discussed it. When he said I broke his heart I felt like crap, but of course I had to go there. I told him at least we were even. He said the heartbreaks weren't on the same level, they were two totally different things. I said that was only to him, not the way I saw it. We both did the unthinkable and no matter what we did today, we couldn't erase the pain from yesterday and how it affects our tomorrow.

****

Kalani asked me if I was sure I wanted to do this. I told her there was only one way to be truly sure. I finally agreed to go out with Anton. I couldn't stand to see him keep hanging on like he was. Either we were going to go our separate ways or give the energy between us a good college try. Anton's nothing like Darryl and for me right now that's a good thing. Every time I see a guy that I honestly think is cute, when I truly ask myself why he's cute to me it's because he reminds me of Darryl in some way. He's tall like Darryl, did something silly like Darryl, looked at me the way Darryl used to. Anton isn't like Darryl at all, maybe that's why I wasn't interested. I decided to open my mind to the possibility, he was definitely determined enough. Anton's request to actually take me out had become part of our routine. He'd find some excuse to take me to a cheaper dinner cause I wouldn't let him take me anywhere nice. Then he'd ask me to let him take me out somewhere nice during the course of our meal. I'd decline citing I wasn't ready, Anton would fake understanding and then he'd wait until the next opportunity to ask me. When he asked me and I didn't reply quickly with my usual no, he acted as if I said no and continued on with the conversation. When he realized I was smiling at him he stopped talking and asked me if I said yes. I shook my head yes, "either that or we've got to stop doing this." He smiled really big, and as he attempted to shake his leg with nervous energy. He hit the table with his knee which made the whole table shake, knocking over his water glass and the contents spilled in his lap. Anton hopped up as ice and water spilled on to the floor.

"See what you do to me." He was completely embarrassed.

I couldn't help it, I laughed and I laughed hard. When he laughed at himself I told myself this could work, he has a sense of humor. Kalani doesn't think it's a good idea, and I'm sure that every time she starts whispering on her phone that's her plotting with Darryl against me. I can't even worry about it. "How do I look?"

Kalani rolled her eyes, "you look fine. When you go out with Darryl can you wear a dress? I'm about sick of you and pants."

"I'm not a girly-girl wearing dresses all the time."

"Dresses don't make you a girly-girl." She exhaled, "it's a waste of breath. Have fun, let me know if you need me to rescue you from the rebound guy." She said loud enough for Anton to hear her from the living room. Anton was still all smiles when I walked into the living room. I apologized for my sister's rudeness, he shrugged it off. He took me to Sausalito to a restaurant by the water. There was live music and drippy candles. It was a lovely and romantic spot. The music was nice and it wasn't so loud that we couldn't have conversation at the table. Anton kept smiling at me and thanking me for FINALLY agreeing to go out with him. It was weird telling a new person about myself. I could pick and choose what I wanted to say and what I didn't. I decided to focus on him and ask him a ton of questions about himself. When he'd ask about me I'd only say as much as I needed to. Anton on the other hand was giving me his whole life story. His parents struggle as an interracial couple, and how bitter the whole experience left his mother. His mother got so depressed that she spiraled out of control. He has no clue who his sister's father is. He said one day she was just pregnant, and then there was a baby. She never said anything about a father, and she would get angry if they asked. He said he's always been the man of his mother's house, not by choice either. I thought about my momma and how she could've let her grief consume her when my father left. I honestly think that because Kalani and I cared enough to try, that gave her the strength to keep moving forward. My Aunt Quilla is the reason she met Jason, and I'm so happy. A woman like my momma deserves to be loved like Jason loves her. Anton's momma wasn't so fortunate and in turn he's had to cope with a lot. He spoke about his momma's addiction matter of factly. Like he was putting it out

321

there so I'd understand right away. He said because of her he rarely drinks. I did my best to let him know it was ok, and he didn't need to worry. When he kissed me goodnight, it was a good kiss, but never better than I've had. When I went to bed I shrugged. I kept telling myself it was fine, and that this could work. When I realized I was trying to convince myself, I listened to my shell for a while, then I rolled over and went to sleep.

****

"I'm so happy you two FINALLY got together!" Anton's best friend declared to our table. "My friend is so happy!"
"Whoa Sean! How many of those have you had?" Anton asked concerned for his friend.
"I don't know!" Then he laughed, his girlfriend Gayle did not look amused. "Kendra, this man thinks you're soooooo beautiful! That's all he talks about!"
I blushed, "thanks? What else does he say?" I said as I laughed.
"AAAA! That's enough man! You're embarrassing me!" Anton said blushing himself. He put his arm around my shoulders and kissed my forehead.
"It's ok! Girls like it when you embarrass yourself over them. It gets you in there!"
"In where?" Gayle asked with attitude. Sean punched his fist out and then pulled it back. "What would you know about it?"
"Just because I turned my life over to God now, doesn't mean I don't know about," then he punched the air. "I was very good in there!"
"You guys don't have sex?" Anton asked with his mouth hanging open.
"Not before marriage. I know a lot of people think it's restrictive or old fashioned, but it really is the right way to handle things." She said
Anton covered my ears, "don't listen to them! Don't give her ideas!"
"Sex should be shared between a husband and wife, without sex in it's proper place it can cause problems." She said like an authority on the matter.
"And love without sex is frustrating!" Sean blurted out.
"Good thing you don't love me." She shot back.
"Not yet, whether I do or I don't depends upon you." Then he got irritated. "This is not a bible session. Anton and me go WAAAY

back! He's respectful of my life choices and I respect his. You just mad because we know what they're doing tonight, and we're going our separate ways." Sean teased her.

"Mad? Ha!" She shifted in her chair, "nothing good comes from NOT doing things God's way. Most people gotta bump their heads up against a brick wall before they understand that. Other people like….." her voice trailed off as she watched someone enter the restaurant.

Anton and I turned to see who she was looking at. I did a double take when I realized it was Darryl walking in with a date. His eyes locked on me and he smiled, then he scanned my table. "Can you add us to this table?" He asked the host pointing to our table. They moved the small table next to us. Darryl held the chair out for his date to sit next to Gayle. Then Darryl sat next to me. "KB! How are you doing?"

Anton leaned forward, "KB?"

"That's what he calls me." My hands instantly turned sweaty.

"Aren't you going to introduce your friend?"

"My bad, this is Brenda. Brenda this is KB, Ant, Some guy I don't know, and Gayle. Long time no see Gayle."

Gayle was all hot and bothered, nothing like her calm reserved self that we just saw a few moments ago. "D! It's been a long time!" She said shifting in her chair.

Brenda and I looked at her completely irritated, "nothing good huh!" I said reminding her of what she was just saying.

"That was a long time ago." She said fanning herself.

"Nice to meet you Brenda, I'm Kendra and this is my boyfriend Anton."

"Nice to meet you." She said trying to act like she didn't already know who I was.

"Boyfriend?" Darryl said like it taste nasty to let the words come out of his mouth. "How long has this been going on?"

"Awhile, how about you and Brenda?"

"Awhile!" She replied shooting Darryl a look.

"So she's your girlfriend?" Gayle asked

"Does it matter?" Darryl said shooting her an irritated look.

"What's wrong with you?" Sean asked Darryl.

"Somebody's twisted!" Darryl said looking at Sean.

"He's been having a hard time. His sister was in a terrible car accident and her friend almost died." I explained.

Darryl looked at Sean for a minute like he was assessing him. Then he turned his attention back to me. "So KB, what have you been up to?"

"School and working, you?"

"Same here." Darryl said

"Where do you work?" Anton asked Darryl.

"Latour Enterprises, you know it?"

"No, what is that?"

"Latour Enterprises is the parent company to so many affiliates. It would take me all night to explain everything to you. I do a little bit of everything there, that's the simplest way to put it." Then he looked at me, "how's business?"

"It's good, I'm hoping to add new staff and expand."

"Hoping?"

"Yes, we're still small. I want to take on some janitorial jobs as well as housekeeping. That will require more staff, but I don't want to take on more staff unless I know for sure that I can get the gigs."

"That's understandable. I may know a way to help you with that, but you gotta call me."

I smiled, "I don't have your number."

Darryl's face turned serious, "KB! Don't be acting brand new just because your friend is sitting right there. You know my number is burned into your heart." He stared at my eyes, "you can't forget me no matter how hard you try."

I felt uncomfortable with him being so bold even in front of Anton and his girl. I put my head down, "don't do that."

"Do what? State facts? The only two people who matter at this table right now is me and you."

"Who are you to her?" Gayle asked

"That is the stupidest question, I guess following the dialog would be too much like right for you." Darryl spit at her.

Darryl was getting irritated, and I'm sure the fact that I was sitting next to Anton wasn't helping his patience level. I touched his hand, "be nice." I patted his hand. Then I looked at Gayle, "we used to date."

"So who's that sitting next to you? Is that your boyfriend?" Darryl asked thoroughly irritated.

"We… we… we" She stammered.

Anton frowned at her reaction to Darryl. "He's not hitting it, that's why you all up in my business huh?" Darryl smiled, "my man you up for the challenge?" He said to Sean.

"Challenge?" Sean asked

"It's time for you to take Sean home. Tell him I'll call him later." Anton commanded Gayle.

"BUT!" She was trying to think of a reason to stay behind.

"Gayle! Take Sean home, we'll see you two later!" Anton said with an about business tone in his voice.

I tried to hold back my smile as Gayle reluctantly did as she was told. "Ant you alright!" Darryl said watching Gayle and Sean leave. "I like the way you handled her." Darryl adjusted in his chair. Brenda was trying to get Darryl's attention without being obvious, but Darryl was too busy looking at me and smiling.

"Look at you! You got your hair all weaved up, long and down your back. Long hair don't care huh?" He smiled.

I touched my hair, "I tried something different."

"Un huh! Trying something different, has got you trying something different." Then he smiled. The waiter came to the table. He took Darryl and Brenda's drink order, and then Anton asked him for the check for our meal. That's when it hit me that Sean left without paying his portion of the tab. When the waiter gave Anton the bill it was over three hundred dollars. I think Anton stopped breathing. If Darryl wasn't sitting here I would've asked him if he was ok, and if he needed me to chip in. I know he wasn't planning on spending four hundred (after tip) on one meal. Our portion of that bill was probably eighty dollars. Miss Gayle had quite a few drinks herself. Note to self, always ask for separate tabs when you go out with alcoholics. Anton put his card in the billfold and he handed it to the waiter. Anton looked stressed, when the waiter came back I knew it was all bad. His card was declined, I didn't look at Anton cause I knew he was embarrassed. I was embarrassed for him. I reached for my purse, "KB what are you doing? What's going on?" Darryl said looking around me.

"Nothing we're just settling the bill." I tried to take embarrassment out of my voice. The waiter started to walk away with another card for Anton.

Darryl told the waiter to come back and he handed Anton his card. He told him the bill is taken care of, then he winked at me. I stood up to leave with Anton. Darryl came in for a hug and he held on a couple of seconds longer than he should've but I felt bad no matter which way you spun it. So I patted his back and thanked him for the hug.

Anton held the door open for me and then he walked kind of slow with me in the cool Berkeley air. "That was so embarrassing. Had I known I was going to be covering that kind of damage I would've brought my card for my other account. You know I have the money, I wasn't prepared for all of this. I'm gonna kill Sean!" Anton makes good money with his business, I know he has the money. And I also know that he tries to live very minimally so that he will have money later. So he only keeps so much money in that account and he had the gas credit card on him.

When we got to my house Kalani had company in her room, so we went in my room. Anton asked me how I was handling seeing Darryl tonight, I shrugged and said it was fine. He asked me if I was ok, and I shook my head yes even though my mind was wandering. That night Anton tried to put it on me and got a cramp in his legs. Bless his little heart for trying to work Darryl out of my brain.

Chapter 20

Nellie

When my momma was released on probation she initially went to a half-way house. I went there to visit her a few times, and then suddenly she was moving into her own apartment. Nothing as fancy as when I was little but her own place all the same. She asked me to help her refresh her memory on the accounting front. Numbers always come to me easily so I was able to help her, she took a couple classes and I helped her with her homework. Then she found a job with a small company. Then she got a nice, but not as nice car as the one she had when I was young. I asked her how she was affording all of these things, and she would never answer me directly. I got that sinking feeling. When Nathan flew out to come spend the weekend with me and momma, the first thing he noticed was daddy's demeanor. He said he was too nice, and that he could tell they were back together. Daddy was extremely nice now, and not pent up and frustrated like he's always been. Now I know why Nathan always stuck by my stepmom's side. She would look at my daddy with so much pain and hurt in her eyes but she wouldn't say anything. Well at least not in front of us. Nathan keeps going off on our momma, and he calls her Mary. One minute we're fine and the next minute he's mad at her. She says that's exactly how she was and sometimes still is with her momma so she understood it. She'd focus on Nathan a lot to help him work through his feelings, but that meant that I had the chance to try to be unselfish which is still a work in progress cause for me, I still feel some kind of way about not being the focus.

Kendra

I smiled even though she was killing my eardrums. "Kendra! Kendra! Kendra! I love saying that, Kendra!" Ms. Tafoya said loud and rowdy.

She was always drunk, high, or both. Anton didn't like coming around more than he had to. He paid her rent, collected her bills, and took her grocery shopping for the month. She would get excited when she saw me. I honestly think the excitement was just a cover up for how self-conscious she felt about herself. The first time I met her, she was sick trying to kick her habit. But when that proved to be too hard she decided she might as well go out with a bang. Anton wasn't ready for me to meet her, and I think he thought I would judge him. But I explained how my momma has siblings that we don't see because of their addictions. I told him every family has at least one. I made his momma feel comfortable and ever since then, she "loves" her some Kendra! She gotta say my name three times in a row at least four times during our visit for no reason. Anton's sister runs through his momma's house from time to time. When she needs a place to sleep, stuff like that, she don't fool with us too much. "Please momma!" Anton was tired, he's been working on a big project that was going to make Tafoya landscaping the company to get.

His momma huffed at him, "do I embarrass you? Do I remind you where you come from? You's black! Black boy!"

"I know where I come from." He said trying to be cool.

"You act all uppity! Like you don't wanna be associated with anything that reminds you of where you come from! I am your reality!"

I exhaled cause this act gets old, "Ms. Tafoya does his daddy being mixed bother you that much?"

"I should've never let him look at me, let alone hump me." She said loudly.

"Aw! Momma!" Anton said like he was about to be sick.

"He forgets he's black too!" Then pain flashed all over her face. "I was too black for them. He forgot that's what he loved about me! Kendra! Kendra! Kendra! Watch out girl, cause he's going forget too."

"Momma I know who I am."

"I'm surprised you have a black girlfriend. He done dated some of everythang!"

"That's good!" I said

"How you figure?"

"You should like and love who you like and love. To limit yourself to one race is ridiculous."

"So I'm ridiculous?"

"If you limit yourself to one race, yes!"

"Little girl I will snatch that weave out of your head so fast!"

I exhaled, "if you were going to do it you wouldn't waste time threatening it. Leave my baby alone!"

She looked at me frowned, then she started cracking up. "See! I love my niggas!" She cracked up laughing. "Anton done got him some of the real real! I bet you put it on him didn't you?" She started dropping it in the middle of the floor. "Did you work it like this Kendra? Kendra? Kendra?"

Anton would not look at his momma. "We're leaving!"

He didn't have to tell me twice. I was out the door trying to keep my lunch down. Anton was quiet as he drove to my parent's house. I couldn't blame him, with a mother like that what could you say? When we got to my parent's house, Jason was in Milton's face threatening his life as usual. I kissed Anton's cheek then I went inside. Kaleah was bouncing her baby looking out the window. I took my nephew from her. "What's wrong?" I asked snuggling the baby.

"I'm pregnant." Kaleah said matter of factly.

"Again?"

"Why can't anyone think of a different response? Yes again!"

"Jason is going to kill Milton this time!" I laughed.

"If he didn't kill Darryl he won't..... JASON!!!!!" She took off running.

I looked out the window and Jason was beating Milton down.

My momma ran to save Milton. "You think this is a game? This is my daughter!" He yelled as he booted Milton.

Needless to say Milton was a lesser of the Mason's. "Jason! Daddy! Please!" Kaleah was grasping anything she could think of to calm him down.

"This is not a game! This is your life baby girl! Why would you share yourself with someone who doesn't appreciate your gift? You're going to have to raise two babies by yourself when he moves on from you just like he's done the others. I WARNED YOU!" Jason said booting him again. "You play these games with those tricks that don't got nobody! I will mess your stuff up!"

"Whoa! Jayman! Who you got?" Aunrey asked as he strolled up. He's sucked his teeth. "Milton I warned you! You stupid!"

"Alright! Chill man! Chill!" He said putting his hands up. "I love her! I'm not going nowhere!"

"Standup and address me like a man then! Don't come to me with that sissy junk!" Jason was so mad he was about to start foaming at the mouth.

Anton and Aunrey stood there watching the whole scene with smirks on their faces. Momma told us to come back inside. When Kalani pulled up with a friend, everybody gasped. Kalani asked us what was wrong, Jason asked her who the guy was in his deep I'm about to beat somebody down voice. Kalani put one finger up. Then she and her friend got back in the car and sped away. Aunrey and Anton were falling all over each other cracking up.

The men were outside long enough for Kalani to come back alone. Anton and Milton stayed in the living room with the baby, while we went into my parent's domain. I wouldn't call it a room. All they needed was a small kitchen in there and they could never come out. It was huge and very warm and inviting in there. Aunrey and Jason turned the couch to face the bed. Then they told us to sit, while my parents sat on the bed and Aunrey stood.

He started pacing when he got nervous. We patiently waited, I had no clue of what he had to tell us. "You all know how much I love you right! We all grew up together more like brothers and sisters than cousins. The only time I feel bad about it is when I wonder if you all would hate me for it." He took a deep breath. He glanced at Kaleah and then he took a deep breath. "Jerry didn't kill himself, I killed him."

All four of us covered our mouths, Jason didn't say anything. He looked from each person's eyes and then he stared at Kaleah. "He came with a gun twice for my auntie! When I came up on him it was him or me. I couldn't let him hurt you all any more than he had done." He looked at Kaleah, "if I had been home that day it wouldn't have gotten as far as it did. I never would've let him hurt you like that." When no one said anything he continued. I looked at Kaleah who had tears streaming down her face as she watched Aunrey. "Auntie he wasn't a man! And well, I....." He stopped talking when Kaleah stood up. She threw her arms around him while she cried. "What the?" He looked at Jason, "a little help?" Then my momma stood up and hugged him while she cried. All four corners were covered with crying females. "Come on you guys! I'm sorry, don't cry!" He said standing in the middle of our tears.

"Don't be sorry baby, did you at least get a couple hits in for me?" My momma said

"Yes auntie I did!" Then he looked at Kaleah, "I know how much he meant to you."

"He was special when he was a real dad. That person he became...." She squeezed him tighter. "Thank you for loving me that much!"
"Me too!" I said.
"Me three!" Kalani said.
"Me four!" My momma said.

Nellie

I invited my stepmom out to lunch just she and I. "What's going on?"
"Nothing baby," she tried to say like everything was fine.
"You're insulting my intelligence. As much as you've always wanted me to keep things real with you. This is your chance to show me how it's done." I watched her face.
My stepmom slouched for a second, "I can tell he's seeing her again. No matter how hard I try he's always got to have her in our lives. Him having her right now is one thing, you see how happy he is. Have you ever seen him like this?"
I shook my head yes, "when I was little."
"Exactly, when he was seeing your momma. But she wants my spot, and Neallan is my husband!" She said in a defeated tone.
"Why do you stick with him if you know that he cheats on you?"
She smiled weakly, "I love your father very much. And I know he loves me, he just has to have Mary. I mean I know she's pretty." She said looking at the table.
"You're pretty too! So he gets to have both of you?"
"As long as she stays in her place and remembers that I am his wife and that I come first, what am I going to do?"
"You could leave him! You deserve so much better!"
"Leave him and go where? Do what? Suffer in silence. I love Neallan, I don't want to be without him. He accepted everything about me and made me his wife! I can work with him on this." She said in defeat.
I adjusted in my seat, "so you're telling me that because of what I've gone through in life when it comes down to it I have to share the spotlight with someone else? That's it?"
She smiled weakly at me, "you're not going to end up with Ahjani are you baby? History won't repeat it's self."
"No thanks to daddy I won't. If we would've had a chance to grow maybe I'd be on his arm right now and not that other chick."

331

She touched my hand, "Ahjani's mom is the reason you two aren't together. She was afraid for her son as any loving and caring mom would've been. Your daddy was ok with you being with Ahjani, he could tell how much that boy cared about you"

I sunk into my seat, "what should I do? Ahjani wants me, but he's in love with his girlfriend."

"If you're not first you pass. Different relationships are made of different things. You don't have to accept your husband cheating on you just because your father cheats on me. However, if you find yourself here you have to make sure he's worth it. I'm still first no matter what your mother does. As long as she understands that, I'll tolerate her existence. The moment she steps outside of her roll, that's when I'll shut it down again." Then she looked at me, "this is my life sweetheart, and it doesn't have to be yours."

"I guess," I said thinking about it.

"Now," she was changing the subject. "Is Marquez coming to the wedding?"

"I haven't talked to him."

"You haven't? Why?" She's the worst actress ever.

I looked at her for a minute. "He hasn't answered my calls. Graduation is coming soon, maybe he decided it would be less drama for him with someone else."

"If you love him, you fight for him. Do you love him?"

"I do," I said shaking my head.

"Call him!"

I picked up my phone, "he hasn't answered my calls." I dialed his number.

He picked up on the first ring, "hello?"

"Where have you been? I've been calling you and calling you!"

"What did you need?"

"I needed you!"

I could hear his smile, "you needed me?"

"Yes!"

"What about D and Ahjani? Ahjani is on his way to greatness!"

"You are greatness! Please never ignore me like that again."

"Why?" His voice echoed.

I looked at my stepmom who was smiling at me, "because you are my one true happiness. Without you I might as well die."

Then he sat in the chair next to me. He smiled at me and kissed me. I was so happy to see him I cried. "Hi!"

"What are you doing here?"

He put a ring box in front of me. "I came to ask you a very important question."

I looked at the box in disbelief, "you want me?" I started crying and I put my head on his shoulder, "don't you want better?"

"There's no one better for me than you." He said kissing my lips.

"Can you even afford me?" I said partly joking.

"Look at the box, we'll need a few years before we're back to your father's standards of living. But if you'll live like we're in college for a few years. I promise we'll be fine."

I opened the box and the most beautiful ring ever sparkled at me. I never thought of anyone wanting me forever, especially with everything that Marquez knows about me. "It's beautiful!"

"Now you can have this if you give me the right answer." He smiled.

"You didn't ask me anything." I teased.

"Will you marry me?"

"YES!" I said with all my heart. "It's just me and you!"

****

Nassya was so excited about our news. Marquez's uncle came over to celebrate with us. I kept looking at my ring in disbelief, I couldn't believe that Marquez loved me that much to actually want to spend the rest of his life with me, and how did he afford this one karat solitaire? When Marquez's uncle mentioned babies I looked at Marquez in fear. I would do it for him, but I'm not gonna lie and say fear wasn't alive and well within me. Marquez held my hand and said we had plenty of time for all of that.

Later on we went to my momma's place and she finally got a chance to meet Marquez. I could see disappointment all over her face when I told her he was still in school and I gave no indication that we would be living high on the hog once he graduated. I tried to hold it back, and shake it off but I couldn't. I went completely off, I thought Marquez was going to tell me not to go off on my momma like that, but he said nothing. I told her that her ridiculous goal for me to marry rich is what ruined my life! I told her if she would've put as much effort into our relationship as mother and daughter, Bobby would've never got to me. My momma turned so red I thought her head was going to pop off. It was like I stepped outside of myself and I went completely off on her holding back nothing. I told her I didn't agree with her sleeping with a married man even if it was my father. He said vows to someone else. I told her at the end of the day she may have moments with him, but his love and allegiance was to my stepmom. Every time she tried to speak, I shut her down. I told her I was done trying to be like her or looking for her approval over my life. I told her about the night I saw her out with Bobby. I told her she could tell everyone he forced her back, but I saw them together and from where I was sitting she was loving every moment of it. My words kept hitting her and hitting her! She had no defense for any of the things I threw at her. Then we left.

That night I couldn't sleep, I kept tossing and turning. Marquez said I needed to get those things off my heart, but they weren't going to make me feel better. We went back to her house in the middle of the night, she was wide-awake as well. She was smoking a cigarette something I never saw her do. I went on her balcony with her where she was smoking. She told me that money doesn't buy you happiness, but the lack of it causes misery. She said that my father's money provided me with a carefree life. She told me to imagine everything we went through and then put money limitations on my father, our lives would've been that much more hectic. She said money isn't everything, but it is important. I told her it was important, but not a priority. Just because a man has money doesn't mean he's going to share it. And even if he does share as she well knows, one day he could stop. My momma apologized to Marquez and then she told us she was happy for us. That's when I noticed her jealousy.

Kendra

I didn't even say hello, "KB!"

"Darryl?"

"Where you at girl? I gotta show you something."

"I'm at Ahjanae's, what is it?"

"I can't even tell you! I gotta show you! I'm on my way!"

I couldn't stop laughing as I told Ahjanae and Audra that Darryl was coming. "You guys still talk?" Audra asked

"Every once in a blue moon we'll have a three or four hour phone conversation. But we don't talk much anymore."

"What does Anton think about that?" Audra asked raising an eyebrow.

"I don't go through his call log, so he can stay out of mine."

The doorbell rang and then I went down to the door. Ryder and Ahjanae moved to Oakland just before the baby was born. Kalani moved into momma's house. I opened the door and Darryl had a big smile on his face with a cake box in his hands. "KB! Prepare yourself!" He said coming in the door.

"What's in the box, cake?" Audra asked.

He sucked his teeth, "I wouldn't be here for any old cake. You need to experience this." He hurried to the kitchen and we gathered around. Darryl paused. "Uh! Hi?" He said to Ahjanae and Audra.

"If you're not sharing you can get out!" Ahjanae said.

Darryl pouted, "I only have one whole cake. You want a nigga to share though?"

"Or you can get out! The choice is yours."

"You know Jen. This baby has made you mean. You're not as nice as you used to be."

Ahjanae put her hands on her hips, "your point? You can't come in my house and think you're not sharing."

"Fine! Jen! Fine!" He shook his head, "Ryder need to hurry up and knock you up again. Your meanness!" He opened the cake box then he got excited! He started jumping up and down. "YOU GUYS DON'T EVEN UNDERSTAND ABOUT THIS CAKE RIGHT HERE!" The cake was pretty but I wasn't understanding. He cut small pieces for each of us. Then he watched us as we all took a taste at the same time. Oh my! When the cake hit my tongue my eyes got big. "OK!" He jumped around. "And now your eyes have been opened! Go find some clothes, you've been walking around naked!" He cracked up.

The cake was moist, and buttery. Sometimes red velvet cake can be bitter probably from the food coloring, but this cake was delicious! The cream cheese icing, the perfect compliment, was not overpowering or too sweet. "Darryl where did you get this?"

"My sister in law made it. She made a bunch of them for my momma's charity event tonight." He said proudly as if he personally selected her. Then he picked up the remaining cake and licked it.

"WHY WOULD YOU DO THAT?" Audra asked angrily.

Darryl gave her crazy eyes, "this is my cake! I'm not sharing!"

"Stingy!" Audra said putting down her fork in her empty plate.

"You done?" He asked her looking at her plate.

"Darryl stop coveting my crumbs you have a whole cake!"

"This is not a game! Are you going to eat those crumbs or not?" When Audra didn't respond he reached for her plate. She laughed, "you are so crazy!"

Darryl hung around for a while, he kept looking at me. I guess waiting for me to say I was leaving. Ryder kept engaging me in conversation so I wouldn't leave on purpose. The looks Darryl kept giving Ryder were priceless. When I said I was leaving he shot up and said he'd walk out with me. "KB, do you remember my cousin Sophia?"

"Of course! The one with the restaurant with all the delicious food."

He smiled, "that's her. Her parents are having an anniversary party in a little bit and I wanted to know if you wanted to come as a friend. Drew is going to be there with Tracy, I want you to meet her. D-Rick's got a girl too."

"So why don't you bring the girl I saw you out with. She's pretty."

"So are you."

"I have a boyfriend."

"I'm saying if the only qualification for going is pretty, then why wouldn't I take you?"

"I think that would cross the boarders of our friendship. Thank you for the invite though."

"How long are you going to keep me benched?"

"Benched?"

"When are you coming back to me?"

"You seem to be doing just fine."

"You're in love with him aren't you?" He asked like it pained him.

"Anton's a good guy."

"How could you fall in love with someone who's not me?" He tried to say without the emotion that came through anyways.

"He's content with one female."

"Good guy, one female, is that all he's got on me?"

"He loves me, and he wants to get married one day."

Darryl opened his eyes wide and gasped, "KB! NO!" I smiled, "you'd marry him?"

"I've thought about it. Darryl we were kids, playing with fire. We made a mess of everything. What sense does it make to hold on to each other when we know in the end one of us is compromising what we really want to make the other person happy. I want to be with someone who truly wants what I want. Besides our history is too painful."

"KB! You're putting me in a dark angry place. I'm everybody's favorite, how could you do this to me?"

"I didn't do anything to you. It's time to be realistic. We aren't a good fit, too much has happened between us."

He pressed his body against mine and pinned me to the car, "too much like what? This?" He said kissing me, I didn't kiss him back. He looked at me, then put his hands all over me. He almost had me out of my shirt in the middle of the street.

"Stop! Stop it Darryl! This doesn't change anything. All this will do is make me feel bad about myself. I'll tell him as soon as I get home. He'll be upset and hurt but it won't break us up. It will give us something else to grow from, and reinforce to me how much he loves me. And you will become the poison that I cannot allow myself to become victim to." Inside I wanted to give in just because of the weakness of it all, but I knew better.

Darryl lifted my chin, there were tears in his eyes, and something I've never seen before. "I'll give you my whole cake, don't stop loving me." He kissed me, "I love you so much!"

"Darryl really? Your whole cake?" I smiled.

"I think of you every time I eat it."

"I'm with Anton, we're in love."

"I'll tolerate his existence for now."

"What happened to not becoming a hoe over you?"

"You're not a hoe, and anything with me is above and beyond any human thinking or understanding. You need to remember why you need to be with me."

"You can't come to the anniversary party. Fine! But you will come to Drew's wedding won't you?"

"Um..."

"KB, I will snap this pretty little neck if you're not there. Your whole family is going to be there, how you not gonna come?"

"I don't want to come with you."

"Yes you do, let's go." He said leading me by the hand.

"Where do you think you're taking me?"

"Come on, you're about to cum with me."

"I don't want to." I said weakly, he smiled. When we got to his car I started freaking out. "My name is not Nellie! I don't find pleasure in hurting people! Anton loves me, and he's been good to me! He doesn't deserve this from me."

"What about ME?"

"You have your hookers!"

"Chicken Heads! Get it right!" Then he walked away from me.

"You're always putting someone ahead of me! And then I'm supposed to just understand?"

"You always come after me when I have a boyfriend!"

"I can fix that for you! I'll shoot him and then you'll be free!" He said reaching in his pocket for his keys.

"Get real Darryl!"

He pointed to his right eye, "look in this eye! LOOK AT IT!" I did, "if I tell you I'm gonna kill someone, I'm gonna do it!"

"What does that eye have to do with that?"

"I wanted you to look at it." He barked.

I tried to hold back my laughter, "you are disturbed!"

"You act like this is news. Cum with me!"

"No! Last time I was with you, you ambushed me! I don't trust you. I shouldn't have trusted you then."

"All these chicken heads screaming my name, crying cause they want me, and KB is too good!"

I shrugged and started walking towards my car, "whatever Darryl! Call one of them!"

"I WANT TO CRASH YOUR CAR!" He yelled while jumping in a circle in the middle of the street. "I know I told you not to be scared of me, but right now I need you to be scared. I'm pretty pissed off and you're not reacting! Could you dial it up just a bit?" I took my keys out, "I need to go home. Go call somebody!" I blew him a kiss and got in my car. The look on his face was beyond pissed off. He stood in the middle of the street watching me. I could hear Ryder's goofy laugh as I drove away.

I checked every window, door, and any other way I thought he could slide into my house. I turned my alarm on, then I locked my door and put a chair up against it. I finally fell asleep when I thought he wasn't coming. At first I thought I was sleeping, but he was messing with my bedroom door. He knocked softly on the door, "KB?" he whispered.

"GO AWAY!" I yelled! "I did not invite you here!"

Still whispering he said, "KB! Don't be like that! I just wanna talk to you!"

"You's a lie! GO AWAY!"

Still whispering, "I'm not leaving ok! I gave you some of my cake, now give me some of yours! It's only fair!"

"I didn't ask for your cake, and you can't have mine!"

Still whispering, "if you don't stop playing I'm gonna break this door down!"

"Then I'll tell my Daddy!"

"AW! KB DON'T TELL JAYMAN ON ME! WE JUST GOT BACK COOL FROM THE LAST TIME! MALCOLM WILL KILL ME! Is that what you want? To have my blood on your hands?"

"It's not my fault if you do not take no for an answer!"

"Don't say that, somebody might hear you and think the wrong thing."

"I'm thinking the wrong thing! I believe I told you goodnight!"

"I'm not leaving! If I got to camp outside this door so be it, but I ain't leaving!"

"Good night Darryl!" I said turning over.

"For real KB? You cold blooded!" It was quiet for a long time, then just as I fell asleep.... "NOW THAT WE'VE COME TO THE END OF THE ROAD! STILL I CAN'T LET GO! IT'S UNNATURAL! YOU BELONG TO ME! I BELONG TO YOUUUUU!"

"SHUT UP DARRYL! SHUT UP! SHUT UP! SHUT UP!" I screamed at him.

"KB, in all seriousness. Can I come sleep with you? I won't do anything, and if you become overwhelmed by my sexiness and attack me, I won't stop that either but this floor is hard and cold. Why you ain't got no carpet?"

"I don't believe you!"

"I promise!"

"Is that supposed to mean something to me?"

He exhaled, "I'm giving you my word." He sounded completely serious. I walked over to the door and opened it. His smile dropped. "The moo-moo!" I rolled my eyes. "It's just as well, I'm too tired to do anything."

"Stop lying!" I said getting in the bed and under the covers. Darryl threw his leg on me and slept with his head on my back. One of the many crazy positions we used to always sleep in.

In the morning, he was at attention and staring at me. I got up brushed my teeth, put on my cleaning clothes and left without a word. "THIS IS WHY MY WOMAN WON'T WORK!" He called after me.

****

"I know you guys have a wedding thing to go to, but you know wedding season is pretty contagious." He got on one knee, "Kendra, I am so in love with you, will you marry me?" I put my hands over my mouth. "I have been in love with you for so long! Never in my wildest dreams did I ever think I would find someone so perfect for me."

"You need to ask my father for permission." I shot back. Everyone continued to smile, but Jason tilted his head. "I spoke with your father and he gave me his blessing. What do you say?" Jason and Ahjanae watched me while everyone prepared their selves for my yes. "Ok!" I said, everyone took that to mean yes. I avoided eye contact with Ahjanae and Jason. I wouldn't look at them all night. Anton came home with me so no one called. I kept looking at the ring in disbelief, it was beautiful. It was everything I dreamed of. Anton is a good man, faithful, loyal, and so sprung off of me it's ridiculous. But I keep feeling like something's missing. My cell rang, "COME OVER NOW! OR ELSE I'M COMING TO YOU!" Ahjanae said then she hung up in my face.

"Who was that?" Anton said putting my plate on the table.

"Ahjanae, everything looks delicious." I said sniffing the aroma.

"Everything ok? That's the shortest conversation I think you two have ever had." He looked concerned.

"We've had shorter. She wants me to come over. I guess I'll go by after work. Your schedule for today?"

"Replanting the shrubbery at El Cerrito Plaza Shopping Center."

"Did you go by and checkout Ms. Agnes' sprinkler?"

"AH! I knew I kept forgetting something."

"Anton! It's been two weeks!"

"I know, I'll go by as soon as we finish." When I didn't say anything he looked at me. "Don't act like that. You know I've been busy."

"On your things, I could've hired someone to go look at it, but you insisted that you could do it. And now it's been two weeks!"

"I've been working hard to cover everything cut me some slack."

His comment wounded me, "I'm not your mother Anton. I don't need you to take care of me!"

"I didn't say that, you're putting words in my mouth. You know I'm not hurting for money like that. I'm just saying that I've been working hard and it honestly slipped my mind."

"FINE! DARRYL! FINE!"

Anton looked at me, "my name is Anton."

"I know what your name is!"

"You just called me Darryl."

"NO I DIDN'T!"

"YES YOU DID!"

"I did?" I felt like crap, "I don't know where that came from."

"You said you were over him!"

"I am, I don't know where that came from." I said shoveling food into my mouth.

"Kendra," He stared at my eyes, "have you?" Then he stopped himself. "I'm not hungry! I'm going to work!"

"Anton, I'm sorry!" I called after him. He was dressed lightning fast, and out the door. I went to the door, "Anton?" He looked at me and then he pulled out of my driveway and went to work.

When I got off work I went to Ahjanae's house. Erin and the baby were in the living room having a good time watching something on TV. "Why did you say ok, if you don't want to marry him?"

"I didn't say I didn't want to marry him."

"You didn't say you did."

"I said ok," I exhaled.

"Ok is not the same as YES!"

"I called him Darryl this morning." I put my head down.

"In bed?"

"No, we were fussing. Rather I was fussing and picked a dumb argument. I wasn't even thinking of Darryl when I said it. Darryl hasn't been calling, he's finally left me alone. I don't know how his name slipped out of my mouth like that."

"What if he called you by his ex's name?"

"I know it's bad! I don't know how to fix this."

"I was calling you to find out if there was really going to be a wedding, now I don't know what to think."

My cellphone rang and it was Jason, "come by the shop."

I looked at Ahjanae, "HELP! Jason wants me to come by the shop! I'm gonna get in trouble!" panic was all over me.

"How would you get in trouble for not wanting to get married?"

"I DO WANT TO GET MARRIED!" I shot back.

"To Anton?"

"Yes," I said in defeat.

"Look! I wanna know what I'm wearing. So either I'm buying bridal magazines or I'm not, make up your mind. Just because you're engaged doesn't mean you have to get married tomorrow. Take your time, and make sure you know for sure."

"Right," I said not understanding how I felt.

I left and went to the Drew's barbershop out here in Oakland. It was closed on Sundays, but Jason was in his office working on something. I knocked on the back door. Jason gave me a hug and told me to have a seat. My bottom barely touched the seat when he started in. "So you don't want to marry Anton?"

"I do."

"No you don't! I'm reading you right now. You said yes to be nice. This is your life, you have to live with your decision not me. You tell me which way this is going down."

"Jason I do love Anton." I said moving around in my chair.

"So don't set a date. Take your time," then he leaned forward. "Don't get anyone killed!"

"Yes daddy," I said swallowing at the thought.

I knew Anton wouldn't be at my house. So I went to his, he was in his backyard working in his garden. He says gardening is stress relief for him. When he heard me coming he looked at me and watched me walk across the yard. "Hey."

"Hey."

"So you're still seeing Darryl?"

"No! I wasn't even thinking about him. I don't know where that came from I promise."

"You're not over him."

"Why are you asking me that?" I said defensively.

He stood up walked up in my face. "It wasn't a question."

"Oh."

"I love you Kendra, I don't have any loose ends to tie up."

I tilted my head at him. There was a girl that he dated and she moved away abruptly. He heard a little later that she had a baby. He said she never said anything to him, but he wondered.

"Really?"

He exhaled, "that's different!"

"Only if you say so. Someone could come demanding child support one day out of the blue. I'd call that a loose end."
"That's a child, that's not my heart. I need to be the only man standing in your heart." He watched my eyes.
I felt guilty as if I had done something. "You want your ring back?"
"If you don't love me, YES! I'm going to be paying a lot of money for that."
"I love you Anton."
"Have you cheated on me?"
"No, I haven't." I could honestly say!
"Have you had sex with Darryl? Has Darryl had sex with you?"
"What? I said no!" I frowned.
"I'm just checking cause I know how females play on words sometimes."
"Only females do that?"
He exhaled, then he kissed me so deeply that my toes curled. "I love you Kendra!"
"I love you..... What's your name again?" I smiled, then I ran.
He chased me, caught me, and picked me up, "you play too much!" Then he kissed me again.

Nellie
"I'm here, can you meet me?" Ahjani said
"You're where?"
"Oakland, we're playing them tomorrow. I need to see you." He said, when I hesitated he asked where I was. When I told him I was home, he said he was coming.
Nassya came home from school and I grabbed her. I told her to stay put and no matter what not to leave me alone with Ahjani. When I opened the door he swept me up and squeezed me tight. He told me he missed me so much. He couldn't believe how big Nassya had gotten. As he was hugging her he caught a glimpse of my ring. "WHAT IS THAT?"
"We need to talk," I said patting the couch for him to sit down.
"Let's go!" Ahjani said pointing at the door.
I shook my head, "no. It has to be here, and Nassya lovingly agreed to stay in the room." Nassya smiled then she put her headphones on. She curled up in the chair and did her homework.

Ahjani looked at me in disbelief. "You think I'm going to hurt you?"

"No, I know I don't need to fear you. I can't trust myself when it comes to you."

"Trust yourself? That's real?" He asked pointing to my ring." You're marrying someone who isn't me?" He looked like he couldn't believe it. "I don't understand Nellie! It's me! We're in love! You can't possibly love whoever he is more than you love me!"

"Come on, you're in love with Olivia and you question me?"

"I don't love her more than I love you! I've always loved you first!"

"She's your girlfriend, if I was truly first you would've broke up with her as soon as you found me. Marquez loves me, I'm first with him. He knows everything about me and he still loves me."

"I still love you!"

"You don't know everything! You could never be here for me like Marquez is."

He kept kissing my lips, "Nellie don't! Don't marry him! I'll marry you! We could go right now, I have the rest of the day off."

"And then what? Olivia's lovingly waiting for you to return to her. Why would you hurt her like that? She doesn't deserve that kind of pain. Be good to her Ahjani, you are not that guy."

"Nellie!" He put his head between my breasts. "My first love! Please! Don't do this!"

I started crying, "Ahjani! It's already done. I love him, he loves me."

"But you love me! Please Nellie!" He said letting his hands roam all over me like my little sister wasn't sitting right there.

"I love you Ahjani, and that's why we AREN'T alone!" I could tell he forgot cause he popped up. His eyes were red now and he had lots of begging left in him. "You have to go," I could feel myself weaken.

"We didn't have breakup sex!" He said grabbing my waist.

"Oh no! I know better! I know what you're capable of." I smiled.

"Nellie please!" He said trying to pull my waist towards him.

"Go marry Olivia. Have a bunch of pretty babies. Maybe our kids will find each other. Then we can have beautiful grandchildren and live on that way."

He blank stared at me, "why would that be satisfying for me?"

"Our granddaughter will be a little me, and you can freely love her up."
"But I want to love you right now." He screamed into my breast, all I felt was hot air. "I hate your father! He should've left us alone!"
I didn't tell him that his momma was the one. Why tell him? If she told him that was on her. Ahjani tried to convince me for another thirty minutes. I can see why D said begging was a turn on. As soon as the door shut, Nassya popped up and ran to the bathroom. When she came back she hugged me and cried with me. She said my conversation didn't look fun, I shook my head no as I continued to cry. When she told me she was proud of me, I squeezed her tight and I cried harder. I felt surprisingly good about myself especially that my little sister was proud of me. That didn't stop me from crying to Marquez. I could hear the smile in his voice. He asked me to come see him. I told him I was on the first thing smoking. I booked my flight out tonight, and I decided to book my return flight while I was there.
When I approached my terminal I felt like someone was watching me. I looked to my left and D was looking at me. He didn't look mad, but he didn't look happy. I smiled then I held up my left hand. D smiled then he walked a little closer. "My man Marquez finally did it huh? Good for him!"
"Finally?" I said smiling at my ring.
"He's been crazy about you since the beginning. Congratulations!"
"Thank you, is this your flight?"
"Yep, taking care of business working overtime. Where you going?"
"To be with Marquez," I blushed.
D smiled, "Noel is in love! Can the world handle that kind of passion?"
I turned my ring on my finger, "Ahjani popped up today. He was begging me not to do it." I said feeling like I was going to cry.
"Adobo is a good guy, but he doesn't understand everything."
I laughed, "what did you call him?"
D laughed, "ya'll too black for me with all these names. How you expect a nigga to keep up?"
"Can you explain it to him?" I pleaded.

"You trying to get me shot. He's not gonna wanna hear nothing from me about you. He's a pretty smart guy, he'll get it, give him some time."

The attendants announced boarding for our flight, D went ahead with all the First Class passengers. I smiled at him as I passed through the cabin. I felt proud of myself for being so controlled in D's presence. I thought I'd attack him if I ever saw him again.

"Good evening ladies and gentlemen. In celebration of Noel's engagement our First Class passenger has purchased a drink for everyone. Noel can you wave your hand?" The flight attendant asked. I blushed as I waved. Then she said something to D. "Ok so the challenge is that if you can make Noel continually blush for ten minutes by congratulating her, he'll buy everyone two drinks!" She looked at her watch, "go!" Everyone was congratulating me and making a big fuss! I could not stop blushing. When they made their mark everyone cheered and everyone was cheering me on. People continued to congratulate me even as we exited off the plane. D was talking to Marquez when I got to the baggage claim area, I could tell by the vibe he was congratulating him. Marquez was smiling at me so big. He picked me up and kissed me deeply!

We went back to his studio apartment and spent an amazing night in. Marquez thanked me for choosing him. I told him that he saw me when I couldn't see myself. I told him I still didn't clearly see myself, but his patience is incomparable. "Speaking about patience, how long do you want to wait for children?"

"Children? How many?"

"Gotta have at least two." He said excitedly. "After that if you wanna stay barefoot and pregnant, I'm fine with it."

"Marquez can you imagine me as someone's mother? The idea of it scares me."

"You're going to be a wonderful mother. Our children will be our love in flesh and blood. We have the example of our parents to know what not to do. We're going to be amazing parents. I know what you're worried about."

"What?"

"Whether you'll pass on your no rhythm, don't worry. They'll have my genes and we'll put them in dance school."

I hit him with my pillow. "Can we have a few years to ourselves first? We need time with just us, and I need time to be selfish."

He smiled, "you wanna be selfish with me?"

I snuggled into his chest, "yes! I love you so much, I can't imagine sharing you."

He kissed me, "I like the sound of that."

The next day he showed me around his campus, he introduced me to all of his friends. I recognized her from the picture. This was my chance to be as kind and patient as Marquez has been. But instead I kissed Marquez who had no idea the girl was looking. I put my hand on his shoulder so she could see my ring. Her face cracked and she sadly hurried away.

****

My whole family all went back down for Marquez's graduation. We met Nathan out there and he introduced us to his fiancé. We were so surprised to find out he even had a girlfriend; they had been together for some time. Instead of one wedding we suddenly had two. Fortunately, Ava had all the planning together. Since we were in Southern California we hit the amusement parks as a family as well. Junior's wedding was in a couple of weeks, and he said this vacation was the perfect opportunity for them to unplug and reconnect from all the chaos that was the planning for their wedding. I started paying attention to all the headache my soon to be sister in-law was going through and I swallowed really big. Marquez said he would be there every step of the way during the planning. We had so much fun in the Southern California sun.

****

Marquez's uncle knocked on the door with a big white envelope in his hands. He knew we had been waiting for his offer letter from his job. Marquez was leaning against the wall and I was leaning against him sitting in between his legs. He put the envelope in my hands and told me to open it. I could feel his heart beating. I opened the envelope and slowly slid the folder out. The folder had characters from their previous blockbuster animated films all over it. The offer letter was on top of everything. We both sat up when we looked at his starting salary. I couldn't believe it! He got company stock, and a signing bonus. No doubt to help him setup house. I hugged and kissed him while he stared at everything in disbelief. "Look at where my doodles have gotten me!"

"You are the best baby! No doubt about it!" He smiled at me then he went back to his letter. "Do you think I should shift gears and go to design school? I love fashion, I could see working in that field."

"If that's what you want to do, you know I'll support you." He
stared at the check, "should we use this money as a deposit on a
house?"

"If that's what you want to do." I rubbed his leg.

"WE! Baby WE!" He kissed me.

Marquez asked his uncle what we should do, and he said he would
match whatever Marquez put down on a purchase as an early
wedding present. When we went to my house, we were telling my
stepmom about Marquez's uncle's offer. My daddy was
"WHISTLING" (something I never heard him do) down the
hallway when he realized we were there. He offered to match
Marquez's uncle's offer as well. Nassya got excited because she
knew she would be decorating soon.

A few days later we met with a realtor and started looking at
homes. We went back and forth for a while until we found a house
that we both liked within our price range. This house had potential
to expand later and to make it even better than it was as is. It was
three bedrooms, and two baths. It had a long driveway and a
detached garage. The backyard was huge, and there was plenty of
room to go back and up. It wasn't too far from Marquez's job, he
said he could come home for lunch for a little afternoon delight,
then he laughed. We made an offer on the house and things moved
rapidly. Before I knew what happened we closed escrow on the
house. The previous owners moved out, and I told Marquez I
wanted to have the house thoroughly cleaned before we moved in.
I went through the yellow pages and I called a few places. I
decided to go with Immaculately Tidy, I liked the tone of the
person over the phone. I left Marquez's name as the client for the
walk through estimate. Nassya had her notepad out and she was
sketching her ideas for the design of the house when the doorbell
rang. I stopped breathing when I opened the door to Kendra and
Kalani. Kendra looked at her clipboard, "we're here for Marquez
Pelayo?"

"That's my fiancé," I said completely nervous.

Kendra looked back at her van like she thought about leaving,
Kalani looked at Kendra. "Business is business! Suck it up!" Then
she looked at me.

I stepped to the side so they could come in. "Come in."

Nassya got so excited when she saw Kendra she screamed and ran
to her. "Oh my goodness! This isn't Nassya? Honey you are so

grown and beautiful!" Kendra said being genuinely nice to my sister. "Do you remember my sister Kalani?"

"A little bit," Nassya said trying to really remember.

"I want a hug too, cause I remember you."

At least they were all smiling. "What you got there?" Kendra asked looking at Nassya's sketch pad.

"Oh this is my sketch pad, I'm coming up with my design for the house."

"You gonna be an interior decorator huh? You were always so stylish when you were little it makes sense." Kendra smiled at her like she was proud of her.

"I can decorate a room, but Princess is my stylist."

Kendra tried to hold on to her smile. "Well I definitely wanna see what you've got planned, I have no doubt it's going to be amazing."

"Ok, so tell us what you would like done and then we'll be out of your hair and we'll send you the estimate." Kalani said.

We went over each room, the crawl space attic, and the basement. Kendra pointed out the air ducts, and Kalani pointed out a mouse hole. She went out to her van and brought back cotton balls and peppermint oil. She put a few drops of peppermint oil on each cotton ball and then she dropped them all over the house. Then she saturated a couple balls and threw them in the holes. She said that was the humane way to get any mice out of the house. She suggested that I have and exterminator come out to go over the house and then if I liked their bid they'd clean up the house. I told Kalani I was going with whatever they estimated. Kendra didn't say anything she stuck to business. She kept giving Nassya hugs and smiling at her though, and I remembered that she was always affectionate like that. I used to try to act like I didn't like it, but what I wouldn't give for a hug from her right now.

When they left Nassya asked me what happened. To put it in it's simplest terms I told her that I tried to take Kendra's man. Nassya looked at me wide eyed and asked me why would I do that to Kendra. I hung my head and I said I was selfish. When Nassya asked me if she ever met him, I lowered my head lower and I shook my head yes. I told her it was D, Nassya gasped. I asked Nassya if she hated me, and she said no. But it wasn't her man that I tried to steal.

****

349

Marquez and I were doing the walk through with Kendra as we reviewed her work. Marquez kept looking at the ceilings and smiling. He said there wasn't a cobweb in sight. The house sparkled from floor to ceiling. I noticed that they touched up the paint on the crown moldings all throughout the house. The house was move in ready. Kendra directed most of her comments to Marquez, she was all business. "So, when's the big day?" She asked but I couldn't tell if she really cared.

"We don't have a date yet, the engagement is new," Marquez said. "Junior got married, I have pictures if you want to see." I said picking my nail hoping she'd say yes.

She shrugged, "yea sure."

"I have to run back to work, but she has the checkbook. Thank you Kendra, the house looks AMAZING!" Marquez said hurrying out the door cause he knew he was lying. He had the day off from work.

When I looked out the window he smiled at me, blew a kiss and quickly walked down the street in the direction of his office. Junior's memory book, which he had made for each of us, was the only book on my bookshelf until I moved in. I gave her the book to look through. Since there was no furniture she stood in the middle of the floor flipping through pictures. She said our dresses were pretty, she said she loved the decor, she said Junior looked very handsome. I thanked her for her kind words. She looked at me long and hard, "was it just sex?"

"For me, only the first time, one hit and I was hooked, he was like crack!" I said hoping she didn't get mad.

She shifted her weight from leg to leg. "Did he tell you he loved you?"

"NEVER! He always reminded me that he was in love with you! I kept attacking him."

She exhaled and looked at the ceiling, "so….. YOU! Were my BEST FRIEND! You knew I liked him and you went after him? How did you get to him without me knowing?"

I felt horrible, "I saw him at Durant Square and we went in the staff only hallway. Then I saw him when he was out with some of his friends. Then I stalked his school until I found him. I'll tell you everything if you want to know."

"Did you ever feel guilty about what you were doing to me?"

"All the time! That's when I stopped coming around or taking your calls. My double life was eating away at me. And I was stupid to think that at some point he would see the light and choose me."

"You mean your light skin?" She squinted her eyes at me.

I put my hands up, "no the figurative light. Like see things my way."

"Your fiancé knows doesn't he?"

"Yes," I said exhaling.

"Good then he'll understand why he has to sleep with me," she said.

Fire turned in my stomach, "WHAT? NO WAY!"

She got angry, "SEE ALL THAT, THAT YOU FEEL RIGHT NOW! MULTIPLY THAT BY A THOUSAND AND YOU'LL ONLY FEEL A FRACTION OF WHAT I FEEL!"

"I'm sorry, you don't have to forgive me. I understand if you never want to forgive me! You don't have to."

"You dang right I don't have to! I ought to beat you up right now, but I don't want to mess up my floors." She giggled by accident.

"You could use my hair as a mop."

"At least it would be good for something." She held on to her smile.

"I like your hair, it looks very natural. Where did you get it done?"

"This shop in Hilltop, Jovance. Have you heard of it?" I shook my head no. "They do it all, natural to weaves and everything in between."

"I like it."

She flipped her hair, "this old thing? Thanks honey." Then we laughed. "Here's your bill."

"Will you come to my wedding?"

Her smile dropped, "no."

Right! What was I thinking? "Right, sorry."

"We stopped being friends the moment you decided to have sex with Darryl. I'm trying to move past it, but we are not friends!"

"Right! I'm sorry. I guess I just thought since Marquez is the male version of you that somehow we could at least be cordial."

"Cordial yes, friends NO!"

"Ok, I understand." I looked around. "Well I'm going to need to get on your client list, because I'm going back to school in the Fall and I'm going to need help keeping up with this place once Nassya finishes decorating it."

"Nellie! Who is paying for all of this? Houses in Berkeley aren't cheap even the fixer-uppers, my bill is a nice piece of change, and now…." She extended her arms.
"I have furniture from my apartment in College. He has furniture from his, and then my parents are going to fill in the gaps."
"Oh, must be nice!"
"Your parents would do the same for you, but I'm sure you refuse. Your place is nice though, from what I can remember."
She smiled, "I do refuse their offers."
"Sometimes you gotta let go and say yes." I smiled.
"I'll remember that."
I got the checkbook and wrote the check for her services. Then I wrote another check for the twenty percent tip. I put a heart and "thank you" in the memo line. Even though she didn't hug me back, I gave her a big hug right before she left.

Kendra
"Good morning Tamille," I said opening the door for the girl who answers the phone for Immaculately Tidy. Tamille handles a lot of our office clerical work and scheduling.
"Good morning," she replied going to the kitchen to put on a pot of coffee. "Before I forget, a request came in yesterday and the requestor wanted the request marked as urgent, did you see my note?" She went to the office and brought out the request log.
"No, I conked out when I came home."
Tamille handed me the log and then Kalani walked in with Andy's donuts. "It's a donut kind of day!" Kalani declared.
I looked at the log and sure enough there was an urgent request from Andrew Wallace. "Did he say why this request is urgent?"
"No, but he wanted you to call him directly."
I got my coffee and a donut, I got a notepad and pen just in case this was an actual business call. Tamille was in my office doing her daily routine, and Kalani was already out on assignment. "This is Andrew," he said in a business tone.
"Hello Drew this is Kendra, you called....."
"Darryl's KB!" His voice smiled. I was going to correct him, but I left it alone. "I've not seen you in ages, I see business is going well."
"It's going, I need to make some moves though. Oh and congratulations on your wedding."

"Thank you, thank you. You're coming to the wedding? I've got Jayman's family on my confirmed list of attendees."

"That's the plan. The Ritz Carlton huh? Look at you all fancy!" I teased.

"My bride wants a formal wedding, so that's what I'm giving her. Please make sure you're in formal attire. There's going to be pictures and I wanna be able to say all my people respected the dress code."

"Oh man! I forgot it was a formal wedding. There isn't much time left, I'll have to get on that."

"I'm gonna pretend you didn't say that. The world should stop spinning because I'm in love and getting married." He laughed, I listened to his tone and I could hear the love all over him. I bet Anton sounds like this when he talks about me. "I can't wait for you to meet her. It's kind of unacceptable that you haven't met her."

"I know right, where have you been?"

Drew exhaled, "up under the love of my life! I am no good at work cause all I think about is her! I......." He chuckled. "Let me stop going all female." He cleared his throat and made his voice deep. "Yes enough of that! So the point of my call. Yes the point! My loft, I need it cleaned. I'm leaving the furniture, and I wanna leave it polished for Darryl. You've seen my place, how much you gonna charge me?"

"No charge, consider it a wedding present."

"Darryl's KB, I appreciate the thought. But I want a real present. I'm only getting married once. I need you to break the bank. Empty out your pockets for me." He laughed, "ok but seriously. Either you name your price or I'll pay what I think you deserve. And don't cut any corners, I want the full treatment. When can you come?"

It's like the three of them were on three different levels. Darryl's the silliest, then Drew but he's not as silly as Darryl. Then D-Rick, who doesn't even smile for more than two seconds once every five years. I liked watching the three of them interact, Darryl brings out the silly in everyone even their father. He may not laugh, or smile, BUT if you pay attention to the things he says he's hilarious.

I told Andrew that I could get there at noon today. He was quiet for a minute, then he said he had meetings all afternoon until early evening. He said he'd have someone meet me. I told him he wasn't slick. He was laughing as he said he didn't know what I was talking about.

I called Anton and talked to him as long as I could before I left. I needed to hear his voice and reconfirm my love for him as a primary thought. When I parked the station wagon Darryl came through the gate in sweats, a wife beater, and yellow gloves. "KB! What happened to your van?"

"Kalani has it on assignment. We got this for when we work separately." I did my best to ignore how beautiful his arms and chest looked in his t-shirt.

"So we're gonna be all alone?" He raised his eyebrows at me.

"Stop playing," I said grabbing my supplies. "It's perfect that you're here. You can move all the heavy furniture out the way." He held his hands up, "I'm already ahead of you." He helped me bring in my supplies and my floor polisher. "So, is it true?" He stared at me.

I didn't feel like playing dumb, "yes." I said messing with my supplies.

"You don't love me anymore?" He was seriously asking.

"How many ways can I tell you how badly you broke my heart?"

"What does that have to do with the love we mutually share?"

"Seriously Darryl? That has everything to do with it." I said keeping my eyes on my supplies.

He walked up behind me and put his arms around me. "You can't marry someone else when you're in love with me. That's a miserable life to have KB."

"I didn't say I was in love with you. You put those words in my mouth."

"The fact that you turned me down says to me that you feel more for him than I wanna give you credit for. I need you to remember that I've chosen you. You know my love is raw and uncut! I'm not going anywhere. You need time, fine I'll give you time. But get real, you can't marry the guy who couldn't cover the bill."

"So what am I supposed to do?"

"Stop worrying about whether you will ever get married, and pay attention to whether or not you can live without me." Then he kissed my cheek.

I stepped out of his arms, and got busy cleaning. Darryl helped me, and he did it quietly. He put on music and that was really the only noise coming from this place. After the floors dried we put all the furniture down. Darryl gave me a cashier's check from Drew. I blinked at the dollar amount on this check, it was six times the amount I would've charge. Darryl asked me when I was going to contact him about business. I had forgotten that I mentioned anything about growing to him. I told him I'd call him after the wedding.

"Darryl you're too volatile for me. I need certain securities that you can't provide for me. You know my life, everything I've been through. No matter how much I used to love you, the fact that you feel like you need to run around with so many women is a red flag for me. I can't choose that kind of instability. I love you for who you are, but you'll never be what I need."

"You don't know what I'll be." He hissed at me.

"Time will tell!" I shrugged, then we put my things back in my car and I left. It was "interesting" spending hours with Darryl in complete seriousness.

****

"Let's go to Elegant Affairs!" One person said and the group agreed.

"I hate to be the party pooper, but I don't want to go there. Too much history." I said not caring that most of them didn't like my comment. I didn't want to run into Darryl there.

"How about Shylight Lounge in Berkeley?" Another person volunteered.

I looked at Anton to say whether he wanted to go there. After all, last time we went there he wasn't prepared for the enormous bill.

"That's fine with me." He said

We were out with Anton's friends. They were all around his age, and I was the baby of the group. Anton's only four years older than me, but you know how some people act like those years are dog years. I don't care cause I'm the only successfully self-employed female here. Shoot, Anton and I are the only self-employed ones amongst our group. All of them turn their noses up at my job, but as soon as they're in a pinch they're begging me to help them and then asking for hook up cause they know me through Anton. They're all ridiculous if you ask me.

"Kendra do you ever wear dresses?" Sean's new girlfriend asked.

"Why does it matter to you what I wear?"

"Did she just get smart with me?" She asked the other lady.

Carey Anderson

I was not in the mood for them tonight. Stop judging me and
everything I do. Anton brought my drink and sat next to me. "Ant
something's wrong with your little girl. You need to check her!"
"Who needs to check whom?" Sean asked walking over.
"Ant needs to check his little girl. She's always getting smart."
"You need to quit messing with her, what's wrong with you?"
Anton said in my defense.
"All I asked her is if she ever wears dresses, my question didn't
warrant a smart response."
"That may be what you said but that's not how you asked me. You
may loud talk them, and disrespect them. But you will not bring
that over here!"
Anton took my drink and set it on the table then he took me on the
small dance floor. He was apologizing for their behavior. I told
him from now on I didn't need to come out with them. It was fine
by me if he went alone.
We were dancing when I noticed Nellie and her fiancé walk in. As
usual Nellie was gorgeous and her man was proud. She didn't see
us when they walked into the lounge area. I pointed and told Anton
that she was Nellie. Then I told him I'd rather spend the evening
with her than his friends. He asked me if I wanted him to take me
home. I said no cause next Saturday I was going to be at the
wedding and I was going to be working hard to cover all my
clients so that I would have no business impact by taking the
weekend off. However, I was serious about hanging with Nellie.
When I left the dance floor I walked over to Nellie, her face lit up
when she saw me. We hugged and then I sat with her and her
fiancé. When Anton brought my drink over I introduced him as my
fiancé. Nellie did a double take then she said a surprised
congratulations. She leaned in and said he was cute, I thanked her.
Anton and Marquez started chatting a courtesy chat at first, but
then it turned into an all-out conversation about Marquez and
Nellie's backyard. Anton showed Marquez pictures on his phone of
my yards and some other yards.
Nellie leaned in concerned, "I know it's none of my business. But
who is this guy?"
I laughed, "my fiancé."
"Really?" She squinted her eyes at me.

I exhaled, "when Kaleah told me she was pregnant I said 'again'?
She got irritated cause everyone was responding that way. Now I
understand the feeling."
"You're an auntie? Tell Kaleah I said congratulations."
I took out my phone showing her pictures of my sweet shuga! She
told me that Nathan was in Vegas with their grandmother, she said
he went back to school, and he was now married and living in
Southern California. She said his wife was nice and really pretty,
but the wedding and everything happened kind of fast. When I
looked confused she explained that she and Nathan have the same
momma and how no one knew until her father blurted it out. I had
to literally shut my mouth as she unloaded telling me everything
that's been happening in her world. I didn't think I had much to
share, but I told her how Jabbar left Ahjanae hanging and how she
ended up with Ryder, how cute their family is, I told her that Jerry
"killed himself" in our backyard after my momma and Jason got
married. We laughed at how Kalani keeps picking these square
guys and trying to help them connect with their inner thug. Audra
is in school in New York and she got a job off Broadway in a
musical. Aunrey got a job at a temp agency in Oakland and he
seems to like it.
Anton never went back to his friends, he was enjoying Marquez's
company. Anton's friends eventually left and the four of us chatted
and had a good time.
"Kendra he's nice, I'm not saying he's not. But I don't understand."
She put her hands out.
"I can't get over it, so what's the point?" I shrugged.
"Kendra! Blame it all on me, forgive him!" She pleaded. I shook
my head no. "You've always been too stubborn," she smiled.
"If you say so."
"Blame me, forgive him, and come to my wedding." She smiled
again.
"When are you getting married?"
She shrugged, "we don't have a date yet. You?"
"Not yet."
We stayed until the lounge was shutting down. Nellie looked sad
when she said maybe we could do this again sometime. When I
said sure, she screamed, threw her arms around me, and squeezed
me.

Nellie

Our house was finally a home. Nassya took pictures of her work for her portfolio. When everyone left, Marquez and I ran around our house like big old kids. I think we had sex on and against every surface imaginable. I couldn't believe it, this was our home, and I share it with a man that I truly love.

My momma came over looking at everything like she expected something to be wrong. Then she said our house was "cute". She would've preferred that we rented one of those expensive apartments off of Bay Street in Emeryville instead of making a practical investment in our future. I counted backwards from ten.

"Why are you so jealous?"

"Of what? This little house?" She blew air.

"That I've got someone who knows all the horrible things about me and still loves me. He loves me so much he wants to MARRY me! You've never been married, not even engaged! Instead of being happy for me you're always competing with me. Can you just be my momma for five minutes and tell me how happy you are for me?"

"He's not even black!"

"That bothers you? Why does it matter? He loves me momma, and I am so in love with him!"

"You're going to have to deal with judgment from other people, and if you ever have babies people will treat them badly as well."

I put my hand on my hip. "This is America momma. Pretty soon there will only be one culture like Puerto Rican, Mexican, etc."

"That's years from now, I'm talking about now."

"Why does that matter momma? Can you be happy for me?"

She rolled her eyes, "so what if I am jealous!"

"Don't make me feel bad for having something good. I'm trying not to be like that anymore."

"Nealesha you're not better than me just because he put a ring on your finger."

"I never said I was or anything like that. Be happy for me momma, please!"

"Fine! I'm happy!" She exaggerated with her hands and rolled her eyes. I know how hard that would've been for me so I let the sarcasm roll off of me.

"I love you momma!" I said throwing my arms around her.

She hugged me tightly back, "I love you baby girl."

Kendra

I barely got a hair appointment for the morning of the wedding. I had the stylist take my weave out, perm my hair, and then cut it in the most beautiful asymmetrical bob. The front hit my shoulders, the most hair I've ever had. My hair was shining bouncing and behaving. I ran over to the mall hoping to find something amazing at the last minute. I should've known better. Everyone else already had their dresses but I was too busy. I knew Drew would talk about me if I showed up in an ordinary dress. I went to Kalani's closet and she had nothing. When I went to my closet there it was. I held my breath hoping it still fit. I zipped my prom dress up and I did a celebratory dance. It still fit perfectly although I knew I've gained a little weight since I wore it last. I did my makeup then I went next door to Kalani's house. She screamed when she saw me. "YOU BETTER GO! YOU BETTER GO!" She screamed as she admired me. "I can't believe you still have that dress."
"Please! Do you know how much this dress cost?" I said looking down at it and admiring it.
"No."
"Me neither," we laughed. "But I know it was expensive."
When we got to my parent's house my momma and Kaleah immediately loved my dress. Jason looked at my dress and frowned, "I thought I told you to burn that dress!" Then he looked at Kalani's equally sexy dress. "What are you two trying to do to me?"
"My dress is ok though right daddy?" Kaleah asked turning in her maternity dress.
"All except that belly!" He said without any joking in his voice.
"Oh!" We all laughed.
When Milton and the baby came, Kaleah rode with them while they followed us to the hotel in San Francisco. Jason passed his keys to the valet and then he proudly took my momma's hand and walked ahead of us. Kalani and I walked around taking in everything. The walls looked like they were made of marble. Everything was chic and trendy. There were signs telling us which way to go. We sat with our family out in the garden area, Ryder and Ahjanae sat their little family by Ryder's family. Jason introduced us to a lot of people. Everyone was dressed formally

and some dresses were sexier than mine so I didn't feel out of
place. Like clockwork at three-fifty they asked everyone to take
their seats cause the wedding was about to begin. Drew looked so
handsome standing there anxious and excited. When Drew's
momma walked down the aisle with his father both of them
seemed like they were in seventh heaven. I heard someone ask how
old Drew's momma was, then they huffed. Everyone looked so
nice, but of course I couldn't take my eyes off of Darryl. He looked
so good in his tux, and he kept smiling like he was waiting for
everyone to get on his level and recognize how good he looked.
Kalani bumped me, "that girl looks just like Chantel Shaw the
singer."
"Right, but that's not her. Chantel isn't that top heavy. But she does
look just like her." I said refocusing my attention on Darryl.
Drew's bride wasn't what I was expecting. I thought she'd be a diva
like his baby momma or Nellie. She was pretty but classic girl next
door pretty. I gave him silent props for picking a real woman with
real curves. After the ceremony, which was quick and straight to
the point, the guests were asked to go to the waiting area. Kalani
grabbed my arm, "OH MY GOODNESS!" She silently screamed
to me. "It's that guy from a long time ago. HE'S STILL FINE!"
"What guy?" Darryl asked bending down to listen to our
conversation.
"Who is that?" Kalani quickly pointed to the guy.
"That's my cousin Tim. He needs some swag in his life. You gonna
turn him out?"
Kalani looked embarrassed, "no!"
"KB! YOU LOVE ME! I knew it! Everyone who doubts me owes
me money. I TOLD THEM YOU STILL LOVE ME! And they
gonna have the nerve to doubt me!" He patted his chest.
"What are you talking about?"
"You're wearing my dress. Are you silently wishing this was our
day?"
"No," I flashed Kalani a look like SAVE ME!
"Darryl somebody is trying to get your attention." Kalani said
pointing to a guy. When we walked into the reception hall it was
beautiful. And just in case I didn't know it before blue and silver
are the wedding colors. I chatted with Ahjanae, Zoey, and Sharon
for a long time. Sharon is as hilarious as Ryder. Ryder was proudly
taking Erin and their son around the room to meet family. Darryl

kept trying to get back to me but people kept calling him over to where they were. Within two minutes he'd have everyone laughing then he'd try to get away again. When they asked everyone to take their seats Darryl dramatically stomped his foot and then huffed all the way back to his seat at the head table. People were cracking up. We ate dinner and after the bride and groom had their first dance everyone started mingling again. The poor bride was meeting so many people I knew she wouldn't remember me. Drew was talking to someone and then D-Rick introduced Kalani and I before he disappeared. She thanked us for coming and she seemed nice. I patted Drew and said congrats while he talked to someone. He looked me up and down, then he gave me a thumbs up. Then he returned to his conversation.

I was minding my own business when I heard, "KB! Dance floor now!" Then Darryl gave the DJ back his microphone. The music changed and I started laughing when the music started playing. Darryl made his way to me, he glided right in front of me when the first verse started. "You've got your problems baby and I've got mine! Let's just end it all by putting it together, yeah. When you say you love me it don't mean a thing, if you cared you'd be there like you used to be....." Some people thought it was just Darryl being Darryl. But the people in the know were cheering him on. Darryl and I stayed on that dance floor all night in our own world. "I know tonight isn't going to end the way I would like it to. But you can at least let me kiss you."

"Jason is watching us!"

He looked at Jason then he smiled. "I'LL TAKE THE LICKS! IT'LL BE WORTH IT!" Darryl and I kissed for not a long long time. But long enough. Darryl put his forehead on mine. "I love you KB!"

"I love you Darryl!"

MORE FROM THE AUTHOR

Thank you for allowing me to entertain you. I hope you have enjoyed reading my current release. If you have not read Volumes I – VIII of the Wallace Family Affairs series, please do so. Click here for a list of all the background stories. Once you have read the background stories, please checkout the current date series Together We Are Strong. Stay tune for more to come shortly.

Wallace Family Affairs
At Last (Click here)
Tracy's Complications (Click here)
Distorted Mirrors (Click here)
Sometimes Love Isn't Enough (Click here)
Love Is Just Enough (Click here)
Just A Friend (Click here)
Invisible (Click here)
Look Beyond Your Eyes (Click here)
No Regrets (Click here)
First You Laugh Then You Cry
A Heart That's Taken (Click here)
Abandoned (Click here)
Last Words (Click here)

Together We Are Strong
Season 1 Present (Click here)
Beyond The Wallace's ~ I Knew You When (**TBD**)
Season 2 What Comes Next (Release **TBD**)

Standalones
Secrets & Lies ~ (**TBD late 2016 release**)
Anthology **Short** Story (Where Love May Find You Collection) ~ (Click here)
Waiting (**TBD**)

Hopefully you've enjoyed all of the background stories for our lovely Wallace's and Latour's. Please tune in for more from the "Together We Are Strong" Wallace & Latour Family Episodes on Amazon.

www.ingramcontent.com/pod-product-compliance
Lightning Source LLC
Chambersburg PA
CBHW051522050726
47503CB00014B/578